Dear Readers,

Some ten years ago, I read a medieval poem full of color and adventure about knights and mysterious ladies. It opened up an unknown world to me, a place of wild, dangerous forests and white castles, of mud and glorious spectacle; a time when blackbirds really were baked in pies. Against this rich and multihued background, I wrote a story about a powerful, devious woman desperate to reach refuge, and a knight—a true knight who never wavered once he swore his heart, a man who could not comprehend deceit.

To do justice to their world, I wove the music of their own medieval words into the dialogue. My favorite response was from a reader who wrote that at first, she had been a bit dubious about the Middle English, but by the end of the book, she was wondering why the man on the six o'clock news didn't talk that way!

I was determined to make my characters' words clear and understandable in the text, even though readers might never have come across them before. But in the edition of *For My Lady's Heart*, I've added a glossary so that you can be certain of their meanings if you have any doubt. In compiling it, I enjoyed revisiting that world and realizing again how much history and how many shades of meaning stand behind the words we have forgotten and the words we still use.

As I wrote about Ruck and Melanthe, a shadow figure appeared in their story: Allegreto, the young assassin who served his father's cruel ambitions. By the time I reached the end, I knew I must eventually give Allegreto his due. Many readers wrote to ask for his story. It took me a long time, but *Shadowheart* was finally published in April 2004. It is dark and beautiful—like Allegreto himself—and I hope you will be as fascinated by his elusive and compelling character as I was.

Yours,

Laura Kinsale

FOR MY
Lady's Heart

LAURA KINSALE

BERKLEY SENSATION, NEW YORK

THE BERKLEY PUBLISHING GROUP
Published by the Penguin Group
Penguin Group (USA) Inc.
375 Hudson Street, New York, New York 10014, USA
Penguin Group (Canada), 90 Eglinton Avenue East, Suite 700, Toronto, Ontario M4P 2Y3, Canada
(a division of Pearson Penguin Canada Inc.)
Penguin Books Ltd., 80 Strand, London WC2R 0RL, England
Penguin Group Ireland, 25 St. Stephen's Green, Dublin 2, Ireland (a division of Penguin Books Ltd.)
Penguin Group (Australia), 250 Camberwell Road, Camberwell, Victoria 3124, Australia
(a division of Pearson Australia Group Pty. Ltd.)
Penguin Books India Pvt. Ltd., 11 Community Centre, Panchsheel Park, New Delhi—110 017, India
Penguin Group (NZ), Cnr. Airborne and Rosedale Roads, Albany, Auckland 1310, New Zealand
(a division of Pearson New Zealand Ltd.)
Penguin Books (South Africa) (Pty.) Ltd., 24 Sturdee Avenue, Rosebank, Johannesburg 2196,
South Africa

Penguin Books Ltd., Registered Offices: 80 Strand, London WC2R 0RL, England

This is a work of fiction. Names, characters, places, and incidents either are the product of the author's imagination or are used fictitiously, and any resemblance to actual persons, living or dead, business establishments, events, or locales is entirely coincidental.

Copyright © 1993, 2004 by Amanda Moor Jay.
Excerpt from *Shadowheart* by Laura Kinsale copyright © 2004 by Amanda Moor Jay.
Cover illustration by Gregg Gulbronson.
Text design by Kristin del Rosario.

PRINTING HISTORY
First Berkley mass market edition / December 1993
Updated Berkley mass market edition / March 2004
Berkley Sensation trade paperback edition / October 2005

Library of Congress Cataloging-in-Publication Data

Kinsale, Laura.
    For my lady's heart / Laura Kinsale.
    p. cm.
    ISBN 0-425-20659-9
    1. Knights and knighthood—Fiction. 2. Middle Ages—Fiction. 3. England—Fiction. I. Title.

PS3561.I573F67 2005
813'.54—dc22

2005047515

PRINTED IN THE UNITED STATES OF AMERICA

10   9   8   7   6   5   4   3   2   1

These old gentle Britons in their days
Of diverse adventures they made lays
Rhymed in their first Briton tongue,
Which lays with their instruments they sung,
Or else read them for their pleasance,
And one of them have I in remembrance,
Which I shall say with good will as I can.
But sires, by cause I am a burel man,
At my beginning first I you beseech,
Have me excused of my rude speech.
I learned never rhetoric, certain;
Thing that I speak, it must be bare and plain.

The Prologue of *The Franklin's Tale*,
from *The Canterbury Tales*
by Geoffrey Chaucer

FOR MY
Lady's Heart

Prologue

———◈———

Where werre, and wrake, and wonder
Bi syþeʒ hatʒ wont þerinne,
And oft boþe blysse and blunder
Ful skete hatʒ skyfted synne.

Where war and wrack and wonder
By sides have been therein,
And oft both bliss and blunder
Full swift have shifted since.

Prologue
Sir Gawain and the Green Knight

THE PILGRIMS LOOKED looked at the sky and the woods
and each other. Anywhere but at the woman in the ditch. The
Free Companies ruled these forests; her screeching might
draw unwelcome attention. As she rolled in the wagon rut,
grinding dirt into her hair, crying out pious revelations with
shrieks and great weepings, her companions leaned against
trees and squatted in the shade, sharing a vessel of warm beer.

Remote thunder murmured as heat clouds piled up over the
endless grim forests of France. It was high summer of
the ninth year after the Great Pestilence. A few yards from the

sobbing female, on the high grassy center of the road, a priest sat removing his sandals and swatting dust off his soles one by one.

Now and then someone glanced into the dark woods. The girl had prophesied that their party of English pilgrims would reach Avignon safe—and though she was prostrated by holy ecstasies in this manner a dozen times a day, moved by the turn of a leaf or the flicker of a sunbeam to fall to her knees in wailing, it was true that they'd not seen or heard a suspicion of outlaws since she'd joined the party at Reims.

"John Hardy!" she moaned, and a man who'd just taken hold of the bottle looked round with dismay.

He drank a deep swig and said, "Ne sermon me not, good sister."

The woman sat up. "I shall so sermon thee, John Hardy!" She wiped at her comely young face, her bright eyes glaring out from amid streaks of dirt. "Thou art intemperate with beer. God is offended with thee."

John Hardy stood up, taking another long drink. "And thou art a silly girl stuffed with silly conceits. What—"

A crash of thunder and a long shrill scream overwhelmed his words. The devout damsel threw herself back down to the ground. "There!" she shouted. "Hearest thou the voice of God? I'm a prophet! Our Lord forewarneth thee—take any drink but pure water in peril of eternal damnation, John Hardy!" The rain clouds rolled low overhead, casting a green dullness on her face. She startled back as a single raindrop struck her. "His blood!" She kissed her palm. "His precious blood!"

"Be naught but the storm overtakin' us, thou great fool woman!" John Hardy swung on the others with vehemence. " 'I'm a prophet!' " he mocked in a high agitated voice. "Belie me if she be not a heretic in our very midst! I'm on to shelter, ere I'm drowned. Who'll be with me?"

The whole company was fervently with him. As they prepared to start on their way, the girl bawled out the sins of each member of the party as they were revealed to her by God: the intemperance of John Hardy, the godless laughing and jesting of Mistress Parke, the carnal lusting of the priest, and the meat on Friday consumed by Thomas O'Linc.

The accused ignored her, taking up the long liripipes that dangled from the crests of their hoods and wrapping the headgear tight as the rain began to fall in earnest. The party moved on into the sudden downpour. The woman could have caught up easily, but she stayed in the ditch, shrieking after them.

In the thunderous gloom the rain began to run in sheets and little streams into the road. She stayed crying, reaching out her hands to the empty track. The last gray outline of the stragglers disappeared around the bend.

A waiting figure detached itself from the shadows beneath the trees. The young knight walked to the edge of the rut and held out his hand. Rain plastered his black hair and molded a fustian pilgrim's robe to his back and shoulders, showing chain mail beneath.

"They ne harketh to me," she sobbed. "They taken no heed!"

"Ye drove them off, Isabelle," he said tonelessly.

"It is their wickedness! They nill heed me! I was having a vision, like to Saint Gertrude's."

His gauntleted hand still held steady, glistening with raindrops. "Is it full finished now?"

"Certes, it is finished," she said testily, allowing him to pull her to her feet. She stepped out of the ditch, leaving her shoe. The knight got down on his knees, his mail chinking faintly, and fished the soggy leather out of a puddle already growing in the mud. She leaned on his shoulder and thrust her foot inside the slipper, wriggling forcefully. He smoothed the wet wrinkles up her ankle. His hand rested on her calf for a moment, and she snatched her leg away. "None of that, sir!"

He lifted his face and looked at her. The rain slipped off strong dark brows and dewed on his black lashes. He was seventeen, and already carried fighting scars, but none visible on his upturned features. Water coursed down, outlining his hard mouth and the sullen cast of his green eyes. The girl pushed away from him sharply.

"I believe thou art Satan Himself, sir, if thou wilt stare at me so vile."

Without a word he got to his feet, readjusting the sword at his hip before he walked away to a bay horse tethered in the shadow of the trees. He brought the stallion up to her. "Will ye ride?"

"The Lord Jesus commanded me walk to Jerusalem."

"Ride," he said "until we comen up with the company once more."

"It were evil for me to riden. I mote walk."

"This forest hides evil enow," he said harshly. "N'would I haf us tarry alone here."

" 'Fear not, in the valley of shadow and death,' " she intoned, catching his hand. She fell to the sodden ground, her wet robe clinging to the feminine contour of her breasts. "Kneel with me. I see the Virgin. Her light shineth all about us. Oh . . . the sweet heavenly light!" She closed her eyes, turning up her face. Her tears began to mingle with the rain-drops.

"Isabelle!" he cried. "Ne cannought we linger here alone! For God's love—move freshly now!" He grabbed her arm and pulled her up. By main force he threw her across the saddle in spite of her struggle. She began to screech, her wet legs bared, sliding from his mailed grip. The horse shied, and she tumbled off the other side. He jerked the reins, barely holding the stallion back from trampling her as it tried to bolt.

She lay limp in the grass. As he dropped to his knees beside her, she rolled feebly onto her back, moaning.

"Lady!" He leaned over her. "Isabelle, luflych—ye be nought harmed?"

She opened her eyes, staring past him. "So sweet. So wondrous sweet, the light."

Rain washed the mud from her face. Her fair blue eyes held a dreamy look, her lashes spiky with wetness, her lips smiling faintly. The pilgrim's hood had fallen open, showing a white, smooth curve of throat. He hung motionless above her a moment, looking down.

Her gaze snapped to his. She shoved at him and scrambled away. "Thou thinkest deadly sin! My love is for the Lord God alone."

The young knight flung himself to his feet. He caught his horse with one hand and the girl with the other, dragging them together. "Mount!" he commanded, baring his teeth with a savagery that cowed her into grasping the stirrup.

"I n'will," she said, trying to turn away.

"Will ye or nill ye!" He hiked her foot, catching her off balance, and propelled her up. She yelped, landing pillion in the high-cantled war saddle, clutching for security as he swung the wild-eyed horse around. The stallion followed him, neck stretched, the black mane lying in sloppy thick straggles against the animal's skin. The knight hauled his horse a few yards down the verge through the wet grass and mud. He stopped, facing stiffly away from her into the rain. "I am nought Satan Himseluen," he said. "I'm your wedded husband, Isabelle!"

"I am wed to Christ," she said righteously. "And oft revealed the truth to thee, sir. Thou hast thy way with me against my will and God's."

He stood still, looking straight ahead. "Six month," he said stonily. "My true wife ye hatz n'been in that time."

Her voice softened a little. "To use me so were the death of thee, husband—so I've prophesied, oft and oft."

He slogged forward. The horse slipped and splashed through a puddle, sending water up, causing the knight's fustian robe to cling over the plated greaves and cuisses that protected his legs. The rain swelled into huge drops. Hail began to spatter against his shoulders, bouncing in pea-size pebbles off his bared black hair.

He made an inarticulate sound and dragged the stallion to the edge of the wood, stopping beneath a massive tree. Isabelle and the horse took up the protected space beneath the heaviest branch, leaving him with the filter of sodden leaves above to break the hail.

She began an exhortation on the sins of the flesh and detailed a vision of Hell recently visited upon her. From this she went on to a revelation of Jesus on the Cross, which, she assured him, God had told her was superior in its brilliance to the similar sight described by Brigit of Sweden. When a hailstone the size of a walnut cracked him on the skull, he cursed aloud and yanked his helmet from the saddle.

Isabelle reproved him for his impious language. He pulled the conical bascinet down over his head. The visor fell shut. He leaned against the tree trunk with a dismal clang: a faceless, motionless, wordless suit of armor, while his wife told a parable of her own devising in which a man who used ungodly maledictions was condemned to dwell in Hell with fiery rats forever eating out his tongue. The music of the hailstones pattered in tinny uneven notes on steel.

She had finished the parable and gone on to predicting what sort of vermin they might expect to find among the infidels when the storm began to lift, leaving the forest and the grassy verge steaming in greens and grays. Light shone on the watery ruts in two twisted ribbons of silver. Like a frost of snow, hail lay amid the foliage, already beginning to melt. The knight pulled off his helmet and tried unsuccessfully to dry it on his robe. Without speaking, he pushed away from the tree and began to walk again, tugging the horse through small lakes beside the road, his spurs catching in the muddy weeds.

Vapor rose from his shoulders. Isabelle plucked at her sodden robe, holding it away from her skin as she talked. She was describing the present state of her soul, in considerable detail, when he stopped suddenly and turned to her.

A breaking shaft of sunlight caught him, banishing the sullen shadows. He looked up at her, young and earnest, interrupting her eloquence. "Isabelle. Say me this." He paused, staring at her intensely. "If outlaws were to fall upon us this moment, and ransom my life against—" The youthfulness vanished from his face in a set scowl. "Against this—that ye takes me again into your bed as husband—then what would you? Would ye see me slayed?"

Her lips pinched. "What vain tale is this?"

"Say the truth of your heart," he insisted. "My life for your vaunted chastity. What best to be done?"

She glared at him. "Thou art a sinner, Ruck."

"The truth!" he shouted passionately. "Have ye no love left for me?"

His words echoed back from the forest, enticement enough to outlaws, but he stood waiting, rigid, with his hand on the bridle.

She began to sway slightly. She lifted her eyes to the glowing clouds. "Alas," she said gently, "but I love thee so steadfast, husband—it were better to beholden thee put to death before my eyes, than we should yielden again to that uncleanness in the eyes of God."

His gaze did not leave her. He stared at her, unblinking, his body still as stone.

She smiled at him and reached down to touch his hand. "Revelation will come to thee."

He caught her fingers and gripped them in his, holding them hard in his armored glove. "Isabelle," he said, in a voice like ruin.

With her free hand she crossed herself. "Let us make troth of chastity both together. Thee I do love dearly, as a mother loveth her son."

He let go of her. For a moment he looked about him in a bewildered way, as if he could not think what to do. Then, abruptly, he began to walk again, pulling the horse in silence.

A cool wind out of the storm caught the knight's dark hair, drying it, blowing it against his ears. The breeze faltered for a moment, playing and veering.

The horse threw up its head. Its nostrils flared.

The knight came alert. He stopped, his hand on his sword hilt. The animal planted its feet, drinking frantically at the uneasy wind, staring at the curve ahead where the road disappeared into deep woods.

There was only silence, and the breeze.

"The Lord God is with us," Isabelle said loudly.

Nothing answered. No arrow flew, no foe came rushing upon them from ambush.

"Get ye after the hind-bow." The knight shoved his helmet down on his head and threw the reins over the horse's ears. As Isabelle floundered out of his way over the cantle, he mounted. She flung her arms about his waist. With his sword drawn he drove his spurs into the nervous stallion, sending it into a sprint with a war cry that resounded in volleys from the trees. The horse cannoned along the road with water flying from its hooves, sweeping round the curve at the howling height of the knight's battle shout.

The sight that met them was no more than a flicker of red mud and slaughter as the horse cleared the first body in a great leap. The animal tried to bolt, but the knight dragged it to a dancing halt amid the stillness.

He said nothing, turning and turning the horse in an agitated circle. The butchered bodies of their former companions wheeled past beneath his gaze, around and around, white dead faces and crimson that ran fresher than the rain.

Isabelle clung to him. "God spared us," she said, with a breathless tone. "Swear *now,* before Jesus Our Saviour, that thou wilt liven chaste!"

He reined the horse hastily among the bodies, leaning down to look for signs of life as the animal pranced in uneasy rhythm, its hooves squelching wet grass and gore. The looters had done thorough work. "God's blood—they been slain but a moment." His voice was tight as he scanned the dark encroaching forest. "The brigands be scarce flown." He turned the stallion away, but at the edge of the clearing he doubled the horse back on the grisly scene again, as if he had not looked upon it long enough to believe.

"Unshriven they died," Isabelle whispered, and murmured a prayer. She had never let go of her grip on his arm, not even to cross herself. "Swear thee now, in thanks for God's mercy and deliverance—thou wilt be chaste evermore."

He was breathing hard, pushing air through his teeth as he looked at what was left of Mistress Parke.

"I swear," he said.

He yanked the horse around and spurred it away down the road in a gallop for their lives.

AVIGNON INTIMIDATED AND disgusted him. In the murky, baking streets below the palace of the Pope, he stood stoically as Isabelle prayed aloud before a splinter of the True Cross. Behind her back a whore with bad skin beckoned to him, striking licentious poses in the doorway, folding her hands in mockery, running her tongue about her dark lips while Isabelle knelt weeping in the unswept dirt. His wife had barely warmed to her devotions, he knew from experience, when the toothless purveyor of the holy relic grew impatient and demanded in crudely descriptive English that she buy it or take herself off. The whore laughed at Isabelle's look of shock; Ruck scowled back and put his hand on his wife's shoulder more gently than he might have.

"Bide ye nought with these hypocrites," he said. "Come."

She stumbled to her feet and stayed near him, uncharacteristically quiet as they made their way through the crowds.

The shadow of the palace fell over them, a massive wall rising sheer above the narrow cobbled street, pocked with arrow slits styled in the shapes of crosses, the fortifications crowned by defensive crenels. Isabelle's body pressed against him. He put his arm about her, shoving back at a stout friar who tried to elbow her aside in passing.

She felt cool and soft under his hand. He was blistering hot in his chain mail and fustian, but dared not leave the armor off and untended as they moved from shrine to shrine, kissing saints' bones and kneeling before images of the Virgin, with Isabelle's tears and cries echoing around the sepulchers. Now this new shrinking, her snugging against him, fitting into the circle of his arm as she'd been used to do made piety even more difficult to maintain.

He tried to subdue his lustful thoughts. He prayed as they joined the stream of supplicants forging up the slope to the palace gate, but he was not such a hand at it as Isabelle. She'd always been a chatterer—it was her voice that had first caught his attention in the Coventry market, a pretty voice and a pretty burgher's daughter, with a giddy laugh and a smile that made his knees weak—he'd felt amazed to win her with nothing to offer but the plans and dreams he lived on as if they were meat and bread.

But there had been only a few sweet weeks of kissing and bedding, with Isabelle as loving and eager for it as himself, before the king's army had called him to France. When he'd come back, knighted on the field at Poitiers, full of the future, triumphant and appalled and eager to bury himself and the bloodshed in the clean tender arms of his wife—he'd come back, and found that God had turned her dizzy prattle into prophecy.

For a sevennight he'd had his way with her, in spite of the weeping, in spite of the praying and begging, in spite of the scolds, but when she'd taken to screaming, he'd found it more than he could endure. He'd thought he ought to beat her; that was her father's advice, and sure it was that Ruck would gladly beat her or mayhap even strangle her when she was in the full flow of pious exhortations—but instead she'd beseeched him to take her on pilgrimage across the heap of war-torn ruins that was France. And here he was, not certain if it was God's will or a girl's, certain only that his heart was full of lechery and his body seethed with need.

They entered the palace through an arch beneath two great conical towers, passing under them to an immense courtyard, larger than any castle he'd ever seen, teeming with beggars and clergy and hooded travelers. The clerics and finer folk seemed to know where to go; the plain pilgrims like themselves wandered with aimless bafflement, or joined a procession that ran twice around the perimeter and ended at a knot of priests and clerks.

Isabelle began to tremble in his arms. He felt her bones dissolve; she sank from his grip to the pavement, with a hundred pairs of feet scuffing busily past. As her wail rose above the noise, people began to pause.

Ruck was growing inured to it. He even began to see the advantages—not a quarter hour elapsed before they had a church official escorting them past the more mundane supplicants and into a great columned and vaulted chamber full of people.

The echoing roar of discourse stopped his ears. The ceiling arched above, studded with brilliant golden stars on a blue field and painted with figures bearing scrolls. He recognized Saint John and the Twenty Prophets. His eyes kept sliding upward, drawn by the gilded radiance, the vivid color— abruptly the clerk pushed him, and he collapsed onto a bench. Isabelle looked back over her shoulder at him with her hand outstretched and her mouth open as she and her escort were engulfed by the crowd.

"Isabelle!" Ruck jumped to his feet. He shoved after them. She had been named heretic for her sermoning more than once. He had to stay near her, explain her to the wary and suspicious. He floundered into a clearing and found himself in the midst of a circle of priests in rich vestments. The robed and tonsured scribe looked up from the lectern with a scowl, the plaintiff ceased his petition and turned, still kneeling before the podium.

Ruck backed out of the gathered court, bowing hastily. He turned and strained to his full height, a head taller than most, looking out over the massed assembly, but Isabelle was gone. A guard stopped him at a side door and pretended not to

understand Ruck's French, gesturing insolently at the benches.
He glared back, repeating himself, raising his voice to a shout.
The guard made an obscene gesture with his finger and jerked
his chin again toward the benches.

A shimmer of color sparkled at the corner of Ruck's eye.
He turned his head reflexively, as if a mirror had flashed.
Space had opened around him. At the edge of it, two spears'
length distant, a lady paused.

She glanced at him and the guard as she might glance at
mongrels scrapping. A princess—mayhap a queen, from the
richness of her dress and jewels—surrounded by her attendants, male and female, secluded amid the crowd like a glitter of silent prismatic light among shadows.

Cold . . . and as her look skimmed past him, his whole
body caught ice and fire.

He dropped to one knee, bowing his head. When he lifted
it, the open space had closed, but still he could see her within
the radius of her courtiers. They appeared to be waiting, like
everyone else, conversing among themselves. One of the men
gave Ruck a brief scornful lift of his brow and turned his
shoulder eloquently.

Ruck came to a sense of himself. He sat down on the bench
by the guard. But he could not keep his gaze away from her.
At first he tried, examining the pillars and carved animals, the
other pilgrims, a passing priest, in between surreptitious
glances at her, but none in her party looked his way again.
Concealed among the throng and the figures passing in and
out the door, he allowed himself to stare.

She carried a hooded white falcon, as indifferently as if the
Pope's hall had been a hunting field. Her throat and shoulders
gleamed pale against a jade gown fashioned like naught he'd
seen in his life—cut low, hugging her waist and hips without
a concealing cotehardi, embroidered down to her hem with
silver dragonflies, each one with a pair of jeweled emerald
eyes, so that the folds sparkled with her every move. A dagger hung on her girdle, smooth ivory crusted with malachite
and rubies. Lavish silver liripipes, worked in a green and silver emblem that he didn't recognize, draped from her elbows
to the floor. Green ribbons with the same emblem laced her

braids, lying against hair as black as the black heavens, coiled smooth as a devil's coronet.

He watched her hands, because he could not bear to look long at her face and did not dare to scan her body for its violent effect on his. The gauntlet and the falcon's hood, bejeweled like all the rest of her, glittered with emeralds on silver. She stroked the bird's breast with white fingers, and from four rods away that steady, gentle caress made him bleed as if from a mortal wound in his chest.

She turned to someone, lifting her finger to hold back the gauzy green veil that fell from her crown of braids to her shoulder—a feminine gesture, a delicacy that commanded and judged and condemned him to an agony of desire. He could not tear his look from her hand as it hovered near her lips: he saw her slight smile for her ladies—so cold, cold . . . she was bright cold; he was ferment. He couldn't comprehend her face. He hardly knew if she was comely or unremarkable. He could not at that moment have described her features, any more than he could have looked straight at the sun to describe it.

"Husband!" Isabelle's voice shocked him. She was there; she caught his hand, falling on her knees beside the bench. "The bishop speaketh with me on the morrow, to hearen my confession, and discourse together as God's servants!" Her blue eyes glowed as she clutched a pass that dangled wax seals. She smiled up at him joyfully. "I told him of thee, Ruck, that thou hast been my good and faithful protector, and he bids thee comen also before him—to confirm thy solemn vow of chastity in the name of Jesus and the Virgin Mary!"

ISABELLE INSISTED THAT he leave off his armor for the interview with the bishop. Her brief timidity, her snugging against Ruck for protection, had vanished. All night she'd sat up praying, pausing only to describe in endless particular the triumph of her examination by the clerks and officials. They had heard of her—her fame had really spread so far!—and wished to prove to their own satisfaction that her visions were of God. They had questioned her fiercely, but she'd known every proper answer, and even given them back some of their own by pointing out an error in their orthodoxy concerning the testament of Saint James.

Ruck had listened with a deep uneasiness inside him. He could not imagine that those arrogant churchmen, with their bright vestments and Latin intonations, had been won over by his wife. Isabelle attracted a certain number of adherents, but they were of kindred mind to her, inclined to ecstasies and spiritual torments. He had not seen a single cleric here who gave the appearance of being any more interested in holy ecstasy than in his dinner.

He'd slept fitfully, dreaming of falcons and female bodies, waking fully aroused. For an instant he'd groped for Isabelle and then opened his eyes and seen her kneeling at the window next to a sleeping tailor. Tears coursed silently down her cheeks. She looked so radiant and anxious, her eyes lifted to the dawn sky, her hands gripped together, that he felt helpless. He wanted this bishop to give her whatever it was that she desired—sainthood, if she asked for it.

He dreaded the interview. He was afraid as he'd never been before a fight; he felt as if he were facing execution. As long as that vow had been private, between him and Isabelle, it had not seemed quite real. There was always the future; there were mitigating circumstances; he had not spoken clearly just *what* he swore to. She might change her mind. They were neither of them so very old yet. Women were erratic, that was known certainly enough. He ought to have beaten her. He ought to have put up with the screams and got her with a child. He ought to have told her that decent women stayed home and didn't drag their husbands over the face of creation in pursuit of canonization. He watched her prayerful tears, his lufsom, his sweet Isabelle, and could have wept himself.

In the great audience hall he was informed he must wait, that only Isabelle was required. A hunchbacked man held out his hand, leaning on his staff, and Ruck put a coin in it. He got a mute nod in return.

All the morning he sat there, feeling naked in his leather gambeson without armor over it, swallowing down apprehension and despair. There was no way he could find out of the thing short of disavowing his own words and revealing himself a false witness in public, before a bishop of the church. Worse, he was afraid that they might trap him into it, perplex him with religious questions and turn him about like a spinning top, as Isabelle could do, until he swore whatever they wished.

Three clerks came for him. He rose and followed them through corridors and up stairs, until they entered a high, square room. His blood beat in his ears. He had an impression of silence and intense color, frescoes on all the walls and many vividly dressed people, before he followed the clerks with his head bared and lowered. He went down on his knees before the bishop without ever looking into the man's face.

"Sire Ruadrik d'Angleterre." The modulated voice spoke in French. Soft slippers and the gold-banded hem of white and red robes were all Ruck could see. "Is it your will that your wife take the veil and the ring, to live chaste henceforth?"

Ruck stared at the slippers. The veil. He lifted his eyes as high as the bishop's knees. Isabelle had never said anything about taking . . .

Was she to leave him? Go into a nunnery?

"He hath sworn." Isabelle's ardent voice reverberated off the high walls. She spoke English, but the interpreter's French words came like a murmured echo.

"Silence, daughter," the bishop said. "Thy husband must speak."

Ruck felt them all looking at him, a crowd of strangers at his back. He hadn't been prepared for this. He felt as if a great hand gripped his throat.

"Do you understand me, Sire Ruadrik? Your wife desires to take the vow of chastity and retire to a life of contemplation. A placement can be made for her among the Franciscans at Saint Cloud, if her situation is your concern."

"Saint Cloud?" he repeated stupidly. He lifted his eyes to find the bishop regarding him with an inquisitive look.

"Do you understand French?" the prelate asked.

"Yea, my lord," Ruck said.

The bishop nodded in approval. " 'The wife hath not the power of her own body, but the husband; likewise also the husband hath not power of his own body, but the wife,' " he intoned. "As Saint Paul sayeth to the Corinthians. She must receive your consent to do this. Is it your will, my son, that your wife take these vows to be chaste?" ·

They were asking his permission. He could say no. He turned his head, and Isabelle was standing wringing her hands, weeping as she had in the dawn, pleading with him silently.

Isabelle. Luflych.

He imagined denying her, holding her by force—imagined saying yes and losing her forever.

She made a deep moan in her throat, as if she were dying, and held out her hands to him in supplication.

He turned his face away from her. He bent his head. "Yea, my lord," he said harshly to the slippers and the golden hem.

The bishop leaned forward. Ruck clasped his hands and put them in the holy man's cool grasp, sealing his consent. Now he had no wife. No true wife. He didn't know if he was married or not.

"You may rise, my son," the bishop said.

Ruck stood. He started to bow and move back, but the prelate raised his hand.

"Sire Ruadrik—do you believe this woman's visions are given to her by God?" he asked mildly.

"Yea, my lord." Ruck knew well enough to answer that in a firm voice. Any other reply, he felt, could be twisted to mean that they were Hell-inspired.

"You follow her in her preachings on that account?"

"She is my wife," Ruck said, and then felt a flush of embarrassment rise in his face. "She was. My lord—I—could not let her go so far alone."

"You did not require her to stay modestly at home?"

He stood in shame, unable to admit that he'd found it impossible to command his own wife. "Her visions enjoin her," he said desperately. "She is God's own servant."

His words died away into a profound silence. He felt they were laughing at him, to offer that as an excuse.

"And you have given a solemn vow of chastity to her some five weeks past, on the road from Reims?"

Ruck gazed helplessly at the bishop.

"In obedience to this woman's visions," the bishop repeated insistently, "you lived chaste in your marriage?"

Ruck lowered his face. "Yea," he mumbled, staring at the bright floor tiles. "My lord."

"Oh, I think not," said a light female voice. "He is not chaste. Indeed, he is an adulterer."

Ruck stiffened at this astonishing accusation. "Nay, I am not—" His fierce denial died on his tongue as he turned to find the lady with the falcon standing not a rod behind him.

She strolled forward, sliding a glance at him over her shoulder while she dropped a token reverence toward the bishop. Her eyes were light, not quite perfect blue, but saturated with the lilac tinge of her dress and lined by black lashes. She seemed ageless, as young as Isabelle and as old as iniquity. The emeralds on the falcon's hood glittered.

Ruck felt his face aflame. "I have not adultered!" he said hoarsely.

"Is not the thought as sinful as the deed, Father?" she asked, addressing the bishop but looking at Ruck, her voice clear enough for her words to resonate from the walls.

"That is true, my lady. But if you have no earthly evidence, it is a matter of absolution between a man and his confessor."

"Of course." She smiled that serene and indifferent smile, lifting her skirts, withdrawing. "I fear that I presumed too far. I wished only to spare Your Holiness the mockery of hearing a solemn vow of chastity made by such a man. He stared at me full bold yesterday in the Hall of Great Audience, causing me much uneasiness of mind."

A low sound of protest escaped Ruck's throat. But he could not deny it. He had stared. He had committed adultery in his heart. He had desired her with an inordinate desire, a mortal passion—her eyes met his as she retired gracefully to one side—he read absolute knowledge there; she laid him bare, and she knew that he knew it.

"I am grieved to hear that you have had any cause for annoyance in the house of God, my lady," the prelate said, not sounding particularly disturbed. "Modesty in manner and dress, daughter, will temper the boldness of ungodly men toward you. But your point is well-taken with regard to the vow. Sire Ruadrik—can you swear to your purity both in thought and in deed?"

Ruck thought God Himself must be subjecting him to this

mortification, holding him to a standard of truth beyond the strength of human flesh. Why else should all these great people take up their time with him? He was nobody, nothing to them.

He could not bring himself to answer, not here in front of everyone. In front of *her*. She might be the agent of God's truth, but he thought no woman had ever appeared more as if she'd been sent by the Arch-Fiend to enthrall a man.

The silence lengthened, condemning him. He looked at her, and at Isabelle's open tear-streaked face. His wife stared back at him.

Ruck closed his eyes. He shook his head no.

"Sire Ruadrik," the archbishop said heavily, "with this admission of impurity, and other considerations, the vow given to your wife must be considered invalid."

As the interpreter translated, Isabelle broke into a great wail.

"Silence!" the archbishop thundered, and even Isabelle drew in her breath in shock at the suddenness of it. In the pause he said, "You must be heard by your confessor, Sire Ruadrik. I leave your penance to him. For the other matter—" He glanced at Isabelle, who had crawled forward and lay tugging at his hem. "In the usual course, one spouse is prevented from taking such a vow of chastity, if the other does not consent to it and vow also the same. Consent alone is not sufficient, as without the consolation of a solemn commitment to live celibate and close to God, the temptations of the flesh may prove too great." He looked at Ruck. "Lacking this true commitment, you will see the wisdom in such requirement, Sire Ruadrik."

Ruck could barely hold the man's eyes. He nodded slightly, burning all over.

The archbishop lifted his hand. "Nevertheless, this woman appears to me to be a special case. With the proper provisions, I am willing to allow that she may be attached to the convent and live in obedience to the rules of the house without her husband's concurrent vow. After I have examined her further in the articles of the faith and found her response to be satisfactory, and the provision for her support has been received, she may be admitted to the order."

When Isabelle heard the translation of this, she kissed the archbishop's hem and showed clear signs of working herself into an ecstasy. The archbishop made a gesture of dismissal. Ruck found himself escorted toward the door.

He wrenched his arm from the clerk's hold and turned back, but people had crowded in. From the corridor all he saw was the lady of the falcon, lifting her hand to her ear with a look of pained sufferance as Isabelle's voice rose to a shriek. The door closed. A clerk accosted him, informing him that an endowment of thirty-seven gold florins had been promised on behalf of Isabelle and would be accepted at once.

Thirty-seven gold florins was all the money that Ruck had, the last of the ransom from the two French knights he'd captured at Poitiers. The clerk took it, counting carefully, biting each coin before he dropped it into the holy purse.

RUCK WALKED TO the hostel as if in a dream. His steps took him first to the stable, to make certain at least of his horse and his sword when everything else seemed a daze.

"Already gone," the hosteler said.

The haze vanished. Ruck grabbed him by the throat, sending his broom flying. "I paid thee, by God!" He threw the man against the wall. *"Where are they?"*

"The priest!" The hosteler scooted hastily out of reach. "The priest came to collect them, gentle sire! Your good wife—" He stumbled to his feet, ducking. "Is not she to go for a nun? He had a bishop's seal! An offering to the church—on her behalf, he said—he told me you had willed it so. A bishop's seal, my lord. I'd not have let them go for less, on my life!"

Ruck felt like a man hit by a pole-ax, still on his feet, but reeling.

"They took my horse?" he asked numbly.

"My lord's arms, too." From a safe distance the hosteler made a sympathetic grunt. "They would fain have me climb upstairs after your mail and helm. Bloodsuckers, the lot of them."

Isabelle had made him leave his armor. She had made a great ado of it.

Thirty-seven gold florins. Exactly what she had known was in his purse. And his horse. His sword. His armor.

He locked his hands over his head and tilted his face to the sky. A howl burst from him, a long bellow that reverberated from the stones like a beast's dumb roar. Impotent tears and fury blurred his vision. He leaned back against the wall and slid down it, sitting in the dirt with his head in his arms.

"Ye might sue for to have the horse back, if it were a mistake, gentle sire," the hosteler offered kindly.

Ruck gave a miserable laugh from the hollow of his arms. "How long would that take?"

"Ah. Who could know? Twain year, mayhap."

"Yea—and cost the price of a dozen horse," he muttered.

"True enough," the hosteler agreed morbidly.

Ruck sat curled, staring into the darkness of his arms, his back against the stone wall. He heard the hosteler go away, heard people talking and passing. Grief and rage spun him. He couldn't move; he had nowhere to go, no wife, no money. Nothing. He couldn't seem to get his mind around the full dimension of it.

A smart prod at his shoulder pushed him half off his balance. He looked up, with no notion of what time had passed, except that the shadows lay longer and deeper on the street.

The prod came again and Ruck grabbed at the staff with an angry oath. Before him stood the hunchbacked mute he'd gifted with a *denier*—and his first thought was that he wished he had the money back again.

The beggar held out a little pouch. Ruck scowled. The hunchback wriggled the pouch and offered it closer. He waited, staring at Ruck expectantly as he accepted it.

The bag contained a folded paper and a small coin. The beggar was still waiting. Ruck held on to the coin for a moment, but futile pride overcame him and he tossed it to the beggar with no good grace. The man grinned and saluted, shuffling away.

Ruck watched his dinner and bed disappear up the narrow street. He unfolded the paper—and jerked, catching at the green glitter that fell from inside.

I charge thee, get thee far hence ere nyt falleth. Fayle not in this.

He gazed at the English words, and the two emeralds in his palm. One was small, no bigger than the lens of a dragonfly. The other was of a size to buy full armor and mount, and pay a squire for a year. A size to adorn a falcon's arrogant crest.

He held the emeralds, watched them wink and catch the light.

He knew what he ought to do. A good man, a virtuous man, would stand up and stride to the palace and throw them in her face. A godly man would not let himself be bound to such a one as she.

He'd given up his wife to God.

And his horse, and his armor, and his money.

Ruck closed his hand on the jewels she sent and swore himself to the Arch-Fiend's daughter.

A ȝere ȝernes ful ȝerne and ȝeldeȝ neuer lyke;
Þe forme to þe fynisment foldeȝ ful selden.
Forþi, þis ȝol ouerȝede, and þe ȝere after,
And vche sesoun serlepes sued after oþer.
                    *
And þus ȝirneȝ þe ȝere in ȝisterdayeȝ mony,
And wynter wyndeȝ aȝayn.

A year turns full turn and yields never like;
The first to the finish conform full seldom.
Forby, this Yule over, and the year after,
And each season separately ensued after other.
                    *
And thus yields the year in yesterdays many,
And winter wendes again.

Sir Gawain and the Green Knight

One

"YEAR'S GIFTS!"

The cry rose with squeals and laughter as the ladies of Bordeaux craned, reaching for the prizes held tauntingly overhead by their gay tormentors. Veils came askew, belts failed and sent misericordes flying in the tussle—in a rush of varicolored silks and furs each gentleman went down in willing defeat, yielding his New Year's keepsake for the price of a kiss.

The first Great Pestilence was twenty and two years gone, the Second Scourge ten Christmases past—but though the French harried Aquitaine's borders and yet another outbreak of the dread black swellings had killed Lancaster's white duchess herself just last year, such dire thoughts were blown to oblivion when the trumpets gave forth a great shout, sounding the arrival of pastries to the hall, fantastic shapes of ships and castles and a stag that bled claret wine when the gilt arrow was plucked from its side.

A mischievous lady was the first to toss an eggshell full of sweet-water at her lord—the carved rafters resounded with glee, and in a moment every man was wiping perfumed drops from his lashes, grinning, demanding another kiss for his misfortune. Some hungry lordling broke the crust of a huge pie and a dozen frogs leapt free, thumping onto the table amid skips and feminine screams. From another pie came a rush of feathered bodies, birds that flew to the light and put out the candles as the company filled the gloom with shrill enjoyment.

The Duke of Lancaster himself sat with languid elegance at the high table of Ombrière, watching critically as kettledrums and the wild high notes of warbling flutes heralded the first course. At the duke's right hand, his most high and honored guest, the Princess Melanthe di Monteverde, overlooked the dim noisy hall with cold indifference. Her white falcon, equally impassive, gripped its carved and painted block with talons dipped in silver. The bannered trumpets sounded once more. All the candles and torches glowed again in magical unison, illuminating the hall and dais as the liveried servants held the lights aloft.

Lancaster smiled, leaning very near Princess Melanthe. "My lady's highness likes not mirth and marvels?"

She gave him a cool glance. "Marvels?" she murmured in a bored tone. "I expect naught less than a unicorn before the sweetmeats."

Lancaster grinned, allowing his shoulder to touch hers as he reached to refill the wine cup they shared. "Too commonplace. Nay, give us a more difficult task, Princess."

Melanthe hid her annoyance. Lancaster was courting her. He would not be snubbed and he would not be forestalled. He took her coldness as challenge; her reluctance as mere dalliance.

"Then, sir—I will have it green," she said smoothly, and to her vexation he laughed aloud.

"Green it shall be." He signaled to an attendant and leaned back to speak in the servant's ear, then gave Melanthe a sidelong smile. "Before sweetmeats, my lady, a green unicorn."

The heavy red-and-blue cloth of his sleeve brushed her arm as he lifted the cup toward her lips, but the bishop on his other side sought him. In his distraction Melanthe took her opportunity to capture the goblet from his hand. She could already see the assembly's reaction to his attentions. Swift as metheglin could intoxicate a man, another horrified report began to spread among the tables below.

It would be a subdued mumble, Melanthe knew, passed over a shared sliver of meat or a finger full of sweet jelly, whispered under laughter with the true discretion of fear. Lancaster was thirty, handsome and vigorous in the full strength of manhood. While his oldest brother the Black Prince lay swollen and confined to his bed with dropsy, it was Lancaster who kept court as Lieutenant of Aquitaine, but who could blame a younger son of the King of England—most surely one of such energy and pride as Lancaster—if his ambitions were for greater things than service to his brother? Everyone knew he would take another highborn heiress after losing his good Duchess Blanche, and no one expected him to dally long about it. But Mary, Mother of God, even for the gain it would bring him, did he truly contemplate the Princess Melanthe?

She could almost hear the whispers as she sat next to him upon the dais and surveyed the company. There—that woman in the blue houpelande, leaning back to speak to the next table—she was no doubt complaining to her neighbor that such a gyrfalcon as Princess Melanthe carried was too great for a woman to fly. Nothing in the duke's mews could match it; not even the Black Prince himself owned such a bird. The insolence, that she would display it so at the duke's own feast! Immodesty! Wicked vanity and arrogance!

Melanthe gave the woman a long dispassionate stare and had the pleasure of watching her victim turn white with dismay at the attention.

Her reputation preceded her.

And those three, the two knights inclining so near to the pretty fair-haired girl between them—Melanthe could see the relish in their faces. Widowed of her Italian prince, the men would say, heiress to all her father's vast English lands . . . and the girl would whisper that Princess Melanthe had caused a maiden to be drowned in her bath for dropping a cake of Castile soap.

From her late husband, someone else would murmur—the income of an Italian city-state; from her English father, lord of Bowland, holdings as large as Lancaster's; she'd taken fifteen lovers and murdered all of them; for a man to smile at her was certain death—here the knights would smirk and grin—

certain, but exquisite, the final price for the paradise he could savor for as long as it pleased her to dally with him.

Melanthe had heard it all, knew what they spoke as well as if she sat among them. But still Lancaster paid her court with polish and wolf's glances, smiles and covetous stares, barely concerned to keep his desire in check. Melanthe knew what they were saying of that, too. She had entrapped him. Ensorcelled him. He'd left off his black mourning; all trace of lingering grief for his beloved Blanche had vanished. He looked at the Princess Melanthe as he looked at her falcon, with the look of a man who has determined what he will have and damn the price.

She only *wished* she might ensorcell him, and turn him to a toad.

Tonight she must act—this public gallantry of his could not be allowed to go on without check. Before the banquet ended, she must spurn him so that he and no one else could doubt it. When she looked out upon the trestles, she saw the assassin who watched her, tame and plump in her own green-and-silver livery, but in truth another spawn of the Riata family, one of the secret wardens set upon her. Only by the mastery of long practice did she maintain her cold serenity against the hard beat of her heart.

The food arrived with full pomp and glitter, loaded onto cloths of purest linen, the procession winding endlessly among the tables. Lancaster offered her the choice dainties from his own fingers. She brought herself to the point of rudeness in response to him—by God's self, must he be so open about it, this determined public pursuit in the face of her expressed displeasure, when he might have had the sense to send his envoy by night and secrecy to measure her willingness?

But he thought it agreeable sport, she saw, a lovers' game of disinterest and affectation. He full expected that she would have him. She had told him more than once that she would have no man, but none here would blame him for his confidence. It was a brilliant match. Their lands marched together in the north of England: the sum of their possessions would rival the king's. By this alliance the duke could make her the greatest lady in Britain—and she could make him greater yet than that.

It was not passion alone that drove him to these smiles and hot looks.

She touched him lightly when he leaned too close, to remind him that they were in the court's view. He grinned, sitting back in obedience, but a moment later he had leaned near again, grasping her hand possessively, holding it in his upon the table in a gesture as clear as a proclamation. The Riata stood up from his seat, mingling with the servants as they passed up and down the hall.

Melanthe made no move to disengage herself. It was a game of hints and inklings between her and the Riata's man—a language of act and counteract. He moved closer, warning her, reminding her of her agreement with Riata and her peril if she thought to wed any man, especially such a one as Lancaster.

She merely looked at the duke's fingers entwined with hers on the white cloth, refusing to show fear. Her heart was beating too hard, but she held to her aloof composure, asking Lancaster for a loaf of trimmed pandemain from the golden platter just set down before them, so that he must let go her hand to serve her properly.

When she looked up, she saw the Riata lingered in a closer place even though the duke had released her. Verily, Lancaster's hopes must be crushed, or she would be fortunate to see the light of another morning.

Gryngolet moved uneasily on her perch at Melanthe's elbow, the falcon's silver bells ringing as she half roused to the sweeping flutter of a sparrow that still flew, panicked, among the roof beams. Noble stewards clustered and moved behind and before the dais, attending the duke and his guests, trimming bread, carving quail: knives and poison and color—she could not keep them all in her eye at once, as adept as she had made herself at such things. The Riata could kill her as well before the entire hall as in some dark passage. It was too dangerous and open a position; she had not chosen it; she had tried to avoid it, but Lancaster's ambitions had overwhelmed her subtleties. She must sit at his high table and deny him to his face.

She had misjudged. These reckless English—she saw that she had been too accustomed to the feints and lethal shadows

of the Italian courts to recall the power of plain English boldness. She would be fortunate to find her way to her chambers
alive in this castle of unfamiliar corners and hidden places.

An ill luck it had been that had brought her to Bordeaux at
all on her way home to England. She'd foreseen this disaster
with Lancaster well enough to avoid the place by intention,
but still had not cared to chance her French welcome and take
the most northern route. She'd skirted Bordeaux, choosing the
road to Limoges—only to meet there the English army just
done with razing the town to ashes.

Lancaster wielded his courtesy with the same skill he han-
dled a sword. She must not rush on her way home to
Bowland, he had insisted graciously—there was to be a New
Year's tournament—she must come to Bordeaux and honor
him with her presence at the celebration. He had the ear of his
father the king, he told her with his elegant hungry smile. He
would write his recommendation that Princess Melanthe be
put in possession of her English inheritance immediately and
without prejudice. That he might, if he chose, equally well
jeopardize her prospects with King Edward needed no such
blunt hinting.

Wherefore, she was here. And Lancaster continued on his
fatal determination, courting her through the service of the
white meats and the red. She lost sight of the Riata, and then
found him again, closer.

The moment approached. Lancaster would ask for her
favor to carry in the tournament tomorrow. He had already
told her that he would fight within the lists. In this public
place, hanged be the man, Lancaster would beg her for a certain token of her regard and force her to a public answer.

There was no eluding it, no hope that he would not. His
intention toward her was in his every compliment and sidelong glance. She had thought of becoming faint and retiring,
but that could only put the thing off until the morrow—
another night on guard against the Riata—and set off a round
of further solicitude from the duke. Beyond that, the Princess
Melanthe did not become faint. It was a weakness. Melanthe
did not choose to show weakness.

She would end with Lancaster a powerful enemy, his lands
marching with hers in bitterness instead of friendship. A man

such as he would not soon forget a woman's public refusal. Among these northerners, chivalry and honor counted for all . . . but the Riata must be shown that she would not have the duke, and must be shown it soon and well.

She suffered Lancaster's attentions to grow more and more direct. She began to encourage him, though he needed no encouragement from her to lead himself to his own humiliation. She was angry at him, but smiled. She regretted him, but she smiled still, ruthless, laughing at his wit, complimenting his banquet. It was no sweet love that drove Lancaster now, but ambition and a man's lust. She could not save him if he would not save himself.

The second course arrived. As a gilded swan was carved before them, the duke grew a little drunk with wine and success. He plucked a subtlety in the shape of a rosebud from the profusion of decoration on the platter and offered it to her with a glance more of affection than desire. Melanthe accepted the almond sweet from his fingers. She looked at him smiling softly upon her and felt a twinge of regret for his spare, comely figure—for women's fancies—things she had heard about him, of the love he bore still for his first wife, things that could not now nor ever be between her and a man.

In exchange for her life—his pride. It seemed a fair enough bargain to Melanthe.

As Lancaster prepared their shared trencher with his own hands, she glimpsed a slim figure in blue-and-yellow hose in the throng below. Allegreto Navona lounged at the edge of the hall, near the great hearth, his black hair and bright hues almost blending into the shapes and figures in the huge tapestry on the wall behind him. The youth was looking toward the dais. As Melanthe accepted the duke's tidbit, Allegreto smiled directly at her.

It was his sweet smirk; charming and sly. She stared at him a moment.

He had succeeded at something. She looked again quickly for the assassin wearing her own green-and-silver livery—there he was, the one Riata watchdog she knew of certainly, still holding checked, still only observing from a distance—Allegreto had not slain or expelled him. Which did not mean that the youth had not bloodied his hands in some other way.

She was torn between anger and relief. She had her own agreement with the Riata. In spite of the unceasing threat of the watchers they had placed on her, she wanted no Riata lives spent, not now. But she could not disclose that to a son of the house of Navona. And a murder in the midst of this banquet, in her retinue . . . it would be offensive; there would be trouble; things were not done so here as they were in Italy, but she could not make Allegreto understand.

She did not acknowledge him with more than a brief look, reserving her pleasure. He made a face of mock disappointment, then lifted his chin in silent mirth. A pair of servants bore huge platters past him. When they had moved beyond, he was gone.

The trumpets sounded.

Melanthe looked up in startlement. They could not yet herald the last course. Over the hum of gossip and feasting came the shouts of men outside the hall. Her hand dropped instinctively to her dagger as the clatter of iron hooves rang against the walls. People gasped; servers scattered out of the great entry doors, spilling platters of sweets and more subtleties. Melanthe reached for Gryngolet's leash.

An apparition burst into the hall. A green-armored knight on a green horse hurdled the stairs, galloping up the center aisle, the ring of hooves suddenly muffled by the woven rushes so that the pair seemed to fly above the earth as ladies screamed and dogs scrambled beneath the tables.

Nothing hampered his drive to the high dais. Not a single knight rose to his lord's defense. Melanthe found herself on her feet alone, gripping her small dagger as Gryngolet roused her feathers and spread her wings in wild alarm.

The horse reached the dais and whirled, half rearing, showing emerald hooves and green legs, the twisting silver horn on its forehead slashing upward. The destrier's braided mane flew out like dyed silk as light sent green reflections from the lustrous armor. Silver bells chimed and jangled from the bridle and caparisons. At the peak of the knight's closed helm flourished a crest of verdant feathers, bound by silver at the base, set with an emerald that sent one bright green flash into her eyes before he brought the horse to a standstill.

The knight was on a level with her, the eye slits in his visor dark with the daunting inhumanity that was the life and power of his kind. The destrier's heavy breath seemed to belong to both of them. He held the reins with gloves of green worked in silver—on his shield the only emblem was a hooded hawk, silver on green. Rich ermine lined his mantle, and all over the horse's caparisons embroidered dragonflies mingled with flowers and birds, silver only: argent and green entire.

Melanthe's hand relaxed slightly on the dagger as she realized that this was not immediate attack. She felt the sudden exposure of standing alone, but it was too late to sit down and hide her reaction. Everyone stared, and after their first startlement, no one appeared dismayed. At the edge of her vision, she could see the duke grinning.

"My lady," Lancaster said into the utter stillness. "Your unicorn comes."

"Mary," Melanthe said. "So it does."

"My liege lady." The knight's voice sounded hollow and harsh from within the helmet. He made a bow in the saddle. The horse danced. "My dread lord."

"Trusty and well-beloved knight." The duke acknowledged him with a lazy nod. "My lady, we call him the Green Sire who rides your unicorn. I fear he will not grace us with his true name."

"Liege lord of my life," the knight said, "I have made a vow."

"Yea, I remember. Not until thou art proved worthy, was it? At least remove thy helm, sir. It alarms the ladies, as thou canst well see." He made a slight gesture toward Melanthe.

The green knight hesitated. Then he seized his helmet and pulled it off his head. The feathers fluttered as he held it under his arm. Melanthe glanced at the emerald that adorned the crest, and looked into his face.

But he kept his eyes well cast down, focused on some spot below the table at Lancaster's feet, showing mostly a head of black hair cut short and unruly. He was clean-shaven, with a strong jaw and strong features, sun- and battle-hardened in a way that was different from the men she was accustomed to—in the way of campaign and *chevauchée*, open-air knight errantry instead of close-handed *duellum* with wits and dagger. Melanthe had an abiding respect for any type of violence;

this type had the benefit of a certain novelty. One could appreciate the theory of chivalrous knighthood . . . one could smile at the idea of a man who would not give his name until he was proven worthy.

Since she felt the urge to smile, she followed the primary rule of her existence and did not do it. Had she followed that principle a moment ago, stifling instinct, she would not now be standing in this foolish and conspicuous way, showing herself the only one who had been so affected by the sensational entrance.

"You desire a unicorn, and I give it you," Lancaster said in high good humor. "The beast is yours to command, Princess."

The knight lifted his head slightly. His face was immobile. A faint tickle of significance stirred in Melanthe's mind, a fleeting thought she could not catch. He was indeed a fine man, tall on his horse, strong of limb, his face that combination of beauty and roughness that provoked the ladies to sighs and the more elegant courtiers to spiteful remarks about vulgarity. The range of expression in the company behind him was of vast interest to Melanthe—and not least intriguing the green knight's own taut countenance. He had a look of extremity on him, some emotion far more intense than mere playacting at marvels before a lady.

"What will you, my lady?" Lancaster asked. "Shall you send them to hunt dragons?"

The knight glanced at Melanthe for an instant, then away, as if the contact startled. His destrier shifted restlessly beneath him, its enameled hooves thumping on the braided rush. The bells jangled. With an abrupt move he yanked one glove from his hand and threw it down before the company. "A challenge!" he shouted. He turned about in the saddle, scanning the hall, rising in his stirrups. "For the honor of my lady, tomorrow I take all who come!"

Lancaster went stiff beside her. He stood up. "Nay, sir," he snapped. "Such is not thy place, to defend Her Highness!"

The knight ignored his liege. "Is this the court of the Black Prince and Lancaster?" he shouted furiously. "Who will fight me for the honor of my lady?"

His voice echoed in the stunned silence of the hall. They stared at him as if he had lost his senses. But comprehension burst upon Melanthe. *This* was the source of Allegreto's mirthful satisfaction—he had created a chance for her.

"Cease thy nonsense!" Lancaster growled in a low voice. "It does thee no credit, sir!"

The green knight had dropped his veneer of submissive respect. His gaze hit Melanthe and skewed away again. He dismounted and went down on his knee before her in a chinking clash of mail. "My lady!" Over the edge of the table she could see that he held his bare hand against his heart, the plumed helmet thrust under his arm. "I crave of you, do me this ease—give me something of your gift, that I might carry the precious prize tomorrow and defend against all comers."

"Thou shalt not do so!" the duke declared, his voice rising. "I carry Her Highness' favor, impudent rogue!"

Melanthe seized her moment. She slanted him a cool look. "Think you so, my lord?" she asked softly.

Lancaster glanced at her, his face growing red. "I—" His jaw went taut. "I am at your service, if you will honor me," he said stiffly.

Melanthe smiled at him. She caught Gryngolet's jesses and pulled the soft white calf's leather loose from about the falcon's legs, slipping her dagger inside to cut the belled bewits and the jesses free. Gryngolet's varvels swung suspended from the ends—two silver rings jeweled with emeralds and diamonds and engraved with Melanthe's name. She slipped the bells from Milan onto the jesses, tying them so that they made a falcon's music—one note striking high and one low— in the rich harmony that belonged to nothing else in heaven or earth.

Lancaster was watching her. She looked at him for a long, significant moment, then turned back to the knight who still knelt below her.

"Green Sire," she declared, "the most precious prize I possess on earth, I give thee for a keepsake, to defend me for my honor on the morrow."

She tossed the jesses with their gems and bells onto the rush before him.

"I challenge for it!" Lancaster exclaimed instantly.

"And I, on my lord's behalf!" A man stood up beyond him on the dais.

"And I!" They were seconded by two more, and then four, knights standing in the hall to shout their dares until the hammer-beams rang.

"Enough!" Lancaster lifted his arm. "It shall be arranged who will fight." He glared down at the green knight. "Rise, then, insolent fellow."

The knight came to his feet, his eyes downcast again. She noticed that he'd had the presence of mind to retrieve his gauntlet along with the jesses while he knelt—not entirely a lack-wit. God only knew how Allegreto had threatened or enticed him to do this thing. The knight stood waiting with a stony stare at his lord's feet, the light on his virid armor sculpting broad curves at his shoulders, chasing silver arcs across his arm-plates. Lancaster could barely keep the fury from his face.

"A most marvelous unicorn," she said with amusement. "My lord's grace is kind, to put him at my service."

Lancaster seemed to find some control of his emotion. He bowed to her, producing a smile that did not quite cover the grim set of his jaw. "I would have counted it worth my life to serve you myself, my lady. But now I count it an honor to win your better regard by trial tomorrow, against this man I had thought under true oath to me."

The green knight looked up, his expression a fascinating play of yearning and pride, of checked temper. "My beloved lord, I wish with my whole heart to please you, but my lady commands me."

"Thou takest too much credit upon thyself, knave!"

The knight glanced to Melanthe; his eyes as green as his armor, human now instead of hidden by steel and darkness. In his intense gaze there was an open dismay of his own defiance before his prince—he looked to her hoping for reprieve, asking her for release from what he had done.

She held him, denying it. Her answer was unrelenting silence.

The knight bowed his head. She could see the taut muscle in his bared neck. "Does my lord bid me serve his pleasure before my lady's?" he asked in a low voice.

It was a futile attempt, hardly more than a strained whisper. Without an appeal from Melanthe herself, Lancaster would not withdraw—could not, not now, when he had agreed to fight.

"I do not well know where thou comest by this notion that Her Highness stoops to command such as thee!" Lancaster snapped.

"From me, mayhap," Melanthe murmured.

The duke gave her a sullen small bow. "Then your wish is mine," he said curtly. "And my command, of course. This man shall ride for you on the morrow, my lady, against myself and all who challenge for your favor."

The green knight lifted chagrined eyes to Melanthe. Holding Gryngolet on her wrist, ignoring Lancaster, she gave her new champion a small smile and dropped a mocking bow of courtesy. "I look forward to such spectacle. Go now and refresh thyself, Green Sire. Attend me in chamber when dinner is done."

"May God reward you, lady," he murmured mechanically, and stood. With an easy move that belied the weight of his armor, he remounted, reining the horse around and spurring it to a gallop. He parted the men-at-arms at the door, vanishing out of the hall with an echo of hooves and bells.

OF COURSE SHE didn't remember him.

Ruck tore the loaf of white bread and shed more crumbs onto his bare chest, causing mute Pierre to gesture and dust him urgently, but there was no time to sit down for a meal as his broken-backed squire wished. His lady—his liege lady, the cherished queen of his heart—commanded him immediately after the dinner; and by the time he'd stabled Hawk, secured his mount's armor and his own, harried Pierre, and sufficiently bullied and bribed the fourth chamberlain for a bath in the midst of a banquet, he could hear the higher note of the trumpets that signified the lord's retirement from the hall.

A light-headed sickness hung in his throat. The dry bread seemed to choke him. It was almost too fantastical to believe that it was her; that she was here. He had never expected it. He hardly knew how to fathom the fact, or what he had just done for her.

Christ—Lancaster's face—but Ruck could not bear to think of it.

"Hie!" He knocked Pierre's hand aside as the squire tried to wipe the shaving soap from him. The barber had been impossible to obtain at such a time. "My hose." He grabbed the towel, cleaned his jaw himself, and finished off the bread before Pierre had the green hose ready for him.

He didn't think she remembered him. He couldn't settle it in his mind. By her young courtier in the yellow-and-blue motley, she had sent him a command to challenge for her. She had looked upon him in the hall with that cool authority . . . as if she knew his vow to her service—as if she expected it. He had a wild thought that she had known all there was to know of him since that day he had first seen her, that his every move for ten and three years had somehow been open to her. Those eyes of hers, 'fore God!

She was here. And in faith, it felt more like a blow to his belly than a boon.

His breath frosted in the cold as he bit into an apple. Holding the fruit between his teeth, he pulled the green hose over his linen. A few gentlemen began to wander out of the great hall to relieve themselves, passing the open door of the buttery where the servants had grudgingly hauled the bathtub for Ruck.

"La la! Seest thou, Christine," said a feminine voice. "He is not green all over!"

Ruck looked up from belting his hose to find a pair of ladies leaning in the door. He didn't know either of them. He dropped the apple from his mouth and caught it in one hand. As he bowed, he grabbed his mantle from Pierre's hands and tossed it around his bare shoulders. "A common man only, madam."

The dark-haired one giggled. The other, the one who'd spoken, was blonde and comely and she knew it; she moved upon him with a flow of brilliant parti-color robes. "Thy form gives thee the lie, sir. Thou art uncommon strong and pleasing." Smiling, she traced him with her forefinger from the base of his throat down to his chest. "And uncommon brave, to proclaim such a challenge."

He lightly clasped her hand and lifted it away from him. "For the honor of Her Highness," he said evenly.

Her smile deepened. "Such wild courage," she murmured, lifting her mouth. "We have heard much of your ferocity in battle. Stay and tell us more."

He looked down at her offered lips, the soft smiling curve. "For God's mercy, you tempt me to dally, but I cannot." He held up the apple, brushed her cheek with the rosy smooth skin, and pressed the fruit into her fingers, setting her away from him. "Accept this, and I know I've shared a sweet with a gracious lady."

A shadow of pique crossed her features. But she stepped back, taking a bite with a crunch of white teeth. "The Princess Melanthe," she said airily. "You know her?"

"I know her," he said.

"Ah. Then you know to accept no apples of love from that one. She poisoned her own husband."

Ruck stiffened. "Madam—it were better that thou speak truth on thy tongue."

"Oh, I speak true enough." She licked a drop of juice from the apple. "Ask it of anyone. She was put to trial for the deed."

He scowled at her for a moment, and then held out his hand to Pierre for his tunic. His squire caught the mantle as Ruck shrugged it off and pulled the green wool over his head. A few more gentlewomen hovered outside.

"She is a sorceress," his blonde temptress said, and looked to the others. "Is she not?"

"That gyrfalcon," another offered. "The bird is her familiar. Never has she flown it in the light of day."

"She bewitched the magistrate to release her—"

"She took her own brother for a lover—"

"Yea, and murdered him with that very dagger at her waist; whilst he was a guest in her husband's house."

"And now on her way to gorge on his birthright! But no Christian knight will escort her hence, for fear of his soul."

"Nay," Ruck objected, "she is a princess."

"A witch! Sir Jean will say you!" Feminine hands urged a knight forward from where he'd been lingering at the edge of the group, trying to woo one of the gentlewomen.

Pierre helped Ruck into his surcoat, smoothing down the cloth-of-silver. Ruck stood facing the other man, his jaw rigid. "Have a care," he said. "The chatter of the women is naught. On behalf of my sworn lady, sir, I will not take thy words so lightly."

"You have sworn to her?" the blonde asked, stepping back.

"Yea. I am her man."

"For the tourney," the other knight said. "My lord the duke will abide no more." He gave Ruck a shrewd grin. "It was a bold stroke you took. He's angry now, but he'll value you to show him at his finest on the morrow."

"I am her man," Ruck repeated.

Sir Jean looked at him. "Nay, you don't mean to be serious in this?"

Ruck stared back, eyes level, showing nothing. "I am sworn to her. I am honored with her gift. I fight for the Princess Melanthe."

The spectators began to depart, withdrawing with sidelong glances and murmurs among them. Ruck threw his mantle round his shoulders and stabbed the pin of his silver brooch through the cloth. When he looked up, he and Pierre were alone in the buttery.

The mute squire elevated his eyebrows expressively. He dug in his apron and held out a leather-bagged amulet.

"She is not a witch," Ruck snapped.

Pierre crossed himself and mimicked a priest blessing the charm.

"Curse thee! *She is my lady!*"

Pierre ducked and genuflected. With a roll of his eyes and a shake of his head, he tucked his saint's tooth away.

Two

"TELL ME," MELANTHE said lightly in Italian. "I can see thou art full of thine own shrewdness."

Allegreto Navona rested against the curve of the spiraling stairwell, his arms crossed, grinning down at her from two steps above. The last thin light fell between them from an arrowslit. "The green man is invincible, my lady," he whispered, leaning as near as he dared while she had Gryngolet on her fist. "Your fine Duke of Lancaster will have his tail feathers plucked tomorrow."

"Will he? After they have sent half their knighthood against my poor—champion?" She made a short laugh. "So I suppose I must title him."

"Nay, you miscalculate your knight, lady. They have another name for him here. They call him after some barbarian tale from the north—*Berserka,* or some such." He gave an elegant shudder. "I'm told it is the north-name of a savage in bear-coats. A warrior who would as soon kill as breathe."

"Berserker," Melanthe said, gazing at Allegreto thoughtfully. "Thou hast busy ears, to know so much of him. Where didst thou find this great warrior?"

"Why, in the stable, my lady, braiding his green destrier's green mane with silver, in preparation to fight in the hastilude tomorrow. A most pure and courteous knight, well-liked by common men-at-arms. He keeps to himself and the footsoldiers and the chapel, and has no traffic with ladies. But when they ordered him to play your unicorn because of his color . . . I thought to take him aside, Your Highness, and tell him of your wishes."

"*My* wishes." She lifted her eyebrows.

"You wished to bestow your tournament favor on him, lady." Allegreto smiled angelically. "Did you not? But he would have none of it, I fear—until I walked with him past the hall. I caused him to look upon you, lady . . . and sweet Mary, I only wish you might have seen his face."

"What was in his face?" she asked sharply.

Allegreto leaned his head back against the curving wall. "Indifference. And then—" He paused. "But what does my lady's grace care of his thoughts? He is only an English barbarian."

She stroked Gryngolet's breast. The gyrfalcon's talons relaxed and tightened on the gauntlet. Allegreto did not change his lazy stance, but he moved a half-step upward.

"Indifference, my lady," he said more respectfully, "until he had a fair sight of you. And then he became just such a witless lover as we needed to dissuade your duke, though he veiled it well."

"Thou promised him no promises," she said coldly.

"Lady, the sight of you is promise enough for a man," Allegreto murmured. "*I* made none, but I cannot vouch for what blissful hopes he might have in his own mind."

She regarded him for a long moment. He was young and beautiful, dark as a demon and as sweetly formed as the Devil could make him. Gryngolet roused her feathers, pure ruthless white. He glanced at the gyrfalcon for the barest instant. Allegreto dreaded naught on earth but three things: the falcon, the plague, and his father. Gryngolet was Melanthe's one true shield against him, for she had no mastery of the plague—and none over Gian Navona, for a certainty.

Prince Ligurio of Monteverde had been dead three months, but for years before he drew his last breath, Melanthe had upheld her husband's place and powers. As he declined into illness and vulnerability, she had defended him by the methods he had taught her himself. He it was who had schooled her to guard her back, who had been her father from the age of twelve when a terrified child had left England to wed a man thirty years her senior; he who had ordered her to deal with the Riata, to tantalize Gian Navona—because the triangle would always hold, there would always be the houses of Riata and Navona and Monteverde like wolves prowling about the same quarry.

Now Prince Ligurio was gone. The triangle of power fell in upon itself, leaving Melanthe between the wolves and the fortune of Monteverde.

She relinquished it to them. She did not want Monteverde, but to yield her claim was as perilous as to contend for it. Like a fox making for a safe earth, she must dodge and deceive and look always behind her as she escaped.

She had bargained with Riata—safe passage to a nunnery in England, in exchange for her quitclaim to Monteverde. She had bargained with Allegreto's father: she had smiled at Gian Navona and promised to be his wife, gladly—so gladly that she would even travel to England first, to confirm her inheritance there, that she might bring that prize, too, with her to their marriage bed.

Promise and promise and promise. They were made to betray, in layer upon layer of deception.

She kept only one, if she died for it. To herself. She was going home—to England and to Bowland. The fox escaped to earth.

"I am displeased with thy interference," she said to Allegreto. "Thou dost not understand the English. If thou thought to discourage the duke by such a challenge—it has done no more than place him so that he must prove his devotion, and now tomorrow I must spurn him yet again."

"I know aught of these boorish English manners, my lady," he said with light malice, "if a man must thrust his attention upon a lady without her encouragement."

"Save thy indignation for a fool who meddles in his mistress's business. I had my own intent with regard to Lancaster."

Allegreto merely grinned at the rebuke. "Not to take him in marriage, lady, so I hope."

"If he will not bring himself to the point and ask, I cannot take him, can I?"

"He will," Allegreto said. He made a mock bow. "But my lady's grace would not break my father's loving heart that has bided so long in silent hope."

Melanthe returned his salute with an affectionate smile. "I will not have Lancaster at any price—but Allegreto, my love—when next thou dost write to thy father, tell Gian that in truth, thou art such a tender gentle boy, there are moments I should rather take thee to husband in his stead."

Allegreto's face did not change. He maintained the pleasant curve of his lips, his dark eyes fathomless. "I would not be so foolish, my lady. That price has indeed been paid already."

Melanthe turned her face. She shamed herself even to taunt Allegreto with it. What Gian Navona had taken of his bastard son, to be certain that Allegreto would sleep chastely in Melanthe's bedchamber, was beyond cost or pity.

"Let us go." She lifted her skirt, stepping upward, but he made a faint hiss of warning and raised his forefinger. Instead of waiting for her to pass, he turned, going lightly up ahead of her, his yellow-and-blue slippers silent on the stone stairs.

Melanthe's pulse heightened. That was her weakness, as the falcon was Allegreto's—she could not for her life keep her heart cool when her mind required it. Through the harder beat in her ears, she turned to listen behind her. "Come, give me a kiss, Allegreto," she said to the empty stairwell, "and let us be gone."

She heard nothing but the rhythm of her own blood. After a moment she stepped up quietly after Allegreto, her hand on her dagger, her eyes on the turning of the newel. This winding stair gave onto the ramparts above and the chapel below, with a door into a small stone passage connecting to her inner apartment. She had not liked the insecure arrangement when she saw it, and she liked it less now.

The door stood open to empty darkness. She hesitated, staring at it, assessing it. Gryngolet preened calmly, but the falcon was no dog to bark at danger. She held aloof from human matters, as did all her kind. Melanthe took her misericorde from its sheath and turned the blade outward. She lifted Gryngolet, ready to fling the falcon safely free if she must.

"Come, lady."

Allegreto's ghostly voice drifted on silence, beckoning her. She took a quiet breath and stepped upward through the door.

He knelt behind it over a deep shadow. Melanthe saw a white shape, a limp palm half-open—and the shadow became a form: the Riata assassin sprawled dead in the half darkness.

There was no blood but on Allegreto's slim dagger; she had seen him practice his thrust on pigs—to make a stab that stopped the life flow instantly—what little gore there was bled to the lungs and not the surface, as he had once informed her with his sweet pride and pleasure in his craft. He was not smiling now, but sober, skilled in his task, stripping the corpse of her livery.

She pressed her lips tight together. "To my garderobe," she murmured. "I'll send Cara and the others away."

He nodded. Melanthe moved quickly back down the stairs to the chapel whence she'd come, spent a moment pretending to pray, and then climbed to her apartments by the grand stair-case. She retired to the solar, demanding a preparation of malvoisie wine sweetened with scented flowers and roses, and peace for her aching head. Her ladies knew better than to be in a hurry to return when she gave such an order.

When she was certainly alone, she unbolted the door onto the passage. Allegreto waited in the darkness, his prey stripped naked at his feet. He hefted the body to his shoulder, adept at that, too, though he staggered a little beneath the weight. "Fat Riata swine," he muttered, and flashed Melanthe a grin over the pale legs of the dead man.

She stood back with an unforgiving stare—which made Allegreto laugh silently. Bravado, perhaps, or real amuse-ment: it was no more possible to know his true feeling than it was for her to reveal the emotion that swirled in her stomach. She would punish him for this murder, because she had ordered him to refrain—but that did not diminish the horrible shock of triumph, the elation of safety, however brief; of knowing the thing done.

He carried the body before her, naked arms dangling—a sight that she disliked—but worse yet was the garderobe, a cold small chamber and a cold stone bench, a revolting moment while Allegreto worked to arrange the Riata's flaccid

torso, forcing it head downward into the shaft of the privy
well, so that it would not wedge in the fall. He gripped it by
the thighs, panting a little with his efforts. The white corpu-
lent limbs scored against stone without bleeding, opposing
him with slack resistance until he had shoved the thing in past
the shoulders to the waist.

He let go. The feet vanished. For a long moment there was
nothing. Then the sound as it hit the river—not what she'd
expected, not a splash, but a boom like a stone catapulted
against steel, echoing and echoing in the rank well.

He crossed himself and knelt before her. "I beg you pray
for me, my lady," he said humbly. "I know I have displeased
you, but I did it for your life."

She said nothing. He rose and caught up the pile of green-
and-silver livery, folding it into neat lengths. From the yellow
shoulder of his doublet, he plucked a loose hair. He held it
over the privy and flicked his fingers, sending the strand drifting into darkness.

Melanthe watched him. She had no nightmares. She never
slept enough to dream.

THE PRINCESS MELANTHE held audience amid Tharsia
silks and exotic courtiers, warmed by a perfumed fire. And of
course she did not remember him.

Ruck had himself not recognized her at once there in the
hall, at a distance, chafed as he'd been by the duke's sudden
demand to appear in full tournament armor for the pleasure of
some highborn lady, distracted by the strange foreign youth
who dogged his heels. He'd thought nothing of the duke's
guests, annoyed by the whelp's insistence that Ruck pause at
the door to look. He had seen only a bored and black-haired
feminine figure on the dais—until she had turned her head
and gazed with that cold irony upon Lancaster himself, had
lifted her fingers to stroke the white falcon's breast—not until
that crystallized moment had her face and the silver-and-
green colors that matched his own burst into recognition.

Now that he saw her again, he could not imagine that he
hadn't instantly perceived the lady of his life. She was precisely as he recalled; all of his dreams, all of his aspirations,
thirteen years of fidelity and devotion come to pass in gem-

stone radiance . . . except that he had thought her hair not quite so dark, and her eyes a paler blue.

In fact, he'd thought her more like Isabelle, only comelier.

She was comely indeed; gloriously, magnificently beautiful, none could gainsay it, but in a bold style that made the ladies' gossip just a trace more credible. Her chamberlain intoned, "The Green Sire, Your Highness," and she didn't even glance up at Ruck from the jewel casket that one of her gentlewomen held before her, merely lifting a hand toward the side of her bed.

He strode to the position. The slender youth who had conveyed her command to Ruck, that he challenge for her favor, showed no such respect. The boy lounged against a carpet-covered chest, decked in hose of one leg yellow and one leg blue. From the extreme edge of his vision, Ruck could see the puppy staring at him. Keeping his eyes straight ahead, he had nothing to look at but his liege lady, and she was a vision like ebony hammered into gold.

She had changed her gown. It was not now the low-cut kirtle of green samite that she had worn in the hall: it was a golden brocade cotehardi, long-sleeved, tight-fitting, trimmed in black, cut open and laced all the way down both sides—and it took him a long moment to realize that she wore nothing beneath it. He could see her white, bared skin all the way from her torso to her ankle.

He strove to keep his face expressionless. He dared not even blink. The sultry room made him hot beneath his ermine mantle. As she chose a necklace and belt of copper gilt and black enamel, the youth at his side moved, sliding a grin at Ruck, lolling across the bed to pluck the jewelry from her hands.

She bent her head as he clasped the necklace at her nape and smoothed his fingers down her throat. He was sixteen, mayhap less, scarce half her age or Ruck's, with black hair and skin as soft as hers. He stroked her as a lover would, bending to fasten the belt about her waist, kissing her shoulder as he did it.

She tilted her head, refusing to look into a mirror held up by one of the ladies. The youth watched Ruck beneath his lashes.

"Let me take down your hair, lady," he said, moving to do it. His fingers worked amid the crown of braids, unpinning them, spreading them. He held a curling lock up to his lips, laughing silently through it at Ruck. "Look you, my love," he said, speaking clear while pretending to whisper in her ear. "The green man wants you."

"So much the worse for him," she said indifferently.

"Only look at him, lady!" The youth was grinning in delight at Ruck. "He wishes that he might embrace you as I do. Just so—" He slipped his fingers around her waist, never taking his black eyes from Ruck.

She brushed his hands away. "Come, leave thy mischief. Dost thou wish to sharpen thy claws on him, Allegreto? Play, then—but recall that he is of use to me." She turned for one instant and met the youth's eyes. "See that thou dost not kill him, or I shall set Gryngolet upon thee."

This threat had a salutary effect upon her young courtier. He glanced at the falcon perched on a high stand at the foot of her bed. "Lady," he said submissively, drawing back from her.

"Do up my hair," she bid him. "The crespin net, I think."

In silence he took the comb and sparkling net from her lady-in-waiting and began to comb out the length of her hair, coiling it deftly.

As he worked, Princess Melanthe lifted her hand, beckoning to Ruck. He moved to the foot of the bed, lowering himself to one knee.

She laughed. "Truly, thou art the most *courteous* knight! Up with thee. I prefer to see the faces of my servants better than the tops of their heads."

He stood up.

"I will lead thy destrier into the lists tomorrow," she informed him. "See that the heralds know it. And thou must wear my favor upon thy lance for the entry—then I wish it brought to me for the nonce."

He bowed.

"Thou speakest English," she said suddenly.

"Yea, madam."

"Excellent. I will from time to time speak to thee in English. I wish to recall it from my childhood. A lesson for thee, Allegreto—always have a care to understand a little of the language of thy servants and dependants, that they may not take undue advantage of thee."

Allegreto pinned her hair, placing the net over it with care. In a subdued tone he said, "You are the source of all light and wisdom, Your Highness."

"Sweet boy, I would not let Gryngolet have thee for aught."

The shadow left his face. He began to knead her shoulders. Ruck lowered his eyes to the foot of the bed. He took a step back, withdrawing.

"Green Sire," she said imperiously, rejecting the youth's attention with an impatient flick of her wrist. "Word has come to my ear that thou art merciless in combat and tourney."

Ruck stood silent. She looked at him full for the first time, scanned him from foot to chest to shoulders in the manner a hosteler might assess a horse. A very faint smile played at her lips as she looked into his eyes, holding him with blue-purple dusk and mystery.

"Excellent," she murmured. "Savagery amuses me. And what glorious feats of arms shall I expect to see executed for my favor?"

That answer he'd considered long and well, knowing the number who were sure to challenge him. "Ten courses with the lance," he said evenly, "five with the ax, and five courses with the sword will be my offer to any knight who strikes my shield. What glory that it please God I may gain is my lady's."

"Well for that." Her smile took on a hint of humor. "My public esteem always stands in some want of luster."

The moment of self-mockery glittered in her eyes and vanished, lost in a graceful lithe motion as she lay back upon the cushions, beckoning for the wine cup held by one of her ladies. He wanted to look away, but it was impossible: the irony and obscurity and dark radiance of her held him.

Lancaster commanded Ruck as his prince and liege, but if she thought of that she gave no sign. She set Ruck square in the sorest dilemma a man could be placed—vassal and servant to opposing masters—though not for war or any great thing did she command him to declare a challenge for her on his own prince, not that Ruck could tell.

Yet he would serve. She was his sworn lady. Beyond doubt

or motive he would obey her. It was not his place to ask for reasons, even if she did not remember him.

And she did not. When she looked at him so negligently, he was certain—almost certain—that she did not.

Two emeralds and thirteen years. But emeralds must be naught to such as she, as he would have been naught so long ago, a ridiculous boy, no one and nothing.

He wore the green jewel on his helmet. He carried her falcon on his shield. Why had she asked for him, if she did not remember?

She bent her head to take a sip from the hammered goblet—and then paused before she tasted it. She stared into the wine for a long moment, her lashes black against skin of down and rose. When she looked up, it was toward the little group of ladies-in-waiting beside her bed, an emotionless sweep that remarked each one of them—and Ruck saw each of them in turn respond with the stone-silent terror of cornered rabbits.

She lowered her eyes to the goblet again, without drinking. "Thou wilt be valiant in my name on the morrow, Green Sire?" she murmured, glancing up at him over the rim.

He gave a slight nod.

"See that it is so." With a gesture she dismissed him. Ruck turned from the sight of Allegreto trifling with a ring on her finger.

At the door he stopped, looking back. "Your Highness," he said quietly.

She glanced up, lifting her brows.

He nodded toward Allegreto and spoke in English. "Ne such as that could nought kill me."

"What did he say?" the youth demanded instantly. "He was looking at me!"

Princess Melanthe turned. "Why, he said that in his devotion to me, Allegreto, he could defeat any man. A most handy green knight, think thee not?"

AS THE KNIGHT departed, Allegreto turned the amethyst over and over on her finger. He leaned near her shoulder, laying his head next to hers. Melanthe lifted the cup of wine to his mouth and said, "Share with me."

He drew in a light breath—and she felt the barely perceptible withdrawal in his muscles. "My lady," he murmured, "I
prefer the sweetness of your lips."

She tilted her head back, allowing him to trace his mouth
down her throat. With a languid move she held out the cup of
wine and lay full back on the pillows. Cara lifted it from her
hand with a deep courtesy, smiling that soft smile of hers,
serene as a painting of the Virgin Mary. Though Melanthe
closed her eyes, she could hear the light rustling and whispers
as her gentlewomen retreated, well-trained to recognize her
inclinations.

Allegreto put his mouth against her ear even before the
ladies had quit the solar. "Donna Cara," he said. "I told you to
be rid of her. Send her away tonight."

Melanthe lay with her eyes closed. She bore his hands on
her, her senses refined to catch the last instant that she must
suffer his touch. The moment she could be certain they were
alone, she flung his arm away and sat up.

"And I told thee to kill no one. Tomorrow thy back will
feel the worse for it."

He hiked himself up to sprawl against the heap of pillows,
impudent. "Nay, lady, you know none of your men will touch
me. They love my father too well."

"Will please the duke to lend me his guardsmen for the
task, I vow." She left the bed and stood by the chest, gazing
down into the goblet of scented wine. The candle beside it
shuddered, reflecting a sinuous half-moon in the dark liquid.
"It is a warning."

"It can be aught else, Your Highness." He rolled to his side
and lay propped on his elbow, only daunted enough to give
her a deferential address. "Bitter almond." He drank a deep
breath. "From here I can descry it."

She gave a humorless smile. "Thou art not so perceptive. I
could not detect it myself but from within the cup."

"It must have been Donna Cara. She's sold herself to Riata
and betrayed you. Mayhap no warning was meant, but a bun-
gle. Stupid Monteverde bitch, she would blunder such work.
Send her away, I tell you."

"Cara!" Melanthe laughed, scorning that. "Thy mind is
occupied past reason with the girl. By thy notion, one moment

she is subtle as a viper and the next so stupid as to poison me
with bane in my wine, as if I could not smell it there!"

"An idiot, she is. Give her to me, and I will teach her to be
sorry for her treachery, so that she will not forget the lesson.
She's not even worth the killing."

"Not worth killing? Why, Allegreto, thou must be feeling
unwell."

He grinned. "Nay, only languishing in tedium. I should
like to torment a Monteverde. It would make a change from
these tiresome Riatas who die so easily."

"Thy malice masters thy wit. Recall that she is my cousin."

He turned onto his back and crossed his leg, looking up at
the canopy. "My malice is bred in me. A Navona must hate
anyone of Monteverde." He glanced toward her with a wry
smile. "Excepting you, my lady, of course."

Melanthe gazed again into the poisoned wine. She moved
her head to bid him rise. "Take it to the garderobe. The cup
will sink. I want no use of it again."

"Yea, my lady." With youthful agility he rolled to his feet
and made a flourishing bow. "A Riata to Hell and a few fish
to Heaven—I call that a fine day's work for one garderobe."

AMID THE CALL of heralds' trumpets echoing high in the
clear cold air, the Black Prince in his litter took the head of the
procession, too ill to ride—barely able to attend at all,
Melanthe had heard. She held her place among the ladies, carrying Gryngolet in emerald hood and a new set of bells and
jesses, watching the chaos in the courtyard become order as
the parade formed.

The duke had overcome his scowls: he held back, greeting
Melanthe with every evidence of high good humor as he drew
rein beside her palfrey. "Good morn, my lady." He glittered in
azure and scarlet, his shield emblazoned by the lions of
England quartered with the fleur-de-lis of France. At his side
a Moorish soldier with a white turban wrapped about his head
walked a real lion on a leash of silk. "The day promises fine
for our entertainments. A place of comfort is prepared for you
upon the *escafaut,* if you will honor us."

"God grant you mercy for your kindness," she said. "I
shall come there when I will."

"I pray it be soon, for my pleasure in your company."

"When I will," she repeated mildly.

He bared his teeth in a grin. "I look forward with delight to that moment, madam. And to these contests."

Melanthe contained her palfrey's restless attempt to touch noses to his bay war-horse. "You're armed to take a part in the combat, my lord." She nodded in approval. "Never yet have I seen a prince of the blood enter the lists. I commend your valor."

"I shall break a lance or two, God willing. My lady's grace will recall that there is a challenge in her honor."

Melanthe smiled serenely. "I recall it."

"Your champion is well-renowned for his skill." He shook his head, careless. "I shall attempt him, but I hold small hope of winning any prize in a joust with the celebrated Green Sire."

His casual tone was meant to give her surprise, she saw, for he looked at her with a glance that did not quite match his jocular indifference.

"But my lord is his liege, are you not?" she said. "I am amazed that you undertake to meet him at all."

"A short match only. *A plaisance,* for your amusement. With blunted weapons, he need not fear to fight his master." He turned his horse, saluting her. "I shall open the jousts and return to your side as soon as I may, my dear Princess!" With a swirl of bright color, he circled and rode rapidly forward, his men and squires and even the lion running behind him to keep up.

At the proper sedate pace, led by a young page, Melanthe's horse moved out at the head of the ladies, passing through the shadow of the gatehouse and the city streets. Townsfolk and spectators lined all the distance, shouting and running along beside the procession. Melanthe eyed them, wary of the high windows with their waving banners, the milling crowds— wary most of all of Cara and her other gentlewomen just behind her.

She could not trust Allegreto's malicious counsel, but neither could she wholly trust Cara, as comely and credulous as her gentlewoman's dark eyes and soft, simple features might be. Any member of her retinue could succumb at any time to treachery or cajolery—the Riata were masters of both.

The assassin's body had been pulled from the river this morning and hauled away to be buried nameless in a paupers' graveyard. Allegreto spent the day in the public stocks for his trouble, dragged bodily out of her bedchamber by Lancaster's men, a small instructive exercise that Melanthe had arranged for him.

The murder had brought no more than a brief respite anyway—a moment's reprieve and then the poisoned wine, to remind her. She was still watched by some creature of the Riata, and with a sharper threat, for now she did not know who it was.

All she knew certainly was that they would see her dead before they saw her married again, carrying her rights with her to a man who would assert her claim to Monteverde. Such a one as Lancaster, ambitious and powerful—or, worse for the Riata by a thousand times—Gian Navona.

It was the imminent threat of Gian that Melanthe had used to bargain with them. She would not marry him, she swore; she would go home to England and enter a nunnery if they would allow her to leave unmolested. Once there, she would resign all right in Monteverde to the Riata—giving over her widow's perilous claim and a further birthright descended four generations through her Monteverde mother—too strong to defeat in a man's hand, too weak to prevail in a woman's.

Beyond Allegreto's dagger, the yet-unwritten quitclaim was all that preserved her life. It perfected the Riata's entitlement, giving them the advantage over Navona. The Riata wanted their paper precedence, but Melanthe was not fool enough to think they would not kill her and forego it if they suspected her treachery.

The true house of Monteverde had already died with Ligurio. She had not given him an heir, only a black-haired daughter, and even that poor hope was lost, smothered in the nursery. He had done what he could to protect Melanthe. He had taught her what she knew: subtlety and corruption, Greek and Latin and astrology, charisma and cunning, strength—he had taught her the lion and the fox; the chameleon of all colors.

All colors but white. Ligurio had trained her to trust no one and nothing, to lie of everything to everyone. And so at the end she had lied to him, too. He had died in the belief that she would take refuge in the veil, retiring to the abbey he had founded in the hills of Tuscany, safe in a comfortable retreat with Monteverde's lands and fortune rendered up to the mother church, invoking all the heavenly power and earthly greed of the men of God. She knew the bitter gall it had been to him to see his house die, but better passed to Heaven than into the hands of his enemies.

Her last gift to Ligurio had been her promise to do as he wished. Gift and lie. She had loved him like a father, but he was gone. She betrayed both Heaven and her husband. The church would not have Monteverde, or Melanthe—but neither would Navona or Riata have them, either.

She could not live a nun. She could not spend her days praying for her dead. They were too many—be likely she would not be able to remember all their names, and would get into a great argument with God over the matter, and expire of black melancholy.

Nay, if she must live inside walls for her protection, then let them be walls of her own choosing, this one time.

THE TOURNAMENT PROCESSION poured out into the great level meadow where a field of color lined the entry to the lists: vivid tents, some orange, some blue and scarlet, some formed like small castles flying pennants from their multitude of peaks. Each bore the owner's arms upon a shield hung at the entrance. In the wake of the heralds' trumpets the parade moved past weapons and armor, caparisoned horses, and squires bowing deep in honor of Prince Edward and his brother.

Melanthe received her homage also, but the cheers dulled as she passed. When she halted before a tent of green trimmed in silver, the voices nearby suspended entirely, creating a void, a space of silence within the music and the throng.

Her green knight stood beside his war-horse, outfitted in full armor, sending silver sparks into the sunshine from the green metal. As she drew up, he bowed on one knee, his bared head bent so that she saw only the tousle of black hair, his mail habergeon and the tan leather-padded edge of his gambeson against his neck. "My liege lady," he said.

"Rise ye, beloved knight," she murmured formally.

With an unmusical sound, the metallic note of armor, he came to his feet. She extended her free hand. Without raising his eyes to hers, he moved near and went down again on one leg to offer his knee as a pillion stone. Melanthe stepped from the saddle to the ground, lightly touching his bare hand for an instant before Cara hurried up to offer her support.

The knight rose. Melanthe soothed Gryngolet with one finger as he caught his horse away from his hunchbacked servant. Cara melted back from close range when the knight led the huge destrier toward them, its caparison of emerald silk and dragonflies rippling at the hem as the war-horse moved.

Having prompted this little play herself, Melanthe saw with wry relief that the twisted unicorn's horn, a yard long, had been replaced by a less threatening pointed cone upon the stallion's faceplate. The destrier's eyes were hidden behind steel blinders. It blew softly and chewed at the bit as the knight attached a silver cord to the bridle, presenting the lead to her with another bow of courtesy.

She had not really expected to be left holding this enormous beast herself, but the broken-backed squire moved away to help his master with pulling the helm and aventail over the knight's head, quickly smoothing any crimp out of the mailed links that fell over his shoulders. Melanthe realized with some surprise that he seemed to have no other servant. He pushed up the visor with his fist, keeping a cautious eye on his horse as he pulled on his gauntlets.

The uneasy moment passed without incident. He caught up the looping reins, holding them together at the stallion's shoulder as he stood by the stirrup. His plated gauntlets were so thick that his fingers seemed set in their half curl, clumsy and skillful at once.

For the first time he looked directly at Melanthe. He said nothing, but there was a level strength in him, something quiet and open, without evasion. He seemed to wait, without expectation, with immeasurable steady patience in his green eyes. As impenetrable and beckoning as the silent shadows of a forest, and yet flickering with hints of secret animation: with its own mysterious life and will.

Unexpectedly Melanthe found she had no ready word, no deceptive smile to return. She felt—as if she had been falling . . . and under his calm regard found herself caught up from the endless drop and placed on solid ground.

The horse threw its head, ringing bells. She shifted her look, the first to break away, and nodded to the knight.

He turned to mount. His squire took hold of the reins below the bit, steadying the destrier. From the block her champion swung up into the tourney saddle, adjusting his body against the high curve of the cantle. The little squire brought the lance. With a move that held the grace of countless repetitions, the hunchback swung the heavy spear aloft in an arc. The weapon slapped into the knight's waiting hand, slipped down against his open palm, and couched in the rest. At the spearpoint the bells of Gryngolet's jesses rang their hunter's music.

He took up his shield with the image of the hooded falcon upon it and looked down upon Melanthe. Sunlight caught the large emerald at the base of his green plumes.

"Say me thy right name," she said in English, in a low voice.

She ·heard herself ask it, heard the intensity of her own voice—standing amid the crowd of onlookers, not even knowing herself why she should care to know.

His armor masked him now; all she saw was his shadowed face within the helm and visor. She thought he would not answer—he had sworn to be nameless, and yet there was no smell of subterfuge about him: an impossible contrast, new to her and unsettling in its strangeness. She felt a bizarre rush of shyness to have pressed him, and turned her face downward.

"Ruck," he said.

She looked up, uncertain of the English word.

"As the black ravens call," he murmured in his own language. His mouth lifted with a half-smile. "Ruck, my lady. Be nought such a fair name, as yours, but runisch."

There was no presumption, no bold arts of love or offers of certain delight. Only that half-smile, rare and sweet, and vanished in a moment—but Melanthe saw then in him what

Allegreto had claimed to see: a man's hunger beneath the reserve.

He sat mounted with his shield and lance, a warrior geared for combat. An uncouth runisch name he might bear, but his armored figure aroused a thought in her that was stunning in its novelty.

She was no longer married. She might take a friend—a lover—if she pleased.

In the same moment that she thought it, she knew the impossibility. Nothing had changed. Gian Navona had grown smoothly savage over the years of waiting for his prize. He tolerated no gallant by her—any man who could not be discouraged in his attentions would meet his fate by some insidious means, so subtle that only gossip and evil tales followed Melanthe. So subtle that she had learned to befriend no one and smiled upon no man, cold as winter now in her heart.

She turned that icy disfavor upon the knight, so that any who watched could see her do it. "I care naught for thy runisch font-name," she said, as if he'd been too dull to understand her. "What is thy court, knight?"

He showed no reaction but a turn of his thick gauntlet, gathering the reins. "My court is yours, my lady," he said in French. "And his who rules the palatine of Lancaster."

"If thou love me as thy liege," she said, "for today thy court is mine alone." She stared at him, to be certain that he took her meaning, a long moment with everything she knew of command in her eyes.

"Yea, then," he said slowly. "Yours only, my lady."

Three

⎯⎯∞∞∞⎯⎯

THEY CALLED HIM by this north-name of *bersaka* with good reason. Melanthe was accustomed to games of combat, the innumerable hastiludes and tournaments and spectacles she had attended, celebrating every occasion from weddings to foreign embassies. *A plaisance*—pleasantries, as Lancaster had promised. But with his blunted tournament weapons, her Green Knight fought as if he meant to kill.

Melanthe had led him last into the lists, holding back until two lines had formed: opposing ranks of destriers and knights, their banners waving gently over the fantastical crests of staghorns and griffons and outlandish beasts, as if each man vied to display a deeper nightmare than the next atop his helm. Down the open space between she led her Green Sire, halting at the center to the sound of scattered cool applause. The moment she had released his horse, a pair of pages in Lancaster's livery hurried up to her, catching her by the hand and escorting her to a place upon the *escafaut* below Prince Edward on his red-draped couch and dais. She curtsied deeply to the prince and princess, then took her seat next to the duke's empty chair.

There was to be no old-fashioned melee. At the stout gate into the tilting ground, a monument of red stone held the insignia of the defenders. As each knight had ridden past in the procession, he had struck the shield of his choice to issue his challenge—and the green shield emblazoned with a silver falcon bore so many sword and lance wounds of challenge that the wood showed through the paint. Not every knight had touched it; many had raised their weapons and brought them down as if they would hit the falcon, then at the last instant held back, bowing deliberately toward Lancaster, and struck some other arms.

But even so, there were no less than a score of rivals beyond the duke himself who had signaled a wish to fight for Melanthe's favor. The trumpets sounded, clearing the lists of all but Lancaster's swarm of attendants and her champion with his single man. As the Green Sire reined his destrier into position, the jeers began. They would not sneer openly at Melanthe, but her champion was fair game, it seemed.

The entire crowd burst into frenzied acclaim for Lancaster as the duke rode forward into place, surrounded by his squires and grooms. The Green Sire made no sign of noticing either applause or taunts; he rested his lance on the ground and slipped Gryngolet's jesses from the tip. The marshal of the lists accepted responsibility for Melanthe's prize, riding back to the *escafaut*. As he handed her the jesses, both combatants lifted their lances in salute.

Melanthe bowed to her champion, ignoring Lancaster.

The trumpets clarioned. The lances swung downward. Both horses roused; the Green Knight's half reared and came down squarely as Lancaster's was already trotting forward. The green destrier sprang off its haunches into a gallop. Lancaster's bay mount hit its stride, rolling the sound of hoofbeats over the stands and the crowd.

An instant before impact, the Green Knight threw his shield away. The crowd roared, obscuring the sound as the lances hit. Lancaster's bounced upward, flying free and solid into the air along with the shattered splinters of his opponent's weapon. The Green Sire pulled up at the far end of the list, carrying half of a demolished tournament spear in one hand.

Tossing away his shield was the entire extent of his consideration for his prince. In five more courses he broke five lances on the duke, and took off Lancaster's helm on the sixth—whereupon the marshal threw down his white arrow to end the match. To Melanthe's displeasure, Lancaster accepted this without demur, not even demanding to go on to the foot combat.

Amid a murmur that spoke faintly of disfavor from the crowd, the duke saluted Melanthe and his brother and left the lists with his retinue.

She had not counted upon such a paltry showing. Not even the partisan onlookers could accuse her of withholding her favor from him without reason. But when he joined her upon the *escafaut,* he seemed unembarrassed—gay, rather, speaking favorably of his opponent's skill to his brother Edward for a moment before he sat down beside Melanthe. The musicians behind them struck up warbling tunes.

"A fair fight, my lady," he said, "though your champion makes no fine distinction between battlefield and tourney. I only hope that he slays none of our guests."

She felt an irritated urge to rise to this bait. "He faced you without shield," she said shortly.

"Yea—so they told me, but indeed I did not know it until he took off my helm, or I should have done the same." He raised his hand for refreshment and took the cup his squire offered, drinking deeply. "Or mayhap not. Mary, I have no desire to be run through in a joust and buried in unconsecrated ground."

He laughed, but there was a glitter of deeper emotion in him. Melanthe watched him as he drained the wine, tossed the cup down, and turned back to the lists with relish. This was some artificial show—she felt it, studying his unabashed countenance. It was not over yet, not at all. Lancaster had no intention of concluding with such a poor display.

She turned a look of better humor upon him. "I will not believe you stand in such peril, sir. Come, you will fight again, will you not?"

The flicker of hesitation told her all that she need know. "Why—nay, madam. I will take my ease at your side, if you will be kind. Here, now comes your champion into the lists again."

A challenger, emblazoned in gold and black and crested by the gilt head of a leopard, was being led into position by two squires, while Melanthe's knight circled his courser and backed it into place. He had resumed his fighting shield. The lances dipped; a gold-and-black squire shouted and stabbed a stick into the rump of the other horse. The animal jumped forward under the goad, galloping wildly, half shying as her champion's stallion bore down upon it.

The green lance caught its target full in the chest. With a jerk he sailed from the saddle as the horse went down. They somersaulted in opposite directions, the destrier hauling itself upright in a flail of hooves and caparisons to trot intemperately about the list, evading attempts to capture it.

"Poorly mounted," Lancaster murmured dryly.

The gold challenger struggled to his feet, pulling off his helmet and demanding his ax. The Green Sire dismounted, changing to a bascinet helm and sending the visor down with a clamp as the hunchback led his mount away. The challenger came at him, swinging a long-handled ax. It whirred past his shoulder as he stepped aside; he lifted his weapon and took a single cut behind his opponent's knees. The other man fell— and one more murderous strike, blade-on to his helmet, slicing an edge through the metal, was enough to make him shout pax. He was bleeding at the temple when his squire pulled off his helmet.

They did not proceed to the sword combat.

While the musicians played harmonious melodies and Melanthe sat calmly beside Lancaster, her champion smashed the pretensions of three more challengers. Two lances were shattered on him, but no contender fought as far as the swords, and one left the first course of axes with a broken hand.

Outside the lists, where common men-at-arms mingled with the squires and pages, there was a small but growing band of onlookers who met the Green Sire's victories with a ragged volley of cheers. Melanthe made no sign herself, but a feeling of pleasant awe began to steal over her, watching him fight. *Berserker,* indeed. It only remained to see that Lancaster be fired to face her champion again.

Melanthe already suspected the duke's intention. To allow a goodly number of challengers, wearing his rival down and painting him invincible at the same time . . . then perhaps a private visitation by some secret "friend," warning him of his prince's displeasure and designed to shake his nerve . . . and somehow Lancaster, fresh from hours of relaxation in the stands, would find a reason to meet the Green Sire at the end of the day.

She could appreciate Lancaster's design. It required a fine judgment—Melanthe smiled inwardly as he lifted a finger to communicate with the marshal of the lists, who instantly caused the heralding of a new set of combatants, allowing the Green Sire his first rest. It would not do to have him appear too easy—and just as vital to properly exhaust him before the *coup de grace.*

Melanthe prepared to ensure that the duke misjudged his moment.

She toyed with the jeweled jesses, turning a disinterested look on the new jousters. "Tell me of my champion," she said. "He is nameless in truth?"

"Nameless, yea, my lady. A nobody. He gives homage and claims our service, but brings no men of his own beyond that malformed squire."

"No lands, then? But such rich gear, and a great war-horse. He has won many prizes in tournament, I expect?"

The duke laughed. "Few enough, for I've better use for him in real fighting, but it is true that when he enters the lists, he prevails. I have sometimes sent him on a dragon hunt, for sport, but he brings me no prize yet."

"And still he has not proved himself worthy of his name?"

Lancaster turned his palm up casually. "The fortunes of war and dragons, my lady. All must await their great chance at honor, if it ever comes." He shrugged. "Haps he has no name. God only must know where he thieved his gear. It's my thought that he's naught but a freeman."

"A freeman!" Melanthe turned in amazement.

"Else why hide his lineage? That falcon device is recorded on no roll of rightful arms, so say the heralds. But the Green Sire has a talent to lead common soldiers. What men he commands, they come to love him, and the French dread his name. No great chivalry in that, but it is a useful art." He leaned back in his chair and smiled. "So we tolerate his odds and his unlawful device and green horse, Princess—and if he likes to call you his liege lady for a fantasy, then we will enjoy the game."

Melanthe swung the jesses lightly between her fingers, drawing them over the back of his hand. "A poor game to the present, my lord! Know you of no man strong enough to win my favor from this odd knight?"

Lancaster caught up the jesses and kissed them. The bells rang brightly. "I shall find one, Princess," he murmured. "Fear not for that."

Furious shouts drowned the music as a fistfight broke out between a foot soldier and a youth from the retinue of a defeated challenger. Lancaster watched until some of the guards had separated them, and then turned again to Melanthe. "Will you take wine, my lady? The dust rises."

At his words, Cara stood up from her stool behind, placing a tray between their chairs to offer the ewer and goblets. As the duke reached to pour, Melanthe sat back in her seat with a pert moue of impatience.

"Nay, sir, I shall not." She waved Cara away. "This sport is too tame. I vow by Saint John, my lord—nothing, food nor drink, shall pass my lips until a new champion wins my admiration."

He lifted his brows, his hand poised with the ewer. "So eager, my lady? The day is long, and the earth dry."

"So it is," she agreed. She trifled with the jesses, allowing the bells to tinkle. "But I am dauntless. Indeed, I challenge you to join me, and dedicate your comfort to this quest. Surely it is little enough to venture"—she glanced at him beneath her lashes—"as you do not bestir yourself to fight for my prize again."

Lancaster's mouth showed a very faint tautening. She saw the struggle in him, pride against guile, but he smiled at last and nodded toward her. "As you will, my lady." He set down the ewer. "By Saint John, I vow it. No food or drink shall I take until you are satisfied with a new champion."

AS THE NOON passed, Melanthe sat upon the *escafaut,* fanning herself conspicuously with a green plume. The day was clement enough that winter clothing weighed heavily; the duke in his blue-and-crimson houpelande was a little flushed at the neck, his crown resting on hair that curled damply, darkèned against his temple. The Black Prince, fretful and complaining of his swollen joints, had retired with his wife, carried in his litter from the stands to the shade of a magnificent tent set a little back from the noise and dirt.

As each new course of jousting sent dust into the air, Melanthe covered her mouth with a scarf and coughed lightly to convey her discomfort. She looked with a great show of longing at a tray of lozenges and cream tarts that passed en route to some other guests. The duke made no such indication of interest, but she was pleased to note that he swallowed once after the wine had traversed their view.

The Green Sire was handily trouncing all comers. Melanthe sighed, watching a knight outfitted in a boar's head helm pick himself up from a fall, the boar's tusks smashed and drooping askew. "I weary of these trials," she said. "Has he some magic, or be your men all weak as willow wands?"

"No magic, my lady, but goodly strength and skill," Lancaster said. "He, too, is mine," he added in a cool reminder.

Melanthe returned a taunting smile to that and casually jingled her bells. The noise of the onlookers grew, a confusion of cheers and scorn, passions flourishing as support for the Green Sire seemed to increase, scattered widely now among the mixed crowd below. Around the stout fence that enclosed the lists, youths and attendants thronged beside men-at-arms, all pressing as close as they could while the next combatant and his retinue surged through the gate.

The Green Sire pulled off his great helm, bending awkwardly to wipe his eyes and forehead with the tail of his tunic. A man-at-arms shouted, ducking through the fence to hand him a clean cloth. His intrusion past the lawful barrier sparked a great roar.

In the stands noble ladies shrilled their disapproval, answered by impudent shouts from some of the common soldiers below. Another scuffle broke out and spread. Melanthe felt the duke tense beside her, but his guards moved quickly, laying about with clubs and staves and hauling the brawlers away.

Lancaster made another subtle signal to the marshal, and

the next challenge heralded was without the Green Sire. Melanthe watched as her champion left the gate. He and his squire were surrounded instantly by soldiers and commoners, who made a phalanx about his horse and escorted him through the mob toward the tents.

"But if you allow him yet more rest, my lord," she complained petulantly, "what chance have these beardless children to defeat him?"

Lancaster swung a goaded look upon her. She swished the plume lightly.

"There are other matches to be fought, Princess," he said. "We have a hundred knights who desire to joust."

"I suppose my champion has not time to fight them all," she murmured. "Though I vow, I had not truly supposed him the greatest of the lot. I believe my father or brother could have knocked him down several times over."

He managed a creditable smile. "Perhaps so, my lady. But the day is not yet gone."

"I despair of surprises at this late hour." She shook her head. "The great days of the tournaments are past. We have only boys' games now. The king your father, God's blessing upon him, would find this a pale image of the splendid spectacles he has hosted."

Lancaster had become quite red now about the neck, but still he only nodded, stiffly polite. "There is naught to surpass the tournaments of our beloved lord the king."

Melanthe gazed upon the pair now thundering toward each other. To her pleasure, and the crowd's sneers, they missed each another entirely—a commonplace in any ordinary *pas de arms,* but the first time it had occurred today. She clucked ruefully. "I suppose the Italians care more for their honor in these matters," she commented. "They take their ease upon the hearth rug instead of in the lists, and joust like gallant men before the ladies."

Lancaster made a sudden move, sitting straighter in his chair. A page moved quickly to him—they bent their heads together for an instant, and then the duke rose. "You will forgive my discourtesy, Your Highness." He bowed deeply. "A summons from my brother the prince—I regret I must leave your companionship awhile."

Melanthe acknowledged him with good grace. "Be pleased to go at once," she said, "with my health and dear friendship, may God keep our esteemed Lord Edward the prince."

He turned, with a degree less than his usual elegance, and strode down the steps behind his page. The musicians continued to play their merry melody. Melanthe looked after him, fanning herself slowly and smiling.

THE CROWD HAD grown dangerously restless with the lesser jousts, and Lancaster was still missing from the *escafaut* by the time the heralds' trumpets blew a great fanfare, silencing the musicians and the noise. The marshal of the lists held up his arms and strode to the center of the ground, his slashed sleeves showing blue under scarlet and his cape flying out behind him.

"Now comes the one who will take their measure!" he shouted. "The one who will take their measure has arrived!"

As he declared the ritual words, old as the legends of King Arthur and Lancelot, the throng burst into frenzy. The discharge of sound beat against Melanthe's ears like the blare of the trumpets themselves.

From between the tents came a knight the color of blood-sunset, galloping with his black lance balanced on one hand above his head, his armor shining reddish gold. He rode a massive black destrier encased in the same shimmering metal. His shield was sable, as dark as his lance and horse, without device or color.

He dragged his mount to a halt at the stone monument. A hush fell over the onlookers, delicious expectation; a carnal pleasure in this drama. The black lance poised—and came down on the silver falcon, rocking it with force of the blow. The shield he had chosen rang with a wooden resonance as the cheers hit a new plane of passion.

A outrance.

The black lance had no safe coronal to blunt it, but a sharp tip. The shield it had struck was not the battered falcon with the hood, but the one that hung above it, with the silver bird of prey unhooded, offering combat *à outrance*—beyond all limits.

A joust of war, fought to the death with real weapons.

His attendants came behind him, a full score, masked, dressed as fools in rainbow colors, playing flutes and hunting horns. The curling toes of their shoes were so long and pointed that they were attached by belled chains at the knee. They made a grotesque fantasy behind the blood-gold knight, an uncanny contrast to his hostile silence.

Amid the cries and tumult, Melanthe's green knight rode out to meet him, armed with a sharpened lance. She pressed her palms together and tasted the salt on her fingertips, then folded her hands and held Gryngolet's jesses motionless in her lap.

The hunting horns mingled their clear notes with the trumpets, rising higher and higher into the air. They broke off one by one, leaving a single carol from the herald's horn to ascend and echo back from the stands and the river and the city walls, dying away like an angel's voice.

The knights saluted Melanthe, the golden one with an extra flourish.

As they faced their mounts toward each other, the Green Sire pulled his arm from within the leather straps and threw his shield away.

He knew it. Melanthe knew it. The crowd guessed it—and burst into a furor of scandalized exaltation as the man hidden inside the ruddy gold armor tossed down his blank shield in answer.

When the lances couched level, an instant of silent anticipation blanketed the onlookers. The black horse threw its head and charged. The Green Sire spurred his destrier. In the hush the thunderous roll of the animals' hooves made the wood beneath Melanthe's feet vibrate.

The lances impacted with the sound of fractured bone, of a hundred hammers against steel. Both knights fell backward and sideways, clinging to smashed lances; hanging half off their mounts against the weight of armor as the onlookers broke into an uproar.

The rainbow attendants rushed to propel their master back into place and supply him with a fresh lance. He was already at the charge before the Green Sire had hauled himself upright and grabbed his new lance from the hunchback. As the green spear swung up, tip to the sky, Melanthe realized that he had it in the wrong hand to meet his opponent.

A sound like a great moan rose from the crowd. His dancing mount froze in place. As the challenger realized his advantage, he aimed for the most vital target, leveling the black lance at his adversary's head. The green knight didn't even attempt to compel his horse forward, but faced the oncoming lance and rider as if he were entranced. The onlookers' groan rose to voluptuous agony.

Then the Green Sire seemed to collapse; an instant before the black spear hit his faceplate, he and his lance both toppled sideways—a sheer perpendicular to his course. As the tip of the black spear grazed his helm, the green lance swung down across his opponent's path.

The rod took the golden knight flat across his belly. In a crash of plated metal he seemed to fly, bent double for a suspended instant across the lance as the green destrier sat down on its haunches, scrambling against the force of the butt end jammed between the Green Sire's thigh and the pommel.

Melanthe found herself on her feet with everyone else. She stared at the fallen knight stretched on his back on the ground. When he moved, rising drunkenly, his golden armor dimmed by dust, she sat down. The green destrier wheeled and galloped after the loose horse, scattering the attendants as if they were colorful leaves.

Leaning to catch the reins, her champion flipped them over the black's head just as his mount danced away from a vicious kick. The horses trotted together to the little hunchback, who took the black as if it were a palfrey instead of a trained warhorse—and the animal lowered its head, submitting instantly, as if it recognized that a man without armor was no enemy. The squire led the captured horse out of the gate. Melanthe looked away from the dirty golden challenger as he swayed to his feet, shaking off his attendants' aid.

The Green Sire sat fixed upon his horse, gazing toward her.

The nameless challenger drew his sword, shouting within his helm. Still her knight did not move, but stared toward Melanthe. The great helm showed only menace, its eyeslits black and empty, but she saw beyond, saw a man on his knees in the great hall, looking up at her with intense entreaty. She allowed herself no change of expression, gazing steadily back.

The red-gold challenger shouted again. Her knight turned and swung down from his horse, jerking his sword from its sheath. His squire ran up to him with his shield and bascinet helm, but the challenger was already running forward, aiming a great swing with a sword that took the sun to its tip, shining murderous steel.

The hunchback ducked away, dragging the destrier with him. Her knight met the blow with an upward cut; the weapons rang and the crowd cheered. Neither man gave way as the blows fell, denting helmets and armor. They fought as barbarians fought, without mercy.

The golden knight slashed over and over at her champion's neck, killing blows, pivoting and swinging back again. He landed a strike that made the Green Sire stumble sideways, but her knight seemed better at mischance even than advantage, turning his swordhand down and slicing sideways, beneath his adversary's arm, cutting through the vambrace strap. The challenger's plate flapped loose, exposing vulnerable chain mail above his elbow.

He did not appear to realize it, whipping his sword again toward his opponent's helmet. It struck, driving a deep dent in the steel—under the force of the blow, the green knight's sword seemed to fly from his hand, but then it was in his left as if he'd snatched it from the air. He brought it overhead, striking an arc downward, the sharpened edge aimed for his adversary's outstretched arm with a force that would slice through chain mail and bone alike.

Sunlight flashed on the broad side of the blade. Melanthe closed her eyes. She heard it hit—and the golden knight's grunt of pain was audible an instant before the throng burst into noisy reaction.

She blinked her eyes open. The challenger was hauling himself up off the ground, but he could not seem to gain any purchase on his sword. The Green Sire stood over him, looking up again at Melanthe. She had full expected to see the blood-gold arm severed and covered in real gore.

But it was still attached to its owner—only rendered useless. The golden knight was groping for his sword with his left hand, his other hanging ineffectually at his side.

The marshall had stepped forward, poised with his white arrow, but the fallen challenger shouted furiously at him. The official hesitated, his hand wavering, and then bowed and stepped back.

The red-gold knight rolled, pushing himself to his feet with his good arm. Melanthe's champion took a step toward her, the black eyeslits in his helm still focused in her direction. She could see his heavy breathing at the edges of his hauberk.

He lifted his hand, palm up in petition.

Melanthe saw the red-gold opponent achieve his feet. He shouted, his words obscured and echoing within the helm, and raised his sword with his left arm.

She ignored her champion's appeal, staring at him coldly.

The challenger ran forward. The Green Sire turned, met the sword, and threw it off. He thrust the tip of his weapon at the golden knight's helm, catching the visor's edge, shoving the whole helmet upward, half off. Blinded, the other man ducked away, flailing his wounded arm and his sword to reset the helm, but another blow took it completely off.

It rolled across the ground. A great roar swelled from the crowd. Lancaster stood swaying in the middle of the dusty list. One of his attendants grabbed the helmet and ran toward him.

Her green knight turned yet again to Melanthe. He lifted his sword and shoved his helmet off his head with both hands; throwing the armor away from him. He pushed back his mail coif. Sweat streaked his face, stained with rust from inside the helm, marking the edge of his curling, half-plastered black hair. He did not look toward Lancaster, but still to her, breathing in great deep gusts.

She watched the attendants rehelm their master, and then met her champion's silent plea with calm indifference. He closed his eyes and turned his face upward, like a man under torture.

The duke rushed at him. Without helm, the Green Sire came on guard. He ducked his liege's left-handed swing and pressed close inside the other man's reach, nullifying the lack of a helmet. Lancaster tried to grapple him with both arms,

but the injured one would not lift past his waist. The duke's
sword cut awkwardly across the back of the Green Sire's
head, spreading crimson on black curls and mail. The blades
locked at their hilts, crossed, pointing at the sky, shaking with
the force of each man's strength.

Lancaster made a hard shove, turning his sword inward
between them, trying to slash it into the green knight's unprotected face. The tip sliced her champion's cheek, but he used
the sudden motion to thrust his elbow back and up in one
vicious lunge, ramming the guard against Lancaster's fist,
breaking the duke's hold on his weapon. The duke made a
desperate recovery, trying to retain his blade. The sword
dropped, the tip lodging for an instant against the earth just as
Lancaster caught it. As he stumbled, the Green Knight's blade
came up broadside against his helmet.

He fell sideways over the lodged sword, his exclamation
of agony audible above the noise as he hit the ground on his
injured side. He rolled onto his back.

The Green Sire stood above his liege, sword point at his
throat. Lancaster lay weaponless, injured, felled—and still
made no surrender. The crowd held its breath so still that the
panting of the two knights seemed the loudest sound.

Her champion looked up at her, holding the sword steady.
The blood on his face and hair was darkening, gathering dust;
he looked like a devil risen from some pit, imploring her to
save him.

"My lady!" The words were an exhalation of despair.

Melanthe lifted her plume and fanned herself. She laughed
aloud, in the silence, so they could all hear.

"Yes, thou mayest have pity upon him," she said, with a
mocking bow of her head.

Her knight pulled his sword from the duke's throat and
flung it half across the list. As Lancaster sat up, the Green Sire
fell on his knees before his prince, head bowed. He pressed
his gauntleted hands over his eyes. Slowly, like a tree falling,
he leaned lower and lower, until his hands and forehead
touched the ground.

"Pax, my dread lord." His muffled voice was agonized.
"Peace unto you."

Painfully Lancaster hauled himself to his feet, standing

against the support of one of his attendants. Still in his helmet, he seemed to overlook the man in the dirt at his feet. He searched out Melanthe on the *escafaut,* and then turned his back to her, walking unsteadily out of the lists with his attendants clustering about him.

Melanthe rose and descended the steps. As she walked toward the gate, youths and men-at-arms and onlookers parted, gazing at her. She moved to the center of the dusty lists, where the green knight still knelt with his face to the ground, blood matting his hair and staining his neck.

"Green Sire," she said mildly.

He sat back, staring for a long moment at the hem of her gown. Then he wiped his gauntlet across his eyes, smearing blood with rust. He turned his face up to her.

All light of worship and chivalry was gone from his look. He was still breathing hard, his teeth pressed together to contain it.

She knelt and reached for his right arm, tying the jesses about the vambrace and mail. The heat of his body radiated from metal armor. Gryngolet's varvels made a silvery plink against his arm, the precious stones casting tiny sprays of light that played over steel, coalescing green and white as the rings came to rest.

On a level with him, she looked up from her task into his eyes. She could not have said what she saw there—hatred or misery or bewilderment—but it was surely not love that stared back at her from under his begrimed black lashes.

From the persistent tickle of recollection, memory sprang sudden and full blown into her mind.

Once, long ago, for a whim, she had pulled a thorn from this lion's paw. She remembered him, she remembered when and where, an image stirred more by his height and bearing and the baffled agony in his face than by his features. Just so he had submitted, disarmed of all defense, as they took away his wife and money from him.

He repaid her today, then, for that emerald on his helm. Whatever precarious place he had striven to gain in Lancaster's heart, with his fighting skills and command of men and vow to find glory, was vanished now. He knelt before her like a man dazed.

Apology sprang to her lips, regret for his maimed honor, his lost prince. It hovered on her tongue.

"Thou art a fool," she murmured instead, "to think a man can serve two masters." She lifted a varvel and let it fall against his armor, smiling. "A splendid fool. Come into my service to stay, be it thy desire."

He stared at her. A sound like a sob escaped him, a deeper breath, harsh through his teeth.

Melanthe rose. She extended her hand, touching his shoulder to make a gesture for the crowd. "Rise."

His squire brought the destrier forward. Melanthe took the silver lead. They smelled of sweat and dust and hot steel, the knight and his mount, perfumed with blood and combat. When he had mounted, she looked up at him.

"If thou art vassal unto me," she said, "I shall love and value thee as Lancaster never could." And with that snare set, she turned before he answered, leaving his hunchbacked squire to lead him from the lists.

"Away, away!" Melanthe held Gryngolet on her wrist, urging the flustered falconers of Ombrière to haste. "I will away!"

She turned her palfrey in the castle's empty courtyard, watched only by her own retinue and a few dumbstruck servants. Outside the walls the sound of the tournament was a distant rise and fall of temper, the tensions between soldiers and squires and townsmen flaring. Melanthe cared nothing for that—it was the duke's difficulty if he could not control his people—she only wanted escape from the tumult, releasing her own tensions in a flying gallop over the countryside with Gryngolet aloft before her.

Allegreto stood sullenly under the arched entrance to the hall, waiting for a horse, one of his eyes turning black from his morning in the town stocks. He had not had a difficult time of it; no taunting of a foreign stranger could equal the excitement of a tournament, but he glared at Melanthe all the same.

Her greyhound strained against its leash as Melanthe felt her heart strain for the open country. She had seen herons and ducks by the river; yesterday Lancaster had given her his leave to take what she could—and if he regretted it now, she was beyond having to care. The falconers, two underlings left behind to mind the mews, finally secured their drum and swung up double onto a thin poorly horse, carrying a trussed chicken in a bag in case the hunt should have no success.

Melanthe reined her palfrey toward the gate. Across the bridge and through the barbican—and she could turn away from tournaments and courts and crowds and pretend she was alone with the open sky. Alone, as Gryngolet flew, but for the escort of hunters and falconers that chased the bird's wild courses.

Melanthe, too, was followed. Allegreto and Cara and a Riata rode behind her; Lancaster and Gian Navona and the ghost of Ligurio hounded her; and another hunted her now— the image of a man in green armor, bending slowly to the ground with his hands covering his eyes.

All of them her constant companions, ever in pursuit, never lost to sight. Spur her horse as she might, she was only free as the falcon flew free—until she killed, or was called back again to the brilliant jewels and feathers of her lure.

Four

A WITCH, SHE was.

Ruck stood beside one of the shadowed columns in the cathedral, staring blindly at the scaffolding beneath a newly installed stained glass window.

He felt robbed. He felt utterly pillaged.

Where was his lady, his bright unblemished lady, lovelokkest of all, who made the blood and boredom and solitary days worth bearing? He hadn't asked that she be with him. He had never thought he was that worthy, but he had held himself to her standard—when they laughed at him, when he hurt for a woman's body to the point of despair, he cleaved to the impossible measure that she set by her own perfection.

He had dreamed about her in his bed or on the cold ground; he saw her beside the Virgin in the churches. He even imagined her with Isabelle in the nunnery, praying for his soul, both of them together, both of them the same, fair blue eyes and fair blond tresses and a face too lovely for any woman on earth . . .

He turned his head and rested his bandaged temple against the pillar. The cut across his skull burned. His cheek stung and throbbed in spite of Pierre's salve.

The reality of Princess Melanthe had been like a bucket of ice-cold water thrown in his face. He was angry at himself, but he reserved his deepest fury and disgust for her—the witch—she probably *had* ensorcelled him. How else could he have managed to forget what she was?

The Arch-Fiend's whore, that was what she was, curling like a silken tiger on the bed with her Satan's cub caressing her. He could not even find the image of fairness anymore. It had vanished from his soul, blasted by the sight of sable hair and eyes the color of unearthly twilight, the deep strange inner hue of hellish flowers. He recognized them now—but he had not remembered them so vivid-dark, or her coldness so numbing.

She had laughed. He could hear it still, like an echo in the empty cold air of the cathedral, floating above the endless murmur of the priests' chantries. The sound was branded on him. He had stood with swordpoint to the throat of his gallant liege, who had fought on wounded, unbowed, with no thought of submission—and she had laughed.

The windows glowed with the last faint light of day, spreading colored radiance over the floors and columns, subtle warmth in the soaring blackness. Beyond the cathedral walls he could hear faint sounds of celebration. A few knights came and went in the nave, kneeling to cleanse themselves with prayer, and one youth had been keeping solitary vigil in the Lady Chapel for hours. Ruck stayed to himself, using the pillar for a prop when his cushion grew too uncomfortable for his knees.

Outside of duty and the exercise yard, he spent most of his waking hours in chapels or cathedrals or churches of one sort or another. At first it had been the hardest effort of his knighthood—tedious to the point of screaming agony—but after thirteen years he had come to peace with the cold stone spaces and the fact that his knees could not support hours on the cushion. He stood now more than he knelt, sparing his frame for the field and fighting, sparing his soul with a regular confession of this small sin. He never even got a real penance, the priests being sympathetic in the matter.

He seldom prayed during his hours in church. Isabelle, he'd thought, would be doing that for him better than he could for himself. He'd often imagined her at it, her face alight and the tears flowing, the other holy women ranged behind her. He felt closer to her in the churches and chapels, where he could banish the faint fear that she never thought about him at all. Sometimes he envisioned her in nun's robes; more often in a sparkling gown of green and silver—and the lonelier the road, the bloodier the combat, the more beautifully and brilliantly she glowed, almost as real as if she stood in the shadows holding her falcon.

It came as a sickening jolt to him now to realize just how often he had confused them in that way. His wife and his nameless liege lady—they had somehow across the years, within the stark isolation of his heart, melded together into a single female image—and he had spent his adult life in rigid devotion to her, celibate, devout, courteous, refusing to stoop to dishonor and bribes of money to win the favor of his prince.

Never had he been invited into his lord's inner chamber— yet he had waited patiently for God to send his chance. He had risen slowly in Lancaster's service, earning his place in spite of the half-concealed amusement. He would lead men-at-arms and archers against the French, he would play at unicorn if he must; dragons he would hunt when his liege commanded. He knew the other knights preferred him safely away from court on such commissions. He was mad in action, so they claimed, dangerous, unreliable. By which they meant that he gave no quarter, demanding surrender when surrender galled them—the only way he had been taught to fight. But he had never lost the certainty that he would find a means of proving himself and winning his lord's boon.

The stained glass panel above him was a lancet, blue and rose, glowing with a painting of the Virgin and Child. Ruck gazed at the Blessed Mother's pensive face as she looked down at the baby Jesus. He ached with grief and anger.

It appalled him to realize what he had done, how the years had gone by, how he had deluded himself and confused *her* with his pure sweet wife. Tainting his memory, his only connection to Isabelle, who even now must be devoting herself to solitary worship. Alone, as he was. He was sure that she must have taken vows of seclusion and silence in the convent, for even though he sent money and tender greetings every year to Saint Cloud, she never wrote him back. He only received an acknowledgment of his gift from the abbess, with no word from Isabelle even by proxy.

Her loss seemed a fresh wound now, stinging as sharp as the cuts on his cheek and head. He missed her—and he could hardly recall her face. All he saw clearly were purple hell-flower eyes and a white flash of skin; all he felt plainly were wrath and anguish and the degrading burn of his body's appetite in spite of everything. He struggled to remember Isabelle, to rededicate himself to the purer image, and could not. She was lost now, by his own folly, as lost as the bright illusion that had sustained him.

Outside the bell rang to signal curfew. Ruck leaned down and retrieved his cushion, scowling at the worn white threads of the embroidered falcon that adorned it. He thought of having it ripped out and replaced with the azure ground and black wolf of Wolfscar, but to take up his own true arms now, in disillusionment instead of honor, seemed the final defilement of his dreams.

He left the falcon be. He left all of his green-and-silver vestiture as it was, determined to wear it as a constant reminder to himself of how a woman—*this* woman—could twist a man's mind into the Fiend's knots.

AS HE PUSHED out the great wooden door onto the stone porch, his head aching, a hard hand cuffed his shoulder. Three guards in Lancaster's livery stood just beside him. They offered silent sketches of bows, and one nodded toward the outer entrance.

Pierre hung back in a corner of the porch, looking terrified. Ruck glanced at him and at the guards.

"Ye alone are summoned, my lord," one of them said. His tone was curt, but not hostile.

Ruck nodded. The door opened to the last of twilight spilling over the city roofs. The streets were already deep in shadow, but sparked with torches and wandering groups of revelers. They showed no sign of extinguishing their fires and going to lodgings in answer to the curfew. It was often so on tournament days, and armed guards usually much in evidence—but this evening every man they passed was armed, common soldiers mixing with the city watch. Colorful retainers of the tourneying knights roamed drunkenly with their swords still at their hips.

"God's love," Ruck muttered, "this is ripe to go ill."

The guard at his side grunted an assent. But he did nothing to urge anyone to go home, only lengthened his stride, grabbing Ruck's elbow to direct him into an alley. As they came out on the other end, a hoarse voice yelled, "Hark ye!" An English soldier came weaving drunkenly toward them. "Our lord!"

His companions followed, their wayward steps enlivened by this new goal. Suddenly Ruck and his escort were surrounded by ungoverned men-at-arms, all of them familiar faces to Ruck, scowling and sullen with drink.

"Unhand our liege, dog!" A soldier tried to pull Lancaster's guard away from Ruck. "Nill ye not take him!"

The guards' hands went instantly to their weapons, but Ruck shoved the soldier back. "I am no liege of thine!" he snapped. "Watch thy tongue, fool. 'Tis stupid with ale."

"He will not have you, my lord," a man shouted from the back, "nor throwen you in prison for his pride!"

Ruck glared. "Get ye gone to your places! The curfew tolled a quarter hour since."

"He will not arrest you!" There were other men accumulating now, attracted to the shouts, crowding nearer. "He goes through us first!"

"Haf ye ran mad?" Ruck exclaimed. "Disperse! I order it!"

Some of the ones nearest him made attempts to turn, as if to obey, but the growing wall of men behind them blocked their way. Lancaster's guards stood with their swords at ready, a tense triangle around him.

"Disperse!" Ruck bellowed. "I am summoned by the duke! Out of my way, whoreson!" He shoved viciously at the soldier nearest. The man lurched backward, creating a momentary opening. Roaring his displeasure and intention, Ruck knocked another one aside. The path begun by force began to open of its own accord. Lancaster's guards came with him, but he stayed in front of them to show that he was not in duress.

The way cleared before him. Though he didn't look, he was aware that the men did not scatter, but only fell back, following close at his escort's heels. He cursed them silently, deliberately taking a route down narrow alleys and close streets to spread them out into a weaker force.

But outside the bannered lodgings of the highest nobles, the curfew was no more in force than in the lower streets, though it was full dark now. Knights and valets reeled in and out of the bright doorways, young squires singing war songs and scuffling. Ruck strode past, his eyes straight ahead, but his luck did not hold. A youth in blue-and-white reached out and grabbed his cloak. He jerked it free, but not before he'd been recognized. Shouts erupted, and as the men-at-arms issued from the narrow passage behind, they began to run, pressing up around Ruck, elbowing the noble retainers back. More men began to pour out of the doorways, filling the street with shouting shadows, with torches and the glint of steel.

Ruck seized a fagot and jumped atop an upended barrel. He lifted it high, waving it, so that sparks flared.

"What folly is this?" he roared. *"Silence!"*

For an instant his voice caught their attention.

"Who are ye?" he shouted. "The duke's soldiers. The duke's knights and their squires. I am the duke's man! He calls me to him. Will you forestall me? Fight among yourseluen, if ye be great fools enow—but hinder me in obeying him, and I'll see every villain of you with your guts strung on the city walls!"

The silence held, a sullen acknowledgment. Threat or no, there was nothing that they wanted better than a reason to brawl, drunk as they were, commoners and gentles alike. He did not stay to see them come to that inevitable conclusion, but tossed the torch into a watering trough below him. It gave him a moment while they were still dazzled blind—he jumped down and slid between the crowd and a building's wall, using the shadows for cover to get away.

•   •   •

THE DUKE OF Lancaster had his arm in a sling. In his capacity as Lieutenant of Aquitaine, he sat sprawled on a throne, the walls and floor of the chamber draped in cloth woven with the arms of England and France. The flood of richly colored squares obscured the shape of the room, so that it seemed to Ruck that he and the men he faced floated in a bowl of gilded red-and-blue. At the duke's side stood his brother the Earl of Cambridge. Ruck recognized their councillors—Sir Robert Knolleys, Thomas Felton, and the Earl of Bohun—men of military craft, veterans of all the savage campaigns of France and Spain.

"Get up, knight," Lancaster said with a deep sigh.

Ruck stood, sliding a secret look toward him. The duke appeared wakeful, but he had a sleepiness about his eyes that Ruck had seen before in men hit upon the head. His councillors had barely glanced at Ruck as he entered, but kept their close attention on Lancaster. Sir Robert scowled, standing by a table set with wine and food.

The duke stared at Ruck for a long time, his eyes half-lidded. "It was," he said slowly, "a good fight."

A great wave of relief fountained through Ruck. He wanted to go down on his knees again and beg forgiveness, but he kept his feet, only saying, "For the honor of the Princess, my dread lord."

Lancaster laid his head back and laughed. His eyes focused from their drift with a sharper look at Ruck. "She has made fools of us both, has she not? Hell-born bitch."

"My lord's grace—" Sir Robert said warningly.

"Ah, but my sentiment will not leave this chamber, if this green fellow hopes to avoid my most grievous displeasure, and such jeopardy for him as that may entail."

"My life is at my lord's pleasure," Ruck said.

Lancaster sat up, leaning forward on his good arm, his mouth tightened against the pain of the movement. "See that thou dost not forget it. What is thy judgment of the temper outside?"

Ruck hesitated. Then he said, "Uneasy, my lord."

"Clear the streets, sire," Felton said.

Lancaster turned a sneer on the constable. "With what?

Your men-at-arms? They're the ones *in* the streets, making mischief in the name of this green nobody."

"They have not been paid, my lord," Felton said, without embarrassment.

"And is that my fault?" Lancaster shouted, and then squeezed his eyes shut, laying his head back. "I'll run my own coffers dry in the defense of your damned Gascon barons."

"The prince your brother—"

"The prince my brother is sick unto death. He is to know nothing of this! Do not disturb him."

There was a little silence. Then the constable said tentatively, "I believe—if my lord's grace appeared with this knight"—he made a faint gesture toward Ruck—"they would obey this man, my lord, if he ordered them to submit to curfew."

"By God," Lancaster exclaimed, "he knocks me off my horse and holds his sword to my neck, and now I'm to stand by him while he gives orders to the men-at-arms? Why not appoint him lieutenant and be done with it?"

Ruck pressed his lips together, appalled. He had felt the threat hovering over him; now it crystallized into real danger. He had never thought Lancaster would imprison him for pride—but suddenly a new and horrifying vista opened.

The duke seemed to catch his mute response, for he looked again at Ruck. He stared for a long, speculative moment, an assessment that chilled Ruck to the bone.

"What thinkest thee, Green Sire," he said, in a serious voice. "Canst thou control them?"

"My lord's grace has the right of it," Ruck said. "Me think it not seemly."

"But thou canst do it?"

"It be unmeet, my lord," Ruck repeated, trying to prevent any note of alarm from entering his voice. "It be not wise."

"But if I cannot command them, nor their own constable here, and thou only canst keep the city from strife and riot?"

Ruck shook his head. "I pray you, dread lord, ask it not of me."

"I ask it of thee. I command thee to take charge of the garrison and the men-at-arms and control them."

Yesterday such a command would have been a wonder for Ruck, a victory. Today it was the edge of a pit: the precipice of war between nobles and common soldiers, rebellion with himself at the center.

"My lord," he burst out, "reconsider! Your head pains you to folly." He sucked in his breath, as if he could take back the brazen words as soon as they escaped.

Lancaster rubbed his face with his good hand and looked to Sir Robert. "My head pains me in truth," he said, with something of a smile. "What think you of him?"

Knolleys shrugged. "He will be a loss to us."

"A loss," Lancaster repeated in a silken voice, looking at Ruck from beneath lazy eyelids. "Well for thee, that thou didst not leap at the command. Some here have counseled me that thou art a sly rebel, Green Sire. That thou hast kept thy name secret for something less than honor, and wormed thy way into a place and gained the love of my men only to inflame disloyalty and rebellion with this spectacle today. That thou hast conspired with the princess to weaken us, in preparation for a French attack tonight or tomorrow."

Ruck dropped to his knees. "Nay, my lord! By Almighty God!"

"Who stands behind the Princess Melanthe, traitor?" Knolleys demanded.

"I know not!" Ruck exclaimed. "I'm no traitor to you, my lord, I swear on my father's soul. Her man told me that she wished me to issue challenge in her name."

"Against thy liege?" Sir Robert demanded. "And thou took her up?"

"My beloved lord, I meant you no insult. I was to challenge all comers. I am sworn to her. Years ago—and far from here. I knew not even her name until yesterday. I never thought to see her again. She was . . ." He paused. "I swore myself to her service. I know not why. It was long ago." He shook his head helplessly. "I cannot explain it, my lord."

Lancaster lifted his brows. "Canst not explain it?" He burst out in caustic laughter and held his head. "Has she bewitched us or besotted us?"

"Send for the inquisitor," his brother said. "If she's a sorceress, he will discover it."

"And whiles? There's no time for the inquisitor."
Lancaster rested his head against the throne. "Much as I
should like to see her burn." He drew a deep breath and
sighed. "But here—I find I cannot imprison or execute my
green companion-in-arms, in spite of my aching head and
dislocate joint. I have a fellow feeling for him, the love-
struck ass. Moreover, it provokes riot."

"Nor let him walk free," Knolleys said.

"Nor let him free, for if he wills or no, the men gather to
him, and with the temper of the nobles, we'd have disorder
enough to burn this city down. I want no rivals to my command. I need my men to fight France, not one another."

Ruck knelt silently, awaiting his fate, watching his future
dissolve before his eyes.

Lancaster gazed at him with that sleepy speculation. "Tell
me, Green Sire, what is it thou hoped to gain of me, to join
my court?"

"My liege . . ." Ruck's voice trailed off. He had not envisioned that his moment with Lancaster would come this way.

"Position? Lands? A fine marriage? I hear that the ladies
admire thee."

"Nay." Ruck lowered his face. "I ask naught of you now,
my lord."

"And I offer naught," Lancaster said, "for I want no more
of thee. I have detained Princess Melanthe at the gate, so that
thou wilt be seen alive and well to escort her into the city. At
dawn thou must be off, with thy princess and all her train."
He smiled sourly. "And look thee to see me at the quay, to bid
you both a cordial farewell."

IT WAS FOR her protection, the message said. Melanthe
pulled her cloak close about her in the cold darkness outside
the city gate. Her little hunting entourage huddled before her.
Behind lay the distant fires and tents of the tourneyers who
had no lodging within the walls. That the gate was still open
this late was strange. The guards were men in Lancaster's
and the prince's livery—not the usual gatekeepers. She could
see torches and hear drunken shouting from within.

If she had had another choice, she would have turned
away. The message—and signs of riot inside—were omi-

nous. She did not think real trouble had erupted yet, but it might flare at any moment. Her presence alone might be enough to spark it. She much doubted that Lancaster's message to await an escort at the gate had been sent with loving concern for her safety.

Gryngolet fluffed her feathers to keep out the cold, perching quietly upon the saddlebow. The greyhound sat shivering. Melanthe had not dressed for darkness. Even in gauntlets, her fingers were cold. She looked into the blackness behind her, sparked by open fires, and admitted wryly to herself that nothing stopped her at the moment from fading into the gloom, as free as she dreamed of being, except for the mystery of how to live as anything but what she was.

"My lady—" One of the guardsmen came striding from beneath the black bulk of the gatehouse over the bridge. "Your escort."

Even as he spoke, the arch brightened with the flare of many torches. At the head of a score of armed men her green knight rode toward her beneath the gate.

The torches behind him lit his mount's breath and his own in transparent gusts of frost. He wore no armor now, only a light helmet over a bandage that shone white across his forehead. The bridge thudded with the sound of hooves and boots.

He never looked directly at her. With a perfunctory bow he made a motion to the men to surround her horse. Placing half of the company before them, and half behind, he wheeled his mount next to hers, swept his sword from its sheath, and shouted the order to march.

She rode beneath the archway beside him. Inside the city walls, the streets were full of men. They stared and shouted and ran beside the company. Melanthe kept her eyes straight ahead and up. Her palfrey felt very small next to the destrier, and the score of men a thin wall against violence. In some of the side streets other knights sat their mounts, swords unsheathed, staring malevolently as her escort passed. Limp bodies lay in doorways—drunk or dead, she could not tell. The high bulk of the keep itself was a welcome sight, until she saw the crowd milling and pressing below it. As her

escort came into view a cheer went up, confounded with outrage and spiced by drink.

The Green Sire shouted an order. The men ahead halted.
He lifted his sword over his head, and the men-at-arms spun
their sharpened pikes, forcing the nearest of the crowd to
give room. The pikes stopped with their points at chest-level,
a bristle of protection.

The castle gates opened slowly amid noise and disordered
motion. He yelled another order, and the men-at-arms began
to move, stabbing into the crowd ahead of them. In the light
of the torches her cavalcade pushed through the mob, encap-
suled by pikesmen. The throng in the street could not seem to
decide if they wished to cheer or resist, swarming back and
forth in ill-tempered confusion, fighting one another, stag-
gering back from the pikes, waving their own weapons in
wild and abortive threats to their neighbors.

Her palfrey danced along beside the war-horse, taking
hopping, frightened steps, half rearing as a man fell between
the pikes and sprawled in front of her. Melanthe gave the
horse a quick spur, and it sprang off its haunches, coming
down on the other side of the prone figure. The palfrey
kicked out as it landed, but Melanthe did not turn to see if the
blow struck. Allegreto's horse crowded behind her; the gate
was overhead at last—and they were through, passing into
the inner courtyard. The gates boomed closed behind them,
shutting out a rising roar.

Her knight dismounted and came to her, offering his knee
and arm. Melanthe took his hand for support. Hers was shaking past her ability to control it. As her feet touched the
ground, she said, "Thou tarried long in coming. I'm nigh
frozen through."

She did not wish him to think that she shivered from fear.
Nor did she thank him. She felt too grateful; she felt as if she
would have liked to stand very close to him, he seemed so
sure and sound, like the enclosing walls of the keep, a circle
of sanctuary in the disorder. For that she gave him a sweeping glance of disdain and started to turn away.

"My lady," he said, "his lordship the duke sends greeting
and message, and desires to know that your hunting was
well."

Melanthe looked back at him. "Well enough," she said. "Two ducks. I will dispatch them to the kitchens. There is a message?"

"Yea, my lady." He looked at her with an expression as opaque as a falcon's steady cold stare. "I am to escort you hence without delay. We leave at dawn, upon the tide."

"Ah." She smiled at him, because he expected her to be shocked. "We are cast out? Crude—but what does an Englishman know of subtlety? Indeed, this is excellent news. Thou shalt make all preparations for our departure to England and attend my chamber at two hours before day-break."

His face was grim. He bent his head in silent assent.

"The duke has denied you, then?" she asked lightly. Melanthe held out her hands in the flicker of torches. "Green Sire, swear troth to me now as liege, and I will love thee better."

His mouth grew harder, as if she offended him. "My lady, I was sworn to your service long since. Your man I am, now and forever." He held her eyes steadily. "As for love—I need no more of such love as my lady's grace has shown me."

Melanthe raised her chin and shifted her look past him. Allegreto stood there, watching with a smirk.

She bestowed a brilliant smile upon her courtier and lowered her hands. "Allegreto. Come, my dear—" She shivered again, turning, pulling her cloak up to her chin. "I want my sheets well warmed tonight."

THE BOATS RODE the current and the outgoing tide downriver, their oars shipped and silent. As the banks of the Garonne slipped away, ever wider, a cold sun rose behind Ruck's little fleet, sucking the wind up the estuary off the sea. It was not to his taste, but he'd reckoned it his duty to sail aboard Princess Melanthe's vessel himself.

He had worked with her steward all night to organize their departure. When he had seen the painted whirlicote Princess Melanthe was to inhabit on the land journey, he'd found that he had to use the duke's patent to commandeer an extra ship only to convey the leather-covered, four-wheeled house and the five horses necessary to draw it.

Ruck had full believed that he would spend hours waiting on his liege lady's convenience, as she did not seem the sort to bestir herself to undue exertion, but Princess Melanthe's attendants outshone even the men-at-arms in their packing and loading efficiency. There was no scurrying back to fetch a lost comb or another pillow. Not one lady slipped away to linger in farewell with some brokenhearted lover. Ruck suspected that they feared their mistress too well to delay her.

The duke had come to see them off as he'd promised, making a great false show of giving the kiss of peace and offering cordial farewells. Ruck had found himself the object of more courtesy from his liege in the cold dawn of his departure than he had received in the whole sum of his years in service to Lancaster. The audience was small, only a few beggars and merchants, and a soldier or two woken from sleeping on the docks, but by noontide the story would have spread throughout the city to gentles and commoners alike: the Green Sire had left Aquitaine in Princess Melanthe's service, alive and without duress. No threat to Lancaster's command, no martyr to his pride—no spark to set rebellion alight.

The Green Sire was nothing to Lancaster, or to anyone else now.

Ruck drew in a slow breath and let it go. He had lost his prince and liege. He had loved a lady who did not exist—but she had seemed so real, he had spent so long devoted to her, that he felt as if death had claimed a piece of his heart.

He sat on deck atop the single high cabin in the stern, very aware of the princess below him. He wondered if she suffered from the seasickness, and had not sufficient imagination to picture such a thing.

Pierre huddled in the tip of the stern, snoring gently. The wind blew in Ruck's face. His men lined the deck, sitting in the protection of the gunwales. He reached over and plucked his flute from Pierre's capacious apron. The squire opened one eye, and then snugged into his cloak again.

In the early light Ruck began to play a sweet, mournful song of the Crusades, of a lover left behind to grief and worry. It seemed to him fit for the gray rise of dawn, slow and yearning, with the sway of the water and the glint of dull light on the helmets and crossbows. Fit for his mood: leaving nowhere, going nowhere.

Below him the curtain over the cabin door flicked. Ruck's note faltered for a bare instant, and then he lowered his eyes and went on playing. It was only her lapdog Allegreto, who climbed the short stairs with a crimson cloak wrapped tight around him. To Ruck's concealed surprise, the youth sat down on the deck at his feet, facing away from him into the wind.

"That is a love song, is it not?" the young courtier asked.

Ruck ignored him, enclosing himself in the melody.

Allegreto sat quietly for a few moments, and then sighed. He looked around at Ruck. "Hast thou ever been in love, Englishman?"

He asked it wearily, as if he were a century old. Ruck made no answer beyond his tune.

Allegreto smiled—an expression that was undeniably charming in spite of his blackened eye. He pushed the wind-blown dark hair from his forehead. "Of course. Thou hast as many years as my lady, and she knows more of love than Venus herself." He leaned back against the gunwale. "Thou knowest she has magic to keep herself always the same. Perhaps she's a thousand years old. Upon hap, if thou wouldst see her in a mirror, she would be no more than a skull, with black holes for eyes and nose."

Ruck lifted his brows skeptically, without losing the cadence of his notes.

Allegreto laughed. "Ah, thou art too astute for me. Thou dost not believe it." With an abrupt intensity he leaned nearer. "Thou wouldst not take her from me?"

Ruck's music wavered for a beat.

Allegreto closed his eyes tightly. "Thou hast—such as I cannot give her," he said in a lowered voice. "I am not so young as I appear."

It took Ruck's mind a long moment to construct that into meaning. He lowered the flute.

Allegreto pulled the red cloak up to his mouth and turned his head away. Ruck stared at the smooth wind-pinkened cheek.

"When I was ten and five," Allegreto said, muffled, as if

in answer to a question. "She preferred me thus." He pulled the cloak closer and then glared over his shoulder. "But still I love her!" he exclaimed fiercely. "I can still love!"

Ruck gazed at him. He could think of nothing more to do than nod in the face of such awful devotion. Allegreto held his eyes for a long moment, and then put his head down in his arms. Amid his shock Ruck felt ashamed of himself. Whatever sacrifices he'd made in the name of his false lady, they had been honorable, and his own choice. He was a whole man. He wet his lips and picked up the flute again, taking refuge in the music.

He had played only a few notes when two sharp thumps came from the deck beneath their feet. Allegreto looked up.

"Oh." He turned to Ruck and smiled sweetly. "I forgot. I was to order thee to cease that dirge and play something more amusing."

Five

THE OLD KING of England was a haggard and drunken shadow of the tall warrior Melanthe remembered. Edward's regal progresses and tournaments lay as gemstones among her childhood, all luster and polished steel and dazzling majesty: her father's red and gold glistening among the other colors, sparks flying from his helmet at a hard strike; her mother's fingers tightening for an instant over Melanthe's hand.

King Edward drank a long swallow of wine and handed the cup aside hastily, gesturing his servant behind his chair when Melanthe entered his royal bedchamber. The king's gray hair lay loose over the broad shoulders that once had borne armor, his mustaches flowing down into his long beard. He had the reddened nose and cheeks of too much drink, but he kept a regal posture in his chair.

A day in London had been ample time for Melanthe to discover that he was in utter thrall to his mistress, a fine female of a stamp that Melanthe understood full well. No one attended the king without consent of the feared and hated Lady Alice—and Melanthe was no exception. Alice Perrers sailed into the chamber on her heels.

"I bring you someone you will like, my dear," Lady Alice said, plucking the goblet from the servant's hand. She leaned over the king's chair and kissed his forehead as she poured him more wine. He smiled dreamily at the ample bosom hovering so near his face. "Here is Lady Melanthe, the daughter of Lord Richard of Bowland, God give his soul rest. She bears gifts for you, and letters from Bordeaux. The duke writes."

"John?" The king's eyes brightened. He held out both his hands. His fingers shook.

Melanthe made a deep courtesy. She rose, giving Lady Alice a significant look before she moved forward to make her offerings.

The mistress had fattened her unofficial power so far that it was said she even sat upon the benches and threatened the justices. But Melanthe could play that game. She had lavished compliments and gifts upon this overripe and overblown person, along with hints that their interests were quite compatible. Lady Alice would not wish any powerful man, most particularly someone like John of Lancaster, to marry Melanthe and combine their great estates into a domain that would challenge the king's.

No more did Melanthe care to marry such a man, she had assured Lady Alice. She had no ambitions beyond her father's inheritance. Her greatest desire was to pay her levies to the king so that he might be enriched, and thus more generous yet in bestowing suitable presents upon his favorites. In her excess of goodwill Melanthe herself would make a generous present to the king's intimates the moment a private audience might be arranged.

Of course, if a private audience was impossible, if Lady Alice did not trust her new friend, then in Melanthe's crushing disappointment and hurt, she feared that she must return in disgrace to Aquitaine, where his lord's grace the duke had been *most* flattering in his attentions.

Lady Alice gave Melanthe a narrow smile as she straightened from bending over the king. With much petting and many careless endearments, she withdrew. He retained her hand in a lamentably fatuous manner, but when she finally departed, leaving only the chamberlain—Alice's man—and the servant, Edward seemed to forget her, leaning forward in his eagerness for his son's letter.

Melanthe made another courtesy and gave him Lancaster's

missive. She could have recited it to him, having made herself
free with the wax seal before they had left Bordeaux. She
watched the king frown over his eldest son's poor health, and
quicken at the news that the prince would return home to
recover. She saw Edward's mouth purse at the report of
the empty treasury in Aquitaine, and the uneasy temper of the
Gascon nobles.

The tournament went unmentioned in the letter, as did the
Green Sire and Lancaster's shoulder and the duke's soured
courting of Melanthe. Lancaster merely recommended her to
his father's favor as the daughter of a loyal and beloved subject, suggesting that she be confirmed in her inheritance with
all due haste—a forbearance that spared everyone, including
himself, considerable embarrassment. Melanthe was greatly
in charity with the duke at present.

"Richard of Bowland, God assoil him!" Edward exclaimed
with pleasure in his voice. He bade Melanthe rise and gave
her a wine-balmed embrace. "Child! And our John has sent
you to us! Tell us of him; in truth, how does he?" He held out
the paper with a sad sigh. "This speaks naught a word of himself."

"My very dear and mighty lord, your son was in great good
humor when I took leave of him, may God defend," she said.

He nodded, pleased, and then seemed to lose the course of
his thought as he stared off into a corner. After a long
moment, he tilted his head toward her as if he were a child
with a secret. "The prince is our pride," he whispered, "but
John is our heart."

Melanthe murmured, "The duke has much the look of his
dear mother the queen, God give her soul rest." Melanthe had
no idea if this were so, having only the haziest recollection of
Queen Phillipa as a plump and smiling personage, but she
added, "He has her eyes, my lord. A very fine figure of a man.
Your majesty may well love him with a full heart."

Edward's lips trembled. "Verily. Verily." He gave a deep
sniff. "You are a good and lovely child. What can we do for
you?"

Melanthe bowed, placing a lavishly bound volume upon
his bed. "My lord would honor me, would you accept this

small gift. It is a work upon falconry, written by a master from the north country."

At Edward's impatient gesture, the king's servant passed the book to him. He turned the leaves, nodding in delight. "A most worthy subject for a treatise. Excellent. Excellent. We are pleased."

Melanthe drew him into a little discussion of hunting birds. After a quarter hour they were great friends. He was well known to have a passion for falconing and hawking.

"And this, sire," she said, when she felt the moment right, "I would convey into your own hand, if you will consent."

She held out a sealed parchment. King Edward accepted the paper, fumbling it open. "What is this, my dear?"

"It is my claim to my husband's estate, quitted into your name, my beloved lord. I am a weak woman; I have not the power to assert it myself, but it is a most valuable right. My husband was the Prince of Monteverde. He had no male heirs to survive him, and I myself have a claim through my mother's blood. All of it I cede to my mighty and esteemed lord, to do with as your majesty might will."

Melanthe was aware of the chamberlain's subtle stir at this news. He stood close to the king, bowing. "May I read the document to you, sire?"

The chamberlain's greedy hand was already upon the quit-claim, but Edward's fingers closed. He held to the document. "Monteverde?" His vague old eyes seemed to sharpen. "We are in debt to Monteverde for a certain sum."

"My lord, I did not know of such a thing," Melanthe lied, dropping into a deep courtesy. Edward was in debt by an impossible amount to the bank of Monteverde, as he was and had always been in debt to the Italian money merchants. "Then I may have even greater hope that my humble gift is of value to my king."

Alice's man made another attempt, not so subtle, to divest Edward of the quitclaim, but the king held it tightly. "You have not asserted your right?" He frowned. "Nay, but—our mind betrays us. Bowland—have you not a brother to act for you? Lionel's friend . . ." He paused, his voice trailing off into an old man's quiver.

Melanthe could see him remember. He had peddled his

second son Lionel to the Viscontis of Milan, in a payment for England's debts—but the most lavish wedding of the age, with gifts of armor and horses and hounds in gemmed collars, cloaks of ermine and pearls, a banquet of thirty courses all gilded with gold leaf and a dowry so huge it had taken two years to barter, had not bought a long and happy life for Lionel. He had died six months later in Italy of an unnamed fever.

And with him Richard, of his closest inner circle, Richard her brother, who had been only five when Melanthe had left England and a stranger of twenty-one when he came to Italy to die. The gossips had said that he had been slain mistakenly, by sharing poisoned drink with Lionel. The gossips had said that Richard had meant to kill his own prince and accidentally killed himself as well. The gossips had said that Melanthe had murdered her brother for his inheritance, uncaring that the prince died with him. The gossips said anything. She watched the king with her heart beating hard.

"May God give both of their souls reprieve." Edward's broad shoulders were drawn inward, his lower lip unsteady. He groped for the wine goblet and drank.

"Amen." She made the cross, drawing a deep breath. "My lord, in my woman's frailty, I have not the courage or desire to act upon my claim to Monteverde. I wish only to return to Bowland and live there unmolested in my widowhood, if it please you. But a man of greater energy and shrewdness than my poor self, sire—such a man as the Duke of Lancaster, say—a lord of your son's natural powers might make a great and useful thing of this claim."

"Verily." The king wiped his eyes. "Verily."

"Your majesty must wish to give the duke much, in return for his dedication to his brother's interests in Aquitaine," Melanthe murmured.

King Edward began to weep at this mention of his son's unswerving loyalty. God knew, Lancaster was truly faithful to his family, bankrupting his own coffers as he was in trying to hold Aquitaine together in their name. For a moment Melanthe feared she had gone too far, that this talk of his sons would send Edward back into maudlin foolishness. But the chamberlain took advantage of the moment to get his claws upon the quitclaim again. The king roused, shaking off his retainer's obtrusive hand with royal contempt, showing a gleam of his former spirit as he stared down at the document with a narrow-eyed examination.

They shall not have it, Ligurio. Melanthe smiled inside herself, her teeth grinding together. *Not Alice Perrers or Riata or Navona either.* Pray God and Fortune, King Edward had resolve enough left in him that he would turn her quitclaim over to his favorite son instead of Alice's brood, and the wolves of Italy would find John of Lancaster in their midst after all. Fair payment it would be to him, she thought, for the dislocate shoulder and humiliation she had caused. By hap someday he would even thank her.

The king looked up at her, his eyes red. "What can we do to show our fondness for you, child?"

"Sire," she said, bowing her head. "My only wish is that I may live alone at Bowland. My marriage is in your majesty's gift."

"You would not be pleased to wed again?"

"Nay, sire, by your leave. In hap, in the fullness of time, at God's hest I will enter a nunnery and devote myself to prayer."

The king nodded, gripping the quitclaim. "So be it. You have our pledge, child—in our affection for you we shall not require you to marry again. Also, we desire that you hold the dignity of your father's offices, in the style of Countess of Bowland, and all other titles with which he was invested." He waved a shaky hand toward the chamberlain. "See that these things are so affirmed by our seal."

Bowing down unto the very floor, Melanthe abandoned the king to Alice's tender avarice. It was vital now to leave London instantly, before Allegreto or the Riata could discover what she had done. She acted by Ligurio's teaching: she kept her goal clear, but the path to reach it shifted on the edge of a moment.

She felt freedom near. On the high empty hills she remembered from her northern childhood she would live, belonging to no one but herself. Of all her father's rich and comfortable manors, she chose cold Bowland Castle as her citadel, as he had done. If she could command Monteverde for the six years of Ligurio's dying, she could hold her father's lands from Bowland, vast though they might be, among these simple-headed Englishmen.

The course she would take to attain her end was still uncertain, but she lived moment to moment as she must. Allegreto was well distracted from his usual vigilance—she had made sure of that before her audience with the king—but how long his fear would divert him she did not know. Always she watched for opportunity, seized on a different ruse, twisted and turned as she saw her chance or felt her danger. She had betrayed every bargain and vow with her quitclaim. Now she lived like quicksilver, breath to breath until she could rid herself of her watchdogs.

LONDON WAS FULL of plague rumors. At Princess Melanthe's command Ruck tracked hearsay through the muddy streets. When he presented himself to attend her at Westminster Palace, Allegreto assailed him in her anteroom.

"What befalls?" the youth demanded, trailing Ruck to her steward. Allegreto had a morbid fear of plague: he talked of it endlessly and had taken to attaching himself to Ruck whenever he was at the palace, as if Ruck had some talisman against it.

"Naught befalls, that I can tell," Ruck said.

"Naught?" Allegreto asked anxiously.

Ruck held out his hand toward the door as the steward announced him. "Am I to report to thy mistress or to thee, whelp?"

"To me, certainly." The princess's voice was elegant and firm. She lowered the book of poetry to her lap.

"My liege lady." Ruck bowed, while Allegreto hovered by his elbow like an importunate child.

"Green Sire," she acknowledged courteously. She was much more sedate in her manner among the English, dressed with rich propriety in blue and white, only a few diamonds sparkling in her necklace and belt. A changeling, taking on the aspect of her surroundings. He felt his own weakness, succumbing to this false look of virtue when he knew the corrupt truth of her.

"You come with what news?" she asked.

"I find no evidence of any epidemic here, Your Highness."

She nodded. "Well enough. It is only gossip as usual, you see, Allegreto." She laid aside the book and gave a little stretch. "I fear you must leave me now to rest. The sea journey still fatigues me."

Ruck started to withdraw, but Allegreto hung on to his arm. "Nay, the truth!" Allegreto demanded. "What dost thou know?"

Ruck frowned at him. "I've said truth. There's no plague in the city."

"Do not conceal it!" Allegreto flung himself onto the bed. "My lady—he must speak."

"Dost thou hide something, sir?" she asked sharply.

Ruck prevented himself from looking directly at her. Out of her presence it was possible to feel disgust, but the sight of her overpowered his better reason. A vision of her had haunted him for ten and three years: the reality cut through illusions to the heart of impure hunger. Her new modesty only made it the worse. He knew more of her, but not enough. He feared that everything could not be enough.

"There is no plague," he repeated. "It is but gossip."

Princess Melanthe tilted her head. "But you believe it will come?"

"How can I know? There's talk of the planets aligned for it."

This news turned Allegreto white. "My lady!"

"There's little enough to that," Ruck said. "I vow the planets predict plague once a month. The astrologers make their living on such gloom."

"Nay!" Allegreto turned to Princess Melanthe. "My lady's charts say the same!"

"Thou must be careful, love," she said. "Very careful. I've cast thy stars again. They exert an ill chance now."

"In Bordeaux they said it had returned in the south!" Allegreto exclaimed.

"Not in Milan," she said soothingly. "The talk there was that it raged among the Danes."

"Mayhap it is all talk," Ruck said.

"Traders will bring it from the north! In death ships!" Allegreto hurled himself off the bed. "Lady, let us fly!"

"Fly where?" she asked calmly.

"Away!" His voice had a frantic undertone. "Out of the city!"

"And suppose it follows us out of the city?" She smiled at him. "By hap thou wilt be fortunate to meet the Heavenly Father while thou art still young and innocent."

The youth made a faint sound, falling to his knees before her. He buried his face against her skirt. Ruck had begun to feel a certain compassion for Allegreto. The indifferent way she mocked his mortal fears might have seemed casual, but Ruck had caught the small cruel narrowing of her eyes as she looked down at her youthful lover. At that instant it was as if she hated him, but then her mouth softened, and she ruffled his hair.

"Fly, then, if it pleases thee," she said. "Return home to Monteverde."

He lifted his face quickly. "Your Highness—we go home?"

"Not I. But I will send thee to safety. Thy father will shield thee in his country villa."

Allegreto stared at her, his fingers gripped in the folds of her dress. "Nay—lady . . ."

She traced her fingers down his face. "Go home. I could not bear to see thy sweet skin swell and blacken," she murmured. "I could not bear to hear thy groans."

His breath came faster. His tongue ran around his lips. "We will go home together, lady. My father will give refuge to us both."

"I've had audience with the king. Wilt thou deny me my lands that he commends to me?"

"But the plague—"

She gave a slight laugh. "There is some privilege in age, my lovely boy. Does it not strike most terribly at the young and handsome such as thee?"

He shook his head, holding her embroidered hem pressed to his mouth. "I cannot leave you, Your Highness."

"The stars augur ill for thee. Wilt thou compel me to follow thy bier?"

He gave a dry sob. "You know I cannot leave you, lady. But let us fly from this city, I beg you."

She sat back, glancing a question at Ruck.

"As soon as Your Highness likes to venture forth," he said bluntly. "But the weather is untoward. We were fortunate in our water crossing. To the north, they say the winter already holds hard. And it were wiser to take time to assemble a large escort for my lady's protection."

Allegreto raised his face, wiping fiercely at the tears that tumbled down his cheeks. "Please—lady—no delay!"

"How long to softer weather?" she asked Ruck.

"Three months, say."

"Three months!" Allegreto cried. He reached for Princess Melanthe's hand and squeezed it between his. "I'll be dead in three months! I feel it!"

She looked down at him for a long moment. His eyes seemed to grow wider, almost fearful, as he held her gaze.

"I am in no hurry to leave," she said indifferently. "The journey will discommode me."

He suddenly snatched his hands away and flung himself from her. "You taunt me!" he shouted. "We'll not stay here, or I'll write to my father!"

"Little use, if thou art to be dead in three months." Princess Melanthe picked up her book and turned a page idly. "With luck he might arrive to pray over thy coffin."

Allegreto seized the book. He ripped out half the vellum, scattering it across the carpets as if the precious leaves were but wheaten chaff. When Princess Melanthe made no reaction, his face seemed to transfigure, altering from smooth beauty to a demon's mask of rage. He leaned over her, grabbed her cheeks between his palms and kissed her, crushing his mouth against hers. Ruck saw her hands clench white on the arms of the chair as the youth bore her head hard back against the carved rest.

Ruck grabbed Allegreto's shoulder and hauled him off. With one shove he sent the youth sprawling backward against the tapestried wall.

"Master thyself!" He held Allegreto by the throat, pressing him to the wall. "Ere thou findest a grave sooner yet!"

Allegreto swallowed beneath his hand, breathing hard. He looked at Ruck with black eyes that had gone empty, as if fear and fury had canceled each other.

The sound of light clapping came from behind. "A most knightly performance, Green Sire! The poor child only wants manners. Haps thou might give him a lesson at thy leisure."

"Tell my lady—" Allegreto said between panting breaths, "tell my lady's grace to think of how she will grieve should I die."

Ruck let him go and stepped back. "This lies between thee and thy mistress." He cast her a hard glance, then bowed. "I await your decision without, madam."

She lifted her hand to bid him stay. "That will not be required. We shall be civilized, shall we not, Allegreto? Begin the preparations to depart for Bowland at once, sir."

"Tomorrow! By secluded ways," Allegreto said, quick and hoarse. "If it please my lady's grace."

She made an impatient flick of her hand. "As thou wilt, then! We take only what men-at-arms you have at present, sir. The rest of my court may follow with my baggage. It will be safer to avoid peopled places, should pestilence somehow run ahead of us."

"Nay, only for his fancy?" Ruck asked in outrage. "Your highness, such a small party—it be nought protection enough!"

"Allegreto wishes to avoid plague."

"Plague is not the only danger to Your Highness," he said harshly, "or the likeliest, for that matter!"

Her lashes lifted. "And what is likelier, sir? Canst thou not master such bandits as the countryside boasts?"

He scowled. "My lady—I think not of outlaws only."

"Of what, then?" she demanded.

"Your Highness holds great wealth and property," he said brusquely.

"Ah. It is my abduction you fear. Well thought, Green Sire, but I have no apprehension of it. Our departure will be quick and quiet, and if we travel by uncommon ways, so much the better to foil any such schemes." She smiled. "And of course, you may spread word that any man who forces me to wed him will rue every day of his short life and die in lingering agony."

Ruck gazed at her. She was so beautiful and so wicked, laughing at him behind that comely innocent smile. It would work, he thought with resentful wonder—between her reputation and her plan to slip away, she would be near as safe from seizure and force as if she traveled with half a thousand men.

He bowed his head. "My lady," he assented grudgingly, "as you say."

Allegreto gave a deep sigh and closed his eyes. He stood against the wall, fresh tears trickling down his cheeks. The pulse in his throat hammered visibly.

Ruck's own heart still thudded with reaction. He had seen little of Princess Melanthe and her courtier so far on the journey—he hoped that he would see little more, if this was to be the way of it. He disliked scenes and ravings intensely.

Six

———∞———

"OEN . . . TWEYE . . . THREN . . . *hie!*" Ruck yelled, driving Hawk forward, dragging at the lead horse's bridle as the line went taut over his saddlebow. The animals threw their heads, blowing great puffs of frost, heaving and struggling as their hooves sank half to the knee in ice water and mud.

Easy enough for the Princess Melanthe to choose to avoid lodging on the way north. She and her attendants sat in the whirlicote, lumbering monster that it was, without even lifting the leather cover to watch. Ruck let the line go lax and backed Hawk again, turning in the saddle to look down the line of five blowing horses to his men wrestling with the tree limbs braced beneath the wheels.

The whirlicote's proud paint and glitter was a sad sight now, covered in dirt, drowned to the axles in the ruts. His sergeant-at-arms, standing to the side and peering underneath, shook his head and straightened. He held up his arm for another try. Ruck turned again.

"Oen—tweye—" As the whirlicote rocked thrice in time, the men chorused in with Ruck's shout, maintaining a miserably determined enthusiasm. "Hie-*uuup!*"

Hawk bowed his gray head and strained. The harnessed horse reared against the yoke and came down with a splash of frigid water that sprayed over Ruck's leg. Shouts erupted behind him. The whirlicote pitched mightily and went nowhere.

He twisted round and saw two of the men sitting on their backsides in ice water. He cursed under his breath, throwing the rope off his saddlebow. Turning Hawk, he rode through the mud to the front of the whirlicote and reached over, pitching back the leather curtain.

A miserable-looking Allegreto huddled nearest the front, cloaked in furs. Her single gentlewoman sat behind him, almost invisible in her wrappings. Ruck leaned farther over. Princess Melanthe reclined on a lounge placed midway back in the vehicle.

"Madam," Ruck said, "methinks, were you to descend, your ease would be well served."

"I am full at ease, kind sir," she replied tranquilly in English.

"Then I pray that you find this place pleasing, Your Highness," he retorted in the same language, "for ne'er shall we nought see another, stay my lady's grace and her company of twenty stone within."

"Twenty stone!" she said, with a light surprise. "Weighen we so much?"

"More," he said.

In the half-light of the whirlicote he could not tell, but he thought that wicked-innocent smile hovered at her lips. "Allegreto will descend," she said in French. "He fancied the journey."

"Yea, he will," Ruck said. "I doubt me this whirlicote goes any farther, laden or nay."

"Thou must try harder, Englishman!" Allegreto shivered and pulled his furs closer.

"Poor Allegreto," Princess Melanthe said. "Art thou cold, my soft southern pet?" She laughed, changing to English again. "Green Knight—do drive out a decree, my litter to the forn."

Allegreto lifted his head. "What did my lady say?" he asked urgently.

She only smiled tauntingly at him. Ruck turned his horse away, issuing orders. As his men set to work on the harness, he rode Hawk to the back of the whirlicote, judging how they might angle her litter so that she didn't have to step into the muddy water to make the change. Allegreto's head popped out from the back opening.

"What did my lady say?" he insisted.

"Canst thou ride a horse, whelp?" Ruck asked.

Allegreto groaned.

"Thou it was who wouldst have us come on roads out of the common way," Ruck reminded him.

"To avoid the pestilence!"

Ruck looked at the bleak and empty country around. The track ran along the dark edge of a forest, with not a habitation to be seen. A hard, cold wind blew off the somber line of mountains that marched away to the west, burning his face. "I think us well secluded from infection," he said blandly.

Allegreto scrambled up and balanced on the wagon's gate, the long toes of his elegant slippers, one yellow and one blue, drooping forlornly over the side.

"I have a fine rouncy for thee, whelp." Ruck tilted his thumb toward a mud-covered harness horse. The sergeant led it up. The animal squelched to a halt and blew a spumy sigh, reaching out a hopeful muzzle toward Allegreto's blue toe.

The youth snatched it back. He looked up at the arriving litter and then over his shoulder into the whirlicote. "My lady, my exquisite gentle lady, I worship you. I live for you. You are more beautiful than the sun, more lovely than—"

"No, thou may not ride in the litter," she said tartly. "Gryngolet will not abide thee at such close quarter."

Allegreto turned back. Ruck held onto Hawk's reins, half expecting another fit of passion, but the youth appeared to resign himself to the limited recourse, choosing to mount rather than risk the falcon's temper—or his lady's. By the time her gentlewoman was transferred to a mule and the litter moved into place, Allegreto was somewhere off amid the pack train, sawing at his horse's reins to turn it away from a donkey loaded with fodder.

Princess Melanthe appeared at the lowered gate of the whirlicote, wrapped in a mantle of ermine and royal blue. Ruck dismounted. In spite of their efforts, there was still a gap the width of a rod across the icy lake between the whirlicote and the litter. He saw nothing else for it—he pulled off his muddy gloves and moved to step into the water and assist her.

"Pray do not," she said, leaning her hand across to catch the top of the litter. She flashed him a smile and with a swift move stepped across the gap.

The litter tilted precariously, and she gave a small squeak, holding to the roof. Ruck dove forward with a splash, catching her. Her body startled him: a brief weight, a soft lithe shape within the voluminous mantle. He hardly realized he was standing to his knees in freezing water. Almost as soon as he touched her, she left his hold, ducking into the litter and lapsing back into the cushions.

Somehow he had her hands in his. They felt so hot that they stung his flesh. He thought: *witch,* to burn so—and then she held his fingers for a moment and murmured in English, "Thy hands are so cold!"

"My feet are colder, madam," he said. He hiked himself out of the ditch and walked away with his legs dripping.

When the litter was marshaled into place and horses harnessed to it, one before and one behind, she summoned him again to her. Even bundled in her furs and hood as she was, Ruck found it hard to behold her face. As he stood by the litter, he let the curtain sag so that all he saw were the damask cushions and her cloak.

"What be your counsel?" she asked quietly in English.

He did not know why she asked his counsel, as she had never yet taken it, not even in so modest a matter as the choice of road.

They had avoided Coventry, they had avoided Stafford, now they swung wide of Chester. In the past ten days she had sometimes wished to go north and sometimes west, as erratic as a belfry bat. They had come so far out of the way to her lands in the north that he had begun to doubt if she had the vaguest notion of where they lay. That, or she had gone witless in her head.

"I caution my lady's grace, let us hie to the nearest manor and crave harbor." He had said it before. It was what they ought to have done all along, if not for her indulgence of Allegreto's overblown terrors. "Yewlow lies east by sunset, do we tarry nought."

"And what ahead?"

"An arm of the sea. Dee quicksands and the Wyrale," he said. "It is wilderness."

"Thou knowest the country?"

"Well, Your Highness."

"Dragon hunting?" she asked mildly.

He did not give her the dignity of an answer to that, although it was true.

Her voice from behind the curtain held a hint of amusement. "So we needen fear no attack by a fiery worm, if we advance."

"Outlaws only, my lady," he said dryly.

She said nothing for a moment. Then he heard her sigh. "Allegreto will be tedious. Can outlaws be worse?"

Ruck glanced at Allegreto pounding vehemently at the poor cart-horse's ribs. "Methinks my lady's grace hatz nought much experience of outlaws."

She gave a low, wry laugh. "And thou but little of Allegreto. But thy fingers are blue with cold, sir. I may be pleased to see thee in bed at Yewlow tonight," she murmured. Where he held the curtain, she caressed the back of his hand.

He jerked away. He remembered what he escorted, that she was hot with an unholy flame and he himself all too quick to set alight. "I feel nought the cold, my lady," he said stiffly, keeping his eyes down.

"Then we pressen ahead, and tarry not, Green Sire."

He heard no regret in her voice, only command, leaving Yewlow and its bed a yawning crevasse of iniquity, a promise of unknown possibilities—or haps just a pallet by the armory fire with his men. Haps she did not know that such as he could hardly expect to be offered a bed of his own, outside of a promiscuous lady's. Haps she had meant nothing by her words, and her touch had been a mischance.

He didn't look on her again. But he felt the deep timbre of desire in his flesh, fire beneath his skin. As he walked away, he thought mad thoughts: that she prolonged the journey on his account, to seduce him or to torture him.

The Wyrale lay before them, a wild place, afforested and forsaken—better to avoid it and backtrack to Chester, but if that was not to be, then in two days' travel they could be across. He had a dozen men, well-armed and passably horsed; without the whirlicote they could make far better speed. He turned to the sergeant-at-arms, charging him to have the vehicle unloaded while the rest of the party moved on.

Then he mounted Hawk and rode back into the train. Catching the reins of Allegreto's packhorse, Ruck yanked the animal around, shouting orders to the company to fall into line. With Allegreto clinging and bouncing and complaining on his rotund mount, Ruck pressed both horses into a mud-splattering canter and took the lead.

THEY CAMPED ON the banks of the great tidal mouth of the river. Eerie vapor lay so heavy in the dawn that his men were sound without sight—he heard their quiet murmurs, voicing fears that they would not have spoken knowing he was near. Through the mask of the sergeant's discipline, Ruck had not fully realized how ready they were to abandon the Princess Melanthe without regret. This wild country made their minds easy prey to dark rumors about the lady and all the fears of feeling themselves far too small a defensive party. The mountains of Wales were invisible, but the weight of them loomed heavily, rebel-haunted as they were even in these latter days of peace. He would not have put it past his men to bolt, but Ruck held the simple mastery of having yet paid only a token of their promised wages.

He'd dealt with such before, and set to work dealing with these, rallying them out of their doubt with an order to break fast with white bread instead of rye. He followed that with a gathering at a little distance from Princess Melanthe's tent, appealing in a quiet voice first to their vanity—ten of them were worth twenty of any others he'd encountered; and then to their greed—an heiress of Princess Melanthe's stature would be generous indeed with her escort, and there were few to share the sum. He refrained from naming a figure, merely conveying the modest opinion that it would be more money than any of them had ever seen in their lives.

They grew better hearty at that, and he set them to polishing the mud off their weapons in preparation to awe the countryside. Though the mist showed no sign of lifting, Ruck sent Pierre off laden with an offering of a fur to the hermit of Holy

Head who acted guide across the sands for those too poor—
or mad—to use the king's ferry nigh to Chester.

The mist hid the water, but the nearness of the sea brought
a drizzling chill, a cold that cut deeper than true frost, seeping
through Ruck's mantle, dampening his skin. He'd already
walked down to the strand, judging the tide. They must be
ready to move as soon as the hermit arrived, but there had yet
been no sigh of stirring from his liege lady—who was no
early riser, he had found.

He saw the gentlewoman leave Princess Melanthe's tent,
but the maid disappeared into the vapor before he caught her
eye. Ruck wavered, standing before the emerald fabric. The
maid had left the flap caught back, showing scarlet lining, the
only blossom of color in the gray atmosphere.

He coughed to reveal himself, and chinked his mailed
hands together, and rattled his foot against a pile of shells,
with no response. He moved back a little, turning half away,
and stole a surreptitious look inside to see if she were yet
awake.

She was not. Amid a pile of featherbeds and furs she slept,
with the whelp's arms tight around her. Allegreto rested his
cheek against her netted hair, his lips curved in a sleeper's
smile.

Ruck turned full away. He stood staring into the blank mist
toward the sea. He felt obscurely angry, and lonely. It was not
a new feeling; he'd felt it half his life, since he'd left his home
and found no place for himself in the world, but not for a long
time had it been so keen and envious.

He was disgusted. He would have run himself on an
enemy's lance before he would live as Allegreto lived. But it
was not the warmth, not the soft place in a silken tent, not
even physical possession of her that he most craved. Nothing
of the truth of Princess Melanthe. What he wanted was that
false and beguiling picture: a slow familiar awakening, sleeping close, trusting; easy smiles and union.

He wanted his wife.

For ten and three years he had believed God had taken
Isabelle for good and sufficient reasons. Sometimes he caught
himself wishing that she'd been taken in truth, that she was
dead instead of in a nunnery, so that he could marry again and

cease wandering in this limbo where his body tortured him and his heart hungered even after such as Princess Melanthe. He couldn't tell that he was becoming better for it; he was becoming worse—he felt himself sinking toward a kiss instead of a shared apple, toward that subtle offer of a bed in Yewlow.

The untarnished image of the lady he served had once sustained him, but it held him no longer. Nay, she drove him now toward infamy herself. The vision of Isabelle alone had never been enough to bind him; he'd needed his liege lady of the hawk to serve, governing himself for her honor. When he tried now to put Isabelle in her place instead, he found an abyss of anger opening up beneath his feet: anger at Isabelle, at the archbishop who'd let her leave him, at God Himself. Without his liege lady, his defense crumbled against the endless question of why, why, why he must live without a wife.

He raised his face to the gray sky and found no answer there. The archbishop had declared his vow before Isabelle invalid, but taken her anyway—leaving Ruck in an impasse he could only understand as God's intention to hold him fast to chastity, archbishop or no.

It seemed too pitiless that he should only be given a few weeks of love in his life and never permitted to seek it again. He had no calling for holy orders, of that he was certain. He felt no urges to preach to the Ninevites—he wouldn't have known what to say to them if he had. He heard no voice telling him to wear sackcloth against his skin or wall himself up as an anchorite.

He was only an ordinary man, and ordinary men were suffered to marry instead of burn, to have sons and daughters, to have a bed and a fire and a wife waiting at the end of the journey.

Without his liege lady to fortify his resolve, he could only cleave to his bitter perfection, hating Isabelle and God . . . or surrender honor and hate himself. He had never thought truly of yielding before, but he thought of it now. He felt the tent and the deep furs behind him, and the whisper of hellfire on the nape of his neck.

•   •   •

MELANTHE FELT THAT today might be the time. Or tomorrow, perhaps. She waited for Allegreto to wake—or perhaps he was awake already: she thought he must sleep no more than she, always on the edge of consciousness, aware of her every move as she was aware of his. They had come to this compromise, that they slept so close that neither could move without the other heeding. She could feel his suspicions growing in the tightness of his arms about her.

To Cara, Melanthe had said this journey would end at an English nunnery, but that was to be kept secret from Allegreto. To Allegreto, she had declared they traveled to her castle at Bowland, and that was to be concealed from Cara. Melanthe herself waited for the moment that she could rid herself of both of them. They did not know the country; they could not speak to the English men-at-arms, and she had kept them strictly away from her knight. She had directed the Green Sire in a fickle course, invoking the fox to confound pursuit, leaving no scent in such places as towns and cities, winding and turning toward the safety of a strong and secluded earth.

She worked upon Allegreto's fears of plague. Like his fear of Gryngolet, it went beyond his reason—Allegreto, who had killed a man before his tenth birthday, would weep at her feet to protect him from plague.

So she thought. Sometimes she feared it was only another illusion, that he and his father were always ahead of her in their intrigues. Gian Navona had his own intentions, driven by passion and mystery, as he had always been.

But the safe earth of Bowland was almost within her reach. Already she had left the whole of her retinue behind in London—they had not anticipated that, for Melanthe traveled always in great state, however quickly she might move. She could not disperse her Italian household entirely yet without suspicion, but to organize their separate journey to Bowland, she had appointed her most hopelessly incompetent and aimless attendant, to be certain they did not arrive ahead of her— if ever, considering Sodorini's truly wonderful lack of efficiency.

Only Allegreto remained. And Cara. Innocent-eyed Cara, who slept in Melanthe's tent and brought her food; who would not be left behind, her devotion to her mistress was so very ardent. This sudden display of mulish loyalty confirmed all suspicions of the girl. Allegreto was right—the Riata had subverted her.

It made no matter. Melanthe was going to be free of her; free of Allegreto; free of any threat of Riata or Navona or Monteverde. Within the walls of Bowland no foreign strangers could pass unnoticed, no Italian assassins could slip past the gate. She had only to arrive there before any enemy, and live enclosed by a fortress of Englishmen loyal to her alone.

Cara returned to the tent. Melanthe pretended to wake, turning and stretching. She sat up, and Allegreto jerked a little, caught half drowsing before he was full awake the next instant, like a cat. He rolled away and made a dismayed mutter when he saw the foulness of the weather outside, catching up his pestilence-apple and holding it to his nose as he left the tent.

"Give you good morn, my lady," Cara said pleasantly, on her knees beside the chest as she laid out Melanthe's clothing. "The hunchbacked man, he brought fresh cockles from a hermit here. She gestured toward a bowl, where they were already washed and opened. "Will you break fast while they are still sweet?"

"Bring them here," Melanthe said. "I'm in no hurry to leave my bed on such a morning. Where is my water? Not heated yet? Go—fetch it at once."

Cara bowed, still on her knees, and scurried out of the tent. Melanthe eyed the cockles.

Though Melanthe had been first cousin to Cara's own mother, the soft-voiced maid was far more dangerous to her life than Allegreto. Cara could hide much behind her mild pleasantries, a sharp eye and perceptive mind the least of it. Yesterday she had asked quietly if she would be allowed to stay and attend her mistress in the English nunnery. Melanthe had returned some careless answer, but verily, should not Cara have shown more curiosity than that about the location and name of this religious house? She had asked no more or less in the whole time they traveled.

Melanthe stared at the cockles. Then she grabbed up the

sandy bag that Cara had laid aside and poured the shellfish in.
Pulling up the silken floor of the tent, she pushed the bag
down into the sand. She heard Allegreto returning and hur-
riedly smoothed the fabric back in place.

She did not bother to tell him of the suspicious cockles.
She was weary of hearing his spiteful accusations against
Cara—and no more did she want to wake and find the maid
dead of poison or a knife. Allegreto, at least, was determined
that Melanthe should live to become his father's wife, at the
cost of any other life but his own.

Forsooth, it was something strange that he had not killed
Cara already.

ONCE ACROSS THE river ford Ruck kept Allegreto close
beside him on the traverse of the sands, dragging the patient
cart horse along at his knee, following hard on the footprints
of the mount in front of him. Ahead, lost in mist, the horses
bearing Princess Melanthe's litter were immediately behind
the hermit's donkey, held narrowly in the track to avoid
quicksands. Each man had strict instructions to keep the man
ahead and behind in sight or send an instant alarm.

Ruck and Allegreto brought up the rear, but the pace was
so sedate that there was never any danger of Hawk falling
behind, even burdened as he was. The war-horse proclaimed
his displeasure at the sluggish speed by leaping from bank to
bank of each sandy tidal stream instead of fording them,
which annoyed Allegreto and his cart horse very much. The
boy was already complaining of saddle sores. He held a
smelling-apple of powders and herbs constantly to his lips to
ward off pestilence. In a muffled voice Allegreto kept Ruck
fully informed of his sentiments regarding the danger of their
position as last in the procession and the folly of allowing a
stranger any contact with the party. He vacillated unhappily
between fear of association with the hermit and desire to cross
the quicksands directly at his heels.

When Ruck saw large broken shells beneath Hawk's
hooves and heard the sound of the mild surf that marked the
solid shore of the Wyrale, he let go of the cart horse's reins
and tossed them at Allegreto. But the youth gave a dismayed
cry as his mount immediately began to fall behind. He

pounded it into a trot, holding the reins out toward Ruck with his free hand.

"Do not leave me!" The order was arrogant and scared, half-stifled through the scented bag. "The vapor! Is it thicker behind us? It breathes poison—dost thou sense it?"

Ruck tendered no opinion on the vapor, but he took back the leading reins. Up a sharp, sandy bank with a heave and a scramble, and they were safe across the mouth of the river, the marsh and bleak forest of the Wyrale before them. He took a quick account of the party as he rode up to Pierre and the hermit, ignoring Allegreto's vociferous objections.

Pierre had thieved something—Ruck could tell by the beatific smile on his squire's lips. He fixed his broken-backed man with a ferocious scowl. Pierre's benevolent smirk faded. No doubt he'd found some mislaid trinket as they broke camp and folded the tents, but Ruck knew, having done it once or twice, that even if he upended Pierre and shook him by the feet, there would be no finding the hidden cache.

The hermit went to his knees, folding his hands for a benediction. Ruck dismounted, kneeling with the rest. Even Allegreto fell to the shelly bank, both hands pressing his herbal over his mouth. During a long prayer of thanksgiving for their successful crossing, Ruck took another count with his head bowed, considering each of the men-at-arms while repeating paternosters, deciding on the day's order of march. Once, his lowered gaze wandered to Princess Melanthe's litter: he saw the curtain pulled slightly back and her eyes upon him instead of closed in prayer.

The curtain dropped, hiding her. Ruck felt his body flush and harden with the chance of what her thoughts might be. She'd been looking at him, staring. He lost the sequence of the prayer, his "amen" coming too late and loud after the rest.

"Thou," Allegreto said imperiously from behind his smelling-apple. "Hermit! Hast thou heard tell of pestilence in this region?"

The man betrayed no sign of understanding. Ruck repeated the question more respectfully, in English, and got a negative shrug.

Allegreto wasn't satisfied. "The atmosphere is corrupted here. I feel it."

"We move onward," Ruck said, to forestall any enlargement on this unsettling topic. He gave orders, placing himself at the head of the cavalcade once more, the litter midway back and protected on both sides. With Allegreto's and Hawk's reins firmly in one hand, Ruck lifted his arm and shouted, *"Avaunt!"*

As they moved off the sandy shore and into the trees, Allegreto leaned forward, holding the rouncy's thick mane, keeping his bag of herbal protection pressed across his mouth and nose as he bumped along. "The recluse was bloodless, thinkest thee not?" he demanded through his bag. "He sickens."

"I saw aught of such," Ruck said in a deliberately disinterested tone.

"He sickens. He was ashen. By nightfall he is dead."

Ruck cast him a glance. "What is this? Thou art now a physician, whelp?"

"The miasma is infectious!" Allegreto insisted. He let go of the horse's mane and dug in his mantle, pulling out another bagged smelling-apple. He offered it to Ruck. "I have three. I've given my lady's grace the other."

Ruck lifted his brow in surprise. "Hast thou no need of it thyself?"

"Take it," Allegreto said. "I wish thee to have it, knight."

Ruck gave him a one-sided smile. "Nay. Keep it for thine own. The plague never touches me."

Allegreto crossed himself. "Say not so! Thou wilt call the wrath of God upon thee!"

"I speak only the truth," Ruck said mildly.

The youth changed hands, holding his apple with the left.

"Cramped arm?" Ruck asked, hard put not to smile.

"Yea," Allegreto said seriously. "It is a most wearing thing to hold."

Ruck raised his hand, signaling a halt. He drew the cart horse up even with him. "Where is thy scarf?" He leaned over and dug under the youth's furs, pulling the dagged silken scarf from his shoulders. With a few knots he made a cup in the middle of the length and reached for Allegreto's smelling-apple. "Hold in thy breath."

The boy reluctantly released the bag, making a small,

choked sound of protest as Ruck dumped out the amber apple. As quickly as he could, Ruck secured the herb bag and apple within the scarf and reached over to tie it round Allegreto's mouth and head.

"There. Thou art safe from pestilent airs, whelp."

Allegreto looked down over his bright blue mask and tucked away his spare bag of herbs. "God grant you mercy," he said behind the scarf, the most courteous words he'd yet spoken to Ruck.

He answered with only a short nod. Allegreto looked foolish in his sapphire kerchief; foolish and young. Ruck wondered if it was possible to make a cuckold of a castrato—his mind pondered on the wordplay until he realized what he was thinking. He slapped Hawk overhard with the reins and yelled the order to move.

"Thou hast seen plague, then?" Allegreto asked from inside his muffle.

"Yea," Ruck said.

"I was but a child when it came again. My father took me into the country, away from the malignant atmosphere."

"Give thanks for that."

"How comes it thou art certain it touches thee not?"

Ruck rode in silence, watching the trees ahead for any sign of hazard.

"Hast thou a charm?"

"Nay. None of man's making."

"What, then?" Allegreto urged. "What protects thee?"

"Nothing." Ruck frowned at the sandy track ahead.

"Something it must be. Tell me." When he got no answer, he raised his voice. "Tell me, Englishman!"

"I know only that all about me died, and I lived," Ruck said at last. "In the last pestilence my man sickened. I stayed with him when the priest refused to come, but it never touched me."

"The hunchback? He sickened and lived? He is protected, too?"

Ruck shrugged.

Allegreto urged his horse a little closer. "By hap thy presence confers some immunity."

"Haps." Ruck looked at him with faint amusement. "Stay close, whelp."

He kept the company to a brisk pace, not caring to tarry long outside the sound of bells and habitation. But the mist yet lay heavy in the late morning, and Princess Melanthe demanded frequent rests from the sway of the litter. Ruck held to his austere outer composure, but he smoldered inside. He was regretting his decision to chance the Wyrale with such a small guard. This persistent vapor could hide too much. It seemed to cling, salty and still, hanging as close as Allegreto clung to Ruck. The company said little, but he could feel their nerves, and Allegreto was strung as tight as a lutestring. Only Princess Melanthe seemed careless of the atmosphere's malevolent influence. Ruck half wondered if she'd called the mist herself.

They left the forest to cross the marsh far later in the afternoon than he had intended. Moorland stretched away into white nothingness ahead. The vapor closed behind them. When the maid sent word forward that Princess Melanthe's falcon was restless and Her Highness wished to pause again, he threw Allegreto's reins to the sergeant-at-arms and dropped back to ride abreast of the litter.

"Your Highness, I pray you," he said to the litter's closed drape, "if it displease you not—I advise all haste to continue."

"Iwysse, then let us do so," she agreed in English, a disembodied voice from the curtain. "I will calm Gryngolet well enough."

Such an easy capitulation was not what he had expected. He was left with an unfocused sense of impatience, a restlessness that seemed to call for something more to be said.

"I mind your safe conduct, madam," he said, as if she had argued with him.

Her fingertips appeared, swathed in ermine, but she did not pull back the drape as the litter rocked along. "I give myself to your will, Green Sire," she answered modestly.

He gazed at the fine elegance of her fingers and looked down at his own mailed glove resting atop Hawk's saddle bow. The contrast, the delicacy of her hand set against his metal-clad, cold-leather fist, sent a surge of carnal agitation through his body.

In a low voice, past the hard rock in his throat, he murmured, "Passing fair ye are, my lady." He stared at the reins in his hand. "My will burns me."

As soon as he said it he wished it retrieved—repelled and aroused at once by his own boldness.

Her fingers disappeared. "Faith, sir," she said in a different tone, "me like not such runisch men as thee. Study thou on my gentle Allegreto and save thy love-talking for thy horse."

For a long instant Ruck listened to the steady thud of Hawk's hooves in the sand. Her words seemed to pass over him—coolly spoken, unreal.

Then mortification flashed through him, a fountain of chagrin. He closed his fist hard on the reins: his large and rough and runisch fist, green and silver in her colors, darkened with mud in her service, stiff with cold, with shame and passion.

"I am at your commandment, Your Highness," he said rigidly and spurred Hawk to the fore.

AS CARA PREPARED Melanthe's bed, she said, "My lady's grace took pleasure in the cockles this morn?"

Melanthe looked up from painting silver gilt on Gryngolet's talons. Her pot gleamed in the light of the half closed lanthorn. "Nay—I had not the stomach for cockles this day. I made a present of them to our knight."

Cara gave it all away—all of it—in the instant of horror that crossed her features. It was gone in a moment, but too late. They both knew. Cara sat still as stone.

Melanthe smiled. "Dost thou suppose he will enjoy them?"

"My lady—" The maid seemed to lose her voice.

"Thou art a very foolish girl," Melanthe said softly. "I believe I shall loose Allegreto on thee."

Cara wet her lips. "My sister." She whispered it. "They have my sister, the Riata."

Melanthe hid a jolt of shock at the news. "Then thy sister is already dead," she said. "Look to thine own life now."

"My lady—ten years have I served you faithfully."

Melanthe gave a quiet laugh. "Naught but a moment it wants, to turn treacherous." She placed a careful brush stroke. "Yes, I believe I shall have Allegreto kill thee. Not tonight. I'm not certain when. But soon. Thou hast served me faithfully for such a span of years, I shall be kind. Thou needst not to beware it long."

Cara was sitting on her knees, staring at the pillow in her hands, panting with fear. Melanthe stirred the silver paint and continued with her task.

"Thou dost love thy sister greatly," Melanthe said in a mild tone.

Cara was shaking visibly. She nodded. A single teardrop of terror gathered and tumbled down her face.

"Such love is ruinous. Thou placed thy own sister in jeopardy by showing it. Now you are both doomed."

Cara's hands squeezed rhythmically on the pillow. Suddenly she turned her face to Melanthe. "You're the spawn of Satan, you and the rest of them," she hissed low. "What do such as you know of love?"

"Why, nothing, of course," Melanthe said, placing a careful stroke of silver. "I take good care to know nothing of it."

Seven

———◦◦◦◦◦———

ALLEGRETO'S DREAD OF plague was such that the youth
forewent his place with the Princess Melanthe and bedded
down so close to his living talisman that his hand curled,
childlike, around Ruck's upper arm. What his mistress thought
of this desertion was left unsaid. Ruck did not see her. As
usual, she left her litter only after her tent was pitched, shifting
from one silken cage to the other without showing herself.

As Ruck lay in the dark with the fire fading, staring
upward into nighttime oblivion, he had a bitter thought that it
might have been to his advantage that Allegreto had left the
tent, if Ruck had possessed foresight enough to discourage
this inconvenient transfer of the youth's attachment to himself—and if she had liked such runisch men as he. But she did
not, and Allegreto went quickly to sleep in the blue mask,
firmly holding to Ruck's arm, as effective as any governess in
protecting his lady.

Not that she required protection, beyond a scornful tongue
and that mocking laugh.

Ruck attempted to form a prayer, asking forgiveness of
Isabelle and God for his carnal lust. But his prayers were
never of the inspired kind; he could not think of much more
to avow than he was full repentant and would do better.

Not that he ever did do better; for every confession day he had a penance laid upon him for lusting in his heart after women. Sometimes for the mortal sin of easing himself, too, which he would have done now, at the price of barring from communion and any number of Ave Marys and hours on his knees before the altar, if Allegreto had not had such tight hold of his right arm. He was not a godly man; his mind went where it would and his body had limits to its rectitude, but he had dishonored himself, and Isabelle, too, this day.

He had the Princess Melanthe to thank for saving him from committing real adultery—and that only because she liked not runisch men. It was no virtue of his own that had saved him. If she were to rise and call him now into her tent, he would go.

He felt sullen and ashamed, thinking of it. He should get away from her. He should go home, having nowhere else pressing to go at the moment.

HE SLEPT BADLY, dreaming plague dreams, old dreams, in which he was lost and searching. The howl of a wolf woke him, shaking him out of uneasy dozing. He lifted his head. The fire had gone to dead coals—there was no sign of a guard. The wind had come up, blowing off the vapor. By the height of the moon over the moorland, it was three hours to dawn. Pierre should already have woken him to share the last and most arduous watch. With a silent curse Ruck slipped out of his warm place. Allegreto's hand fell away from him.

He stood up in the frigid night, sliding his feet into icy boots. He'd ordered a double watch—but by moonlight he could see the silvered wind-sweep of marsh reeds and the whole company sound asleep. The hourglass glinted softly next to Pierre's place, white sand all fallen through. A loose tie fluttered on Princess Melanthe's tent.

He gave the fur-covered lump that was Pierre a light kick. It did not move. Ruck leaned down and tossed the mantle away.

A smell of vomit assailed him. Pierre lay with a terrible arch to his twisted back, his dead eyes rolled up to show the whites in the dim moonlight, a sheen of sweat on his face and his open mouth full of dark spittle. Ruck swallowed a gag and threw the fur back over him.

He turned away and stood for a full minute, drinking draughts of clear night wind. The fear of plague held him frozen on the edge of frenzy: the lifelong terror—to be left alone, to be the last, to die that way . . .

The moon hung over him, cold and sane. He stared at it, struggling with himself.

Allegreto was sitting up, a faint outline against the light mist that still clung to the grass. Ruck felt the youth staring at him.

He suddenly began to tremble, letting go of his breath.

Not plague. It was not plague. The stink was wrong.

Ruck had smelled pestilence until the fetid black odor had burned itself into his brain—and this was not it. The loathsome stench of plague made poor Pierre's disgorgement seem halfway sweet. Ruck looked down at the shapeless mass and saw what his mind had not recorded a moment before—the white shapes of two opened cockleshells lying on the dark ground.

Horrible enough, if Pierre had purloined spoilt cockles and then choked on his own vomit, unable to call for help—but not plague. Not plague. Ruck took a deep breath. The reality of his man's death was beginning to reach him. Pierre, who had been with him for thirteen years, who filched small things, never more than a penny's worth, who'd learned to squire from Ruck, who'd always been an enigma, mute, faithful as a dog was faithful, but with no outward sign of affection.

Ruck glanced toward Allegreto. The youth was no longer visible sitting up against the mist. Ruck hoped he'd gone back to sleep. He bent down and gathered the furs about Pierre, keeping the small body wrapped close. His mind flashed over possibilities, trying to think of a way to hide this and prevent panic. Allegreto's fears and mask had the rest on tenterhooks—Ruck saw now that he should not have suffered any talk of plague at all.

"Is he dead?"

The youth's suffocated voice startled him, coming from behind, at a distance. Another man stirred.

"Of putrid shellfish," Ruck said quietly. "He could not call us. He choked, God give his soul rest."

"Thou liest," Allegreto hissed. "I saw him when thou lifted the mantle! He's warpened with death agonies. Has he the swellings?"

"Nay. Come thee and see for thyself." Ruck laid the body back down and threw off the cover. Now that he recognized what it was not, the smell was bearable.

Allegreto stumbled backward with a little cry, waking another man.

"Silence!" Ruck hissed. "Listen to me. There's no black eruption. The smell be not of plague, but only plain vomit. Not six hours past he was fit and walking like the rest of you. He stole cockles from the hermit and ate them. The shells are here on the ground. None other ate such, did they?"

No one answered. He knew they were all awake now. He tossed the blanket back over Pierre's dead face.

"He choked to death," he said softly. "Too quick it killed him, for to be plague."

"Nay, I saw it take a priest in half an hour," came a shaky voice from somewhere in the shadows. "There were no black boils. He fell dead over the man he'd come to shrive."

"'Tis winter," said someone else. "The cockles be sweet now."

"The stench is wrong," Ruck said.

They simply stared at him.

"Henri," he snapped in a low voice. "Thou quitted watch without the next man wakened." He took a stride, hauling the culprit out of his coverings by his collar. Before Henri had a chance to cower away, Ruck backhanded him so hard that he fell over his heels. "Tom Walter!" He scanned the dark for his sergeant. The man scrambled up. "Tie him, and John who was on duty with him. Ten lashes at first light. Relight the fire. And if any speak so loud as to wake Her Highness, tie him, too, and he shall have twenty." He swung his hand toward Allegreto. "Watch this one, also."

He paused, to see if they would defy him, but Walter was moving toward John to obey. Allegreto was only a motionless shape in the dark.

Ruck looked toward the tent and saw a pale face thrust

between the drapes at the entrance. He lowered his voice to a bare murmur. "My lady—she has not been disturbed?"

"Indeed, she has." It was the princess's amused voice. "How could I sleep in this uproar? What passes? Where is Allegreto?"

Her courtier made a faint sound, barely articulate.

"Your Highness, it is nothing," Ruck said. "I beg you will return to your rest."

Instead she pulled a cloak about her and emerged from the tent, standing alone without her gentlewoman. "What is it?" she asked, in sharper tone.

"My squire has died in the night."

She sucked in a breath, staring at him.

"My lady!" Allegreto's moan was like grief, like a plea for mercy, as if she could save him. "The pestilence."

"He died not of the pestilence, Your Highness," Ruck said. "The smell is wrong."

"The smell!" she repeated blankly.

"Yea, my lady. Have you never smelled the plague stench?"

She stood silent a moment, then lifted her hand. "Uncover him," she said.

"Nay, there is no need. He grew sick on cockles," he said, "and gagged to death."

"Uncover him," she snapped.

Setting his jaw, Ruck leaned down. Let her look then, if she must, and choke on her revulsion.

But she did not cringe back from the body. Instead, she went forward, gesturing. "A light."

None of the men moved. Ruck finally squatted down and lit the lanthorn himself. He opened the light on the corpse. Princess Melanthe gazed down at it. She knelt and lifted Pierre's stiffened hand. "Poor man. He suffered, I fear."

For a moment Ruck thought it was real, this sympathy, the echo of regret in her voice a true emotion. Then she rose, turning toward Allegreto.

"Come to bed, my love. There is nothing to be done for him." She walked toward her young courtier. Allegreto made a gurgling gasp and backed away from her. She beckoned.

"Come, do not be foolish. The man died of cockles. Come lie down with me now."

"Lady—" It was a whisper of horror.

Ruck watched her advancing slowly upon him, driving him to frenzy apurpose. Only for the cruelty of it—she must be as certain as Ruck there was no pestilence, or she would not have touched Pierre.

"Dost thou not love me, Allegreto?" she murmured in a hurt voice, moving toward him with her hand extended. "But I love thee still."

Allegreto groaned, beyond any reason. He scrambled back from her. "Touch me not!" he cried. "Get away!"

She stopped. Over the moonlit distance he had made between them, they gazed at each other.

"I won't come," he said in a deathly voice. "I won't come."

Princess Melanthe swayed slightly. She turned to Ruck. "Help me—help me to my place. I do not feel strong."

Before Ruck could respond, she fell to her knees. He moved on instinct, catching her limp body in his arms as she toppled. He rose with her, shocked beyond feeling, staring down at the pale column of her exposed throat.

Fear hit him again like a hammer. He carried her, seeing nothing but her arm hanging lax over his in the moonlight, hearing nothing but his heart in his ears, turning blindly for the tent. As he laid her down on the featherbed, he called for her gentlewoman—he thought he shouted it, but he could not hear anything over his heart.

No one answered. In the utter blackness of the tent he could see nothing; he groped for a lanthorn, sparking the flint and steel by fumbling. As the light rose, he looked toward her.

She was smiling at him. She sat up on her elbows and lifted her finger to her lips for silence.

Ruck's jaw went slack—and then stiffened in outrage. He shoved himself off the ground, standing with his head against the silken roof. She raised her hand, as if to hold him, but Ruck was too furious. He took up the lanthorn, flung back the cloth, and strode outside in a black temper.

"My lady is in fine health," he uttered through his teeth,

jerking his head toward Pierre's body. "I need two men to bury him."

In the tallow light no one moved. Allegreto shrank into the shadows, and even the sergeant took a step backward.

"He'll haunt us," someone muttered.

"Accursed be you all!" Ruck snarled. "I want no succour from a pack of cowards, then. I'll leave him myself with the monks." He lifted Pierre again, turning toward Hawk. "Loosen his fetterlock," he ordered the nearest man, who covered his mouth and nose with his chaperon as he obeyed.

The horse disliked the load, flaring its nostrils and drawing in suspicious noisy draughts of air, but Hawk was accustomed enough to the smell of death to bear his burden. Ruck took his lead and turned him toward the trickle of hazy moonlight that fell onto that track, heading toward a dim black line of trees in the distance, silently asking pardon of God and Pierre's soul for what he was about to do.

There were no monks, not within his reach, for though he knew there was a priory at the headland, it was yet so far away that he could not hear the bells. But he wanted no more of these whining fears of hauntings and pestilence. In his anger he wanted isolation in which to lay Pierre to rest. He wanted the comfort of driving a spade deep in the ground until he was weary with it, his muscles hurting instead of his spirit.

He wasn't afraid of ghosts—he'd buried all his family in unconsecrated ground and found their only haunting to be the gentle, lost voices in his plague dreams. Poor silent Pierre didn't even have a voice to haunt dreams, unless his soul found one with the wild wolves that ran free in this place, the way he had never been able to run in life.

MELANTHE SLEPT. SHE kept trying to rally, rising to the weary surface and failing, losing herself again in the sweet dreamless warmth. With her wakening mind she knew she must not let sleep have her, but she had lost the will to fight it, falling back, luxurious collapse into rest and safety.

Full light flooded the tent, coloring everything with a rosy tint, when she finally held herself awake. The light shocked her; she made the effort to pull herself from the depths. It was difficult, as it had never been before. She had slept oversound, and the slumber still sucked at her.

The difference came slowly. She realized that she was alone. Without Allegreto's restless clinging presence at her side, without Cara's quiet rustle.

The whole camp was unusually quiet. Her Green Knight always did his best to restrain the men, she knew, attempting to serve his indolent lady by maintaining peace of a morning—little as he might approve of her slothful habits—but this morning he had succeeded well beyond his usual measure. There was only a faint chink of harness, none of the low talk and dragging sounds of packing and loading.

She must have outslept all. Or they were still confounded by the night's events and sat bemused. She sighed and stretched, enjoying the soft liberty of the furs.

Melanthe smiled as she thought of her knight, how he would lift that one dark eyebrow, conveying utter disdain while he spoke in the most courteous of phrases. He scorned her, this green man—scorned and still desired her.

It was a compound new to Melanthe. She was not accustomed to disdain, not at least from the men who wanted her. She might already have pursued the matter in some way, if not for Allegreto. And Gian.

Pulling an ermine about her shoulders against the icy air, she sat up. There was still no sound from outside, nor any scent of toast browning at the fire—nor even the scent of a fire at all.

The strangeness struck her. Her heart began to thump. The poisoned cockles—had any but the hunchback eaten them? Wild thoughts possessed her. Allegreto, nightwalker, assassin, capable of any butchery, had been driven half to madness by the fear she had roused in him. And this was wilderness, the knight had said, a place beyond the king's control, resort of outlaws.

She looked quickly around—but there—there was Gryngolet, sitting hooded and calm on her perch. Melanthe slipped her dagger from beneath her pillow and left the furs, shivering. She broke open a chest, ransacking it for something to pull over her nakedness. The azure wool of a heavy tunic prickled her skin through linen. Her hands had begun to shake a little, suddenly anticipating what nightmare she might find outside.

Covered, she knelt at the opening of the tent and listened. A horse blew softly, champing its bit, but there was no other sound of man or beast. She held the dagger at ready and pulled the drape slightly aside.

A few feet away she saw a man's mail sabaton, old-fashioned, with a blunted toe. An upright leg—through a slightly wider slit, she could see two armored legs—he sat motionless on a half-rotted log a few yards from the tent. She closed her eyes, fortifying her mind for any horror—a dead man tied into a lifelike position, a decapitated torso. She lifted her head a little and saw the hem of a green-and-silver coat of arms.

One toe moved, pushing a cockleshell a fraction of an inch, first one way, then the other.

Relief shuddered through her. She had half expected a bloodbath and bodies in the sand—she had not even trusted those greaves and knee poleyns to belong to a still-living man until she had seen the faint, ordinary movement.

It was her knight, then, fretted with her. Following on the surge of reprieve, Melanthe felt an odd spurt of good humor. Had she slept so late that he'd sent all the others ahead and stayed to scold her?

The idea pleased her, but she recognized the absurdity of it instantly. He would do no such thing—it was not his nature to openly rebuke his liege, and she had given him provocation enough. She found slippers and pulled them on, grabbed a mantle, and pushed aside the curtain, emerging from the tent.

His war-horse, its green-dyed coat long since washed to a handsomer gray, pricked its ears toward her as it stood by the log. The knight sat for a moment with no expression, his breath frosting, his helm in his lap. He looked up at her.

It was the only time in her life that any man but her husband or her father had not risen to greet her. That jolted her, made the empty, trampled clearing of marsh grass stranger yet, eerie in its silence and the blank way that he looked at her.

"They have fled," he said. Then he seemed to come to himself and stood with a metallic sound. "My lady—I beg your forgiveness."

"Fled?" she echoed. "All of them?"

She stared around the barren camp. The only horse was his. They had ransacked the supplies and taken the animals, leaving bags and bundles broken open.

"Allegreto?" she asked breathlessly.

His brows drew together. "He is gone, madam."

She gripped the dagger, holding her hands pressed over it. "Gone."

His scowl deepened. He nodded, watching her.

"He is gone?" She could hardly bring herself to speak. "How long?"

"I know not. Two hours I was absent, before dawn." He made a slight gesture toward the ground. "The tracks—they scattered apart from one another. Your maid, also. This talk of plague—it inflamed a terror."

She was alone. Free. She had done it. But she had not meant to do it so completely.

She met his green eyes and saw everything he thought of her. She let him think it. In his armor he stood perfectly still, black-haired and silent, a solidly potent presence on this empty moor.

Allegreto was truly gone. He had left her.

"Where went he? What will happen to him?" She stared at the horizon.

"I cannot say which marks are his, Your Highness. We can wait here. Mayhap he will grow frightened and return."

Melanthe kept gazing at the horizon, the empty horizon.

"I would seek him for you, my lady," he said, "but I cannot leave you alone."

"Do not leave me!" she said.

He dipped his dark head. "Nay, Your Highness."

She looked about her again. It was so strange: she had never in her life been alone—never without attendants, never with one man, not even in her husband's bedchamber where his pages always slept on pallets beside the bed. The sky suddenly seemed bigger, dizzyingly huge, the moorland vast.

"God shield me," she whispered. How beautiful it was, how quiet, only the wind and the wild fowl speaking far off at that strand of silver light where the sky came down to the land.

"By hap they will all come into their senses and return to us," he said.

She realized that he was trying to reassure her. She turned to him. "Nay—they will not, between fear of plague and retribution."

"Then they live outlawed," he said simply.

His plain view of things seemed oddly befitting in this place, but she said, "I cannot comprehend Allegreto as an outlaw."

He did not return her faint smile. In his expression she saw the truth of what he thought of Allegreto's prospects in the wilderness.

"What threatens?" she asked quickly.

He hesitated. "Bogs and quicksands," he said at last. "Brigands. Poison water." He shifted, making that faint armor noise. "I heard wolves in the night."

She pulled her lip through her teeth. "Melike not to linger here," she said, changing to English because it somehow soothed her to hear him speak in his own tongue, a thin common thread between them.

"I ne like it nought myseluen," he agreed, shifting language in response as he always did, "but we shall dwell here for today, so that they moten come again to us if they so will."

Melanthe shivered in the wind, pushing her hands beneath her mantle. "Thou art too merciful," she said. "Traitors deserven no such indulgence."

Ruck watched her hug her arms about herself. He narrowed his eyes. "Indulgence they shall nought have, Your Highness. But it were your lo—" He almost said "lover," but it curdled on his tongue. "—your courtier who unnerved them." It was she herself had been the one to set the seal on the party's panic, with her spiteful games, but he did not say so. "Away from Allegreto, they mayen think well again."

She stared toward the horizon. She seemed smaller somehow than she had seemed before to Ruck, the cloak bundled around her, less elegant and imperious.

"Allegreto," she echoed, as if her tongue were not her own. She made a sound of frenzied laughter, and then stopped it, biting hard on her lower lip. Her knees seemed to give

beneath her. She sat down on the ground and stared at the
horizon, rocking. Then she leapt up again. "I see him!"

Ruck turned sharply. He squinted, scanning the moor—
and saw the flicker of yellow motion. "Nay, Your Highness. It
be no more than a plover bird." He looked back at her, but she
had already sagged to the ground again. One lock of her dark
hair had escaped the golden net that confined it, flying across
her cheek in the cold breeze. He feared she was sickening in
her mind for her lover—she seemed so lost and bewildered.

"We shall not stonden here," she said. "We shall not wait
for them."

"How wende we without an escort? My lady has nought
e'en her maid."

"I say we shall not wait!" she exclaimed. But when she
looked at him, it was a confused look, with no command in it.
"I never thought—I ne meant not them *all* to go!"

Ruck made no answer. She was no more reasonable now
in her reaction than Allegreto had been in his last night, like a
wicked spoiled child who had taunted her playmates until
they fled, and now could not fix between anger and tears. The
fugitives had taken the animals but bothered to load nothing
heavy in their haste. He unpacked a wooden cup and filled it
at the ale keg. As she sat huddled on the bare ground, he
squatted beside her.

"Will you break fast, lady?"

She accepted the ale, drank a few sips, and handed it back
to him. He watched her shiver inside the fur mantle. It was
cold, but not so cold as to make her shake in that way.

"It would be no great thing to finden us," she said in a troubled tone, glancing at the tent with its bright unnatural hues.

He drained the rest of the ale. "Forsooth, we are easy seen.
It is best in this place to hiden such color, and layen doon and
watch." He stood up and went to the tent. He was about to
duck inside when she suddenly rose, slipping past him.

As he held back the drape, she emerged with the gyrfalcon
on her gauntleted wrist. Her gestures had slowed; she moved
softly with the bird as she transferred it. "Bring the block.
Gryngolet will keepen watch."

Ruck obeyed, approving the idea. He shoved the spike of
the cone-shaped block firmly into the sand.

Princess Melanthe established the falcon, crooning as she removed the hood. "'Ware for thy favorite," she murmured. "'Ware Allegreto."

The gyrfalcon stretched her wings wide, milky white, her bells tinkling. The bright, dark eyes focused briefly on Ruck and then beyond, fixing on the distance.

"Is a noble bird," he said, in spite of himself.

"Grant merci, sir." She seemed more composed now, not so shaken as she had been but a moment before. "I had her gift of a Northman." She glanced at Ruck. "He were near as tall as thee, but fair."

Her slanting look at him seemed to hold some message. This tall, fair Northman had been another of her lovers, he reckoned. He felt irritated and runisch. To give her a gift of such value had not occurred to him.

"He died in bed by a bodkin knife," she said, as if it were a piece of light gossip. "I believe his soul went into Gryngolet."

Ruck crossed himself in reflex at the blasphemy, but he did not rebuke it.

"If Allegreto comes, Gryngolet will knowen," she added enigmatically.

"Well for it." Not only her witch's familiar, the falcon, but a jealous lover, too. He grabbed the handle of the chest inside her tent and hauled it out. "I can turn hand then, and gear us to wenden when we will."

Ruck went about his work moodily, with half an eye to the horizon. He rolled her furs and piled them on the chest outside, then kicked each of the tent pegs loose in turn. As the bright pavilion fell in on itself, he pulled off his gloves with his teeth and stuffed them under his arm, grimacing at the taste of metal and sand. He squatted and began to untie the ropes.

He looked up to see Princess Melanthe huddled at the other side of the cloth, engaged on the same task.

"Fie, madam," he said in astonishment, "I shall do the labor."

She was having little success with the tight knot. He stood up and caught the rope, pulling the stake from her hands.

"Your Highness, it be nought seemly," he said, vexed. He

caught her elbow and drew her up. With a little force he guided her away from the tent, releasing her immediately.

"I ne like not this waiting," she said, holding her fingers clasped tight together. "When mayen we go?"

"If they return nought by morn, then we depart." He spread her furs on the log, searched inside her chest, found a book, and handed it to her. "One night be enow to spenden alone in the Wyrale."

He bent knee briefly before her, then stood up and went back to work, releasing the pegs and pitching the corners of the tent toward the middle, folding it together into a tight package. From the corner of his eye as he secured the ties, he could see her sitting upon the furs. The shivers caught up with her sometimes, making the open book shake.

"We wait for naught," she said suddenly. "If so be they have lost their fear of plague, they fearen their punishment too well to comen again."

He rose from binding the tent. "They fears, right enow. But in the cold light of morn a man reflects that he hatz both wife and child, and cares nought to liven outlawed from God and home." The corner of his mouth lifted as he stood straight, setting his hand at his waist. "Wherefore, my lady, he bethinks him of a story, of how the others fled, but he alone among them watz a brave man, and ran after, to bringen them back. But he lost his way in the darkness, and only now comes to us again as fast he may find us."

The reluctant shadow of a smile crossed her features. "The duke did say thou art a master of men."

He gave a slight shrug. "It is what I would do, were I one of them."

"Nay," she said. "Green Sire, thou wouldst not—for thou didst not run away to begin." She laid the volume aside. "But a gift thou hast, to read the hearts of lesser men."

He did not trust her compliments. "They are soldiers," he said. "More like to me than to my lady's grace."

She turned her eyes to him, her eyes the color of purple dusk, and gazed at him as if she were only just seeing him for the first time. She had looked at him so once before, as she had prepared to lead him into tournament, a glance that wished to see through to his heart. She had asked him his name then—as if she cared what it might be.

"Per chance so." She gave another peculiar laugh. "Per chance not. I have some talents in common with base liars and cowards—more than I think me thou hast."

Her fingers plucked at one another, her jeweled rings glistening. She looked away, staring out past him at the distant trees beyond the marshland. The wind blew more strands of her dark hair from under the furred hood. She brushed them back without elegance.

Ruck realized he was watching her, standing still, as if he did not know what else to do with himself.

"I am always lying, green man," she said, without taking her eyes from the distance. "Always. Remember that I told thee."

He turned and slung a bag of bedding onto Hawk's rump. He went on packing, hot in his heart and his loins, half-frozen by the cold wind on his runisch fingers.

THE KNIGHT HAD no more to say; he merely finished his work and sat on the ground, leaning against the pile of baggage he'd made, facing away from her and Gryngolet to look out on the northern horizon. His destrier stood loaded as if they might leave at a moment, the most tangible evidence of his expectations.

Melanthe pretended to ignore him, as he appeared to ignore her after their first brief moments of intercourse. The circumstance was too singular; she suspected he had no more been so utterly alone with a lady than she had been with any man.

In the long hours of waiting a peculiar curiosity possessed her. She wondered at his age, if he had children, brothers, a favorite dish. She did not ask. She never asked such things, but found them out by secret ways if she felt the need. They were powerful holds, the small details, the life and loves of a man—things to exploit and manipulate. She did not wish to use him that way; she only wished to know.

But she took care to deny such an alien impulse, and let him keep court with her as stately as if they were in the palaces of kings. Already she had said more than was wont—

why she had warned him of her lying, she could not fathom. She had simply said it, hearing herself with wonder as she did.

At noontide he rolled over and knelt, rifling among the bags. Wordlessly he brought her an orange, a soft herb cheese, and wine, along with five almonds and a twisted stick of violet sugar. He laid them on a cloth on the ground, proffering a napkin and an ewer of rose water drawn from a silver cask. Melanthe dipped her fingers in the frigid water and dried them hastily. On his knees he cut a tiny bite from each food, tasting it himself before he offered it to her.

She accepted this solemn ritual. It was a strange moment, a regal distance between them—and yet he knew what she customarily ate for a midday meal as well as if he'd shared it with her himself a hundred times before. When he came in his ceremonial tasting to the sugar *penidia,* he paused, looking down at the delicate and costly sweet.

"Me think it nought seemly that I spend a portion of such on myseluen, Your Highness," he said.

"Spend it all on thyself, knight," she said. "It is thine to savor. And it pleases me to give the orange to thee, also."

He glanced up at her. She saw for a bare instant the stark blaze of his desire, the quick touch of his green eyes on every part of her face, on her lips and cheeks and brow—almost palpable, vivid as the powerful beat of a falcon, light as the brush of hunter's wings.

He looked down again.

"Grant merci, my lady," he said briefly, and withdrew with a bow, taking up his place again by the baggage.

As if a little distance released him from court manners, he sat propped up in a relaxed fashion, his legs bent to accommodate roweled spurs, his armor plates shining dully in the hazy sun. His helmet rested on the ground within easy reach. Roughly cut black locks spilled over the folds of the chain mail hood at his nape. When he tilted back his head and drained a mug of ale, she had a great impulse to reach her hand out and caress his windblown hair.

Queer reticence possessed her at such thoughts, and she could not even look at him in secret. Her mind distrusted; her heart could hardly bear to acknowledge the thought that

Allegreto would not return, that Cara was gone—she was at last free of it all.

She put her face in her hands suddenly. For a long time she stared at the black inside of her cold palms, feeling the winter wind chapping her skin, breathing short hot breaths of agitation.

She did not dare to plan beyond the instant, leaving decision in the hands of her knight. She heard him come to his feet, chinking armor and spurs, and still she did not lower her hands, unable to admit light to her eyes.

"Your Highness," he said quietly. "I mote sleepen now, so that I can keep the watch tonight."

She drew her palms down and looked up at him. He stood a few feet away holding the ewer, wary observation in his face. Melanthe had another lunatic urge to laugh at the way they prowled and met and recoiled from each other. Instead she nodded, lowering her eyes.

Without a word he knelt again before her and offered the ewer. When she had ceremoniously dipped the tips of her fingers, he cleared the cloth of her half-eaten meal. She stuffed her cold hands into her furs and watched him bed down in full armor beside his sword and helm. He turned his back to her, pillowing his head on a pack saddle.

She envied him his easy sleep. She felt as if she had never had enough.

RUCK ATE HER discarded orange by moonlight and the sound of wolves. A few hundred yards away he could just see the spark of the three fires that he kept going in their original camp, returning at intervals to add fuel and stand a brief watch. His men would reappear tonight, he felt, those who could. The fires were to reassure them—and give the impression of a well-manned camp to any others.

He would have moved farther from the flames, beacon and decoy that they were, but the wolves hunted close. He'd made Princess Melanthe's bed here in the dark. Cold, perhaps, but more likely to be overlooked if something human took him. The wolves would find her no matter where she hid.

He sucked the fruit, allowing the rich bitter juice to run on his tongue. He'd had oranges in Aquitaine a few times, at feasts and Christmas—but to eat one every day as she did was something utterly beyond his experience. And the *penidia*: he'd never tasted white sugar but once, a score and more Christmases gone, a child at the high board with his father and mother.

He held the fragile stick to his nose, smelling his own fingers, smoke and orange, and on the sugar a very faint scent of flowers. He closed his eyes and touched his tongue to it. It was a thousand times sweeter than the fruit, flooding his mouth with potent flavor, erotic as sin and springtime.

He lowered it and looked away from the fires, into the darkness. She was there, close to him, though he could see nothing but blackness.

He lifted his hands again. He did not eat the sugar stick, but sat with it cupped to his mouth, watching the dark and the fires, breathing the scent of a world beyond his reach.

Eight

AN INSTANT OF sleep, it seemed, and the urgent voice was at Melanthe's ear, whispering out of the dark.

"Your Highness, we moten get us gone." He laid a heavy hand on her shoulder. "Lady, wake ye, all haste!"

His urgency drove through the waves of sleep. She rolled toward him, allowing frigid air to hit her face. In the moonlight he was leaning down over her, very close, his breath frosting about her face. She could hear voices somewhere in the night.

"We are marked," he murmured harshly, grasping her arm amid the furs, pulling her upright. "Come!"

She was sitting, but he did not even give her time to rise. He thrust his arms beneath the furs, lifting her all in a bundle. Melanthe gave a small cry of surprise. His arms tightened as he made a hiss to silence her. The featherbed slipped away, but he did not stop. He carried her to the horse—and Melanthe wakened fully to the sense of things now. She took hold of the saddle and dragged the furs about her shoulders, struggling into position atop the lumpy bags as he pushed her up. He mounted before her. She fumbled to take hold of his sword belt beneath his mantle, grabbing it just in time to save herself as he spurred the destrier hard, clapping his hand over hers as the horse leapt forward.

They rode through the dark as if the Wild Hunt were at their heels. Melanthe saw nothing, her face pressed into his cloak as the freezing wind whipped her, clinging for her life with the reckless pace. He'd loaded the stallion with this in his mind, for though she bumped and swayed, the bags formed a slight hollow that let her keep her seat. But there was no margin for modesty or coyness in the full-tilt sprint— she locked both her hands in his belt and felt his glove gripped tight over them, stiff leather and freezing metal pressing her arms into the hard plates at his belly.

Her chin and face jolted against his shoulder armor, padded only by his mantle. The furs slipped, but she loosened her hold with one hand long enough to grab them back, depending on to his grasp to anchor her. The horse twisted and turned in the darkness on some frenzied path of its own, but the knight rode as if he had the mind of the beast itself, holding her with him when the strength of her own fingers began to fail.

A sudden falter threw her forward onto his back. The stallion stumbled and came almost to a halt, the marsh sucking at its hooves. With a shaft of horror Melanthe felt its haunches begin to sink beneath her—before she could find the voice to cry out, the knight let go of her and raised both arms. She felt his body drive; he gave a great shout, and the horse reared, leaping and floundering forward. Melanthe grappled to keep her hold, cutting her fingers, pinching them painfully against the sharp-edged metal belt as he bent at the waist and impelled the destrier forward into another rearing leap.

With a jolt and a heave, the horse scrambled free. Melanthe gave a faint mew, holding on as the animal broke again into a gallop. The knight's hand closed on hers, locking her fingers into his glove, crushing her fingers between his. She hid her face against his back, concentrating on the pain, welcoming it as the only thing that assured her she would not fall.

After an eternity of this mad race, she felt the stallion's endurance wane. She could hear its laboring breath and feel the slowing pace. She cracked her eyes open and saw the barest hint of dawn light. It almost vanished as they plunged into the gloom of tall trees, but when she turned her head to look behind she could see silhouettes of trunks against gray mist.

The horse shied, a great leap sideways that nearly hurled her loose from her clinging perch. The knight grabbed her, holding her arm so tight that she gave a desperate squeak. He dragged her upright, settling the horse to a walk.

It came to an abrupt halt. He swore quietly on Saint Mary.

Melanthe was panting as hard as the horse. She could not seem to command her fingers. They were frozen to his belt and armor; she could not spread them open, she could only droop against his back, staring mindlessly at the barely perceptible dawn.

A bird called amid the barren branches, and suddenly motion returned to her fingers. "Gryngolet!" she gasped, shoving herself awkwardly away.

"I cut the falcon free," he said softly. "Be still."

He was looking ahead of them. Melanthe realized that the horse's ears were pricked—she closed her hands again on his belt, but he brushed them aside and dismounted, dropping the destrier's reins over its head to trail on the ground.

"Move nought," he murmured, and drew his sword. She watched him duck off the faint track into a thicket of branches, each step a gentle chink.

Then, in the growing light, she saw it. Between the winterbare twigs, a spot of bright yellow and blue.

Allegreto.

Her heart began to pound as if it would explode. She held her bloody hands around her stomach, huddling in the furs.

She heard the knight's quiet steps move about beyond the tangle of branches. Allegreto was utterly motionless—hiding—she could not see him, only that splash of color through the thicket and the mist. She had a horrible fear for her knight walking into murderous ambush.

"Do not kill him!" she cried fiercely in French. "Or I shall see thee flayed alive."

The footsteps paused.

"It is too late, madam," the knight said in a cold voice. "He is dead."

Melanthe froze in place. She stared at the patch of yellow and blue.

Then she slid from the horse, pushing back branches, shoving them away as they whipped in her eyes and stung her cheeks. But the knight met her, stepping solidly before her, turning her with a rough push.

"Ye ne wants to see it," he said in English.

She turned back, trying to pass. "I mote see him!"

"Nay, madam." He held her firmly. "Wolves."

Her panting breath frosted between them as she stared up into his eyes. He shifted his gaze, tilting his head toward something beside her.

She followed his look. On a low branch, brushing her skirt, hung a tangle of black hair dirtied with blood and fallen leaves.

"Your maid," he said quietly. "Her gown is there, too." Melanthe turned her head aside and down. Nausea swept over her. She tore herself from the knight's grasp and floundered through the brush. Leaning against the stallion's steaming flank, she bent over, shuddering. But the tangle of hair had clung to her skirt—she shook it frantically, panting in great hysterical gulps. Still it clung. The cold air seemed to draw slimy fingers over her flushed cheeks, as if the bloody hairs touched her face. She shrieked, flapping the azure wool, shaking harder and harder, but the black tangle adhered to her. She turned, as if she could run from it, and collided with the knight.

"Off!" she cried, her voice peaking shrilly. "Take it off me!"

She held out her skirt, her hands trembling. When he hesitated, she screamed at him, "There! *There!* Dost thou see it?"

He reached down and plucked the black mass from her skirt, then took a step back, casting it away. Melanthe didn't look to see where it went.

"Is there more?" She lifted her dress toward him with a frenzied move. "I feel it!"

The knight pulled off his gloves and put his hand on her

shoulder. He bent a little and with his other hand smoothed over her skirts. He turned her, running his bare palm briskly over all of the woolen folds, her sides, her back and hips. "Nay, my lady. No more."

She retched, falling to her knees, holding her hands over her stomach.

"Oh, God," she moaned, and began to laugh. "Allegreto!"

The crazed hilarity echoed in the barren wood. Ruck stood over her, looking down at the vulnerable white nape of her neck beneath the bedraggled netting that barely contained her hair. He retrieved the furs she'd dropped. Kneeling, he wrapped them about her and lifted her onto Hawk as he'd done before. She made no resistance, reaching for him even as he mounted. She slid her arms around him, clinging hard, still laughing and sobbing dry half sobs.

ALLEGRETO AND THE maid *would* haunt him, Ruck feared. He chose not to linger even to bury the remains, anxious to lengthen the distance between themselves and the camp. His men had indeed come back in the night, some of them—bound and at knifepoint, held by the felons who haunted this ungoverned wilderness. He had not waited to watch. Small enough torture it would want to loosen his soldiers' tongues about whose camp it was and what a prize was ripe for the taking in Princess Melanthe if she could be found. He could do no more for his hostage men than he could do for Allegreto and the maid. His whole charge lay now with the princess.

She clung to his waist, leaning hard against him as he guided Hawk through the woods. Over the soft thud of the stallion's hooves on the damp, littered ground, he heard her breathing, still punctuated by small gasps and shudders, the residue of her fearful fit of grief for her young lover.

They passed between fir and barren oaks and birches, the frigid morning sun laying bars of light and shadow across Hawk's path. Ruck kept a wide watch, turning to inspect underbrush and thickets as they passed, careful of ambush. Once a red deer broke cover and crashed away from them, leaving his heart speeding.

His frosting breath curled about his face and vanished. In

hopes of confounding pursuit, he made for the priory at the headland instead of going east out of the Wyrale, but as the morning rose a fear grew in him that he had lost his direction, for still he could not hear the bells.

Near midday they came abruptly out of the wood to the edge of a low cliff, where the wind off the sea blew in his face. Below, the forest thinned to bogs and fenny copses that ended in a range of sandhills; beyond, the western sea, running brisk with whitecaps. To the south, far across the estuary of the Dee, the Welsh peaks made a line of misty gray.

He turned Hawk away from them, heading north along the ledge. Ruck was uneasy with the wilderness silence. On the back slope of the hill the land dropped down to an inlet of another great river. Rising above the leafless birches, the square bell tower of rose-colored stone marked the priory not a mile away. And yet he heard nothing.

They came across a narrow, sandy track that led downward off the slope. He urged Hawk to a slow canter, ducking branches as the path took them again into the woods. Princess Melanthe held to him, quiet now.

He brought Hawk to a quick halt at the edge of the trees. In a burst of noise a flock of wild geese took wing from the deserted garden plots.

Beyond the fallow earth lay the priory, sharp sandstone walls rising clear of the wasteland, the imposition of God on the wilderness. The bell tower stood solid and lofty, crowned foursquare by spires, with the domestic ranges huddling in its shadow. Ruck had not seen the priory for half a dozen years, and then only for a night's lodging before the monks ferried him across the river. Ten and six habited brothers and a few laymen had occupied it then, a small house—but at least they had kept the garden plots neat and enriched, and their livestock fed.

Now only a single white goose, wings clipped, was left behind on the empty field. It waddled toward where Hawk stood, honking impatiently.

Ruck examined the open space and all the distance along the trees. "Wait here with the horse," he said softly. He dismounted, tossing Hawk's reins over a branch to make the destrier stand. Halfway across the field the goose paused, turning a bright eye toward Ruck.

Using the thickets of bog myrtle as cover, he circled the priory's cleared land, moving out toward the river. The ferry landing was deserted. Only one of the monks' sturdy rafts lay beached, tied by a thick, sandy snake of hemp to its high-tide mooring.

Ruck squinted up at the priory. It was possible that behind the walls and heavy doors, the monks worshiped as usual, that it was simply happenstance—or fear of outlaws—that kept all inside, including the lay brothers, on this winter day.

But there were no bells.

For a long while he lay in a copse and watched. The white goose poked and prodded in the open ground, feeding near Hawk. When he was sure Nones had passed, with no bell rung and no sign or sound of human voice, Ruck finally decided to chance crossing to the gate beneath the guesthouse. The goose came hurrying after him, demanding and impudent, nipping at his heels. He knocked the bird aside, but it followed, making loud claims on his charity.

Before the gate he paused with his hand lifted—and then pulled the bell rope thrice in slow time. The sound seemed huge and clear, though it was only the gate bell and not the tower.

There was no answer. He gave the gate a push, but it was barred from inside.

The goose renewed its excited honking. Ruck turned, walking along the wall and around the corner to the church porch with the goose following doggedly. He shoved at the outer door. It gave easily beneath his effort, squeaking wide on strap hinges. Beyond, the church doors stood open, revealing the tall, stark void rising in ranks of double arches that demanded the eye follow them to the great window where the white light shone down, jeweled with the small figures of saints.

Ruck swept a wary glance about the sanctuary. It stood silent after the echoes of his entry died away.

It seemed sacrilegious to go armed into a church, but he made a brief obeisance, crossing himself and asking pardon in respect of the holy place. He walked to the side aisle. The sound of his steps on the stone-tiled floor came back in more reverberations, each finished by the jangle of his spurs.

He unbarred the side door and opened it onto the cloister. The monks' carrels and book cupboards stood unused, but there was a volume lying open upon a lectern, with parchment beside it and an inkpot still uncapped, as if a black-robed figure had left it just a moment before. Loose chickens scratched in the dirt.

"Oyeh!" Ruck called. "Haylle, good monks!"

He had no answer, nor truly expected one. Moving quickly, he crossed the cloister-garth, ducking through a barrel-vaulted passage that brought him out on the stableyard behind the guesthouse and refectory.

The livestock was missing, but he saw no sign of struggle. There were still cattle tracks in the mud, a few days old at most. A green-glazed jug sat on a bench, full of soured milk.

Ruck swore softly on Saint Julian. He strode back through the vaulted slype and stopped, looking hard at each window over the cloister arches. He began an examination of the undercroft, though the doors were locked and the narrow cracks between boards showed only blackness inside. The parchment upon the abandoned lectern rustled lightly in the silent air.

Ruck walked to the podium. He put his hand on the parchment. He was no scholar to have studied Latin; he read French and English, but little more. Nevertheless he ran his gloved finger down what was clearly a letter, scowling over each word. He skimmed the salutation, which directed the missive to the bishop of Chester. From liturgies he recognized the words for "humble brethren beseech you," and "hear us," and a reference to "after Christmas." With difficulty he followed a passage describing a brother—the cellarer, he thought—a trip, the village of Lyerpool, and something about a swine and candles.

The next sentence said that all at Lyerpool were dead or ailing.

Ruck read it again, his finger on each word. *Mortuum,* he was certain of that. *Omnis* and *invalidus* he knew, also. He could not translate it any other way.

A slow dread began to grow in him as he passed his finger down the page. *Miasma malignus. Pestis.*

He pushed away so hard and suddenly that he overturned the lectern. It crashed upon the stone, the dry inkpot shattered. Chickens clucked and fluttered overtop one another in alarm. Ruck walked swiftly along the cloister. The cemetery lay beyond the eastern range. He found admission beside the chapter house, another dark passage that opened to winter grass beyond.

In the open ground there were ten new graves. On the far side of the chapter house, over a wall, he counted two more in the burying ground for laymen. Twelve—and the others fled. He stood by the wall and put his forehead down on his locked fists.

He tried to conjure Isabelle's glowing features, tried to ask her to beg God to spare His children. Or if the pestilence must come again to castigate mankind, to let it take Ruck this time, so that he would not have to watch the whole world die around him once more. He was as wicked as any other; he deserved affliction as surely as the next man.

And yet he did not mean it. He could not see Isabelle in his mind, not anymore, and the willful flame of life burned stubbornly, deaf to fear and fueled by flesh—he realized amid his despair that he was hungry. The Princess Melanthe was in his charge, another link to human clay. She was worldly passion, hot desire—and like enough she would be glad to eat, as well.

HE CAUGHT UP Hawk's reins, untangling them from the brush. "Come, be no cause for us to biden here."

He said nothing of plague. She asked naught, only looked down at him from the pillion with strange innocence, as if she did not comprehend the truth of their situation even yet. She held the furs awkwardly about her shoulders, her fingers pale and stained with dried blood beneath their load of glittering rings. Her eyes seemed sooty dark instead of clear, tiny lines at the corners that he had not noticed before. The cold made her cheeks red, marring their smooth whiteness. With wonder he realized that she was not now so very beautiful as he had thought.

No longer a princess—only a woman, not even comely, but cold and apprehensive. And instead of repelling him, it made all his senses rise a hundredfold in response, hot greed to protect and possess her, things beyond honor or vows.

With a sudden move he turned his face away from her. He gathered Hawk's reins and led the horse out of the trees down to the ferry landing. Across the river Mercy, a mile distant, the castle of Lyerpool was a silent gray shadow; no ships lying in the water below it; no sign of life that he could discern on the other side.

"We moten cross while the tide runs in," he said, halting the destrier.

He raised his arms to her. She shifted her skirts, showing a flash of her white hose and green long-toed boots. She put her hands on his shoulders, but he barely felt that through his armor; his mind was fastened on the brief image of her boots and ankles, trimmed in silver and fine as an elven's slippers.

He released her instantly, but she did not move away, only took hold of his sword belt and stood beside him. The furs dropped to the ground.

He reached up and yanked the ties free on the bags, searching out her cloak. The emerald wool came loose in a puff of breeze as he dragged it down.

She still held to his belt, as if loath to let go. The shock of her lover's death, the sudden transition in circumstances from rich comfort to cold peril—he would not have blamed any woman who succumbed to distress. But since the fit had left her, she seemed subdued, even sleepy, indifferent to time or destination.

When she made no move away from him, he stepped back, disengaging her hand from his belt as gently as he could, careful not to crush her fingers in the metal of his gloves.

"Be nought fearful, lady," he said. "Put on the cloak and go aboard."

She seemed not to hear him. He swept the cloak around her shoulders and caught her up in his arms.

The raft was near to floating in the rise of the tide. His stride cleared a half yard of shallows as he sprang onto the boards. He set her on her feet, holding her muffled female figure steady as the casks and boards rocked beneath them.

"My lady—" He kept his hands on her shoulders. "Are ye ill?"

"Nay," she said remotely. "Where do we go?"

"Across the river, Your Highness."

"The monks—" Her eyes came to his, wide and dark. "Were they dead?"

He hesitated for a long moment. "Yea, madam. Dead or departed."

She seemed bewildered at that, like a child that had been asked an incomprehensible question. She turned away from him and sank down into a huddle on the boards.

Ruck watched her for a moment. "I will keep you, lady. I swear it."

He jumped ashore to unload their meager baggage and toss it onto the raft. Experienced in water passages, Hawk made no objection to being led into the shallows and onto the unsteady surface: the horse put his big hoof on the boards and pulled it off again, then came in one great splattering lunge that tipped the raft, grounding it at one corner. He stood splay-legged and wild-eyed, until Ruck dressed the horse in his *chaufrain,* with its blinding pieces that narrowed his vision.

Hawk calmed immediately, as if what he could not see did not exist. Ruck led him a few steps, refloating the grounded casks by shifting the horse's weight.

The princess sat with the baggage. Ruck cast off the hempen line, took up a pole, and shoved, pushing them away from the shallows. The raft spun gently. He walked to the other side and poled there.

They drifted into open water. He unlashed the great oar that propelled and steered the unwieldy vessel, letting it swing loose between the thole-pins. When he looked up to make certain of the princess, he saw that she had settled herself against the bags, her cloak wrapped about her. She was gazing into the water.

He grasped the thick paddle with both hands and put his back into rowing. The next time he looked toward her, she had fallen fast asleep.

●　　●　　●

THE RAFT SPUN slowly across the river, carried sometimes upstream on the tide, and sometimes downstream on a
wayward current. Ruck could not guide the vessel with the
skill the monks had used: even with the great oar, the casks
drifted at the mercy of the water, so that it took a long time
to cross. The incoming stream and a wind off the sea over-
bore the current, propelling them up the estuary, away from
Lyerpool and the priory. Ruck thought he saw a figure moving in the village, but he could not be sure, and soon enough
even the castle was lost to sight.

He took a landing where it came. Along a shoreline of
coppice and reeds, the raft hit bottom. He poled it in as close
as he could, and still had to wade through a spear's length of
shallows.

The princess seemed reluctant to wake, huddling herself
closer when he knelt and spoke to her. He pulled off his glove
and pressed his hand to her forehead, but she was cool, her
skin chapped with wind, not fever. "Ne may I sleepen?" she
mumbled plaintively when he touched her. "I want to sleepen
a little while."

He did not disagree, just picked her up and carried her
again. The motion seemed to revive her a little; she sat in the
sandy clearing he'd chosen for their camp with her arms
clasped about her knees. She watched him silently as he
slogged back and forth, moving the bags ashore.

Then, as he knelt to fetter Hawk, she turned sharply, her
eyes on the shoreline of the Wyrale. "Listen!"

Ruck hurled himself to his feet, grabbing his sword. As he
stood, he heard bells, dreamlike and soft; and at the same
moment saw the white speck flash against dark trees.

"Gryngolet," she whispered, with her eyes fixed on the
distance.

Almost as if it heard the longing in her voice, the pale falcon soared upward, turning black against the sky, and dipped
into a wheeling curve toward them. It skimmed across the
river with powerful fast beats, striking upward again, spiraling above them until it was naught but an atom in the winter-
blue heights.

"She waits on us!" The princess sprang to her feet. "The
lure—before she rakes away!"

Ruck dropped his sword. Both of them pounced upon the bags, tearing through them for the falcon's furniture. Ruck found the hawking-pouch, proffering it with a muttered prayer of thanks that he'd brought it. She snatched the prize from his hands.

White leather it was, embroidered in silver and jeweled like all the rest of her possessions. Emeralds caught the sun and sparkled on her gauntlet as she thrust her hand into the heavy glove. Even the lure itself was decorated with tiny gems at the ring and fastened along the shafts of the heron's feathers, with one splendid diamond blazing on the body.

She looked up. Ruck watched her face as she followed the falcon's tower. He had thought her not so beautiful in the unsparing light of day, but he found himself mistaken again. Witchlike, she had transformed herself to loveliness once more, as the falcon changed its nature from earthbound to sky-free in one leap.

He turned to find the bird and could not see it, the black speck gone so high it was beyond sight. Her hand swept upward. The sun took the lure as it arced over their heads, scattering brilliant light. Hawk pricked his ears at the faint rush of the cord and feathers spinning through the air. The princess kept her face to the sky, her arm outstretched against the blue, her gauntlets sparkling, green fire and silver flying from her fist.

She called her falcon, spinning the lure; a carol of love, half laughter—and the bird came, dropping hard from the sky.

Ruck heard the stoop before he saw it. The bells screamed one long, high note as the falcon hurtled downward, a prick on the blue that became a dot, a lancet, an arrow bolt, a scythe, its wings bowed close in two thousand feet of fall. The lure rose to it, aflame with emeralds.

At the instant of strike, a fan of white burst open, wings spread wide against the glitter as the hit sent a crack of sound echoing across the water; the lure shot downward and the falcon threw up into the air, jesses dangling. The lure impacted the ground, spraying sand, and sailed off again under Princess Melanthe's hand on the cord.

They began a dance, the woman and the bird, a swinging

and sweeping dance that defied the compass of the earth, marked by the flash of emeralds, the bells, and the white glory of the falcon's twisting flight as it drove and stooped and chased the toll. Around and around the lure spun, beckoning and evading, mercurial, up and down and doubled back, the falcon keen and nimble in pursuit—an eternity— and yet before Ruck could take his eyes from them, before he could imprint the picture on his mind, before he could overcome the irresistible rise of his heart at the sight of the falcon's dance, it was over.

She ended the flight in a fashion he had never seen. Instead of letting the toll drop onto the ground for the falcon to take, she swung the lure up and caught it into her other hand, lifting it like a pagan priestess calling to the sun. The bird shot past, chopping once at the feathered toll with her talons. Then she swung wide and slanted back, checking hard.

With wings outspread the falcon came to the glove, silvered talons open to grip fast. In a regal sweep she settled, folding her wings and reaching greedily for the lure.

"Poor Gryngolet!" The princess was breathless, laughing and weeping at once. "Poor Gryngolet, my beauty, my love! 'Tis a foul trick, I vow. We have no garnish for your reward."

The falcon spread her wings again, screaming angrily and striking the meatless lure at this injustice, but her mistress had a secure hold on the jesses that Ruck had severed to cut the bird free. The falcon's complaints ceased as the princess deftly slipped a hood over its head.

Now that the moment was over, Ruck found his heart thudding in reaction. He could not believe what he had seen, that tremendous stoop from such a height and the dance that followed. The gyrfalcon sat quietly, unresisting as the princess caught the braces, drawing the gaily plumed hood closed. One-handed, she tied the shortened jesses to the glittering varvels and leash, using her teeth to finish off the tightening of the knots.

Ruck picked up the fallen toll. Its feathers were battered, one broken. The big diamond had fallen off, and emeralds hung loose by metallic threads. He looked about him on the ground, searching for the lost gem. When he saw a white glint in the sand, he pulled off his glove and reached down.

"Keep it. It is thine," she said as he rose with the diamond between his thumb and fingers. "A token." She was smiling. Glowing, her eyes shining with tears of elation. "So thou wilt not forget her flight."

The gem lay in his palm, a gulf between them, a distance beyond comprehension—so careless was she of such stones, to hazard them as decoration for a falcon's lure, to give them in casual remembrance—as generous as the greatest lord Ruck could imagine. He did not know if the king himself did such things.

"My lady, I need me no token to mind such a sight. As help me God on high, I shall ne'er forgetten it."

"Ne the less," she said, "keep it." She turned her attention to the falcon, leaving him with his hand extended.

He felt vaguely insulted, though there was nothing slighting in her manner, or in the gift itself. It was the first time she had given any sign that he was due anything at all for his service.

Not that he served her for a reward. He did not expect or wish any recompense for honor. But she did not endow him for his fidelity; she only gave a token of remembrance as a gracious lady might—and that made him more sullen yet, for she obviously expected nothing in exchange. Why should she, when she would see that he had naught to his name that was worthy of a lady?

He watched her cherishing the gyrfalcon and remembered the tall fair Northman who had given the bird to her. A man of sense would have felt uneasy—that stupendous flight could have been sorcery—but instead all he felt was churlish. He thought of what he had: his horse, his sword, the jeweled bells and jesses that were her own present. The field armor that he wore. His other set, the ornate tournament trappings that had cost him his first five years of ransoms and jousts, and bore the emerald she had given him . . . left behind for bandits to plunder.

He had nothing deserving of her notice that had not come to him at her own hest, and so he was angry at her.

Holding himself stiffly courteous, he said, "I crave no gift of you, before God, my lady—and naught will I taken. My whole care is for your well faring. Go we on to a safe place tomorrow."

She turned from the falcon, but did not lift her eyes to his. For a moment she watched the long wind ripples on the river. Her face altered, the warmth in her passing to an ivory stillness. "There was a castle," she said. "And a town."

In the deep oppression of her spirit, he had not thought she had perceived them.

"Lyerpool," he said quietly.

"Will we go there?"

Below the river's surface, beneath the sparkle of the sunlight, the depths lay black and unplumbed, like old fears.

"Nay, my lady. Nought there, I think."

"They died of pestilence, did they not?" Her voice made a queer upward break. "The monks."

"Yea, my lady."

She sat down on a bank of sand, staring at the falcon. "I brought it," she said. "I have brought it back."

All of his suspicions rushed over him again. The clinging mist, her secrets, her dark hair and purple eyes—hellmarks, drawing and repelling him at once. A changeling. A witch.

"I teased and beleaguered Allegreto with it so." She held the falcon on her fist, biting her lower lip, rocking faintly. "Now he's dead, and pestilence comes. It is God's judgment on me."

Ruck's mouth flattened as his mistrust deflated into exasperation. "Your Highness, I ne think me that God would bringen down plague on all mankind only for your foolish wickedness."

For a long moment she remained rocking, each sway a little greater than the last, until she was nodding her head. She began to smile again. "Be my sins so trifling? By hap I am not to blame for plague, but only for the excess of lice this winter."

"Certain it is that you are to blame for our present state," he muttered. "My liege lady."

She stood, taking up the falcon. "Thou art impudent, knight."

"If my lady japes at sin and pestilence, is her servant to be less bold?"

"Avoi, I wist thou art but a saucy knave, hid in a loyal servant's clothes!"

His moment of insurrection already mortified him. He became very interested in putting the fetters on Hawk. "Lady, there be no humor in it. We ne haf no escort, my lady, nor sufficient food to eaten, nor now'r safe to go."

"Why then," she said, "I will call thee Ruck by name, sir, and thou wilt call me Little Ned, thy varlet and squire. Gryngolet will be known as 'Horse,' and the horse will continue as Hawk, that we mayen have a pleasant balance. And we will all hunt dragons together."

His mouth tightened. He could not tell by her tone if she was making jest of him. He held out the stone. "Nill I nought accept this. My lady should stowen the thing safe away."

She ignored it. "Yea, Ruck and Little Ned and Horse and Hawk." She was suddenly smiling, beautiful again, beautiful and ordinary at once with her smile. He wondered if he would ever resolve on which.

"My lady's brain is fevered," he said.

" 'Ned,' if thou please. Thou art to put a degree more of contempt in thy voice. 'Ned, thou worthless churl, thy witless brain is fevered!' "

"My lady—"

"Ned."

"I ne cannought call you Ned, my lady!"

"Pray, why not?"

He lifted his eyes to Heaven, unable to compose an answer to such a question. Retrieving the falcon-pouch, he dropped the stone and lure inside.

"Tom, then," she said. "I will answer me to Tom, and on hunting of dragons will we wenden. Thou art our master and guide, Ruck, for thy experience of fiery worms and diverse other monsters."

"We nill nought hunt dragons, my lady," he said impatiently.

"We have nowhere safe to go. Nowhere but wilderness and wasteland empty of people." She paused with the gyrfalcon still on her fist, her body shaking again with that tremor that was too deep for cold. But she smiled, her eyes dry, fierce as the falcon in her spirit. "So say me true, Ruck— what better business hast thou on the morrow than to fare with me for to slayen dragons?"

Nine

CARA COULD NOT control the shivers. It was not the cold, though the air in the abandoned smithy was cold enough. It was that she wore the clothes of a dead woman, and that Gian Navona's bastard son kept looking at her as if he expected her to stop her shaking. She was terrified of Allegreto; she wished he had left her with the bandits—no, she did not wish that— God save her, she was going mad. She would wander the countryside, tearing her hair and crying at the moon in grief. It was her penance, just vengeance upon her for trying to poison her mistress.

She wept for herself and for Elena. Little Elena, mischievous and quiet by turns, Elena with her ears too big and her chin too pointed and still pretty—Cara loved her and she was doomed, as the princess had said, because Cara had not succeeded at her task. But Allegreto told her that Princess Melanthe was dead anyway, of plague. Would the Riata accept that?

No. It would not be enough. There would never be enough. She saw past it now, saw what her mistress had meant—why should the Riata loose their grip on her, when they could keep Elena, when they had such a hold as love upon Cara to make her do their bidding?

"Cease this weeping," Allegreto said tautly. He looked at her again and stood up from the block of iron he had been resting upon. Even in the bandit's dull woolens, he had his father's arrogant nobility and the grace of a fallen angel. His legs were muddy to the knees from floundering in the bogs.

"I'm sorry. I'm trying." She held her fist hard against her mouth in the attempt. Another sob escaped.

"Stupid Monteverde bitch," he said.

"I'm sorry!" she cried. "I'm sorry I'm Monteverde! I'm sorry I can't stop weeping! I don't know why you troubled to save anyone but yourself from those thieving brutes!"

He stared at her sullenly. Then he lowered his dark lashes and looked away. "Are you rested? I want to go on."

Hunger gnawed at her, and her legs were cramped and aching. Her bare feet bled in the dead woman's rough shoes. "Go, then. It's nothing to me."

He leaned over her and jerked her chin up. "What is this—another puling, weeping Monteverde? Christ, I wonder that your father found the vigor to get you on your mother. By hap he didn't, but let a Navona do the work."

Cara tore her chin from his fingers, scrambling to her feet. "Don't touch me. And I would not brag so of Navona vigor were I you, gelding!"

In the half-light of the smithy, his teeth showed in a feral grin. "Careful, Monteverde, or I'll prove myself intact on you. How would you like a Navona babe?"

"Idle threat!" she snapped.

"Shall I show you?" He reached as if to untie his hose.

Cara could not contain her breath of shock. "Liar! Cursed Navona, your own father would never have let you near my mistress if you were whole. You slept with her!"

His mouth hardened. "My father has reason enough to trust me." He shrugged, dropping his hand. "And the Princess Melanthe was as hard as this anvil. Stupid girl, she was old! We did no more than mock at love, she and I, to preserve her from Riata and the silly Monteverde geese who do their bidding."

"I don't believe it."

"It's not her I ever wanted." He looked down at Cara, just a little taller than she, his face smooth and youthful, but with cheekbones shaded by the promise of maturity. "How many years do you think I have?"

She shrugged. "I know not, nor care. Enough for every evil."

"Sixteen on Saint Agatha's day," he said.

"Nay," she said. She had thought him twenty and more, caught forever at the cusp of adulthood, his voice a young man's, his body still a youth's but with a full-grown control, matured beyond the gawkiness of adolescence.

But when she looked at him, she could see it. Like a trick of the light, his aspect altered before her eyes, and she saw a tall boy, a year younger than herself, well-grown for his age, with his frame filling rapidly into manhood.

"I don't believe you," she said, but her voice wavered.

He gave a short laugh. "Well, it matters not what you believe. If you are alive in a year or two, Monteverde goose, which I doubt, you may see for yourself. This play must have come to an end soon enough, for no eunuch grows a beard. I see that I shall have to grow mine to my knees now, just to prove my sex."

"A beard will suit you ill," she said caustically.

He gave her an odd look. He touched his jaw, drawing his fingers down it as if he already felt the coarsening.

"Navona peacock! Of course you would not wish to cover up your beauty!"

His dark eyes searched hers for a moment. Then he smiled, sweetness tinged with some strange melancholy of his own. "Nay," he said slowly, "haps I would not. Come, feeble Monteverde, I see you have made your feet. Walk with me, and if I please, I may discover you something to eat." He grinned, a flash in the shadow. "Even if I have to kill another outlaw for you, and his lady, too, for to take it."

RUCK HAD BROUGHT only delicacies for food, oranges and nuts and spiced sugar, having presumed that there would be refuge and keep at the priory. He had intended the luxuries as gifts for the house—instead they were all that was to be had for supper. The twilight was coming on too deep to hunt, and his stomach was hollow with complaint.

He was unrelentingly formal in his manners with the

princess, trying to regain the proper distance between them, but she seemed to have taken a capricious dislike to ceremony. In the sunset that lit the river gold and turned the coppice along the shoreline to black lace, she would not sit as a gentle lady and be served. After seeing her falcon established upon a bow perch made of a green alder branch, its ends thrust into the ground, she persisted in collecting deadwood for the fire and winter grass for the horse.

"My lady soils her gloves," he said in disapproval as she dumped handfuls of greenery at Hawk's nose. "I bid Your Highness sitten adown, if it please you nought ill."

The destrier lipped up her offering eagerly and lifted his head, pushing at her shoulder. She stumbled a step under the hard nudge and dusted the clinging stems from her gloves. "The horse mote eaten."

"He's fettered. A little distance he can wander, to finden the same fodder you bring him, lady, and more."

Hawk had already dropped his head and begun nosing and cropping at the tender winter shoots around a sandy hummock. She looked at the horse and said, "Oh," as if such a novel notion had never occurred to her.

"Your Highness mote eaten, also," he said. "If you be pleased to sitten adown, so I may attend you."

He opened his hand toward where he had made a seat from his saddle and some furs and carefully positioned it upwind of the smoking fire. It was the third time he had made the suggestion, but he managed, with some effort, to keep his voice mild.

She smiled, with the golden light on her face. "I do not wish for thy attendance, worthy knight, but for pleasure I will beg thee to bear me company at table."

He bowed stiffly. "Nought to your honor be it, to sup with your servant. Do sit ye adown, if it please."

"I will sit me down if thou wilt," she said.

He held fast to form. "I think it nought seemly, my lady."

Her lips tightened stubbornly. She stooped and began tugging at grass, gathering more into her hands. Sand clung to the damp hem of her cloak and skirt. Green stained her white gloves. She carried the fodder to Hawk, and then picked up a stick from the kindle pile. She tossed that on the fire and chose another, struggling to break a branch that was too thick for her to snap.

"Iwysse—I will sit!" Ruck crossed his legs and dropped down onto the ground. This newest vagary of hers, this acting as if she were no greater than he, vexed and baffled him. Instead of feminine tears and terror, peril seemed to make her foolish in her mind.

When she dropped the stick and sat beside him, he regretted his capitulation, for she ignored the saddle and took up a place much too close, so close that her folded knees almost touched his. Her cloak did, a bedraggled ermine corner lying in a casual sweep over his knee poleyn.

"My lady, I made a fitter seat for you," he protested.

"The sand is soft enough." She picked up the knife. "Come, we will counsel together. I pray thee, what best us to do?"

"Hunt dragons, I trove," he muttered. "Wherefore should we nought, if Your Highness will gaderen fodder and sitten upon the ground like unto a bondman's wife?"

She held out to him a segment of orange. "Yea, we will hunt us firedrakes—wherefore not?"

"Because I'm nought doted in my head, even if you are so." He bit into the orange unthinking, and then realized that she was not yet served. He lowered it hastily, appalled at himself and aggrieved at her for luring him into it by taking no notice of his misdemeanor at all. She peeled the rind and offered the whole fruit to him as if she full expected him to eat before her.

He refused to do it, but sat sternly with the food in his hands, waiting.

"Tell me, art thou at my hest, knight?" she asked.

"By right I am yours, lady," he said swiftly, "in high and in low."

She smiled. "This is low."

"What is your will?"

"That thou wilt eat till thou art sated and leave to me the remainder, forwhy I do not wish thee to wax faint from hunger in this wild place. I doubt not thou wouldst swoon just as a dragon fell upon us, which would be inconvenient, as I am no master of a sword."

He turned the orange in his hand. "I grant my lady that she is no swordman"—he laid it back upon the cloth—"but I deem it no more convenient that my lady be brought low of a fainting-fit herseluen, and I haf to carry her."

"For one avowed at my bidding"—she snatched up the fruit—"thou art as obstinate as a wooden ox!"

Her white teeth sank into the orange. She ate it all. While he watched, she finished the second orange and peeled the third, ate one segment of it and threw the rest over her shoulder, where it plopped into the muddy shallows of the river. Then she nibbled at the almonds until she had consumed them. She tasted the sugar, made a face, and ground the remainder into the sand.

Ruck looked down at the bare cloth. She had eaten or destroyed everything.

"If thou wouldst have a forpampered princess, then thou shalt have one, knight. I am mistress of that craft."

Ruck said nothing. He stared grimly into the darkening woods that lined the shore.

"If thou wouldst have a companion of sensible wits," she said, "then save this overweening indulgence for the court. It is thine to choose."

He looked over his shoulder into the twilight shadows where she had thrown the last orange. "My lady, I say you troth, I haf nought seen no such thing as common wit in you yet."

She drew in her breath at that. He expected temper, but instead the silence expanded between them. Darkness had fallen enough that he could see only the shape of her face, not the contours.

Her soft laugh surprised him. "Yea, so I imagine," she murmured. "Poor knight—thou must be sore dismayed to have ward of me in this desert."

He could think of no answer that would combine truth and courtesy but to say, "I am sworn to you, my lady."

"Ne cannot I conceive how that came to be, but verily—I think it better fortune than I deserve." She made a faint sound of rue. "And how do I favor thee, but to make thee go hungry in my temper? I am full sorry."

Ruck scowled. He picked up the stick she had dropped and cracked it in two. "I reck nought of it, lady."

"Tomorrow, Gryngolet takes a duck. It is thine."

"Less does my belly concern me than your safety." He held the sticks between his fists, frowning down at them. "We're far out of the way to my lady's lands, or any dwelling that I know from my faring in this country. In faith, is near forsaken since the Great Death, without souls enow to keepen the weeds back." He hesitated, and then broke the wood again over his knee and tossed the staves on the fire. "Of fortified places, there's aught but Lyerpool, if any souls be left alive there. To sayen troth, Your Highness, I fear pestilence more than any desert."

"Allegreto said me that thou art exempt from it."

"Yea, I am." He looked up at her. "Can my lady sayen the same?"

Full dark had fallen. The firelight played on the curve of her face, shadowing her lashes. "But thou wilt keepen me," she said softly. "I place my whole trust in thee."

"Best to put your faith in God's design, my lady," he replied in a rough tone.

She smiled, her skin kindled rose by the fire, her hair black shade. "Forbye, monkish man, what art thou if not part of God's design?"

He felt anything but monkish, sitting beside her, all semblance of respectable reserve between them in ruins. It seemed to him that God's design must be to make him live a lifetime of temptation, the half of it condensed into this moment, when it would be no more than a movement of his hand to touch her.

"Haply I might be part of God's scheme, too," she mused, "though I've not much odor of sanctity, I trow."

He turned his face away from the firelight, unable to disagree with that even for courtesy.

"Well, I have endowed an abbey, so let it be a secret betwix us," she said, as if he had assented aloud. "The nuns have made an eloquent record of my faith and good works. We would not wish to casten doubt on such a pleasant document."

He tried to think of his empty belly, which was her perverse doing, and failing that, of the danger that she was to his soul. He tried to hope that she would move away from him, and instead could not stop gazing at her, at any part of her that he could see while he turned his face away, even if it was only the ermine fringe of her cloak.

With the corner of his eye he saw her yawn deeply. The ermine fell from his knee as she drew her cloak close about her.

"Sore weary I am," she murmured, leaning back against the fur-covered seat he'd made for her.

"I will lay you a place to bed, Your Highness." But he did not rise, unable to shake off the witching of her nearness. He was weary himself, and hungry. And when she closed her eyes, with her chin tucked down against the folds of the cloak, he could watch her without her knowing.

"Thou mote be wondrous sleepy thyself, knight," she mumbled. "It is my turn to stay waking."

"Nay," he said quietly. "I will keep thee, lady."

A faint smile curved her lips. She let go a long, deep sigh.

MELANTHE SLEPT EASY against the hard lump of the saddle as she had never slept in silk and featherbeds. She was vaguely aware of awakening sometime in the dark, with the knight arranging furs and a softer cushion for her head. She knew him by the light chink of his armor and the scent of orange and leather and metal as he tucked something soft beneath her cheek—Ruck, she thought with cloudy fondness, and felt pleased and secure.

"Grant merci," she said, but if he heard her he did not answer. For a few instants she saw him through leaden eyes, down beside her on his heels, with one knee pressed into the sand, the firelight gleaming on the curved fan of his poleyn.

Thou wilt keep me . . . She dreamed of his dark silhouetted figure beside her all night, and slept sound in the wilderness.

THERE WAS NO start or dread in waking. The first thing she saw was Gryngolet, and the next was her knight, squatting at the river edge bare-chested, splashing water against his face. With his back to her, he shuddered in the cold like a wet dog, flinging droplets from his fingers as he whooshed a harsh breath of air between his teeth. The steam made a frosty curl against the bright river and vanished.

He held a razor to his face, and then cursed softly.

Melanthe saw a scarlet welling of blood mingle with the wetness at the edge of his jaw.

She sat up. "What art thou about?"

He startled and grabbed up his tunic, pulling it over his head as he turned. The linen clung to his chest, showing damp through it, and the dark lump of some amulet he wore. Blood from the place he had nicked himself trickled down to a pale band of reddish-orange that ringed his throat where sweat had rusted his mail and stained the linen and his skin.

"My lady—your pardon—I thought you heedless in slumber."

She squinted at the sun overhead, surprised at the height of it. "Have I slept so long!"

He turned, gathering up his surcoat and armor. "Anon I go a way off, my lady, and dress my horse."

She realized that he was offering her a discreet spell of privacy. As he turned and walked away, he wiped at the nick on his jaw and smeared bloody fingerprints on the hem of his linen shirt.

"What thou art dire in need of, Sir Ruck," Melanthe murmured into the furs, "is a neat, goodly housewife to love thee." She smiled, sinking down in her warm coverings. "I will arrange it for thee."

From the river she heard the dim conversation of ducks and geese. She pushed her nose out of the furs, welcoming the chill morning air. It made the moment real, an awakening from deep nightmare into life: this was sure fact, this cold morning, this river and woods and this muddy sand, the small smoking flame in a circle of gray and black ash, the curling rinds of oranges on a cloth spread on the ground—no servants to distrust, no Allegreto, nor slim daggers or poison, no Navona or Riata or Monteverde. Only her knight nearby to keep her from all harm.

In the warm security of it she flipped the fur back over her cold nose and closed her eyes. Her body relaxed in the soft haven. She lay slipping, half dreaming, letting the silent river take her safely again.

RUCK DONNED HIS armor, watered Hawk, checked the horse's hooves, and curried his coat. He took his time, yawning, lingering until he was certain that he could not possibly shame either of them by returning while she was still in the midst of her gearing.

As he led the horse back, he made sure that they raised a noise, rattling dead reeds as they passed through. He called softly, not caring to advertise their presence too much abroad, neither to outlaws nor to the great flocks of ducks that floated and fed near shore. He was looking forward to breaking his fast.

On the sandy bank where they had made camp between the water and the coppice-alders, there was no sign of her. A spark of alarm flared in him. He dropped Hawk's lead and strode forward.

Just as he drew a breath to shout for her, he glanced down. He froze half a step from treading on where she lay, still wrapped about in furs and cushions.

He gazed at her, incredulous. She had gone back to sleep! Here in this desolate place, on a saddle, as if at any moment they might not be set upon by perils human or unhuman.

He sat down hard on a hummock. He had never in his life known man nor woman to sleep so much as the Princess Melanthe.

He put his jaw on his fists. He waited. As the shadows grew shorter, the ducks floated past and flew on, at first a few pairs, and then covies, and then whole flocks, as if at some soundless call to the distance. The noise of their wings resounded across the water, feathered thunder. The gyrfalcon roused eagerly, standing first on one foot and then the other upon the bowed stave, but its mistress did not wake.

After a long time Ruck picked up a pebble and aimed it for a point a few feet away from her head.

It hit the sand with a light plop. She didn't move.

His belly growled. He tried a slightly larger pebble, a little closer.

MELANTHE DREAMED IT was beginning to rain. She heard the single drops and felt their airy impact on her coverings. A faint stinging drop struck her hair and she jerked awake.

She sat up, scrambling to pull her hood over her head, looking about for shelter.

On a grassy tussock a little distance from her, she saw the knight hastily lower his hand. He was full dressed and armored; he stood up, flashing her a look as guilty as a thieving boy caught up a pear tree, before he fell to one knee and lowered his face in formal respect.

There was not a cloud in the cold sky. The tanned folds of the fur overtop her were littered with tiny pebbles, as if it had rained stones.

"Knave!" she gasped in laughing outrage. "Thinkest thou to cower behind this meek bow?" She threw off the furs and scooped up a handful of sand, sending it toward him in an extravagant spray.

He flinched back, lifting his arm against the shower. She sat up on her knees and dug both hands into the ground. Her second discharge spewed over him, making him duck his head. Melanthe took advantage, laughing and scooting forward, kicking up a relentless cloud of sand with her hands as he tried to rise and step back, his arms up to defend himself. Awkward in his armor, he tripped over his spurs, falling on his seat with a surprised grunt.

She gave a hoot of victory and tried to stand in preparation to launch a triumphant volley from both hands. Her cloak tangled underfoot and she lunged forward, saving herself and losing her balance, catching on the cloak in half steps as she tottered wildly. She loosed the sand, sprawling full atop him with a cry of merriment, grit in her mouth and under her palms, a bruising impact against hard metal. The jar knocked him back against the tussock as they fell together.

It took the breath from her. She blinked her eyes open, pushing herself up against his shoulders.

He lay with a look of utter consternation, his face close to hers. No humor answered her amusement. He was frozen still beneath her hands.

She felt the short rise and fall of his breath under her. Dirty sand dusted his cheek and brow. His green eyes, so close to hers, refused to see her. He stared past her and tightened his mouth, as if she were some enemy set to slay him.

A terrible abandon seized her. She could do anything here in the empty wilderness; she did not have to lie—

She bent and kissed his mouth, fierce as Gryngolet, senseless and violent as Allegreto in a temper, forcing herself on him. He made a despairing sound, half turning; but she followed, letting her weight fall against the rigid curve of his breastplate beneath the tunic, sliding her hands up beside his head.

He was breathing hard into her mouth, kissing her and pulling back at the same time, opposing his own action. He might have pushed her off with a fraction of his strength, but Melanthe held him with only her fingers spread in his hair.

She softened her touch, brushing her lips featherlight where she had pressed ruthlessly a moment before, exploring his jaw, tasting grit and dirt and the faint, rusty note of blood. He held motionless, arrested in a straining tension.

She pulled back a little. His mouth was drawn into tautness. His eyes glittered with water, the black lashes spiking together. He brought his hand up and pushed back her hood. He touched her hair, lightly, and curled his fist and dropped it.

"I beseech thee," he uttered from deep in his throat. He closed his eyes. "I beseech thee. Lady—I cry peace."

"A bargain," she said. "One kiss of thine—and I will let thee go."

"Nay." He moistened his lips. "Ne can I play a courtier's game." He would not look at her. "I cannought, lady, for God's love."

"Why, monkish man? Because thou art my servant? One kiss. I command thee."

"One!" He gave a bitter laugh and laid his head back. He squeezed his eyes hard, baring his teeth like a man in pain. A drop rolled from the corner of his lashes down his temple. "Kill me now, my lady, and let me live in Hell, and you will be kinder."

She pushed herself from him and sat back. Immediately he rolled away, shoving to his feet. Without looking at her he walked to the furs and hauled his saddle from beneath them. He shouldered it, carrying it to his horse.

Melanthe looked down at her palms. Sand clung there, the same sand that seasoned her tongue with the taste of him and cleaved in ragged arcs to the back of his tunic where he'd lain pressed against the ground.

She blushed hot.

To fling sand at him—to press her mouth against his as if she could be part of him by doing it—to force herself upon him—the clumsiness appalled her.

The wilderness abruptly seemed a strange surrounding, and herself stranger yet.

She had known that he wanted her. A hundred men had wanted her. She trifled gracefully with them. In smooth gallantries she had heard her beauty praised, her hair adored and her lips cherished, her eyes compared to jewels and stars. Every gift and finery had been proffered, extravagant self-destruction threatened if she withheld her favors. She toyed and smiled and refused, binding them on a velvet leash.

But she dared not look in mirrors; she had never been certain if she was truly so tempting in herself, or only the irresistible symbol of her power and position.

And she had not known that she wanted him.

Until now, when she had gazed down at his face, into another kind of mirror—and thought that all before had been the mere shadow of this desire.

She stood, shaken and mortified. He did not look at her, but went about his work with grim concentration, as if absorbed in it beyond thought.

She brushed sand from her cloak and strode toward the high reeds and blessed privacy.

Ruck stilled as he heard her go, sitting on his heels above the soft furs where she'd slept. He bent his head.

His soul seemed near to shattering within him. With laughter she smashed his shield to splinters. She lay upon him, careless as a child—reckless as a whore.

He touched his jaw where she had touched it, drew his fist down his own skin where her mouth had brushed him, and then stared at his knuckles.

As long as she held aloof and disdained him, he was safe. Her tempers and arrogance defended him; her station was a wall between them even in this desert; if he felt himself weakening, he had only to recall that she liked her not rough and runisch men.

But nothing could save him if she was to cast this spell of laughter. That was where her power lay, he thought, not in charms and incantations—she had laughed at Lancaster and brought a king's son to his knees; she laughed now and Ruck was lost, helpless as one of Circe's beasts.

And he hungered for his downfall. The ache in his belly was nothing to the tension of waiting, to the hot pain of love's appetite. A lance through his body was nothing to it.

He closed his eyes. He'd sworn himself to the Devil's daughter. Thirteen years—ill-omened number—and she came for him again.

Ten

THE BIRD MUST be fed. That demand went unspoken. All the gems on the princess's gauntlet and lure, all the books left behind in her chests, all her furs and pearl-encrusted gowns were not worth the price of the white gyrfalcon. Ruck's empty stomach, the question of where safety lay, the awareness and awkwardness between the two of them—all of that diminished before the first necessity of properly keeping the falcon.

She had not been fed for two days; she was in highest flying condition, restless, showing herself ready to hunt by her roused feathers and fretful talons. Ruck had some hope of what was left, after the falcon had taken its reward, although by now he thought that the princess must be hungry again, too. He waited silently while she prepared, changing the jesses and examining the leash and hood.

The huge flocks that had floated so close early in the dawn had vanished but for a few stragglers. In spite of her command of the falcon's lure, he was not certain what sort of hunter the princess might be in a true quest for food—her morning indolence did not promise great skill or experience of more than ladies' crossbows and deer-parks. But he was no master falconer himself. He looked on their situation beside the wide estuary with misgiving—it seemed to him that the fowl must flush away from shore, and the strike be made inevitably over water.

He had once been in the courtyard when Lancaster and his brother the prince had returned from a day of flying a score of high-bred falcons at crane and heron. Among the large and colorful party, there had been dripping servants, damp courtiers, wet dogs, and great good humor—on a temperate day with the castle and a warm fire at hand.

Here they had no dogs or servants to retrieve if the gyr-falcon lost its prey over the depths. And as the only courtier present, Ruck felt he would be exceedingly fortunate if he did not have to swim.

Perhaps she had witchcraft to enchant the quarry. She seemed confident enough as she swerved and bent ahead of him through the reeds and coppice, carrying the hooded fal-con. The hawking-pouch hung over her shoulder, gems shin-ing under her cloak as it flared, so that as she moved she seemed some Valkyrie of ancient dreams, a silent war-maiden striding to battle. Ruck moved quietly behind. He had taken off his spurs and stripped himself of plate and mail for stealth, wearing only his leather gambeson and sword.

Beside a brushy bank she paused, staring out through a dense clump of leafless alders. Ruck saw the pair of mallards floating fifty feet from shore. What he did not see was any hope that they would flush in the desirable direction.

"These will do," she murmured, so low he could barely hear. She slanted a glance at him. "Look thee to biden there, in the farthest reeds, for to await my sign. We will not delayen till she towers up so high this time.

He inspected the stand of reeds, gauging a hidden path to it. "What sign?"

"A blackbird's call."

"Lady"—he squinted through the branches and whispered barely above the sound of his own breath—"hatz ye a sorcery to direct them?"

She gave him such a look askance that he felt chagrined and added in haste, "Were I to swimmen, I may sink or take ill and leave my lady without protector."

Her lilac gaze seemed to cut a hole through him. "Or get thee wet!" she mocked.

It did not seem such a jest to him. He muttered tautly, "The weeds I wear be all I haf, my lady."

Her lip curled. "So I will not watch thee strip, monkish man, dost thou dislike it."

She had not the modesty of a stoat. He set his jaw, feeling the burn of mortification—worse, feeling his own body's instant reaction to such words. Even she seemed to feel it; her eyes sliding abruptly away from his.

She nodded toward a layer of cobbles and gravel in the sand bank. "Thou art master stone-hurler of our little company. Cast one up so comes it down beyond the ducks. Mayhap it hies them toward us."

Ruck thought even a mild charm had a better chance than that. "Lady—only a natural magic. A small one. God will forgive us."

She lifted her fine eyebrows. "I perceive thou art monkish only when it agrees thee."

"I am no monk," Ruck muttered, having rapidly tired of that neke-name.

"No more am I witch." She stared at him, her eyes level. "I await thy readiness."

Ruck set his jaw and squatted by the bank, prying out two cobbles that filled his hand, round and heavy to land with a generous splash. Bent low, he moved out of the coppice and down amongst the reeds, parting them slowly as he passed through. His feet sank into sandy mud; he had to lift each one carefully to avoid a loud sucking. Cold water quickly began to seep into his boots.

MELANTHE HAD A secret sympathy for his disinclination to enter the cold river—though she would have smothered herself in a hair shirt before she would have said so aloud. But she had no magic beyond her wits and Gryngolet's to please him. The falcon had experience enough to wait until her quarry was over land to strike. The ducks, though, would likely flush into the wind which came down the wide length of the river, and, if they were wary and wise, fly within its compass, never leaving the safety of water below them. Lady

Fortune had provided mallards, big fowl confident of their own size and speed, furnishing the only hope that the quarry might chance an overland passage to escape. They belonged to Gryngolet then, for in level flight she could outfly any other bird under God's Heaven.

Impossible to guess how far away the kill might occur in that case. In more common circumstance—a well-mounted party with falconers, beaters, servants, and hounds—following the gyrfalcon on such a cross-country chase was a joy. But that was sport; the catch less to be admired than the elegance of the flight, the valor of the bird. They hunted in earnest now. Gryngolet must make a quick slaying, or there would be no dinner and haps no falcon, either, once she was beyond sight and sound of the lure.

Melanthe kept a divided watch between the mallards that still fed peacefully off the bank and the faint sway of reeds that marked the knight's passage. It was a delicate moment: if she dallied too long, the ducks might flush and be lost before the falcon was ready, but if she unhooded Gryngolet and cast her off too soon, the anxious and hungry falcon might lose patience with waiting for her quarry to be served and rake off on her own hunt.

The reeds had ceased swaying. Melanthe saw the mallard drake glance alertly toward shore and begin to paddle away. She caught Gryngolet's brace in her teeth and struck the hood. Lifting her arm a little, she faced the wind and gently plucked the hood free by its green feathered plume.

The gyrfalcon slowly roused, expanding herself. She muted. Melanthe did not take her eyes from the ducks, but from the edge of her vision she could see Gryngolet survey the horizon deliberately. Her feathers tightened, and she roused again. Melanthe opened her glove, losing her hold on the jesses.

Gryngolet spread her wings and bounded upward.

The ducks began to paddle faster, making wide V's in their wakes. They would be soon out of reach of stone or yell; already they were almost too far from the bank to fear it more than the white shadow of death overhead. Melanthe glanced up, saw Gryngolet circling out wide and returning at a few hundred feet. She gave a low blackbird's whistle.

The knight should have exploded into motion, shouting and waving, throwing stones or any other maneuver that would frighten the ducks into flight.

"Go!" she whispered under her breath.

Instead, that light sway in the reeds was silent, moving, paralleling the bank until it was directly before her and she lost sight of the subtle movement through the interlacing of coppice twigs and branches.

"God's bones!" she hissed between her teeth. She whistled again.

Gryngolet circled idly; falling downwind as she waited, losing position. The ducks still paddled, gliding farther and farther beyond flushing. Melanthe made a faint whimper of dismay in her throat. She reached for the lure at her belt, preparing to call the falcon down before she raked away.

A boom of feathers erupted from the reeds. Like a huge ghost, a gray heron—king of river quarry—leapt into the air with a shriek, the knight hallowing and waving as the bird lumbered along the edge of the reeds, running with wings outstretched, trying to regain the safety of the thick cover. The knight drew back his arm and hurled a stone, fired the second one after it a with a powerful heave of his arm, sending the heron clawing upward, gaining the sky in great ringing circles.

Gryngolet snapped to business; she instantly began a kindred spiral. For a hundred beats of Melanthe's heart the two birds circled for advantage, their flights arcing over the bank and then back above the river as they gyrated upward, Gryngolet ever gaining, passing the desperate heron, mounting aloft.

Suddenly the gyrfalcon seemed to capsize, overturning, empowering her downward plunge with three mighty strokes of her wings before she fell into her stoop. She hit the heron like Vulcan's lightning hammer; threw upward, rolled over, smashed a daring mallard that had risen before Melanthe even perceived it, and then drove straight back up and turned head-on into the second duck as it pumped for the horizon. They met with a crack like solid stones colliding. The mallard exploded in feathers.

The two ducks dropped dead well out in the river, but the

big heron tumbled and listed, shedding feathers, collapsing
into the reeds as Gryngolet wheeled and followed it down.
The falcon and the huge wildfowl disappeared, battling,
Gryngolet shrieking defiance of her quarry's superior size
and strength. Melanthe heard a great splash as she broke out
of the coppice running.

She pulled her skirts up, elbowing branches and reeds
aside, racing for Gryngolet's life. Wild plashing and screeching came from the reeds. She saw stalks fall, swept aside as
if by a scythe, and despaired of the falcon's survival of such
a combat. "Towe-towe-towe, *hawk!*" She cried Gryngolet to
her as if she could save her that way.

She stumbled on the long toes of her boots and slid in
thick mud, gained her feet, trying to run, ignoring the water
that poured in at her ankles. The reeds ahead swayed violently. Suddenly the splashing ceased, an instant of silence
that stopped her heart. Then Gryngolet screamed again with
lunatic frenzy. Melanthe whipped the stems aside and came
upon the battleground.

The gyrfalcon was mantled, her wings arched in a white
canopy as she stood shrieking atop the heron's body. The
knight lay full length, facedown in three inches of water, with
one arm over the heron and its broken neck between his fists.

Gryngolet had footed his elbow, seizing it with a savage
shrill of anger, one claw buried in her quarry and the other in
his leather-covered arm as if to fend him off. Ruck had his
face turned away from her, hiding it in the crook of his other
arm as he yelled muffled curses in answer to the falcon's
screams.

Melanthe pressed her fingers over her mouth. She suffocated an appalling urge to burst out laughing.

"Stand up," she said unsteadily. "Get off her dinner, and
she will let thee go."

Slowly, shielding his face, he humped himself to his knees
while Gryngolet screamed. Water poured off the front of him
and dripped on the gyrfalcon, startling her into a moment of
confounded silence. Then she bated ferociously, attacking
him with both feet. He stood up with her hanging upside
down off his elbow, shrieking and flapping as if she were
demented. Melanthe jammed her fingers harder over her

mouth to contain herself, holding back hilarity with fierce resolution.

The knight gave her a look as malevolent as the falcon's rage. He appeared to know there was nothing to be done until Gryngolet decided to let go—which she did, with startling suddenness, dropping in a delicate sweep onto her prize. She mantled over the dead heron's body again, staring suspiciously at the knight.

He moved back promptly, shoving aside the reeds and slogging away without a word. Melanthe slipped her knife from her belt and lifted her skirt. She made in quietly, sliding her bare hand into the cold water to lift the heron's head and cut it off. Gryngolet, recalling her manners, accepted that as her rightful due, stepping onto the gauntlet like a high-born lady.

With the falcon busy tearing feathers and skin, Melanthe stood. She dragged the heron by its feet. It was the largest she had ever seen, a weight that felt well over a full stone as she pulled it up on the dry bank.

She dressed it there, giving Gryngolet bone marrow and the heart. The falcon ate eagerly, then paused, mantling covetously over the spoils again as it stared behind Melanthe.

She turned. The knight stalked barefooted up through the reeds, soaked, wearing only linen that molded to him so perfectly he might have had on nothing at all. Every muscle showed as he moved, every feature, his ribs and chest, his waist, his thick calves and thighs, even tarse and stones. His shoulders gleamed wetly, big and straight beneath the dripping tails of his rough black locks.

She was accustomed to men who diminished by a third when they shed their armor, but he almost seemed larger, looming up over her as she knelt beside Gryngolet. He dangled the mallards by the neck in one hand, his sword and leather gambeson wadded together under the other arm. His small amulet pouch swung from his wrist, the leather darkened with wet. He did not appear mirthful.

He cast the ducks down beside her and stood dripping. Melanthe looked at his bare muddy feet and saw a shudder run up through his whole body. She raised her face warily.

He squatted beside her, his eyes for a moment on

Gryngolet, who was rending her food with renewed energy, glancing frequently at the knight as if she were determined to consume it before he could steal it from her.

A slow grin lifted his mouth. "Little warrior," he said, smiling his rare smile. "Three in one flight!"

Melanthe watched him, feeling things in her heart that frightened her, emotion that all her instinct and experience warned her against.

She looked from his face to his body, stifling sentiment in cold observation of muck and clammy wet—and not even that could rescue her from folly. He was a pleasure for a woman to look upon, as elegant and fine in his body as a great horse was elegant, without padding or puff, startling in his grace and muscle. She had been married at twelve to a prince thirty years older and courted in halls of the highest fashion—she had not until this moment understood the plain, powerful comeliness of a dripping and muddy man.

He seemed at ease, as if he thought the linen clothed him as well wet as dry. He had only to look down at himself to find his mistake—but with a rueful inner smile, Melanthe thought that even the evidence of his eyes might not convince him, if he would put his faith in such flimsy things as honor and courtesy and linen, principles as liable to evaporate under the force of reality as the cloth was prone to become transparent in water.

Another shudder passed through him. She stood, unpinning her cloak, and thrust it at him. "There—wrap thyself. And do not dispute and debate me!" she added. "Thy bones rattle from the chill."

He rose, sweeping the mantle around his shoulders. "Nay, lady," he said meekly.

She hesitated, and then said, "She did not hurt thee?"

He turned a thumb toward the pile of stiffened leather. "Before I won my spurs, I used that for armor. Good *cuir bouilli* will turn off hard steel."

"N'will it turn off a catarrh," she said. "Come back to dry at the fire, ere thou begin to cough and croak."

SHE COULD SLIT the wing-bone of a heron for the marrow, but she did not know that green wood wouldn't burn.

She had cut the hearts out of all the fowl, but could not clean them without direction, ending with duck down clinging to her nose, sneezing and struggling to bat it away. The necessity of a spit for roasting did not occur to her until she had already plucked both mallards.

Ruck sat with his mantle and hers both wrapped about him, squinting against the smoky fire she had built, offering advice when she applied to him. By the time they had reached their camp, he had not been able to control his shaking—he had to remove his wet linen. While he was encumbered by the need to hold both mantles close about him to cover himself, she became housewifely in her waywardness—if any housewife could be so inept at some of the tasks as she was.

Reasoning that she would soon tire of such an arduous game, he silenced his objections. But as the ducks roasted amid billowing smoke, burning on one side and raw on the other, she seemed in high humor, binding the heron's feet to an alder branch, undaunted by the fact that she could not reach high enough to prevent its severed neck from dragging the ground. She held another branch curved down, trying to bend the bird's knees over it.

Ruck watched her struggle for a few moments. "My lady—" he began.

She turned her head. The twig she was holding broke off in her hand and the branch snapped aloft, the heron's wings smacking her face as it passed. It hit the top of its arc, bounced off the branch, and fell into the sand.

Ruck kept his expression sedate, as if he had not even noticed.

She sighed, bending down to pick it up by the neck. "For to be tender, I thought to hengen the bird a day or two."

"Is a witty idea," he acknowledged, "but we wenden us today. I'll tie it to the baggage."

She dropped the bird on the ground, as if someone else would pick it up, and came to sit down beside him. Ruck shifted his weight, withdrawing as well as he could without standing up to move. He was wary of her, that she might make love to him again. He did not wish to be teased and tempted. He could not endure it. She was a rich and gentle lady; she might be delighted by the amusements and pleasures that men made with women in the court, but Ruck had never partaken of those pastimes. He knew his own limits.

As she settled cross-legged beside him like a lad, he realized that she herself had always been his armor against seduction. His true lady.

"Where go we?" she asked, turning up her eyes to him, pretty flower eyes, witching eyes.

"A safe place."

"How can we knowen where is safety? Even mine own castle at Bowland—" She frowned. "Pestilence may be there, too, or in the country between. How can we knowen?"

Such feminine uncertainty made him feel protective and suspicious at once. His own responses to her he did not trust; how so, when he could look at her and see that she was ordinary and yet think her comelych beyond telling?

He scowled at the ground before him. "I have heard me, madam, that there are some can go in the air at night—to far places, where they learn there what they please and return ere morning."

Her expression changed, drew stiff and harsh. "Why say thee so to me?"

"Oft have I thought me that you are a witch." He said it outright. He was determined to know, yea or nay, even if she should slay him for it. "How else could you hold me so long—and still yet? If be enchantment, I pray to God that you release me."

She pressed her lips together. Then she lifted her arms and cried, "White Paternoster, Saint Peter's brother, open Heaven's gates and strike Hell's gates and let this crying child creep to its own mother, White Paternoster, Amen!" She spread her fingers. She clapped three times, and dropped her hands. "There, tiresome monkish man—thou art released from such spells as I have at my command."

With a shower of sand she stood up and stalked away. Ruck pulled the cloak up around him, leaning on his knees, watching her. She spun the spit—the first time she had done it—and looked with dismay on the blackened skin of the ducks.

"Mary and Joseph! Ruined!" She let go of the stick, and

the awkwardly spitted fowls fell back with their burned sides to the fire. Then she cast Ruck a venomous look and held out her fingertips toward the fire, wriggling them and chanting some weird garble of sound.

She lifted the spit from the wobbly supports she'd made, and one carcass fell off into the flames.

"Well, it is no matter," she said lightly, fishing the duck from the coals and rolling it out onto the sand. She pushed it with a stick onto the cloth that they ate from and picked it up. She set the half-charred fowl before him, spreading out the cloth with great care and standing back with a flourish. "I have conjured three fiends and worked a great incantation, and enchanted it to be cooked to perfection."

He gazed down at it for a long moment. "Better to have turned the spit," he said wryly.

"Thou shouldst have said so. I could have ordered Beelzebub to do it."

He lifted his eyes. She looked straight at him, with no warding for speaking the Devil's name, her mouth set, her eyes bright with challenge.

"Allegreto said my lady is a witch. And Lancaster's counselors. All at court said so."

Her lips tightened dangerously. "And what sayest thou, knight?"

He stared at her, his imperious liege lady, beautiful and plain, with her jeweled gauntlets and her hair astray and a great black smudge of ash on her cheek. Her own cloak he wore about his shoulders, and the duck she had hunted lay before him. Her gyrfalcon held the soul of a dead lover, and her eyes, her eyes, they saw through him like a lance, and crinkled at the corners when she laughed.

"Ne do I know why I love you!" he exclaimed, sweeping the mantles around him as he rose. "Ne do I know why I swore to you; why I ne'er accepted any man's challenge that might release me from it! Ne'er did I want to be released. Ne do I nought still, if it cost my soul. And I cannought say why, but that you have beguiled me with some hellish power."

"Flatterer!" she murmured, mocking, but her face was terrible and cold.

He turned away from her. "I know a place safe," he said.

"Safe from pestilence and all hazard." He frowned at the river. "But ne will I taken a witch there."

"Iwysse, then there is no more to be said." Her voice was cool and haughty. "If a woman bewhile a man, a witch mote she be."

"If ye says me you are nought, my lady—" He paused. Ripples blew across the water, the cold wind stung his face. "I will believe you."

He waited, watching the water and the dark line of trees that marked the far shore of the Wyrale. The wind shifted, sending another sparkle of ripples at an angle to the first set, scenting the air about him with smoke.

He turned. She stood with her arms hugged about herself, her brows drawn together in icy disdain, black and arched, delicate as the tips of a nymph's infernal wings.

"Haps I am a witch," she said. "I tell thee true, Green Sire—I have cheated demons, and still I am alive."

He could believe she had. He thought, were he some minor devil, that he would look on her and be afraid. She discharged power; he could dream that he saw it in a radiance about her, even here, even stripped of jewels and silver trappings, if he let his imagination run away with his sense.

"Is no sin to escheaten demons," he said gruffly. "Only to yielden service to them."

"My husband taught me many things. Readings from the Greek—astrology and alchemy and such, matters of natural philosophy, but never did we call on any power but God's mercy that I know. Test me on my knowledge, if thou wilt."

"Ne haf I no command of such. Battle I know, and a sword. Naught of natural philosophy."

She lifted her chin. "I make no protection-spells."

He did not wish her to be a witch. In his heart he longed to prove her innocent. But he said stubbornly, "By logic, that is no more than evidence that ye desires nought to maken them."

She narrowed her eyes. "Then what proofs wilt thou have, if thou art so prudent? Wilt thou bind me and throw me in the river, or have me to clasp a red-hot staff?" She pointed at his sword. "Heat it in the fire, then, and test me! And then haps I will testen thee the same; Sir Ruck of No Place, for ne do I know why I took notice of thee and gave thee jewels in Avignon when thou wert but a shabby stranger to mine eyes! Haps thou worked a charm on *me* and stole my gems by magic craft!"

"Not I!" he uttered. "I'm no—" He stopped, his hands tightening in sudden realization.

She remembered. Embarrassed heat suffused him, thinking of the raw youth he had been, of how he had let Isabelle be taken from him—of the nameless lady of the falcon and her accusation of adulterous lust against him. "A strong memory, my lady hatz," he said grimly.

"I recall every evil deed I've done in my life," she said. "No great difficulty is it, to rememberen a good one."

"A good deed, lady? To shame me before the church? To name me adulterer in my thoughts?"

She paused. And then her lips curved upward gently, as if the recollection pleased her. "Yea . . . I remember that. I saved thee."

"Saved me!" With a harsh chuckle he pulled the woolens close about him. "My lady saved me of a wife and a family, so did she, and set me for to liven alone as I do. He swept a stilted bow. "May God grant you mercy for such a favor!"

"Wee loo, what a sad monkish man it is."

"I am no monk!" he exclaimed in irritation, turning his shoulder to her.

"In faith melikes to hear thee know it." Her tone had warmed. "If I caused thee aught such injury as to compel thee to liven alone, Sir Ruck—I will repair it and looken about me in my household for a suitable spouse to comfort thee."

He whirled back to face her. "Mock me nought, my lady, if it please you!"

Her brows lifted at his vehemence. "I mean no mockery. I bethought me just this morn that I would looken out a good-wife for to cherish thee."

"You have forgotten," he said shortly. "I haf me a wife, my lady."

For a clear instant her startlement was palpable. Then she gave him an accomplished smile, of the kind that court ladies excelled in. "But how is this? I had thought thee a single man."

It seemed impossible that she did not remember, if she recalled the rest. But her face was puzzled and attentive, a faint shadow of question in the tilt of her head.

"My wife tooken nun's vows." Ruck inhaled cold air. His breath iced around him as he let it go. "She is—a sister of Saint Cloud." A little of the wonder and agony of it always crept into him when he spoke of Isabelle, thinking of the radiant image that forever knelt and prayed in his mind.

"Is she indeed?" Her voice became vague as she knelt beside the half-burned carcass of the duck. "And is she well there?"

"Yea," he said. "Very well."

"I am pleased that she writes good word of her health," she said in an idle way as she pulled the wing of the duck between her thumb and forefinger, examining the scorched area.

"She ne writes me nought," he added stiffly, "for her mind is fixed on God."

"Iwysse, I am sure thy wife is a most holy personage," she said, inspecting the duck with immoderate concentration. "She married thee, did she not?" she murmured.

His mouth grew hard. "I send money for her support each year. The abbess would advise me if aught were ill."

"For certes. There is no doubt of it." She looked up at him with a brilliant smile. "Now say me true, Sir Ruck—dost thou suppose this duck can be saved?"

He stalked away from her, leaning down to sweep up the heron from the sand as he passed it. "I'm dry now for to dress. I'll wash this when I'm geared, and roast it, so that we may eaten ere we starve of hunger."

IN THE THIN peasant clothes, without furs or camelot, Cara could barely move her fingers. All night she had lain on the bare ground, the cold seeping up through her. She had not been able to curl tight enough to warm herself. It seemed that she ought to have died, but it was worse to be alive in this horrible country, with this dreadful companion, in these hideous clothes, and no other choice that she could fathom.

If Allegreto felt the cold as she did, he had some way to

conceal it. He never shivered. She wondered if he was a demon.

The bare trees and spiky bushes reached out claws to tear her. They had yet to see a living soul, or a dead one either, only one village in deserted ruin, but the overgrown path out of it must lead somewhere, she told herself. What she would do when she arrived there, she had no notion, but the hope of food and warmth was enough to move her.

Yesterday she had wished to die, but the process seemed so endless and miserable that she had given up on it. At first light, too cold to sleep, she had heard Allegreto rise, and had stumbled to her feet and trudged behind him without a word, without even a prayer, until the suspicion that she might be following a real demon to the abyss made her recite aves with silent diligence.

He did not change shape or disappear, though he stopped and waited for her when she fell behind. She limped up to him, and he made a face at her. With renewed hate for him, she lifted her head and passed by.

He gripped her from behind. Before Cara could even scream, sure that this was the end, that he would transform to a fiend and rend her to bits, he stopped her mouth with his hand.

She felt his breath rise and fall against her back, but he made no sound. Only when the thump of her own heartbeat slowed did she hear the chinking creak of a harnessed animal.

A woman's voice muttered, then gave a sharp command. The clear sound of a blade scraping against hard soil rang through the cold morning air.

Cara exhaled relief. No bandit, then, but an ordinary peasant. She waited for Allegreto to realize it and release her, but his body grew even more tense. He gripped her harder. She felt a tremor grow in him.

They stood there, frozen, for endless moments.

Finally she lifted her hand and pulled his away. He did not object; he freed her all at once, staring through the trees.

He was dazed by terror. She could see it. Like a rabbit panting beneath a circling hawk, he was arrested in place, only the white puffs of his breath showing life.

Cara began to laugh.

She could not help herself. The frenzied hilarity echoed about her, a sound halfway to weeping, an echo as if someone else answered.

He was afraid of the plague. She almost pitied him.

"I'll go first," she said. "I don't care how I die."

She hobbled on, but he caught her again. "No. Cara—wait."

He had such urgency about him that she halted. He held her hand, wrapping it between both of his, pressing a small bag into her fingers. "You stay here. Use this."

He left her standing alone with the herbal purse. With his silent ease and muddy leggings, he moved ahead. A thicket swallowed him, as this heavy English wood ate everything a few yards away.

Cara looked down at the bag. It was one of the perfumes against pestilence that he had about him always—he must have taken it back when he'd killed their bandit guard and his mistress. She threw it down. Even the thought repelled her, made her remember stumbling over the woman's body in the dark as Allegreto had urged her with him, the sick shame of being stripped of everything she wore down to her shift; the dread of worse, but by God's mercy the bandit's drab had put a violent stop to that, boxing her man's ears and covering Cara in her own filthy rags.

The woman had treated her with an uncouth kindness, talking in this ugly English speech, stroking the silk again and again as she paraded back and forth between lamplit bushes in Cara's gown, almost pretty in her awe and pleasure in it. She must not have looked at Allegreto's black eyes, Cara thought, or she would have seen death watching her.

With a half-mad chuckle, Cara picked up the perfumed bag again. How amusing, that death was afraid of the plague. How gallant of him, to leave his charm to protect her. How courageous, to approach some poor peasant woman only trying to plow the icy clods!

She would save this for him, his little shield. She carefully dusted off the bits of leaf. She chuckled again, baring her teeth. God's corpus, any more of this reckless chivalry, and she would be like to think the Navona loved her.

"Monteverde!" His voice from the path ahead was triumphant. She limped quickly forward, favoring the worst of the blisters on both her heels. In a clearing the peasant plow and ox stood abandoned. Allegreto held up a food pouch with a grin.

"They ran before I showed myself," he said. "By hap your laughing sounded like some fiend out of the wood. Ghastly enough it was."

She ignored his mockery. "There must be a village nearby," she said. "We can buy shelter, if you thought to recover more than your plague apple from the thieves and got my silver, too."

"Silver enough," he said, looking into the pouch. "But we shan't chance a village."

"Please yourself, wretched Navona, but give me my money. I don't fear pestilence so much that I want to sleep on the ground again tonight, or steal food from churls. I'm going to the village."

He glanced up at her. "Nay—you would not."

"I will."

"I tell you, I won't go in amongst people!"

"Then do not, for God's grace. We shall part here, and gladly. As soon as you give me my coin."

He turned a sullen shoulder. "Monteverde goose! You would not last a day without me."

"What is that to you, Navona?" she snapped. "I don't even owe you thanks for freeing me—you and yours have done me more mischief than you could ever repay!"

"Go then!" He dropped the food pouch and strode away over the frozen dirt. "It's nothing to me. Nothing!"

"My silver!"

He stopped, slanting a look over his shoulder. "I don't work for free, *carissima*. It's mine now."

She held the herb bag behind her. "A fair exchange. Your plague perfume for my silver."

"I'll buy another herbal."

"Without going in amongst people?"

He turned slowly to face her, a look upon him that sent a

chill to her heart. "Monteverde goose," he said softly, "I can take it from you before you can draw breath."

"Then slit my throat if you must!" she cried defiantly. "And be damned for it! Plague or murder, it makes no mind to me. I am dead no matter what I do." Her voice began to quaver on the last words, and she shut her mouth, lifting her chin.

Allegreto was impossible to read, his black eyes watching her. "You work for the Riata, don't you?" he asked slowly. Cara tried to stare him down. For a moment he only studied her—then something in his expression changed, grew more penetrating.

"I didn't see you when we found the hunchback dead." He said it with a voice of discovery. His hand curled over his dagger. "You were already gone from the camp."

She managed to keep her breathing even. If her life was over, she should commit her soul to God, but in the moment of peril all she could do was think that he was too young and comely to be what he was.

"And you took money with you—you knew you were leaving. You were already running. Oh, Mary, Mother of God—" He took a step. *"Why?"*

She did not answer him. She only closed her eyes and waited for him to kill her.

"What did you do? Was it poison?" A note of panic hovered in his question. "Did you try to poison her?"

His concern for his evil mistress sent a spurt of wild rage flooding through her. "Yea, you harlot—I tried to poison her. And if she hadn't sickened for death of plague as you tell me, I would try again, God forgive me, to save my sister!"

In three steps he had her: "Was it the cockles?"

She tried to jerk free, and could not. He shook her until her teeth rattled and her head rang, and stopped with a jerk.

"Was it the cockles?" he asked, in a voice so quiet and soft that it turned her limbs into water.

She nodded, trembling. He stared down at her with horror, with that same frenzy that he had of plague.

"God save me." He let her go and turned, breathing like a winded stag. "She's not dead. Oh, Mary; oh, God and Jesus, she contrived it. She isn't dead." He dropped to his knees, his fists pressed to the side of his head. As Cara watched in shock, he tore his fingers down his face, drawing blood. "I let her fly, she's not dead, she's not dead, she's not dead! My father!" With a mortal groan he lifted his face to Heaven. "Lord God have mercy on me!"

Eleven

———⊸⊱⊰⊷———

THIN GOLDEN CHAINS fastened to her garters held up the long muddy toes of Melanthe's boots. They were not intended for the march; she could feel every pebble and twig through the soft soles, but she barely noticed that. It was too good to be free.

She had no fear. That was not quite rational, she knew—her knight was plainly of the opinion that there was much to cause alarm, but such was the disposition of any worthy watchdog. She enjoyed treading along beside him, skirting grass tussocks and pushing branches aside, hiking her skirt to leap little puddles and rivulets. In spite of her gown, she was not much more encumbered than he in his armor. She guessed it must weigh half a hundred pounds and surely affected his stride, checking him to a speed she had no trouble to maintain.

They did not speak to each other beyond necessity. Although the hunt had seemed to Melanthe to have created some momentary degree of intimacy, softening the edge of awkwardness between them, he had stung her with his suspicions. She supposed that she would not look him out a wife after all.

His mail chinked in a rhythm that worked its way into her brain in the hours of silent march. The horse's hoofbeats changed from soft thumps to thuds as the marshland rose to higher ground. Meadow gave way to open woods, gray and black, straight young birch trees like a thousand cathedral columns springing up from a strange undulating floor of hawthorns and green winter grass.

"Tilled field," he said, breaking the quiet. He gestured with his mailed hand to the furrows and edges that spread like huge ripples in the earth, the massive ghosts of peasants' plows, birch trunks growing out of the spines and hollows.

"Mary," Melanthe said softly. "Abandoned?"

"Yea. Twenty year and more, hap, on measure of the trees."

"The Death."

"Yea, my lady. Was never a much peopled place, I think. What souls were left—" He shrugged. "Why keep it, when they mayen find better livelihood to the east, where men were wanted to worken easier lands?"

She nodded. So it had been everywhere, the marginal surrendered to desert when there were barely enough people to till the richest fields. She had been nine years old. Her mother had died and left Melanthe and her little brother, Richard. Her father had wept, and never married again, nor smiled as gaily—and wept once more a few years later when Melanthe set out for Italy in the rich train Prince Ligurio had sent for her.

She had never seen her father after that day. But he had remembered her. He had not blamed her for Richard's death. In his will he had confirmed her as the heiress of Bowland. She could not recall his face—Richard's boyish grin intruded, Richard of the fond smiles and songs for the ladies. In the few months that Melanthe had kept him with her, she had basked in those smiles. She had loved him so easily, known him so surely, as if they had never been parted.

Another life. Other places.

She had been afraid. She had always been afraid, every minute, every hour of eighteen years since she had left home.

She felt a fierce will that the plague might kill them all, Navona and Riata, while she sojourned here in isolation and wildness. Haps she would never return, not even to Bowland.

She and her knight would hunt dragons and battle wildmen of the woods, and never go back to the world of human things.

Here was nothing but peace, that she could see, and what danger there might be was her knight's charge and not her own. She wanted peace. Even more than she wanted Bowland.

She gazed at the silent English woods. When he had first told her what the peculiar ridges were, she had felt a quick superstitious dread of such eerie signs of long-dead men. But as she looked on them now, they seemed to signify the weakness of human power in this place, where trees grew without effort from the heart of men's hardest labor.

"In such remote desert we moten find us a damsel in sore straits, Green Sire, and rescue her," she said.

"We moten find us safe haven, lady," he said, pulling the horse on.

Melanthe picked up her skirt and came abreast of him. They climbed up a plow ridge and went down the side. "Nay—a damsel, passing fair, and in distress."

"Full enow in distress is my lady, I trove. We need none other."

She tugged her skirt free of a thornbush. "Alack, sir, art thou satisfied with such a small aventure? Where is our venomous serpent? Our fiery worm?"

"Ne does nought my lady wish to meet a dragon, in troth."

"Thou woundest me! I do."

He shook his head. "Ye knows nought of what you say."

She looked toward him, intrigued by the note of certainty in his voice. "Hast thou seen one?"

"Yea, my lady."

He said it in the same dispassionate tone that he might have said he thought it like to come on rain. Melanthe pursed her lips. "Thou wilt not fool me, Sir Ruck. My husband said that all such beasts were drowned in the Deluge."

He gave a faint snort and glanced at her. "I thought I heard my lady say that she wished to war with one such."

"Tush, I am but a woman," she said lightly, "full of a woman's fantasies."

"Oho," he said, and nothing more.

They walked along in silence. Melanthe freed herself from another thorn.

She listened to the steady chink of his mail. They went up one side of the ridges and down the other, up and down and up and down again. She slanted him a sideways look.

"So, knight—where didst thou beholden this dragon?"

He nodded in the direction that they walked. "To the north. Not far from here."

"Fye upon thee! Thou undertake to frighten me!"

"Hah! My lady hatz no proper dread, nought of wolves nor outlaws. Wherefore should I wist a firedrake might make you shrink?"

"No firedrake abides in Britain yet," she insisted. "My husband said me so. They are now all in Ethiopis and India and hot places."

He walked steadily onward. "Haps I slayed the last one," he said. "Haps it were nought the last, though I've seen none since. I ne wit that your lord husband could know so much of it, lest he spent the years that I haf done in the hunting of the beasts."

"He read deeply. It may be that thou wast mistaken in what animal thou slayed. 'Tis said the likeness of a dragon can be forged on the carcass of a great ray."

He halted and turned with an exclamation of disgust. "It were nought a fish!"

Melanthe stopped, facing him, her curiosity fully roused. "Descrive it me."

"N'ill I," he said, turning to go on.

She put her hand on his arm. "Sir Ruck, if it thee like and please," she said, with her best coaxing grace, "tell me of thy dragon that thou slayed."

He began to walk. But he glanced aside at her and did not pull away from her touch. "It was in a hard winter," he said. "The bulls came and bears, and boars from the high fells. Only a man outlawed would occupy such a wasted place as this. But the warring did nought wrathe me as the winter, so much. Shed the clouds sleet, and I sleeped, my lady, on the raw rocks, rigged in my arms, with hard icicles henged over my head like serpents' teeth. It was too terrible to say a tenth of it." He nodded toward the grass that carpeted the undulating forest floor. "Nought as now."

"But say me of the dragon." She walked beside him, balancing on the top of a ridge while he went in the furrow, her hand resting on his shoulder. "How did it appear?"

"My lady, if ye would discover what manner of beast it was, then would ye nought knowen its habitation, and what weather likes it? So I am telling you."

"Ah. I crave thy pardon. The winter was a harsh one, then, that drove the wild creatures down from the hills. Dragons, I've read in the beastiaries, dwell in sweltery places."

"Swelter did I nought, my lady, that eventide. For harbor I halted in a hollow below cliff, where the stones sloped down perilous steep. I fettered Hawk, to forage for his fodder, could he finden it, but I broke nought e'en hard bread to brace me. Black night befell us, of all brightness wanting." He stared ahead as he walked, his eyes narrowing, as if he could see it. "Thus in pain and plight full unpleasant in troth, I dropped down as were dead and lifeless, but that I shivered and shooken, sore with cold."

Melanthe pulled her mantle closer about her as they came to the end of the curving ridge. At the base of it a tumbled wall of stone was succumbing to hawthorn, and beyond that the furrows lay perpendicular to those they traversed. He turned along the wall, taking Melanthe's arm and prompting her to walk before him down the trench.

"Weary sleep shunned me, I say you, my lady. Blew aghlich airs out of that black atmosphere, tolling awful tunes to terrify a hunter." A freshening breeze swept the bare branches above. He raised his eyes, watching them. "I believe it was the breath of the beast."

Melanthe glanced up. The shadow of new clouds raced across the woods, throwing a chill into the wind. At her feet she realized there was a subtle dirt track in the bottom of the furrow, as if theirs were not the only feet that passed this way.

"Were there lightnings?" she asked. "Haps it were an unseasonal storm, far off."

"Yea, there were lightnings, my lady," he said from behind her. "Lightnings and luminaries as the long hours passed. My bed of boulders grew to burn me. Sat I straight up, with my skin blistering, smarted by hot steel where skimmed my armor. And I heard then a hiss, my lady, so hideous and vast that my heart haled to the heels of my feet."

"The wind might make such a noise."

"Came it out of the cliff, from a cavern deep, and a wind with it as you wis, my lady, wrothly reeking."

"Of burning brimstone, I trove?"

"Nay—" He paused, and then said thoughtfully, "More like to the smell of a siege in the summer heat—when the bodies of the dead grow bloated and burn with the sack of the city."

"By God's self," Melanthe murmured. "How pleasant."

"My lady has read of some beast with such a breath?" he asked.

"Several might have such," she said. "A manticore, a griffin. They are found in Ethiopis. The basilisk of India may kill by no more than its smell."

"Ne slayed by the scent of this serpent was I. I shocked out my sword from the sheath, my lady. The rocks rained down about me, for rattled the earth itseluen. The air grew ardent, and out of the opening, coiling and curling like a cable, a great serpent came—colored comelych blue, and carried into the sky."

She stopped, holding up her skirt as she looked around at him.

"O'er the wall, my lady, if it please you," he said in an ordinary tone, with a slight bow of his head.

Melanthe looked down and saw that the faint dirt track made a turn at a place where the stones were broken down. He gripped her arm to steady her as she stepped across, and then tugged the horse after them through the gap.

As its last great hoof cleared the stones and thumped down into a bed of damp leaves, she said, "It was colored like the sky?"

"Yea, but shining, my lady. In the night it nigh glared."

"Shining!" She frowned. "The serpent called the Scytale glows, so that it may stupefy its victim by its splendor."

"Bedazzled was I to beholden it, my lady."

"And the air about it grew hot?"

He made a heartfelt sound of assent. "Heat such as Hell

mote hurl, my lady. All my iron afflicted me, as if afire was I. By what work I wielded my sword, I wot nought. Marks it made upon my palm for months thereafter."

She chewed her lip. "A basilisk might cause such. They have been known to burn people up. I read naught of their color as blue. They're striped in white. But they have wings and might fly." The slope of the land rose as they walked. She followed the path over another ridge and furrow.

"Wings it wore, yea," he said, "but it wafted as if the air arched it aloft, like autumn leafs, for its bulk was too big to bravely fly on wing. It shrieked as the sound of . . . as the sound of . . ." He paused for a long moment. "I know nought. I ne can think of no word. As the sound of . . ."

Melanthe kept walking, scouring her memory for what she had read of these things in the beastiaries, barely listening to him as he repeated the phrase beneath his breath.

"As the sound of—a scythe on a whetstone!" he exclaimed, with the tone of having solved some puzzle. "It shrieked as the sound of a scythe on a whetstone."

She tripped over a root and caught herself. As she looked up she realized that the ridges and furrows ended here. A darker forest lay ahead, the trunks older, thick and gnarled. She hesitated.

The steady beat of the destrier's hooves came to a halt behind her. "Will my lady riden now?" he asked.

Melanthe was not so certain that she wished to lead the way afoot into this woods. She nodded. He put his hands at her waist and lifted her up to sit aside on the saddle next to Gryngolet. For a moment he looked up at her, a phantom of his uncommon smile in his eyes.

It was an impossible thing to resist. She smiled back, but he cast down his look, moving away to lead the horse into the deeper wood.

They traveled steadily, following a muddy path that skirted bogs and roots, as sinuous as his dragon. The rhythm was brisker now, for she realized that he was after all not so weighted down by his armor that he could not stride along at a far more active pace than hers. She ducked branches, deep in thought as she listened to him, unable to conceive of what beast he had actually slain. His description was detailed enough: its size immense, its scales blue, its breath fetid, and the air about it scorching; its aspect like a great serpent, but head broad and flat, more like to a lizard with the teeth of a wolf, wings too small to hold it aloft.

She allowed for exaggeration—what hunter did not make his boar larger and fiercer with the telling?—but the more she pressed him for particular attributes, the more she began to think that he had killed a very large basilisk. Until he showed her the scars beneath Hawk's coat, three long ridges full two inches apart, that the monster had made as it fell upon the horse from its fiery height. Then her opinion wavered.

"A griffon hates horses," she speculated. "But sayest thou its head was like to a lizard? Not an eagle?"

"Nay, my lady, nonsuch like. But my horse hatz the heart of an eagle. Sprang he up with a scream, striving to kill. Such strength did he spend that he splintered his chain. His loose fetter he flung, to flay as if were a weapon. He smote the serpent and slashed it in its loathly eye. The dragon rebounded with a roar, ripping his hide." He laid his hand on Hawk's shoulder over the old scars, passing his palm down the horse's coat as he walked. "I plunged to impale the paunch that it bared. Mother Mary blessed me, I believe, and abetted me in that moment, for my sword struck the scales and slipped betwixt. Bright blood boiled forth, but the creature coiled about my cuirass, choking my breath, wringing life from my limbs and light from my eyes. I descried my sword divided and dragged from my hand. I felt the fetid air as the fangs locked upon my feet, in the way that a snake feeds on a field mouse."

He stopped speaking. Melanthe realized that her hands clenched the saddle, gripping it as if she could throw off the deathly coils herself.

"What didst thou do?" she asked, loosening her grip.

"I submitted my soul to Mary's sweet mercy." He glanced back at her. "Next I knew, I lay near dead. Beside me the beast was buckled, embedded with my sword in its breast, its lifeblood all about me. My sabatons it had sucked off my soles and swallowed my legs to the knee. I wrenched free and withdrew, and bowed down to bear thanks to God the

Almighty. And thus in another day this aventure betided," he said. "I abidingly thereof bear witness, my lady."

"Depardeu! What became of the creature?"

"I will show you, my lady."

"Wee loo! Show me?"

He nodded ahead. "My lady sees before us, through the trees? There is a chapel. Peraventure, the creature's bones lie there yet."

SHE SLID FROM the saddle even before he could help her down. In the afternoon shadow the little chapel was a dark smudge against the boggy woods, an old and unadorned rectangle of slate, windowless. With an echoing scrape of wood on stone, the knight pushed open the door and stood back to let her pass.

She saw it immediately. The skull lay in the shaft of light from the door, enthroned upon a wide bench below the crude altar. It was huge, and nothing like a basilisk's eagle head. Just as he had said, a long and pointed snout, with great eye and nostril hollows and vicious teeth like no living creature she had ever seen. Remains of its spine lay scattered in a rough line down the bench. A fan of thinner bones, like an enormous hand or a wing, was assembled carefully on a nearby table.

"It is a dragon." Melanthe strode into the church, stripping off her gloves, leaving the knight leaning upon the door to hold it open. She bent over the skull.

In the half-light it was bleached bone, the sunken eye holes deep caverns of black. But at the first touch, Melanthe sucked a hissing breath.

Stone. No real skeleton, but heavy and hard, solid inside where a skull would be gaping. The eye hollows, the backbone, the teeth—all white lime rock, impossible to misjudge.

She whirled to face him. He was still leaning on the door, his arms crossed, the faintest suggestion of an upward curve at the corner of his mouth.

"Thou lied to me." She narrowed her eyes at him. "Is naught but a rock!"

His mouth twitched.

"Thou lied to me!"

"My lady wished a firedrake." His hidden smirk became a grin.

"Thou knew that I believed thee. Thou took delight in it. Thou lied to me!" Her vehement words returned, fierce whispers echoing against the walls and floor, *lied-lied-lied.*

"Lied?" The door scraped as he pulled back his weight in the face of her sudden advance. "A tale, my lady, that I made for your pleasure. In verse—" He gave a modest shrug. "Of a kind."

"Verse! I—" She stopped. She remembered him searching for a word to describe the dragon, repeating the phrase under his breath, until he came out with the same sounds echoing and compounding through the sentence, rhyming at the head of words instead of the tail, like the old poetry. In the peculiar convoluted idiom that was his normal English, she had barely noticed.

He was still smiling at the floor. He thought it amusing. In a voice as cold as the dragon stone, she said, "If I find thee in a lie to me again, knight, thou wilt rue it to thy early death."

Ruck raised his eyes, his humor expiring. She was white, staring at him with her chin set and trembling.

"As thou livest," she said through clenched teeth, "never lie to me, in revel or no. Swear it now."

"Lady—" He had meant only to make a mirth. She did not understand.

"Kneel!" she commanded.

He hesitated. He expected her to smile. He thought she would say that she made merry of him, and laugh as she had when she threw the sand.

"On thy knees, knave!" She pointed at the floor. Her hand shook. "Abase thyself!"

Shock welled in him, and resentment, warring with his honor that was bound to her homage. Slowly he stood straight from the door.

"In the name of what you hold most dear," she cried, "before God!"

In outrage he slammed one gloved fist inside the other. The harsh metal sound of it rang in the little chapel, violence and submission joined as he gripped his hands together and lowered himself before her. The whip of his pride kept his head upright. He could see her fingers, balled tight in fear or rage or some emotion beyond his comprehension.

"Ne'er will I speaken false to you, my lady," he said briefly.

"Swear it!" Her voice rose nearly to a shriek. "Swear upon what you love as your life!"

He flung himself to his feet. "On my lady's heart, then, I swear!" he shouted. "Fore God, n'ill I ne lie to you, nought while I live! I ne have nought lied, never! Was but a tale. A lay—for the delight of it, no more than that!"

She glared at him. Then she turned away, pacing to the stone dragon, her cloak sweeping the floor. She drew a breath. Slowly, as if she had to will it, her hands stretched open at her sides.

She spoke more quietly. "I depend upon thee for truth." She looked back at him. Her lilac eyes were intense, outlined in black. "There is but one person on the earth that I trust, and that is thee."

If she had said some incantation, some unholy powerful mutter, if she had spilled blood and boiled toads, stolen his hair and molded his figure in wax, she could not have bound him so well and finally. He felt love like pain, love for her when still he did not know who or what she was.

She said in a smaller voice, "Thou didst not tell me it was a poem."

"My lady—" He made a miserable bitter laugh. "Were no true poem, but a ragged thing, made out of my head. I will nought be false with you, my lady—ne'er, nor devise no lay again."

Her furred cloak rustled. He watched her as she ran her finger down the dragon skull. "Was somewhat agreeable a tale," she said. "Thou mayest devise such—but tell me." She looked up at him. "Certes tell me when thou speakest not in troth."

He bowed his head, just barely, in acknowledgment. He was angry at her, at himself, and still more mortified. The weariness of two nights without sleep marred his judgment; he did not know why he had hazarded to speak in sport to her, or even half in sport. "Were a stupid jape, my lady."

"Only say me." She seemed almost penitent. "Only warn me."

"Yea, my lady."

With an unnatural bright smile she stroked the dragon skull. "This is a monstrous creation. How came it here, knowest thou?"

"I found it. In a place to the south, cemented in a shelf above a rockfall. Whiles, I carried it about as a penance. Weighs it sore, my lady. But a priest was here then, and he gave me absolution to dedicate it to the glory of Saint George's chapel, which he said this was."

"A penance!" She took on the smooth light manner of a court lady. "When hast thou ever sinned, monkish man?"

His mouth tightened. He disliked her mockery the most when she ridiculed the virtue that he fought so hard to preserve against her. Sin and dishonor and temptation incarnate she was, with her elven's boots and her black hair drifting free of its golden net. "Daily, my lady," he murmured.

"Daily!" she echoed, glancing at him and then down at the dragon.

He followed the slow caress of her fingertip across the stone, a carnal thing, simple and compelling. "Every hour, my lady," he said low, "and every minute."

She tapped the skull briskly. "Forsooth, I believe mote be a true dragon. Drowned in the Deluge. Or haps it stole a very ugly damsel by mischance, poor creature, and congealed to stone when it looked upon her. Some of us needen no knight to fly to our rescue."

"More like it were the Deluge, my lady."

She regarded her own hand as if it interested her greatly. "Sober and chaste, monkish man. That is what they sayen of thee." A subtle smile marked her lips. "What lady's heart didst thou swear upon, Green Sire?"

"My lady wife's," he said. It was not a falsehood. He was sure it was the truth. It must be the truth.

"Alas." She lifted one brow. "I may but mourn it was not mine."

"If I say you troth, my lady, ne can I nought flatteren, also," he said stubbornly.

Pink flushed her cheek. "In faith, I am honestly answered for my ungrace in asking."

Ruck had not spoken false. He must have sworn upon

Isabelle, for she was his wife. But he looked at Princess Melanthe's face, and he could not remember Isabelle. Had not been able to remember, not for years.

"What wants ye of me, my liege lady?" he asked harshly. "Dalliaunce and kisses?"

"Yea," she said, without looking up. "Yea, I think I want those things of thee, otherwise would I not bear myself so bold. Such is not like me. But I am not sure."

He had never known a woman to be so open about it, or so maddening. His heart thudded slow, but his blood felt too hot for his veins.

She made a peculiar laugh. "Too strange it is—I have said in my heart that now I am free, now I have no need to deceive. Now I can speak always in troth—and I find I cannot distinguish what is true and what is not." She faced him openly. "I have forgotten how."

The painted cross stood behind her, simple and stark. To cool himself, Ruck said, "The priests would tell my lady to pray and find God's troth."

"So they would. And then take themselves off to their dinners and concubines." She lifted her chin and threw back her shoulders with a little shrug. "But lo—thou art a man with a nun for a wife," she said. "Avoi, I know not what the world comes to, with these upside-down arrangements!"

"My lady," he said, "up swa downer is it, that so worthy as you would incline to so poor as your knight."

"Ah." She rested against the table and looked about the little shadowed space, opening her hand. "But among these hundred of suitors, thou art my favorite, Sir Ruck."

He did not know how he was to go on with her so near to him. She stood in this chapel, all but offering herself to be his lover. Never would he have looked so high above him, even had he succumbed to love-amour, but it was she who chose.

He closed his fist around the hasp of the door. "These are foolish matters," he said abruptly. "The night comes on too swift."

"And what if I made thee a greater man? I have lands escheated to me, with yet no lord. I will maken thee a present of them."

She stung his pride with that. "I am lord in my own lands, my lady, and my father before me. I need no whore-toll."

Her swift look made him instantly regret that he had said so much. She said mildly, "What lands are these?"

He held the door wide. "If my lady does please to pass?"

"Whence hails thee?" she demanded, without moving.

Ruck stood silently, angry at himself. He felt her study penetrate him.

"Thou speakest the north in every syllable."

"Yea, a rude and runisch northeron I am, lady. Avoi, will you come then, ere I cast you o'er my saddle and ravish you off to the wilderness, for to take my will like a wild man?"

She laughed aloud. "Nay, not while all is upside down." She came to him, a sweep of cloak and warmth out of the shadow, taking hold of both his arms. "I will take *thee* captive, and have my will here and now, for I cannot cast thee upon a horse to ravish thee away, and we are in wilderness already."

She leaned up and kissed him, all softness and glee, so that he was powerless, captive in truth. He was instantly beyond thinking of spells and enchantment: what she willed, he willed. He held his arm under her back and lifted her against him, hungry for her body against his, despairing that his armor screened all sensation of it.

"My lady," he mumbled on her cheek, when her indrawn gasp for breath broke the kiss. "It is a church."

"Then release me, monkish man, and I will lead thee astray outside."

He relaxed his arm. She slipped down, laughing still, and he followed her like a mongrel dog would follow a kind-hearted village girl in hopes of a scrap of bread, dragging the door in closed behind him.

She turned and met him, another stand on tiptoe—he could not feel her, but he could not even think of her body, her breasts, without his member going full and stiff. He pressed his gloved palms wide under her arms, taking her up against him again. He leaned back hard on the door of the chapel, drawing her whole weight on himself so that he had some crude sense of her through his plated armor.

Her lips met his, so sweet that he knew it was a magic that could kill him and make him glad to die. He felt her slip and try to keep her place. Without lifting his mouth from hers he slid his back down the church door and sat upon the step, holding her between his legs.

She stood on her knees, cupping his face in her hands, smiling down at him. He came a little to his senses.

"I have a wife," he said to the white soft skin below her ear. "I ne cannought do this."

"It is none of thy doing. Thou art seized and cruelly assaulted." Her breath caressed the corner of his mouth. "I perceive thou art a princess in disguise, Green Sire, with vast properties in unknown places. Haps I shall force thee to marry me for thy fortune."

He tipped his head against the door, evading her, breathing roughly with the effort of containing his desire. "Would be sore disappointed in your bargain, my lady, I fear."

She sat back, catching his chin between her fingers, examining his face solemnly. "A beauteous fair damsel thou art not, forsooth. But 'tis a poor marriage founded on a comely countenance, so they sayen. I'll have thee for thy riches."

He shook his head, half smiling at her in spite of himself, pulling her hands down from his face and holding them gently in his mailed gloves. "Lady, ye knows nought how thin you draw this thread."

"By hap I wish it thin," she murmured. She lifted her lashes, looking into his eyes. "Haps I desire it broken asunder."

She was so close to him that he could see each fine black brushstroke that formed her brows and lashes. In the lengthening afternoon shadow, her skin seemed like snow under moonlight, her eyes that strange deep hue, the color of flowers that bloomed in the winter dark, more rare than any dragon or basilisk or unicorn could be rare.

He felt as if he himself must break asunder, the unbending rectitude and loneliness of thirteen impossible years razed at a stroke, consumed by the clear invitation in her words and her eyes. "I pray you, think wiser, my lady," he said roughly. "It is this strange place and time. I am far beneath you. Yourseluen said ye be nought certain of your desire." He curled his hands about hers. "My liege lady, my luflych, when we wend us back to court, your pride and your honor were mortified, to know you kept close company with such as I am."

She was silent, her hands unresisting in his. Tiny strands of her hair had long since come free of her netted braids, floating about her cheeks and temple. Slipping her hands free, she spread her fingers over his dirty gauntlets.

"Nay, I would be proud," she whispered. "I would be proud, when I think of such worse as I have kept company with." She bit her lips with a faint sound. "Oh, thy good conscience will make me weep."

He lowered his head, gazing down at her hands. "Ne'er in my life, my lady, could I believe this much would come to pass, that I could e'en touch you."

She skimmed her fingertips over his hands and his arms, up to his shoulders, over mail and plate, following with her eyes. He saw tears, which amazed him. He shook his head. "No, lady—do nought; nought for such a thing."

She leaned forward and kissed him. The sweetness ran down through him, unbearable. He put his arms about her and buried his face in the side of her throat to avoid her. "I beseech you, my lady," he said. "It will ruin us. It will be the ruin of us both."

She pressed her head hard against him. He could feel the silent unevenness of each indrawn breath, and her tears that trickled down below his ear and under his gorget. He sat holding her, waiting, because to say her nay again was more than he could do; he was body and soul at her will now, heedless of rank or witchery, of honor or his wife.

She set her palms against him and pushed back. He let her go, opening his arms.

"Thou art mistaken," she said fiercely. "Both of us would it not ruin, no—but only thee, and that I ne will not have. Naught will we say more of keeping company, but as sure friends and companions. Little thou may reckon it, but my friendship is worth something in the world. I will stand thy true friend, Sir Ruck, in all that may pass."

He put his hand to her cheek and throat, resting it softly there, isolated forever from the feel of her by layers of metal and leather, by what he was, and had been, which was noth-

ing. "I am your true servaunt. I will lay down my life for you
if you ask it."

She made a teary grimace. "Well, ne do I not ask it! Pray
keep thyself alive and well, Sir Ruck, if thou dost not wish to
displease me most grievously." She wiped hard at her eyes
and swallowed. Then she pushed away from him and rose,
holding her hands tucked close beneath her arms, her head
bent. She shivered, but did not draw her cloak about her.

Ruck stood. His hands were open. He would have pulled
her into his arms and warmed her. All night he would have
embraced her, lain down with her and kept company with her,
held her so near that she was one with him. But his fingers
closed, empty.

"I could weep myseluen, lady," he said, "for wanting what
you would give me."

She laughed, still crying. "Oh, honor and a silver tongue,
too! Look what a lover I have lost."

"My lady—naught is lost. I am with you yet, and always,
to serve you and sayen you ne'er false. I swear it upon what I
hold more precious than my life—" He reached out and
touched her, laid his hand above her breast, against the soft
green felt and ermine.

She raised her eyes. Even through his heavy gauntlet, he
could feel her pulse.

"For my lady's heart," he said. "My life, my troth, and my
honor. For your heart I swear it, and none other."

Twelve

⸙

MELANTHE SAT WITH her mantle wrapped close about her, her back against the chapel wall, watching the frigid dusk come down. Her head felt dull with the unfamiliar aftermath of tears, her eyes heavy, but she was not melancholy.

Her knight lay across the door, his head on his arm, padded by his cloak. The steady sound of his breathing was the only noise but for the destrier cropping grass outside the open portal, and the occasional tinkle of Gryngolet's bells. Each soft chime brought a sharper breath and a suspension from him, as if he listened for peril even in sleep—then a shift of his body, and a long deep exhalation like a sigh.

She was to wake him before full dark gathered, so that he might sit up again all through the night on watch. He had gone to sleep with his back to her, but soon enough his movements had turned him so that she could just see his face in the last of the light. He looked exactly what he was: a weary man-at-arms, shabby and handsome, resigned to sleeping in armor on stone. The strong lines of his face were no softer in sleep: only his lips, slightly parted, and the smoothing of the stern lines about his eyes and brows made him seem younger, more like to the youth who had stared at her so hotly those many seasons ago in the Pope's palace.

He had amused her then, and flattered her—such a look, and from a boy who had not even anything to gain by it. She had noticed him. And when she had seen what mischief they were about, the bishops and priests, she had saved him, little though he appeared to know or thank her.

She had felt then a hundred years older than he, though she'd been only seventeen herself. She felt a thousand now—and yet new, in some strange way younger and more reckless than she had ever been. She felt, for the first time in her life, in love with a man.

Ligurio she had respected, loved in mind and in soul: teacher, father, companion, and lifeline. And before she had learned better, she had found friendship and a sparking attraction with the smiling Dane who had given her Gryngolet, but that memory was no peaceful one.

She gazed at the long shadowed teeth of the dragon stone, burying her cold nose in ermine. The Northman had taught her to hunt, disciplined her to the exacting task of training a wild *passager* trapped after its first moult, revealed to her the hours of freedom in a falcon's courses. She had not betrayed Ligurio with him, nor thought of it. It had not been more than a girl's infatuation. It had not had time to become more, before Melanthe had discovered the Northman slain in her own bed. The lady asleep with him put on a great shrieking show to find that the man beside her was murdered, just as if she had not slipped in the knife herself. Melanthe had been fifteen, Prince Ligurio's still-virgin bride, in wit as well as body. Her husband had had to explain it to her.

That was the first she had truly understood of Gian Navona's cold lunatic passion for all that Monteverde owned. For her. Before it, she had only known him as a courteous and clever man who sometime supped with her husband, and had once shown her a cunning hand trick of making a living flower appear in a bowl of glass.

In many ways, that was all she knew of Gian still. And yet he had made her what she was, as surely as Ligurio's careful lessons. Prince Ligurio taught her how to swim; Gian Navona was the sea—tide and current and storm, treacherous depth and smiling surface, and creatures dwelling beneath that haunted dreams. She learned never to rest, never to float, never to cling to what appeared solid. She learned that he would not abide her to smile upon any man.

The dragon stared back at her from black eyeholes. The long line of its teeth could have been a deathly grin. She wondered if it had amused Gian, to dispatch his own mistress to end Melanthe's innocence in seduction and blood. She wondered how far ahead he planned; if he had intended even then to sire a bastard on the woman and train him up to be another beautiful murdering viper, to castrate him and set him guard upon Melanthe, at her table and in her bed, tainting the very air she breathed with bloodshed. She wondered if he found it all some lurid jest, and sat alone in his palazzo and laughed.

Gryngolet, the Northman's gift—the white gyrfalcon had hated Allegreto from the day he had come into Monteverde, a boy with the mind and countenance of the fallen archangel himself. Melanthe also had hated him. He had the look of his mother on him—murderess—Melanthe could see her magnificent frantic face even now, tearing her hair in her fraudulent horror.

But Ligurio had commanded Melanthe to keep Allegreto close, for her life. Her husband was failing in health, and the balance was all, the eternal balance between Navona and Riata and Monteverde. Allegreto was an assassin to keep her from assassination, a bargain Ligurio had made with Gian to protect her, taking advantage of Navona's passion to guard her from other enemies who had less than no use for her alive. Her husband had accepted the boy, even been kind to him. Melanthe had suffered him, dreaming of the day she would be free.

Dreaming of this day, when she could put such memories behind her.

Gryngolet's bells jingled again, and the knight adjusted his arm. He made a low sound. His mouth curved, just visible above the crook of his elbow, a trace of his uncommon smile. Melanthe rested her cheek on the soft trim of her mantle, happily assotted with him. The comlokkest man on earth, the most honorable, humble, gracious, the strongest, the best-spoken, the finest warrior—she diverted herself with heaping extravagant merits upon his slumbering person.

He snorted, denying such exalted perfection in an ordinary man's sleep, lifting his hand as if to reverse his arm beneath his head. The move seemed to expire halfway. His gauntlet wavered, balanced in mid-arc, the heavy mail and leather curl of his fingers drooping, declining slowly sideways. The back of his glove came to rest on the stone with a soft chink.

She loved the sound of him. The sound of his armor, the sound of his breathing, the sound of his voice speaking English. Forsooth, she loved him.

Having come to this insight, she felt that she must proceed with great care. She found herself somewhat bewildered by it; unable to reconcile such an intangible force with all of her plans and designs.

She ought to be thinking. The whole world would not die of plague; it had not the first time, nor the second, and it would not this time, either. Pestilence came now by fits and starts, killing five here, fifty there, no more than one or two in another place. She could not suppose that God would elect to erase the names of Navona and Riata from the earth merely to save her trouble.

Iwysse, she doubted that God had much use for her at all, in spite of her abbeys. She was unrepentant. She was pleased to look at the sleeping masculine form of her knight. She sore desired him in a most sinful and earthly way, and she was not the least sorry for it.

Her foremost care had been to arrive safely and without interference at Bowland Castle, where amid the native Englishmen, any agents sent by Gian or Riata would be easy to discern and dispatch. But she found that this ambition had now palled, replaced by an acute desire, amazing in its quaintness, to remain in the wasteland with Sir Ruck d'Somewhere, the lord—and his father before him—of imaginary places.

She smiled wryly, thinking of the quick pride with which he'd refused her offer of lands. He spoke himself well enough, like a gentle man, but she remembered his wife—a burgher's daughter if there had ever been one—and was inclined to agree with Lancaster's guess that the Green Sire's splendid tournament armor hid a man baseborn. He had almost admitted as much, had he not, in refusing her?

It was a sign of her corrupted nature, she supposed, that she did not care a whiff for his birth. Haps he was misbegot of some knight too poor to provide for him, but Lancaster was overharsh in judging him a freeman—no son of villeins would be endured by the men-at-arms as their master, far less tolerated by the knights and ladies of court.

Nay, he had gentle manners: a quiet dignity about him, even now in his shabbiness, and a nobleman's way with a good horse. He was a poet of sorts. He had been brought up in a lord's household, of that she felt certain, though in the end it made no matter. She was the Earl of Bowland's daughter, wife to a prince, cousin of counts and kings. As well fall in love with a monk or a merchant, or a cowherd, for that, as with this obscure and humble knight.

Ligurio had taught her many things, but inordinate tenderness and renunciation had not been among them. She was not accustomed to denying herself any worldly richness or temporal pleasure, unless it be in sure disfavor to her own interests. If she had not taken lovers, it was not for virtue or self-constraint, or even concern for the skins of the many men who had offered themselves, but because of the terrible weakness such a union must create.

It was strength that she needed, not weakness. She had meant to use him, this chivalrous, nameless warrior. She had meant to make him love her if she could, daze and blind him, bind him without mercy to her service. She would need such as he, to protect her and act for her.

And she had done it. He had mistrusted her, accused her of witchery, reserved something of himself in spite of his sworn allegiance—but she was certain of him now. She cared nothing that he spoke of this wife of his, beyond that it proved the unlimited bounds of his loyalty once he gave his heart. She would free him of that vain covenant when the time came.

For now she was charitable as she had never been, yielding her own wish to his welfare. She would not repay his service with encumbrance, his honor with dishonor. She would not be the ruin of him, but the making. And haps if she was so, if she gave him the opportunity to rise that Lancaster had denied, if by her support he made a superior marriage to some lady of her choosing and gained land and a higher place, if she educated his children and sponsored them to a better elevation yet . . .

She gazed across the cold barren space between them, two yards and forever. If she did all that for him, then haps her life would not be without some worth in the end, or so vain in the years to come as it seemed now to be.

RUCK WOKE TO the music of hunting horns. With an oath he rolled over and shoved upright. He'd been so deep in sleep that for a moment he blinked in the morning light and stared about himself, unable to recall this place.

Then he saw the princess curled in her mantle, slumbering in a drooping huddle against the wall. She had not woken him.

"Christ's love!" He staggered to his feet. He'd slept the night through like a dead man.

A horn called again, a mote and a rechase—and he realized that the sound had been reverberating in his dreams since before he'd come awake. Another followed: relays, he thought, with the quarry sighted. Two motes more, to call the berner with the hounds, and a distant *yut yut yut* in answer.

He stared unseeing out the door, listening for the direction that they took. All was silence for long moments—and then the sudden bell of a rache, far off, farther than the last relay. Another hound joined in, and the pack took up their song. Two horns blew the chase, acknowledged by a *hou hou hooouuu*—more distant yet—and the whole hunt was laid out like a map in his mind.

"We! Lady!" He wasted no time in formalities, but shook her by the shoulder, all but dragging her to her feet.

She gave him one wild look, as if she, too, could not find her bearings—and then her expression relaxed, focusing on him.

He was already gathering up their gear. "A hunt," he said. "Get ye and the falcon to horse, all speed, and chaunce we will meet them in the chase."

"Meet them?" She stood as if bewildered. "But pestilence—"

"Sick men do nought hunt. The falcon, lady. Hood her, so that we may hie us in haste." He tossed the hawking-bag to her. "A lord it will be, haps even the king's men, to hunt here with hounds. Good hostel we'll plead, on your behalf. Freshly now, my lady, ere we lose the horns."

Already they grew fainter, the song of the raches almost vanished. As she took up her bird, he forced the buckle of his sword belt closed. He grabbed his helm, not taking time to put it on, and jostled her out the door before him.

MELANTHE RODE ASTRIDE behind Sir Ruck, for she could not have balanced Gryngolet on her fist and held to his waist on the pillion. They came upon a straggler first, a sullen vewterer swinging the loose leashes of his hounds, walking as if he had no urgent desire to catch up with his dogs even though the horns had already blown the death. She peered over Sir Ruck's shoulder as he reined the horse to a walk.

The vewterer had not even turned to look at them when the destrier broke out from the heavy underbrush behind him, but only moved aside from the path, making way.

"*Ave,* good sir," her knight said in English, bringing them up beside him.

The huntsman turned, as if the address startled him. He ducked into a bow, kneeling with his face down.

"Rise." Sir Ruck gave a flick of his hand. "What quarry?"

"M'lord, the great hart, m'lord." He got to his feet, his eyes still downcast.

"Hart!" Sir Ruck exclaimed. "But 'tis fermysoun time!"

The vewterer cast up a quick, keen glance, and then dropped his gaze to the ground again. He shrugged. "My master would have the hart even in forbidden season, good sir, nor be not induced from it, though we had the tracks and bed of a singular boar."

"Avoi," Sir Ruck said with a soft note of distaste. The source of the man's brooding aspect came clear. No proper huntsman would be proud of his lord for taking a male red deer out of season.

Without lifting his face, the vewterer gave them a sidelong look. "Good sir, I beg your pardon," he said humbly. He sent a dour glance directly at Melanthe. "Methinks ye were not at assembly this morn, good sir, to lend your wisdom to the choosing of the quarry."

There was a very faint note of accusation beneath his exaggerated humility. She realized that he must believe Sir Ruck to be one of his lord's guests, who should have been present at the early morning meal, examining the various droppings that had been brought back from the forest and adding his opinion as to which forecast the likeliest game. No doubt the huntsman felt that here was a man who would have put the weight of his argument against the hart, and counted it in the way of a betrayal that Sir Ruck had not been present to do so.

As to that hostile glance at *her*—she bit her lips against a smile and laid her head against his back. "Why, did we lie abed too long, my dear?" she murmured.

He turned his head quickly, flushing hot red from his throat to his cheek. The huntsman tapped his coiled leashes against his leg and all but rolled his eyes.

"I wist nought thy lord's name, sir," Ruck said brusquely. "We comen to crave harbor of him, if he will it. Wouldst thou go on errand, good sir, to seek our welcome?"

The vewterer lifted his head and looked at them straight for the first time. She could see him taking in their baggage and Sir Ruck's armor. His eyes lingered on Gryngolet with puzzled wonder. "Yea, by Saint Peter, my lord," he mumbled, and stooped into another bow before he turned and went ahead of them at a quick jog.

Sir Ruck followed, keeping the horse to a sedate walk. Another great fanfare began. The woods echoed with a united long blare of many horns and the baying and barking of hounds. It lasted as long as the air could hold in a man's chest, and then, all broke off together into friendly shouting and a few yips. Winding through the underbrush by a path of snapped branches where the hunters had passed, they came upon the boisterous gathering around the unmade hart and a hastily built fire.

The hounds were in the midst of their *curee,* climbing over one another in their eagerness to reach the mixture of bread and blood set aside for them as reward. Horses and men stood about, the soberly dressed huntsmen all business with the hounds and the deer, the few guests notable for their laughter and amorous attention to the several ladies among the group. The vewterer had sought out a neat, compact young man who stood by the fire and the carcass, nibbling at the roasted delicacies reserved to him from the *fourchée* stick.

The laughter quieted, leaving only the yelps and growls of the hounds as the destrier came to a halt.

The young man touched his beard, watching Sir Ruck and Melanthe as his vewterer knelt before him. The words were too soft to hear, but the master's astonishment was hidden somewhat better than his servant's. He thrust the stick at an aide and strode forward to meet them.

"Henry of Torbec, sir, your own servant." He swept a courtly bow. "I hold sway in this land. You're welcome to welde my house and my home as you likes. All is your own and your lady's, may God protect her."

"The Lord on high reward you," Sir Ruck said with great formality. "Displease you ne'er would I, worthy lord, but I mote withhold my name and my house until I am shown deserving. Some thereby call me for my color green."

A hum of interest animated the bystanders. The lord of Torbec smiled, looking about at his guests. "Green! Is marvelous in truth, that such an excellent green knight comes among us. You keep this fair lady from peril by your quest?"

Sir Ruck was silent for a moment. Melanthe expected that he would announce her with some brilliance, he was always so concerned for her high estate. Instead he merely shrugged. "She is my leman," he said.

The whole company broke into appreciative laughter. Henry of Torbec said, "By God, here is a shrewd man, who ne denies to himself no comfort in his undertaking!" He gave Melanthe a knowing survey, as if she were a horse or hound. "Ye deck her right richly, knight."

The way Hawk stood, Gryngolet was still hidden from him and the others behind the bulk of Sir Ruck's armor and mantle. Melanthe lowered the falcon farther yet, resting her gauntlet upon her knee and drawing her elbow slowly back into her cloak, so that the folds fell over the gyrfalcon's white plumage. Sir Ruck turned his head briefly and took a glancing, casual note of her move. This sudden descent from princess to common wench warned her full well that he was not at ease.

"From the warring in France, I brought her menskeful things and gifts," he said.

"You've been in France?" Henry asked swiftly.

"At Poitiers."

"Poitiers!" Henry gave a short laugh. "So long ago?"

"Yea," Sir Ruck said without elaboration.

"Ye know not my brother Geoffrey, then."

"A large country, France," Sir Ruck said. "Ne haf I nought the honor to meeten with all good men who serve the high king there."

"And wendeth ye how since Poitiers, green knight?"

"Over allwhere," he said. "Lately on my left half I held Lyerpool, but entered nought, for I feared sickness there. The priory is forsaken. Had ye news of it?"

Henry scowled. "Nay—forsaken?" He looked to his aides. "Is Downy ne come of Lyerpool not yet?"

Heads shook. Henry gave an oath, as if he had already known the answer. He stepped back from the horse.

"Ye ne did not enter the town, sir?" he demanded.

"As I am a knight and Christian, I say you I did nought. The pestilence ne touches me, but I feared for my damisel. She would fain have me take her within the gate, for she delights to display her rich weed to plain country maids." He shrugged again. "Women haf them no wit, depardeu. Fair wide did we disturb around Lyerpool."

Henry appeared to think that a convincing tale. "Well done, sir. I thank you to bringen this warning." His scowl had faded and he seemed to become quite cheerful. "Hie, men, fette the venison and let us turn to home. Green knight, you honor me, to join my guests."

As the hunters fell to work, Melanthe felt Sir Ruck reach under his arm and take hold of the edge of her cloak. He pulled it forward, tucking a fold into his sword belt, so that Gryngolet was enclosed fully. Melanthe leaned on his back, as if he were caressing her, and said softly in French, "Jeopardy?"

He did not answer, but only reached back and gave her a light bob upon the cheek. "Possess thyself in patience, wench," he said aloud in English. "Thou'lt haf a wash and a bed soon enow."

Melanthe bore it, but she wound her finger in one of the black curls at the nape of his neck and gave it a cautionary tug.

Except to bend his head and pull free, he ignored her while the huntsmen coupled their hounds and the guests mounted. The other women rode pillion, pitched up into place giggling and ardent, with open kisses for their swains. Henry took up a plump blonde maid, no lady, grinning as he rode past. Sir Ruck let Hawk fall in with the other horses. They strung out in a file between the trees.

It was country manners, but no more licentious than many a hunt Melanthe had attended where the hunters had been more interested in their lovers' breasts than in the breaking of the kill, openly fondling one another during the hounds' *curee*. As they rode, Sir Ruck turned his head, reaching for her. Melanthe obligingly leaned nearer, and he put his mouth against the corner of hers, holding his glove over her ear as if to steady her. A day's bristle of beard grazed her skin.

"Sir Geoffrey of Torbec is with Lancaster," he said in French, moving his lips on hers.

Melanthe hugged herself close, leaning her chin on his shoulder. She kissed his cheek and whispered in his ear, "His brother?"

He caught her hand and brought it up to his lips. "Geoffrey has no brother," he murmured into her palm.

"Fie, sir!" She snatched her fingers away.

"So acquit thyseluen in meekness according to thy place, wench." His voice carried in reproving English. "We are nought now alone in the woods, for thee to play off thy noble airs."

She saw Henry lift his hand. "Hold the yoke fast upon her neck, green knight!" he called back in warm humor. "Iwysse, it were wise to keepen such proud women low in their conceit."

Masculine whistles and agreement ran up and down the line. Melanthe slid her fingers into Sir Ruck's hair. "If thou namest me wench again, sir," she said affectionately aloud, "I will see thee racked and flayed."

He looked over his shoulder at her, lifting an eyebrow. "God shield me, wench."

That raised a general laugh. Henry gave his own lady a pinch and slapped his horse's rump, sending it into a trot as they turned onto a better path.

TORBEC MANOR HAD new earthworks and a gatehouse with a door of fresh planks bossed in dark gray iron still shiny from the hammer. Inside, buildings of plaster and lath extended from the old stone hall, ranging about the dirt yard.

Henry had another fanfare blown as they entered the gate, all horns in unison, though there appeared to be no lady of the house waiting to greet the returning hunt. The hounds, freed from their couplings, streamed past the horses toward a kennel-yard fenced against the wall. At the gate, one gallant played with a big lop-eared lymer from his horse, offering the scenting hound a wadded lady's scarf, and then hiding it about his person—a poor game, Melanthe thought, for a hunting dog that ought to concentrate on the smell of its quarry alone.

Sir Ruck seemed to have a particular interest in this kennel, or the scaffold beyond it that supported men at work on the masonry. They appeared to be about repairs. It was not a highly fortified place. He turned away.

Amid the general turmoil of arrival, Henry assigned a servant to them. As the man came forward, kneeling and eyeing Hawk warily, Sir Ruck unpinned his mantle, letting it fall back.

"This needs mending, wench," he said over his shoulder to Melanthe. "Let me see it nought till thy work is done."

Melanthe gathered the mantle, using it to muffle Gryngolet, holding falcon and cloak in a bundle against her breast. The gyrfalcon's talons gripped hard on her glove, and the bells gave a muffled plink, but Gryngolet made no other protest.

Sir Ruck dismounted, swinging his leg high over the saddlebow and dropping to the ground beside her, lifting his arm before the servant could step forward to offer aid. "Come, wench."

Melanthe held her armful of falcon and wool close to her breast as he pulled her down. "I am counting every one, thou shouldst knowen," she said, smiling up at him as her feet touched the ground.

He tapped her cheek with mailed knuckles. "Counting what, wench?"

"Six," she said sweetly, turning to follow the rest into the hall.

He put his hand on her shoulder. "Do nought stray off from me, wench."

"Oh, think thee that I jape?" She stopped. "Seven."

In his eyes was that subtle hint of a smile she was coming to recognize. "Keep thee close. In faith, thou art the comlokkest wench in this company. I be jealous over thee."

"Ah," she said mildly, "four limbs broken, two eyes put out, and thy nose cut off. But eight—wee loo, I shall have to put my mind to eight and show a little invention."

He went down on his knee and hung his head. "Truly, I am villainous," he said in extravagant humility. "I beg my lady's grace. Ye are a true gentlewoman, and no common wench."

One of the other females clapped. "Now shall we have some noble talking! Certain it is that your lady is the more gracious, sir, and deserves dainty words."

Amid feminine acclaim, the men groaned. "I warned you," Henry complained from the hall door. "Now will they all wax wondrous proud, these women, and want us to lie abed and write them poetry!"

Sir Ruck stood up and gave Melanthe a light push. "Nay, nought poetry," he said.

Henry laughed and shrugged. "Haps not. Bid you enter, my lady, and I pray my hall be not too common for your comfort!"

RUCK DID NOT think they had a chance of concealing the gyrfalcon for long. He had a tale prepared for the moment of discovery, but saw no reason to tell it sooner than he must. They would not linger in this place. Ruck disliked the look of it. Henry was preparing for defense—piercing arrowslits in his wall and strengthening his gatehouse and outer works— by hap it was only with the outlaws of the Wyrale in mind, but Sir Geoffrey of Torbec had no brother that Ruck knew.

Still, the servants did not appear misused. The only evidence of distaste for Henry that Ruck had seen was the huntsman's contempt for taking hart out of season. Hospitable the man might be, and affable, but it told something of his nature that he would choose to hunt a hart in fermysoun over a boar fitting to the season.

His guests appeared to be no more than a pack of gaily dressed young ruffians, idle sons of squires and country knights. If the nearness of pestilence concerned them, they answered it with mirth and jest, as some were always wont to do. Still, Ruck looked them over to see if he might make use of a pair or three as an escort. They might be bored and willing, he thought, if he made it worth their while.

As they entered the hall, Henry gave orders that as an honored guest, Ruck be conducted to a private chamber. The princess walked ahead of him past servants setting up the trestle tables in the hall, her muddied ermine sweeping the woven rushes, the gold fret in her hair catching what light there was falling down from the smoke hole in the roof. She did not make a half-convincing wench. It was impossible to pass her off as lowborn; clearly she had sense enough not even to attempt it. But she might be as haughty as she pleased; Ruck had no fear that she would be unmasked. It was all too fantastical. What should these men think, that the heiress of the Earl of Bowland would ride out of the woods mounted astride behind a wandering knight? If he had proclaimed her by name, he could not imagine that they would have believed him.

Ruck was surprised to find himself and his leman favored with a solar room, where the winter sun fell through a barred window onto the bedcurtains and a pair of stools. There was even a chair. The servant knelt before it.

Ruck strode forward and sat down. While the princess stood holding her burden, he thrust out his feet and let the attendant pull off his steel sabatons, then waved the man away. "My woman will despoil me of my harness."

The servant bowed. "Will you have a bath of water, sir?"

"Certes he will!" the princess ordered, gesturing briskly, "Needst thou ask such a witless question? Neither hot ne cold, but temperate, with balms as my lord likes. A fire mote be laid here in the chimney and the bath placed before it. Bring him spices, do ye have them, with good wine."

"Yea, my lady." The servant seemed to hunch before such sharp and easy command.

She followed him as he retreated toward the door. "And rich robes, to the honor of this house. And cushions for his comfort. And—iwysse, inquire of thy master, fool—if he has sojourned in the halls of great men, he will know alwise what is required. See that thou dost not return ere all is suitably in order for a guest of my lord's estate!"

"Yea, my lady. Anon, my lady." The door closed behind him as he bowed out hastily, muttering compliance. Princess Melanthe secured the hasp with her free hand.

"That should keep him some little while," she said, throwing the cloak off her falcon. "If they can find thee a rag worthy of the wearing in this place, I were seized with surprise."

The bird roused and stretched her wings. Ruck stood. Princess Melanthe caused the hooded falcon to step backward onto the arm of the chair he had emptied and then gave him a dry look of question.

"We stay only the night, my lady," he said in answer. He pulled off his gauntlets and opened the buttons on his armor-coat, shrugging it from his shoulders. "If the bird be remarked—I descried and trapped her in the forest, and return her now to the master who was named on her varvels. I do not show her much abroad, for her value is too great to risk."

She took up his cloak and arranged it as if it had been casually flung over the chair back, cascading down to form a tent over the falcon. "The huntsman saw her," she said.

"Yea." Reaching awkwardly behind his shoulder, Ruck tried to unbuckle his cuirass, managing only the uppermost clasp. "But I think me he says little to his lord, for he is too shamed and wroth over the hart. E'en does he, what of it?" He gave up on the buckles, leaned against the wall, and bent down to unfasten his greaves.

"I like it not. Let us fly soon."

He looked up at her. She stood in the middle of the room, staring about at the walls and window with a troubled aspect. "My lady," he said. He straightened and walked to her. "Ye be nought at ease?"

"Nay." She lifted her eyes to his, and then averted them. "Nay, in truth I am not easy in this chamber."

He paused. Awkward silence swallowed the room. She stripped the hawking gauntlet from her hand and cast it down.

"Rather would ye bed with the ladies?" he asked.

"Nay!" she said quickly, and then gave a short laugh. "Ladies, are they? And thou namest *me* wench."

He could see apprehension concealed beneath her taut mirth. He did what he should not have; he put his hand to her cheek, caressing her skin with the pad of his thumb. "My lady, only for your safekeeping."

"Nonetheless, I take account of all these wenches on thy tongue," she said, with determined irony in the curve of her lips. "Thou wilt getten above thyself."

"Nay," he whispered. "Always at your command, sweet lady."

"Ah, God." A small sound came from her throat. "I'm frightened here. Must we have people and intrigue? The forest was better. I would rather have us sleepen upon the ground than be slain in a soft bed."

"What fantasy is this?" He took her face between his hands. "By hap this man n'is nought as good alloy as the sterling, but what would gain him to slay us?"

A barely perceptible tremor passed through her. For a moment she stared up into his eyes, and then let go a sharp sigh. "Nothing," she said. "Nothing. I am witless."

"I will sleep before the door tonight. Ye are safe." The urge to enfold her in his arms near took possession of him. His body read the same longing in hers: she stood still, yet it was as if she were drawn invisibly toward him, as if she waited for him.

Fine as the edge of a blade, the moment held him in balance. He looked at the fingers of his own hands against her skin, not daring to seek her eyes. The sight of his flesh touching hers seemed illusion, shameless confidence, as if he truly possessed the right.

He dropped his hands.

"Will ye given help to me, my lady?" Making effort at a smile, he turned aside. "Be I nought above myseluen to asken it, wench—the buckles."

Thirteen

———∞∞∞———

To WEAR ROBES, however common the woven stuff and decoration might be in Princess Melanthe's estimation, was a luxury that never palled for Ruck. Seldom enough did he leave off his armor in the usual way of things; in the past fortnight he had slept and lived in it as if he were on the march. But for the moment he did not have to tolerate the seam in the *cuir bouilli* where the leather corner had pulled loose and curled when it dried, chafing his left armpit with every step, or ignore the pinch of the cuisses' straps behind his thighs, or bide the clumsy weight of chain mail over every inch of his body. He felt light, as if he were made of thistle silk.

His head felt a little light as well as his body, after whiling the afternoon at Henry's table. Ruck had joined the company's meal alone, leaving Princess Melanthe in their chamber. Staring down into his wine cup, he grew warm thinking of her. She had watched the servant bathe him and dress him, sitting cross-legged upon the bed in that way she did—more wench than gentle lady in that pose, he thought pungently—giving keen orders for his care, insisting upon bobbaunce and pomp as if he were some prince. She had even rejected the first robes they brought, sending back for a better selection. Ruck suspected he was wearing Henry's best Christmas houpelande of blue wool and miniver, chosen by her with disdain from among the sparse variety.

The household seemed torn between resentment at such treatment by a stranger's concubine and awe of her manners. Word had clearly gotten back to Henry. The young man who styled himself the lord of Torbec leaned close at the table and murmured that he supposed Ruck's lady had been some time at court. Ruck had merely shrugged. Henry, wearing an avid look, had ventured the conjecture that she was accustomed to the favor of great men. Ruck leaned back with his wine cup and smiled. "Yea, and cost me the Fiend's expense, she does, to keep her as she's wont," he had said, to dampen any covetous ideas.

"Witterly, I can believe it," Henry said, losing his eagerness and turning to his unpolished country maid with a little better cheer.

A bachelor's hall it was, full of hunting dogs and weaponry, with no mistress to foster seemliness or hold the rougher games in check. After a plain and abundant dinner, no one answered the bell for Nones or left to train in the yard. Instead, they spent all the day and into the evening talking of hunt and battle, arguing the merits of Bordeaux steel against the German, wrestling between themselves or, near as ungently, with their willing ladies.

Ruck offered no opinion on the question of the best steel, though they pressed him for his judgment. He listened to them talk. They had the restless violent vigor of youth, and words enough to spend about weapons and fighting, but no more discipline than a band of untaught mongrels; half wolf and half cur, without the sense to know that only because they sat at table in drink and idle discourse about a warrior's concerns, they were not, ergo, great warriors themselves. He might have made much of them, given the time. But he counted them useless for his immediate need, too full of themselves to be trusted.

Arrowslits in the wall or no, Sir Geoffrey of Torbec would make short work of these infant brigands when he returned from Gascony. However that might be, alone and responsible for the princess, Ruck did not care to stir the hornet's nest.

He sat without saying much, though he took care to be a

pleasant guest, not to smile too little or drink too lightly or leave too soon. At evensong he rose, standing carefully to surmount the turngiddy feel of the wine in his head, and shamed them into mass only by asking the way to the chapel.

HE CAME AT dusk, at last. Melanthe was furious, mad with waiting. She rose and went forward as the servant lit him into the chamber with a branch of candles. As if she were the fondest of lovers, she put her arms about him, stood on tiptoe, and hissed French in his ear. "There are spying holes."

He looked down at her. In the falling shadows his face was handsome; his breath heavy with wine. If he heeded her warning, or had even heard it, he made no sign. He sighed and stood holding her, his hands clasped around her hips.

"I am old," he said gloomily.

Melanthe commanded the servant with a gesture, dismissing him. She had intended to point out to Sir Ruck the carved masks in the wall, where the peeks were concealed, but she hesitated.

"Old," he said. "Three ten years."

She pushed back. "No more old than I, then," she retorted in French, disengaging herself. "So spare my feelings and say no more of it. Come and sit thee down."

There had been watchers off and on at the holes all the day. She could not hazard speaking to him openly, even in French. And she had never seen him in his cups; she did not know how much wit she might expect of him. Haps it were better to curb any discourse and put him readily to bed.

His fingers twined loosely in hers, he let her lead him. He did not sit, but looked at the bed as if it were the grave of a long-lost faithful hound. He shook his head, pulling his hand from hers and reaching for his sword that lay with his armor. "The door," he said, using English. "For your safe keep, my lady."

"My safe keep!" she responded lightly, as if he japed. "What safer than thy close embrace? Best-loved, come thee all haste to bed."

"To bed?" With a newly aware look, he stopped in the midst of a half turn away. "Lady?"

She tilted her head toward the masks, smiling. He only

gazed at her carefully, with the diligent attention of a man mindful of his dazed condition.

"My truelove, my honeycomb—" She put her arms about him again, and leaned until he took a step backward. "Lovedear, sweeting, ne let us not linger in disport and speech as is our wont. I can govern my ardor no longer. I crave a kiss for thy courtesy." Fervently she embraced him, pressing him off balance in the zeal of kisses that she showered over his chin and throat, pushing him step by wavering step until his back met the wall beneath the masks.

Before she could point upward, he grasped her close and hard, making a sudden mockery of her wiles. The abrupt grip stole her balance. His hands spread across her loins, pulling her against his body. With a low, hoarse sound he buried his face in her neck and made a motion of pure lust, straining her to him.

It was no counterfeit passion or monkish restraint. Through the muffling robes, his full member thrust between them. His fingers pressed into her, spreading her buttocks, touching her in a way no man had ever dared touch her. He pushed his knee into the space between her legs, forcing her to open for him as if she were an unwilling whore.

Melanthe drew in a sharp breath as the embrace spun beyond familiar ground. He lifted his head, resting it back against the wall, his eyes closed. But he did not let her go. His hips moved in a pushing stir against hers, without shame, rubbing the firm bulk of his tarse to her belly, even against her privy-most quaint.

Kisses she knew, and courtiers' games of dalliance, but nothing of a man's member beyond the cramp and discomfort of her husband's bodily company, so long past and fleeting that it seemed to have no share of this. A spring of delicious sensation arose from this touching, ungentle though it was, a delight in fleshly vices. She let it take her, became his common wench and leman in truth, as light as these brazen country maids whose loves made no difference to the world beyond their beds.

He was wanton drunk; she knew it, but she made no warning or protest when he sought her lips and kissed her, searching inward with his tongue, wine-flavored and reckless in his trespass. She took his tongue into her mouth and pressed her lap to his in pleasure, welcoming the hunger in him.

His open hands slid across her hips and up to her waist. Her hair was loose. She had left off her heavy azure gown after her bath, to be brushed and cleaned, changing it for a lent one of scarlet that was made for close measure and immodest display.

He ran his hands up and down her sides, from her hips to her breasts. "I haf seen this," he said, his mouth close to hers. "Your white skin." There was a doted awe in his voice. "Your body all bare, below thy mantle."

She smiled, tilting her head back. *"Suis-je belle?"*

"Ye are beauteous," he said, closing his fingers on her hair. "By Christ, ye are beauteous."

From overhead issued a feminine giggle, smothered but distinct. His hands leapt away from Melanthe; he jerked upright, searching the shadowed chamber with appalled bewilderment.

Melanthe put her fist under his jaw and made him look upward. Faint light from the hidden holes illuminated odd shadows, picking out detail in the dusk.

She didn't know if he would recognize what he saw, but just as she was about to lean forward and whisper to him, the strange glimmer vanished as the spy pressed to the peek again, blocking it. Sir Ruck went stiff, turning his shoulder to the wall and staring up.

"Hanged be they," he breathed, his lip curling.

She put her hand over his mouth, leaning close to his ear. "They ne cannot see us here beneath it. Only hear."

Immediately he looked over her head, about the room, not too much in his wine to reason that there would be another peek to cover the blind position. Melanthe knew where it was, but she had already pulled the bed curtain a little way, as if by chance, just blocking the line of sight to where they stood.

His lashes lowered in wine-maze. He gazed down at her, then lifted his eyebrows and blinked, like a man struggling to wake from a walking dream.

She brushed back a rough black curl that had fallen over his ear, brazen wench that she was. "I will serven as thy chamberlain, beau sir, to prepare thee for bed. Come."

•   •   •

IF NOT FOR the wine in his head, Ruck thought, he would
have found a more reasonable means of dealing with the spyholes. He wanted to. He thought of covering them, but she
distracted him, doing out the candles, leaving only the firelight that sprang in crimson arcs over the folds of her gown.
It was cut low across her shoulders and back, the gown; he
watched the curve of her breasts as she leaned to take up a
mantle that had been warming by the chimney, her black hair
falling in a cascade across her shoulder—and then remembered again that he was thinking of some cheat for the spying.

Darkness would do it, but there was the fire. He might
bank that, take up his place on guard by the door; she was like
a living flame in crimson.

He could not keep his mind fixed, not with her beckoning
him near the fire. He went, light of weight in his body and
brain, soft wool brushing his skin. He sat on the stool and let
her pull the robes off over his head. His linen lay drying
before the hearth after washing—beneath the robes he wore
only slippers and socks for his feet. She had seen him in his
bath, his body and the scars of fighting that he carried, but it
embarrassed him anew and painfully now to be exposed, his
scars and his lust together, unworthy of her.

She laid the warmed mantle over his shoulders. He
dragged it around to cover him as she knelt and drew the
socks from his feet, massaging them like a fond wife. Her
hands moved up his calf, and then his thigh. He felt helpless,
in utter wonder of what she might do next. Certes he had
taken too much wine. He could not think in straight lines.

"Right seldom do I drink so deep," he muttered.

"Avoi, I hope thou art not unabled." She touched him
beneath the mantle, caressing her hand boldly over his yard.
He clapped his fingers on her wrist, sucking in his breath.

"In good order, so I see!" she said laughingly, rubbing her
palm against his rigid part in spite of his resistance.

"My lady—" he said.

She stood on her knees on the rush mat, putting her free
arm about his neck. "Thou hast named me common wench all
the day—so now I am becomen one." Leaning close to his ear,
she whispered, "These spies, they moten see loveplay, forsooth? That I am no more than thy leman?"

They must see it? He thought there was some flaw in that reasoning, and arrant iniquity, but her seeking touch seduced him from the last of his wit. She was not tender; her handling was without art to the point of hurting him, but it was *her* hand upon him, and her body leaning close, and he could achieve no more than to pull each breath into his chest with a harsh sound.

"Ye are shameless," he said with effort. "Ah . . . Mary and Jesus."

She hid her face in his shoulder, but she did not stop her unchaste behavior. Then she twisted her wrist free of his hold and took his hand against her, strangely innocent in the way she held it over her womb, stilling her whole body, waiting.

The power of his will broke. He stood, lifting her up in his arms. His limbs acted without his reason—he carried her to the bed. The mantle fell from his shoulders, cold air on his skin as he lay down with her.

Then he let her go and sat up, yanking the bedcurtains closed, shutting out the spyholes, enclosing and muffling the bed in heavily quilted winter hangings.

He stayed sitting up in the bed. He would wait until the fire died and the light was gone, he thought desperately, and then he would take his sword and lie by the door. He would pray. He tried to pray now, his arms gripped about his knees, his forehead down upon them, but his brains spun with drink and passion.

He would think of other things. Important things—where they must go now, whether the falcon had been discovered, how far beyond Lyerpool the plague had spread, if it had spread at all. Her leg rested against his hip. He felt her sit up beside him, running her fingertip down the leather cord about his neck, brushing her mouth against his ear, and then he could not think at all.

"I will go," he whispered. "Lady, I am drunk; do nought kiss me."

"Thou like me not?" she murmured.

"Ye slays me, my lady." He turned his face from her. "Ye slays my reason. I am in wine. I will dishonor you."

She rested her forehead on his bare shoulder and ran her

fingertips down his back. "I wish it," she said, so low that he could hardly hear.

"Nay," he said. "I will nought."

Her hand curled around his arm. She rocked him, her face still pressed to his skin, like a child entreating.

"Ah, lady. I love you too well."

Her fingers slipped away. She was silent, still leaning her forehead against him.

"Who would know?" she asked, muffled. "Once. Only once. For this one night."

He drew a deep breath, speaking low. "My sweet lady, ye hatz a demon of hell in you, that takes hold of your tongue sometimes and tempts me beyond what I can bear."

"'Tis no demon. It is me." Her hand crept up and twined with his. "I have been so much alone. You do not know." She squeezed his fingers. "I did not know, until I found thee."

"My luflych, my precious lady, I have me a wife."

She was still for a long moment. Then she said, "Is that why thou wilt deny me? For thy wife?"

"For my wife. And for the dishonor to you."

"Dost thou love her still?"

He gave a bitter chuckle. "Ten and three years has it been. I ne cannought e'en see her face in my head. But she is my wife, before God and man, for we were rightly wed."

"I thought her a nun."

"Yea," he said.

She lifted her head. In the blackness of the heavy curtains, he could see nothing, only feel her.

"But ne'er have I adultered, or profaned my vows." He paused, gripping his hand tight in hers. "Nought with my body."

She stroked his hair, and his back. "Ah, what have they done to thee, these priests?" she whispered sadly. "Hast thou lived in this thought, that thou art wed and yet bound to be chaste, since that day I saw thee last?"

"In troth," he said, "I have lived in thought of you." He pulled from her and lay back on the bed, staring into darkness. "Awake and asleep, I have thought of you. Else I were dead of despair a hundred times, I think me, if I had nought you in my mind to bind me to virtue." He shook his head. "I am no monkish man, I tell you, lady."

She gave a bewildered soft laugh. "Ne do I understand thee not. *I* bind thee to purity? Thou jape me."

"I swore to you, my lady, in Avignon. When you sent the stones. Then I thought—but I was in a frenzy; I recall it little, but that I swore my life to you. I sold the lesser emerald for arms and a horse, and took me to fighten tournies for the prizes, and then to my liege prince when I had some money and good means to show myseluen. I made your falcon my device and took your gemstone for my color. And when my body tempted me, I thought of you and Isabelle my wife, I thought how you both were pure and good and blameless, better than me, and I mote live with honor for your sake, because I was her husband and your man."

"Depardeu," she murmured. "Thy wife—and I? Blameless and pure? Thou art a blind man."

"I knew naught else to do." He pressed the heels of his hands over his eyes. "And it is impossible, it is nought the same, now that—"

He broke off and blew all the air from his chest in a rough sigh.

"Now that thou knowest me for myself," she said with a tone he could not read, whether amused or sad or bitter, or all three.

"I love you, my lady," he said, his voice suppressed. " 'Tis all certain that I know. With my heart, with my body, though I've nought the right to thinken of it, though you are too high—in faith, though I burn in Hell for it." He swallowed. "God forgive me that I say such things. I'm in drink enow to drownen me."

She lay down beside him, half on top of him, her arm across his shoulders. "Dost thou love me?" she whispered, with an intensity that made him turn his face toward her in the dark.

He lifted his hand—he allowed himself that for the fierce plea in her voice—and brushed the back of his fingers over her cheek. "Beyond reason."

"Oh," she said, and buried her face in his shoulder, hugging herself close. "Yesterday I was a witch in thy estimate."

"Yea, and now ye be a wanton wench, and in a moment ye will be a haughty princess, and I know nought what next to plague and bemaze me."

"Thy lover."

"Nay, lady." He started to rise.

She caught him, holding tight. "No. Do not go."

"I will keep watch by the door."

"No. I will ne be able to sleepen, be thou not near where I can reach thee."

"Lady," he said, "for all the hours ye sleeps, me think this one night be nought such a great loss."

Still she held him. "I can't *sleep*." Her voice was soft, but her fingers had the grip of real dismay.

"God shield, am I to lie beside you in a bed all the night?" he asked. "Have mercy on me."

"I cannot." She would not cease; she pulled him slowly downward. "I cannot have mercy. Please thee—stay."

"Enow!" he said harshly. His shoulder sank into the featherbed. He turned his face to the bolster. "Only touch me nought then, my lady, for your pity."

She let go. He felt her roll over away from him. She was angry, he thought, child-geared in her tempers as only those of high estate could be. But she asked too much; to lie here beside her—in bed, unclothed, as if they were married. He was already mired in mortal lust; now she would have him pay his soul for fornication. God have mercy on him if he died this night, for he was bound for everlasting flames.

Yet she lay still in the blackness, without word or demand, and it gradually came into his head that she was weeping. He listened, trying to subdue the sound of his own breath. He could hear nothing.

She said she had been alone until she had found him. He closed his eyes. Lone he had lived all his life, it seemed, dwelling among dreams of things to come. They were all of them shattered now, lost to her whims—he had hated her for that, and hated her yet, but love and hate turned so close in his heart that they seemed to dazzle him together as one passion. He could tell them apart no more than he knew if she was beautiful or plain—she was neither, more than both, his very self, that he might love or hate as he pleased, but could not disown short of the grave.

He reached out his hand. It came to rest on her hair that was loose, spreading over the pillow. She lay silent. Softly, haltingly, he found the shape of her with his fingertips, her temple, her brow. He touched her cheek and lashes, and felt warm tears.

"I ne did not give thee leave to handle me at thy whim, knave," she said sharply.

He moved, folding her in his arms. "I knew you would come the high princess soon enow," he said with a painful laugh. He leaned near and rocked her against his chest. "My lady queen, your tears are liken to an arrow through my body."

"Pouf," she said. "Monkish man."

He crushed her to him and rubbed his cheek against her hair. "Do you want my honor? I give it you, I will forlie and adulter with you, my lady, then—and God and the Fiend torment me as they will."

He felt her turn toward his face, though he could not see her in the dark. For a long moment she lay very still.

"Were I thy wife, would not be sin," she whispered.

He made a bitter sound of mirth. "Yea—and were I king of all England and France, and a free man."

She put her hands up, seizing his face between her palms. "Listen to me."

The sudden urgency caught his full heed. He waited, but she said nothing. Her fingers moved restlessly, forming fists against his face and opening again.

"Ah," she said, "I know not how . . . it frightens me to wound thee. Best-loved, my true and loyal friend, hast thou never guessed all these years why I denounced thee in Avignon? Why I sent thee thence in haste?"

In a far deep place inside himself, he felt his soul arrested. Slightly he shook his head.

"Thy wife—thinkest thou that they released her to this convent at Saint Cloud? Nay, they sent her to the Congregation of the Holy Office. They sent her to the inquisitors, and they would have sent thee, too, if thou hadst shown that her preachings and raving had convinced thee of aught.

They could not bide her, do you see? A woman to preach, to interpret Scripture—to demand of thee her own oath within thy marriage."

"Nay," he breathed. "Nay—the archbishop—he said a place was made for her at Saint Cloud. I paid for it! For her keep—my money and my horse and arms."

She did not answer. In the hush he thought of the letters he'd sent, the money, every year with no word of reply.

"Oh, Mary, Mother of God—where is she?" He sat up, gripping her shoulders.

She stroked her palms up and down his face.

Ruck groaned. He let go of her and rolled away, trying to find the breath that seemed suddenly to have left his lungs. "Imprisoned?"

But he knew she was not imprisoned. He knew by the silence, by the way the princess did not move or touch him, only waited.

"I forsook her." His body began to shake, his hands clenching and unclenching, beyond his command. "Helas, I abandoned her."

"Listen to me." Her cold voice abruptly cut like a scourge. "She abandoned thee. I heard her, if thou hast forgot. She was no saint, nor holy woman, nor even a fit wife for such as thee."

"Her visions—"

"Pah!" she spat. "They weren no more of God than a peacock's preenings. I tell thee, sir, when I married I did not love my husband, but I gave back to him the same honor and duty that he gave to me. I did not weep and scream and claim God sent some handy vision to free me from my vows. Nor do the world of women, but live the half of them without complaint in such subjection as thou canst not conceive, not one in ten thousand so fortunate as she!" Her voice was a throbbing hiss. "I loved my husband well enough in the end, but the life that I have lived for his sake—I would have given my soul to have thy wife's place instead, with a good steadfast man to defenden me and children of my own. And she foreswore thee, for her vain pride, no more, so that she mote be called sainted and pure by such foolish sots as would drivel upon her holiness. By Christ, I would have burned her myself, had she taken thee adown with her as she was wont to do!"

He took a shuddering breath of air. "She was burned?"

"Yea," she said in a calmer voice. "I am sorry. There was naught to be done for her, for she brought it upon herself. They declared her a Beguine, an adherent of the Free Spirit."

"Isabelle," he said. Horror crept over him. "In God's name, to burn!" He began to breathe faster, seeing the image of it, hearing it.

"Ne did she not suffer," the princess said in a steady voice. "She was given a posset to stupefy her, even before she heard the sentence passed, and kept so to the end. I have no doubt she went to sleep still in full assurance she was regarded as a saint."

He turned toward her in the dark. "You know it so, my lady?"

"Yea. I know it."

He stared at her, at the source of her cold and even voice. "I do nought believe you."

"Then I will given thee the name of the priest I paid to intoxicate her. He was Fra Marcus Rovere then; now he is a cardinal deacon at Avignon."

"You—" He felt benumbed. "Why?"

"Why! I know not why! Because her witless husband loved her, stupid man, and I knew thou couldst do naught. Because my window gave out on the court, and I ne did nought wish my nap disturbed. Why else?"

He lay back, his hands pressed to his skull. No tears came to his eyes. He thought of the times he had wished Isabelle dead, to free him, and the penance he had done for it. Of how she had been a burgher's daughter—never could he have brought her openly to Lancaster's court even before she came to believe she was consecrated to God, never could he have held a knight's place there with a baseborn woman to wife. He thought of the first days of their marriage, his joy in her body and her smile, the end of his loneliness, it had seemed, and in his first battle the worst, most shameful unvoiced fear, not of pain, which he knew well enough, nor of dying itself, but of dying before he might bed her again, couple with her on the pillows and look at her.

She was the only woman he had ever lain with in his life—and she had been dead for thirteen years, ashes and charred bone.

He heard the sound he made, a meaningless dry moan like a man at the last reach of his strength. He should weep. But plaint and lament choked in his throat. He could only lie and hold his hands to his head as if he could imprison the mêlée of thoughts there, his muscles straining with each indrawn breath.

"I cannought remember her face!" he cried. "Oh, sweet Mary save me, I can only see you."

"Shhh." She put her finger to his lips. "Hush." She rubbed the side of his face in a quiet cadence, a firm chafing pressure. "That is not marvelous. Iwysse, I am here with thee, best-loved. Is no more than that."

He reached up and caught her arms. "Do nought stray out from my shield, my lady," he said fiercely. He pulled her down against him. "Leave me nought."

"Never," she said. "If it be within my power, never."

Her breath stirred lightly on his face. She lay half atop him, the wool of her gown spread over his leg and thigh. He held her there.

"Nor will I leave you." He bound her wrists in both his hands. "Ne'er, lady, lest ye sends me from you."

The rise and fall of his chest lifted her, so close she was. Though he could barely see her as but a blacker shadow on blackness, he felt her weight, her hushed submission to his grasp. Her loose hair fell down between them, as if she were a maid. As if she were his wife.

"Lady," he whispered, "God shield me, I have thoughts in my head that are very madness."

"What is thy true name and place?" she asked softly.

A distant part of him seemed to know what came to him, what gift of unthinkable value, but his tongue felt near too numb to form the words. "Ruadrik," he said in a dry throat. "Wolfscar."

His hands where they gripped her arms were trembling. Only her steadiness held him motionless.

"Sir Ruadrik of Wolfscar," she said, "here I take thee, if thou will it, as my husband, to have and to holden, at bed and at board, for better for worsen, in sickness and health, til death us depart, and of this I give thee my faith. Dost thou will it?"

Only a little shiver beneath his hands and a break in her final question gave a hint that she was not calm.

"My lady, it is madness."

Her body tightened in his arms. "Dost thou will it?"

He stared up into the dark at her, bereft of words.

"Dost thou believe it is no bargain for me?" she asked in a voice spun as fragile as glass. "I told thee what I would give to be wife to thee. Dost thou will it?"

"Lady—have a care of your words, and make game of me nought, for I haf the will in my heart to answer you in troth."

"In troth have I spoken. Here and now I take thee, Ruadrik of Wolfscar, as my wedded husband, if thou wilt have me."

He turned his right hand, lacing his fingers into hers. "Lady Melanthe—Princess—" His voice failed as the immensity of it overcame him. He swallowed. "Princess of Monteverde, Countess of Bowland—my lady—I humbly take you—take thee—ah, God forgive me, but I take thee with my whole heart, though I be nought worthy, I take thee as my wedded wife to have and to hold, for fairer or fouler, in sickness and in health—for my life so long as I shall have it. Thereto I plight thee my troth." He closed his fist hard over her fingers. "I have no ring. By my right hand I wed thee, and by my right hand I honor thee with the whole of my gold and silver, and by my right hand I dow thee with all that is mine."

For a long moment neither of them moved or spoke. Beyond the heavy curtains there was a faint sigh of coals falling in upon themselves.

"Ne do I have flowers, nor a garland to kiss thee through," he murmured, cupping her face. He leaned up and pressed his lips softly against hers. At first she seemed frozen, cool as marble, and a bolt of apprehension passed through his heart, for fear that she had done it all as a mocking jape—but then she gave a low whimper and kissed him in return, hard and ruthless, as her kisses were wont to be. She put her arms about his shoulders and held to him tightly, her face pressed into his throat.

He lay gazing upward, full of bliss and horror. The world

seemed to go in a slow spin about him. He did not know if it was drink or amazement.

Then he embraced her and rolled her onto her back, overlying her, using his hands to master the awkward tangle of her skirts, his rigid tarse to search out her place urgently. He mounted her, sinking inside with a groan like a beast. A fearsome ache of pleasure shot from his belly through his limbs. It drowned his senses; from a distance he felt her clutch at him, heard her swift breath—but with all the strength in him he could not stop to satisfy her. With a violent thrust he spilled his seed in her womb.

He used and possessed her to bind his right, before God, sealing her beyond resort or recourse as his wife. And when it was finished, he laid his face against her breast and wept for Isabelle, for joy, and for mortal dread of what they had just done.

Fourteen

SHE HELD HIM as he grieved, and lay waking long after the shudders of rough sobs had passed through him. He wept like a man who had lost child and kin and future. And then he slept profoundly, weight upon her such that she could hardly breathe, but she never ceased stroking her fingers through his hair.

She was jealous of his silly and dangerous wife, that he mourned her so. And yet Melanthe thought that it was his lost years and distorted vision that he mourned—pure and gentle nun that he had seemed to make the woman out for be. Melanthe remembered a shrieking and offensive female, full of herself and her prophecy, and a part of her longed to recall it to him in forceful detail. But she thought, with a little wonder at herself, that she did not care so much for her own discontent, if to undeceive him would cause him further pain.

Lying with him seemed enough. It was entirely new to her, so different was he from Ligurio, and from Allegreto's lithe and constant tension that had haunted all her nights. Ligurio had been gentler, without urgency, courteous in his dealing with her. She suspected now that he had already been ill when he had consummated their marriage, coming to her bed for the first time on her sixteenth birthday, and seldom enough in the year after, until he had not come at all.

She felt now as she thought other women must, with her lover sprawled warm and heavy upon her in trusting insensibility. Where Allegreto had the supple light shape of a beardless youth, Ruadrik's arms and shoulders were solid, hard-muscled, his cheek prickly on her bared breast and his leg a dense weight across her thigh. Even to bed, Allegreto wore hose stuffed to make him appear full intact and more; Sir Ruadrik lay with the broad expanse of his back naked to the night air, quite undeniably whole and male, having wept and gone to sleep still filling her, sliding gradually free until she felt the strange touch of his parts, heated between their bodies, a feather brush now where he had been stiff, a gentle pressure instead of invasion.

She ran her fingers down his body and then pressed her arms lightly around him. She hoped his man's sperm engendered a child in her already; and let the king . . .

God shield them, let the king and the court not know until she had time to consider. Never until this extraordinary hour had it come into her mind to make a secret marriage, and to such a man as this. It was incredible. She would have scorned to ashes the witlessness of any other woman who was so foolhardy assotted of a lover as to put her possessions in such peril.

Neither crown nor church would dispute her right to marry—but to wed without the king's permission, to carry her vassal lands with her to a man without her liege lord's approval—that was another offense entirely. Not a jury in the land would uphold her claim to such a thing She might find herself a poor goodwife in truth for this night's work.

And yet she cared naught. If she could have him lie over her all the nights of her life, if she could bear his children—iwysse, she would sweep the hearth herself if she must.

But she wound her fingers through his hair and considered. It was perhaps not so impossible a thing that she had done. The old king, assotted himself, might be persuaded to smile upon her, a weak-willed and love-smitten female. It was not a match that would threaten any royal power or prerogative. Indeed there were advantages. She had not thought of marrying because she had never thought she would care to marry again. Certain she had never had the uncouth thought she would marry beneath herself, or relinquish her lawful right to refuse any man below her station.

But now that she gave her attention to the matter, she saw that to make a humble marriage was not an ill solution. She would have a man's protection, and the crown would have the certainty that she could not join her property to another great domain that might threaten the throne. Wherever this place of his might be, this Wolfscar, she had never heard of it. Another Torbec, no doubt, some remote and paltry manor he would be glad to forget.

And there was Gian . . . but Allegreto was dead, and Gian had lost his ability to daunt her, so far away he was. She had left him with the smiling promise that she would return to him with control of her English possessions and income, for the greater glory of Monteverde. It would take him a long time to fathom that she did not intend to come back, if he fathomed it at all. Every man had one blindness, Ligurio had taught her, no matter how clever he might be. Gian's was Monteverde. When he learned where her quitclaim had gone, he could turn his obsession to a new center and leave her in peace to marry whom she pleased.

Not that he was like to leave her entirely in peace, but his reach was not long enough to be fearsome here. And he was not a man who wasted his energy in any task, including revenge, that did not move him toward his goal.

Yes, a mere goodwife of far distant England, quitted of all claim to Monteverde, was of little interest to Gian Navona. And the king was pliable, his favorites unprincipled and open to bribe.

Melanthe smiled, smoothing her husband's unruly hair. She toyed with one lock that would not lie straight, curling and uncurling it about her forefinger as she fell into sleep.

IN THE FRIGID dawn light of the stables, Ruck saw to Hawk's keep, giving the horse-groom twopence for his work. The man had cleaned Hawk's harness, for which Ruck was grateful—between his headache and his gritty eyes and the uneasiness of his belly, it was all he could do to examine the gear. Bending to pick up the destrier's hooves was beyond his power without feeling as if his stomach would bolk.

He would have thought the past night a dream, but for the way he felt this morning. Sometimes he still thought he must have imagined it in a drunken haze, but it had been no fantasy that he had woken this morning with the Princess Melanthe's hair spread across his arm and her body curled into his embrace.

He walked back into the yard, holding his cold fingers stuffed under his arms, and stood staring up at the window of the room where they had slept. Where she slumbered still, languid and warm as he had left the bed.

When he had married Isabelle, her father had given a betrothal feast, and they had lived together in his house. There was to have been a mass and wedding on the church porch, and another greater celebration, but when Ruck had gotten the opportunity to go to France, they had hurried the thing forward and wed in the street instead, so that if he were killed all her friends and relatives would know her a lady and his true wife. Her father had been anxious for a public show of that.

The burgher had wanted his grandchildren to be called gentle and had been furious when he heard that Isabelle had left Ruck for a nunnery. The man had dragged Ruck into the same street and declared to all the passersby that he washed his hands of his daughter. Ruck had visited him twice after, but it had been no comfortable thing. When he went a third time, and found that the man had died of an ague, Ruck had not been over sorry to be relieved of the duty.

Everything about his first marriage had been open and public. But he knew this second one to be as binding. He had heard of men divorced from a wife when another woman had sworn to earlier vows spoken rightly, witnessed or no, whether it be in a tavern or under a tree or in bed.

It was a true thing, sealing them until death.

He had meant it to be.

This morning, feeling stuporous and ill, he could not believe he had possessed the boldness. He pushed his hair back with cold-clumsy fingers, wondering if she would laugh at him now, and say that she had slipped in some stipulation that he had not heard—she married him if he would bring her the Holy Grail, or some such thing as peasants said to one another when they were playing May games.

It did not matter, he thought sullenly. He had spent thirteen years as one half of a marriage—if he was to spend the remainder of his life the same, what of it?

He nodded to one of the young hedge knights who crossed the yard yawning and carrying a mug of ale. The fellow gave Ruck a grin and a shove on the shoulder as he passed. "Long night in the lists?"

Ruck caught his arm, took the mug, and drained it, ignoring the yelp of protest. He stood still, trying to decide if he would cast or not, concluded that he would not, and opened his eyes. He handed the mug back. "Grant merci."

This one was not quite as old as his friends, sandy-haired and high-colored, wearing a doublet of surpassing shortness over flesh-toned hose. He gave a cheerful, wry shrug. "And welcome."

Ruck paused. He looked the young man in the eye. "Take heed," he said quietly. "Ne do nought be here amongst this company when Sir Geoffrey returns."

The youngster gazed at him warily.

"There will be a fight." Ruck nodded toward the hall. "They will lose."

"What dost thou know of it?"

Ruck put the heels of his hands to his eyes, rubbing. "Enow."

"Art thou from Sir Geoffrey?"

He dropped his hands and grimaced. "No. It is only free advice. My thanks to thee for the ale."

He walked on, turning in to the door of the hall.

MELANTHE WAS DRESSED in her own gown again. She had not let it out of her sight, not with these "ladies" so willing to help, offering to take things away to mend or brush. The day before, to evade their endeavors, Melanthe had made a show of being afraid of Sir Ruck, who had given all her clothes to her and demanded that she repair his cloak with her own hands. The other women had nodded in ready understanding of that and agreed that she would be prudent not to risk his temper.

Obtaining a pair of scissors, Melanthe had sat down in the tall-backed chair and spread the corner of the mantle across her lap, pretending to work it, managing to cut off Gryngolet's bells under cover of the wool. She sewed them to the collar tips, remarking that the embellishment had been about to fall off the cloak earlier, and it was well that she'd noticed and thought to pull them free and secure them in a pocket.

The ladies had showed little interest in the bells or the plain mantle. They were far more fascinated by her ermine and her jeweled gloves, brushing them reverently and remarking on the great French lady who must have owned them. But even that attraction had not kept them when the shout had gone up demanding their attendance on their lordships in the hall. With smiles and chortles they had flocked down the stairs, leaving Melanthe and Gryngolet in peace but for the spy peeks.

She was well-pleased to be departing this place, and worked to have what little there was to do in readiness before Ruck came back. Gryngolet had fouled the floor beneath the chair arm, but Melanthe obscured that by turning over the rush mat. No one seemed to be at the peeks this morning—all lying abed dissipated from drink, she supposed. She was surprised that Ruck had managed to rise and dress and leave the solar before she woke.

She was not concerned that he had gone far, for his armor and sword remained. But the sun was well up and the yard full of servants' voices before he returned to their chamber.

As he came in, she looked up quickly, finding her heart abruptly in her throat. She had a smile ready, but he did not smile, or even look at her. He glanced toward the peekholes and then walked over to his armor and bent to pick up the plate.

A strange alarm possessed her. She looked at him with a feeling of having gone too fast. Was she married to this man—actually bound—united to him for all of the unknown future?

"We wenden us the moment ye are ready, my lady," he said to the cuirass in his hands. There was no welcome or fondness in his voice, only a stiff and brooding subservience.

"Good morn," she said. "Husband."

He held the armor, his head bent. She could see color in his neck.

He lowered the cuirass. Quietly and fiercely, without lifting his eyes, he said, "Yea, husband. I swore nought in jest, my lady, though ye may regret it this morn."

She pressed her lips together. The fear rose higher in her, the realization that she had given him a power over her; that even if she should regret it, she could not undo it. Bone-deep, she felt the weakness he represented. She had made a vow to him. And worse, oh, worst of all—she had let herself love him.

He threw the armor down with a clash and a wordless curse. He turned his face from her, setting his arm against the bedpost.

"If I say to thee"—Melanthe's voice was unsteady—"that I cherish and love thee, but that I am frightened at the weight of it—wouldst thou understand me?"

He leaned his forehead against the post. "Frightened!" he said with a muffled laugh. "I am so seized with love that I haf me a mortal dread e'en to looken at you."

She took a soft step toward him. "Dread of a mere wench . . . and thy wife?"

He turned. Without lifting his head, he reached out and pulled her close to his chest. He held her tight. Melanthe leaned her head on his shoulder.

"I know nought what we are to do," he muttered. "I know nought what can come of this."

"Let us be gone from here in haste," she said.

He released her. "Yea, my lady. I haf packed us food from the larder here—we will make away and come to your hold at Bowland."

Melanthe did not say that she would rather have dwelt alone with him in the forest for the rest of her life. He would not understand her; he would think her reluctant because of him. She watched him as he donned his armor, helping him with the buckles and straps that he could not reach.

When he had his plate and mail upon him, she held up his surcoat. He stepped back, sliding his arms into the sleeve holes. Melanthe buttoned him down the front and then brushed the wrinkles out. It seemed a wifely thing to do.

• • •

As Sir Ruck made farewells in the yard, standing beside Hawk and speaking a courteous word to each of the men, Melanthe lingered on the steps to the hall porch. She carried Gryngolet in the bundled cloak—feeling too noticeable to stand beside Ruck amid the company of guests and servants.

She did not care for these knights, if knights they could be called. Ruffians, more like, playing at fine manners. One of them stood near, attempting to lovetalk her, but Melanthe ignored him haughtily. He was a good-looking wretch who clearly fancied himself with the ladies, his chestnut hair curled and his doublet padded out like a pouting pigeon. She would have eaten him alive in Italy, led him on and made such a mock of him that he could not have shown his face in public after, but now she wished only to be gone.

He came up onto the porch, disposing himself so that he showed a fine length of hose and slender leg. "My heart was full broke," he said, "that thou didst not come down to the hall yesterday, lovely. And now thou art on thy way."

Melanthe gave him a look of disdain. She would not retreat a step, lest he think he had success at stalking her.

He moved about behind, into the shadow of the porch. "A kiss to God-speed thee, sweetheart." He laid a hand on her shoulder. "Look, he's not watching."

"Thy swaddling drags, infant."

His hand dropped away. She took the moment to move out of the cover, but before she could advance, he gripped her arm. It was the one on which she held Gryngolet; she stopped, unable to jerk free without risking the falcon. In the moment of her hesitation, he hauled her up into the porch and pressed her back to the wall, holding her shoulders.

"Scream if thou wilt," he said. "It is fifteen to one against him." He grinned in the half-light. "Haps I'll give thee a better parting gift than a kiss, my duck, here and now."

Her free hand was already on her dagger. She saw a figure behind him, but Melanthe made a cut just to instruct the fellow. He jumped back with a shriek into Sir Ruck's arms.

"Thy duck renays thy gift, infant," she said coldly.

He was bleeding from a light slash across his upper thigh. Sir Ruck scowled fiercely, gripping the man, but the corners of his mouth would not quite turn downward.

"Vicious bitch!" Her bleeding gallant made a lunge toward her, but could not free himself.

"Give thanks that I ne did not prune thee entire," she said, and swept away, off the porch.

"Bitch!" A scuffle sounded behind her. "Thieving, whoring bitch—stop her! Henry! There's something in that bundle!"

Melanthe halted. They stood about her, some grinning, some grim. Henry looked at her and then up at the porch. "In the bundle? Nay, sir—is this how you return my hospitality? To steal from me?"

Sir Ruck let go of his prisoner and strode down the steps. "Ne would I. Only the food ye ha'e offered us freely do we take, and God give you grace for it. Naught that she carries belongs to thee, in faith."

"Let us see it then."

"I will tell you what she holds," Ruck said. "It is a falcon that I recovered in the forest. We take her to her rightful owner."

"A falcon!" Clearly they had had no such notion. Henry looked about him and then insisted, "Nay, I will see it."

Melanthe glanced at Sir Ruck. He nodded at her. "Uncover her, then."

She was wary of this, but saw no choice. Gently she lifted the folds of the mantle, allowing Gryngolet's hooded head to appear. She kept the wool draped over the rest of her, hoping that would be enough. It was a plain white hunting hood, adorned only with some silver leaf and green and white plumes. She did not allow the snowy feathers of the gyrfalcon's shoulders to show.

A ripple of regard passed through the company. Gryngolet turned her head, opening her beak to the cold air.

"What, a falcon peregrine, by Christ? Why did ye not say? We would have put her in the mews last night. Who owns her?"

"A lord of the midlands," Ruck said shortly. "I durst nought mix her with other birds, sir, if it offend you nought."

Henry shrugged. "Our hawks are in health," he said with a little indignation.

"She n'is nought mine," he said. "I mote take extraordinary care."

"Yea, there will be a reward in this—" Henry paused. He grinned. "Whose is she?"

The light of greed in his eyes was unmistakable. Ruck walked to his destrier's head, taking the reins. "Come," he said to Melanthe. "Sir, I recovered the falcon, and such reward as there might be, though I think it be little enow but a few shillings and thanks, belongs to me."

"Is she the king's?" Henry demanded. "Hold the horse, Tom!"

"Nought the king's, nay."

Sir Ruck caught Melanthe at the waist and lifted her, but Henry lunged forward, pulling him backward off balance. Melanthe's feet hit the ground; she stumbled for balance, clutching Gryngolet to her breast.

Henry grabbed her arm. "I'll see the varvels for myself," he snapped.

Melanthe held the gyrfalcon close. "Here—" She flicked the wool mantle back from her wrist, revealing Gryngolet's jesses dangling from within her closed gauntlet. "Canst thou read, my prince?"

Henry cast her a bristling glance and caught the leash, holding it out to peer closely at the flat rings of the varvels where her name was engraved. Like the hood, they were extras for the field that she carried in her hawking bag, made of silver but unadorned.

"Is in Latin. Pri—ah . . . Mont—verd?" He dropped the jesses. "Never have I heard tell of the man. Where dwells he?" Before anyone could answer, he grabbed a jess again and reexamined it. "Princ—i—pissa? Is he a prince, by God?"

"A princess," said the bleeding gallant. "A foreigner."

Henry scowled. "Foreign."

"Let me see." Her troublesome lecher moved closer, taking up the jesses. He examined them both. " 'Bow'—the leash has rubbed the letters. 'Count—of Bow and—' "

"Give me the bird, wench, and mount." Ruck held out his thickly gloved fist. "Ne do nought stond there, as if thou be rooted to the ground."

"Hold!" Henry gripped his wrist. "Ye've had my hospitality, ye and your leman, green fellow, without e'en the courtesy of your name. Do ye deny me a small token of your thanks?"

Ruck tore his hand from the other man's grasp. "If it is the falcon you desire, n'is nought mine to give."

Henry smiled. "Only let me carry it. A prince's falcon. When will I have such a chance?"

Sir Ruck stared for a moment at him, and then looked at Melanthe. "Let him carry it, then."

She drew in her breath, standing still.

"Give me the leash, wench, and mount," Ruck snapped. "Do as I say!"

She let the folded leash drop from her lower fingers, gathering it untidily in her fist.

"Bring me my glove!" Henry ordered. "All haste!" A servant ran. "Strike the hood. Let me see her."

Melanthe glanced at Ruck, feeling her heartbeat rise. "I know not how."

"Nay, I've had nonsense enow of thee," he said as he moved close. He drew the braces open himself, took the plumes between his fingers and lifted the hood. He reached to slip the wool from Gryngolet's shoulders, but now that the gyrfalcon could see, her patience reached its limit. She screamed, lifting her wings. Without thinking, Melanthe let the mantle drop, fearing she would bate and tangle in it, breaking feathers.

Gryngolet's white plumage glowed, marked only by the dark, shining fury in her eyes as she rowed the air, shrieking her displeasure with this place and her treatment.

In the astounded silence her shrilling was the only sound. Even the loose dogs stopped and looked up. Sir Ruck was the single human who moved, closing his hands about Gryngolet's body the moment that she folded her wings.

"Mount!" he said through his teeth as the gyrfalcon shrieked again. He lifted her from Melanthe's fist.

He was looking at Melanthe as vehemently as the trapped falcon stared at her tormentors. A boy ran up with Lord Henry's glove and bag. Melanthe held to Gryngolet's tangled leash, and let go. She gave Ruck a beseeching look, not to lose her dearest treasure.

But he only glared at her and jerked his head toward the destrier.

"A white gyr," Henry breathed reverently, pulling on his

gauntlet. "Pure white, by all that's holy!" He took the jesses and wadded leash as Sir Ruck set the falcon upon his hand. "Ah . . . depardeu, she is glorious."

"I haf heard the penalty for theft of such," Sir Ruck said. "An ounce of flesh cut from the thief's breast and fed to the bird." He put his hands at Melanthe's waist and lifted her up onto the pillion.

"Nay, do you think I mean to stealen her?" Henry asked with a false and sweet indignation. He reached to untangle the leash, but Gryngolet bit wildly at him, almost bating off his fist. He jerked his hand away with a curse.

Sir Ruck was still looking up, scowling intently. Melanthe shifted her leg across the horse and sat astride.

"I think you too wise a man, my lord," he said, mounting up before her and glancing down at Henry. "Now ye hatz carried her, we will take her back to her true owner."

The lord of Torbec was still trying to straighten the leash. Unable to risk his free hand near the bird, he opened his lower fingers to let the tether fall free of its tangle. Melanthe saw him do it; she saw Gryngolet bate again, thrusting off, her powerful wings scooping air—and the falcon bounded free, tearing the twisted leash from his loose fingers and carrying it away.

Henry clutched at thin air, as if he could grab her, but she was gone, pumping up over the stables and the wall. "A lure!" he shouted. "Oh, Christ—here—bring her in!"

A chorus of whistles and frantic shouts followed Gryngolet. Sir Ruck reached back and grabbed Melanthe's arm, gripping so tightly that a whimper of pain escaped her instead of the cry to call the falcon home that sprang to her throat.

"Please!" she hissed. Gryngolet had swung back, circling and playing in lazy drifts over the yard, still gripping the tangle of leash, unaccustomed to being flown from inside manor walls where dogs and people were milling in confusion.

"Get back, give me room!" Henry held up a leather lure, with a hastily attached garnish of meat from the mews. He shouted and whistled, whirling the temptation overhead as the company scattered.

The falcon dropped playfully toward the toll and rolled out

of her stoop halfway, dancing upward over the hall roof. She circled the yard, ringing up to a higher pitch before she stooped again. Henry threw down the lure as she came.

Ruck still held Melanthe in a death grip. Gryngolet dived on the downed lure and made a cut at it, leash and all, then passed right on over the gatehouse. She soared, silent without her bells. She was in one of her mirthful moods, twisting and pumping lazily, looking back at them as if in jest.

Henry whistled frantically, swinging the toll again. Melanthe's heart was in her mouth. She feared the garnish was of pork, a meat that Gryngolet loathed. With no bells to locate the falcon, the dangling leash was a death warrant for her if she escaped now—she would catch it in a tree and hang head downward until she died.

Gryngolet turned back. She almost came to light on the gatehouse, then changed her mind, nearly catching a loop of the leash on an empty banner pole. Curious of the whistling, the gyrfalcon sailed over them, looking for the other hunting birds that she would expect to see among the company—for Melanthe's usual call was no whistle, but her own voice.

The lure spun. Gryngolet trifled about it. She swung in dilatory circles just over their heads. After a few rings she began to ignore the lure and tighten her compass, centering on Melanthe.

Everyone in the yard stared in silence as the falcon swung about her, disdaining the meat, passing Melanthe's head so close she could feel the windy whisper. Sir Ruck kept her hand forced down.

"*Princess!*" It was the chestnut-haired gallant shouting. "Shut the gate! Look at it—Christ's rood, she's a princess!" He began to run for the passage. "That bird belongs to *her!*"

Ruck released her hand. Instantly Melanthe lifted it, calling Gryngolet urgently to her fist as he spurred the horse. There were men already running toward the gatehouse, Henry yelling frenzied commands, a sudden tumult, shouts of *"Princess!"* and "To ransom!"

Gryngolet came, landing just as the destrier lunged into motion. Melanthe grappled for the tangled leash; in the sudden thrust forward the gyrfalcon near fell backward, beating her wings, but her talons gripped and Melanthe swung her arm back to absorb the force.

A pair of men almost reached the gate too soon, but a blond youth in skin-toned hose collided with them, such a bumble that it was as if he'd intended it, sending them all sprawling to the ground only a foot from the horse's massive hooves. Hawk swept past them.

His hooves hit the bridge like the sound of boulders rolling, a pounding rumble and then the wind as he lengthened his stride to a gallop beyond the walls.

SIR RUCK GUIDED the stallion out from among the trees into an abandoned charcoal burners' clearing. They had made haste some distance down the road from the manor of Torbec and finally slowed to a walk, allowing Melanthe a few moments to untangle the leash and jesses she'd been gripping and arrange herself and Gryngolet to more secure positions. When he'd turned the horse off the road, circling back through the forest, Melanthe had realized for the first time that they had been fleeing in the same direction they had first come to Torbec.

They had traveled without speaking. Melanthe did not know whether they passed near again to Torbec; the woods were thick and crossed by many paths. He had reined the horse sometimes left and sometimes right, halting now and then to shade his eyes and look up through the bare branches at the winter sun. His mantle was missing, dropped in the yard in the wrangling over Gryngolet, and the light gleamed on his shoulder harness, showing scratches and the arcs of cleaning scours in the green-tinged plate.

In the deserted clearing they dismounted. Gryngolet was flustered and hungry, and Melanthe felt likewise. Sir Ruck reached for the bag of foodstuffs. "Sit you, my lady, if you will, and take refreshment."

He nodded toward a thronelike seat that had been cut out of a tree stump. Melanthe perched Gryngolet there on the tall back of it, tying the leash to a heavy shoot that had sprouted from the old roots. He brought the bag and handed her a piece of rolled fustian.

"I did steal something of Henry after all," he said. "Two cockerels fresh from a hen's nest, for the bird."

Melanthe accepted the packet, drawing a deep breath. "Almost were we without need of food for her."

He shrugged. "With a choice betwixt the two of you to bringen out of there—" He hesitated. "In faith, I reckon that a wife warms me more pleasantly than a falcon, my lady."

Immediately he turned away, as if he shied from his brash speaking. He squatted down and held the food bag open, scowling into it.

Melanthe felt the touch of shyness, too. She laid one of the cockerels across her glove and offered it to Gryngolet, then sat down on the edge of the tree stump, taking refuge in a pragmatic tone. "We could have ransomed her back, if that little mar-hawk of a lord could have retained her long enough." She made herself look at him, though his head was still bent over the food. "Sir Ruadrik, I have been in consideration of our nuptial contract."

His hand arrested in his laying out of bread and cheese. Then he went on with the task, saying nothing. He rose and bent knee before her, offering food on a white cloth. Melanthe took it on her lap.

"There are many matters to be studied," she said. "My dower and thy courtesy, and—how best to reconcile the king that we have married without his license."

"My lady wife." He stood up. "I ne haf thought on naught else all this morn. If ye wish it—" He stared past her at the ground, his face grim and empty of emotion. "There was no witness on earth to our vows. Nill I nought hold you fast to your words, do you think on them today, that they were said in haste or to your harm. It is a poor cheap for thee, such a marriage. All the advantage be mine, though I seek it nought. I ask nothing of thy wealth; I will have none of it, and yet still I know that the king may in his anger strippen thee of what is rightfully thine. Therefore, I will release thee from any duty or avowel to me, if thou wish it so." He raised his eyes to meet hers, his jaw firm-set. "As for myseluen—if be so much as high treason that I haf married thee, then I will die for it, but ne'er will I forswear it."

"How then could I do less for thee?" she asked softly.

He turned away to the horse, removing its bit so it could graze. With his back to her he said, "God save us both."

"Amen," she said. "Have a little faith in my wits, too. I have me more than the king."

He remained gazing at the horse and then looked over his shoulder with a slight smile. "My lady, look what you come to—" He shook his head, opening his arms to take in the clearing. "A stump for a chair and me for a husband. There be peahens with greater wits than yours."

"A poor comment on the king," she said.

He turned, with a serious look. "When I haf my lady safe, I will go and supplicate of him at any price, that thou moste nought be disseized of thy possessions and title on account of me."

"Nay, leave the king to me." She frowned thoughtfully at the black mound of a decaying charcoal kiln. "I think His Majesty may be appeased, if the thing is laid before him deftly. And even should he not, or someone else make trouble—well, I have searched on the matter in my heart." She took a deep breath. "I have said that my estates are of no great concern to me. I will sweepen the hearth myself if I mote."

He laughed aloud, a sound that rang in the little clearing— the first time Melanthe had ever heard his uncontained amusement.

She turned in indignation. "Thinkest thee I would not?"

He was grinning at her. "I think me thou wouldst maffle the business right royally, madam."

"Pah." She flicked her fingers and ate a bit of cheese. "How difficult can it be?"

He came to her and took her face between his bare hands. "Ye ne were born to sweepen a hearth. I'm nought so poor that my wife mote be a chare woman, but n'would I haf thy property reduced one shilling by cause of me."

"Think again on it. The favor of kings be not meanly bought. For such a crime as this, gifts and presents moten be spent to appease him." She lifted her brows. "Lest thou wouldst rather forswear this marriage thyself, so that I may keep all."

His gaze traced her face. "I have said that I will nought, for my life."

Melanthe dropped her gaze. "Speak not of such cost; I dislike it." She reached up and pulled him down toward her. "Enough of heavy words. Sit by me, beau knight, and let me feed thee milk and honey with my own fingers."

He sank down cross-legged beside the stump, leaning his shoulder on it. "Hard cheese and havercake, it looks to me."

"Ah, but I have said a great spell and turned it to honeycomb." She passed him down a lump of cheese and broken bread.

With his thumb he splintered a bite from the dry edge of the cheese and ate it. "Nay, hard and sour as e'er." He turned, stretching out a leg, his back against the tree. "This is poor witchcraft, wench." He laid his head against her hip. "I've seen better at the market fair."

"Dost thou know why I love thee?" she asked.

"In faith, I cannought believe that you do, far the less why."

She curled her forefinger in his hair and tugged. "By hap one day I shall tell thee."

He was silent. She felt him turn his head, and looked down. He was gazing toward the edge of the clearing.

"I hear a hound," he said.

He rolled to his knees and held still, listening. Melanthe heard it then, too, a far-off bell.

"That lymer." He threw himself to his feet. "Christus."

THEY DID NOT stop for dusk or night, only a short rest and feeding for the horse, with oaten bread and the tough cheese for themselves, and water from a stream where they rode down the middle until it was too dark to be safe. At first Melanthe had not believed that experienced hunting hounds could be coaxed to track them—they were not deer, or even coney, but she remembered the lymer and the gallant's game with a lady's scarf—that chestnut-haired carpet knight it had been, the one she'd cut, and Melanthe could well believe he would be glad to turn his sport with the hound to account against her.

Sir Ruck's mantle, dropped in the yard, must have the scent of herself and him and the horse all thick upon it. The whole pack would follow the lymer's lead. And even had she not believed it, the persistent music of the hounds, distant, sometimes lost, but coming always from the trail behind, would have convinced her.

Ruck had hours since turned Hawk west to the sunset, away from the course to her castle, away from Torbec and the hounds. The coast would lie before them, she knew not how far, but she did not question him. Indeed, by nightfall she was too weary of holding to him and supporting Gryngolet and listening for the hounds to think beyond fear and aching muscle. It was a thing of peculiar horror, to be hunted so. She clutched tight when they came to a stretch of road and galloped, and then strained her ears to hear over the heavy breath of the horse when he let Hawk drop to a walk and turn into the woods again. She feared coming to the sea, being trapped between water and hounds. She feared that the destrier was slowed, that its strength could not hold against its double burden. Ruck halted for another rest and without a word untied the baggage behind her pillion.

They abandoned it, food and all. They mounted again with only Gryngolet and what they wore—his armor and her gown and cloak, and the hawking bag strapped over Melanthe's shoulder. The big horse went on into the darkening night with its flanks moist and smelling of sweat.

She lost all track of time, jerking awake and dozing, so that it all became a ghastly dream, in which the voices of the hounds got confused with the wind, and she thought she heard them howling so close that she gave a start and a low cry— and felt herself in a black roaring confusion, until her mazed mind recognized that they had come out of the trees onto a shore swept by a dry tempest, the waves like a great slow heartbeat, showing long pale lines in the blackness.

She held Gryngolet in her lap, hiding her face behind his shoulders to escape the stinging wind. She could no longer hear the hounds; she could hear nothing but the gale and the sea. The horse rocked beneath her, a steady surge, and she fell asleep again—drifting, sleeping, riding into an endless baying nightmare.

RUCK THANKED GOD who had led him in the right direction. When they had reached the strand, he'd not known how far north or south they might have come. But he had not taken time to wonder and guess; he just prayed—and Hawk had plodded on a loose rein through deep sandhills, veering away from the worst of the wind to the right instead of left, and so they had gone north looking for what Ruck meant to find.

He had found it. The steady creak and groan of a shuttered window made Hawk prick his ears. The night was moonless, but the sand and clouds reflected back on one another, showing the vague outlines of pale things and black massive shadows.

He dismounted, and the princess wrenched upright, mumbling, "I hear them."

"Nay, we've left the hounds behind," he said, though he knew that he might be wrong. He believed that the sand and wind would scour their scent, but he wasn't certain. "Hold here." He pushed the reins into her free hand.

She took them. Ruck hoped that at least she would not fall off if she went to sleep again. Hawk stood with his head down, his tail sweeping up against his haunches, as if he did not care to take another step. Ruck left them there and slogged through the sand toward the salterns, taking care to squint ahead and avoid the pools and trenches of the saltworks as he made his way to the single hut.

Fifteen

THINGS SEEMED TO Melanthe to happen in disconnected
scenes, the hounds and the wind and the shore in the freezing
darkness, and then a strange figure, shagged and silent, barely
seen, a woodwose, a wildman of the desert, mad rocking and
water and a sturdy boat—and colder, colder, wet spray that
made her huddle into her cloak—she did not have Gryngolet,
but somehow she remembered that all was right; Ruck said
so, when she asked—then the first light of dawn, the world a
sickening sway of wind and wave.

Sea loathing and lassitude and cold kept her immobile,
hunched in the tiny cover for the endless voyage, while the
woodwose shouted incomprehensible orders at Ruck and they
worked together against the wind and spray, sailing and hauling upon the ropes, manning oars to point the vessel over
waves that seemed too tall for it, carrying her she knew not
where, nor hardly cared. Hawk stood with his head encased in
armor, his legs braced and his nose lowered to the deck.

Near sunset the awful rocking abated. She found the
strength to open her eyes and crawl from the small shelter into
the open, looking blearily upon an unfamiliar shoreline, crys-
talline with black trees that somehow glittered, mountains

behind them, rising to ponderous heights dusted a spectral white.

She came a little more into her wits as they landed, the boat sweeping and bobbing on the swells that rolled into a protected inlet of a small bay. They had to disembark onto a sandbar. It thrust out into the inlet from overhanging trees, their lower limbs drooping down near the water, every twig and branch encased in clear ice to form strange white cascades against the dark wood.

Sir Ruck hurried her, lifting her bodily onto the sand and glancing often toward the opposite shore of the bay. The horse came calmly off the grounded boat, as if it splashed from vessel into shallow water half the days of its life. Without a word the woodwose, as coarse and savage-looking in the day as in the dark, handed over Gryngolet, her body encased in a falconer's sock, and pushed off his craft with an oar.

Ruck slapped the destrier's rump, sending it into a heavy trot ahead of them. The horse thudded toward the trees, a pale form in the failing light, and vanished in the space of a blink.

Melanthe looked over her shoulder, squinting her gritty eyes at the other shore. A mile off or more across the sands, she thought she could see low buildings and signs of active cultivation. But he did not allow her to linger and study.

"It is the abbey land," he said, with a soft contempt in his voice. "The house of Saint Mary. N'would I nought haf us apperceived."

"Where go we?"

He held her arm and looked into her face as if he would speak—then gave her a light push, turning her ahead of him. "Into the forest," he said. "Make haste, my lady."

THOUGH THEY HAD left the hounds of Torbec far behind across open water, he mounted them upon the horse again and did not stop to rest. They rode all night—or if they didn't, Melanthe knew nothing of it. Poor long-suffering Gryngolet lay secured behind the pillion, girded in her linen sock with her hooded head emerging from one end and her feet and tail from the other. Melanthe held onto the high back of the saddle. She kept falling asleep and starting awake as she lost her balance, until he said, "Lay your arms about me."

She slipped her arms around his waist and leaned her head on his back. He held both her hands clasped securely under his. It was cold and uncomfortable, with only his surcoat to pad the hard backplate of his cuirass, but Melanthe must have slept long and deep there, for when next she roused, the slant of the ground had steepened, and dawn light filtered black into gray around them.

The forest itself was so dark and thick that it seemed the horse was plowing through massive brambles and hollies without a path or sign of passage. And yet, none of the thorns pricked them, or even caught her cloak. The destrier stepped steadily ahead, turning often, making into dark caverns of winter foliage like tunnels, finding easy degrees up a cliff where icicles hung down from rocks directly over their heads. The horse labored, blowing puffs of steam, its iron shoes ringing sometimes on hard stone and other times thudding on moss. The sound of the wind in the branches overhead grew stronger as they gained height. Melanthe could look down and see dusts of gritty snow on every tree and evergreen, but no sign of where they had come.

Ahead, the woods seemed brighter, the trees smaller, driven into hunted shapes by the wind. Sharp rocks made huge flat-sided teeth, as if a dragon of the earth bared its fangs. The destrier heaved up over a shelf and passed between two huge masses of slate, the gray slabs angling down to the ground like a great V-shaped gate.

The sound of the wind suddenly dimmed. Hawk's iron shoes echoed in the defile. They emerged into a little dark snow-spattered wood hidden in the cleft. Beside a mountain tarn, purplish black and still beneath a clear sheen of ice, Sir Ruck halted the blowing horse at last.

"We will letten the horse rest and drink," he said, helping her down. "Are ye thirsty?"

She shook her head, wrapping her cloak tight about her, and sat down on a rock. He produced a havercake from some unknown pocket and offered it to her. As Melanthe crunched on it glumly, he led the horse to the tarn and broke the surface with his heel. The sound cracked against the cliffs and reverberated back as jags of white splintered across the pond. There appeared to be no exit from the coombe, and no

entrance, either, though she stared at the place she thought
they had come in.

"Where are we?" she asked, brushing crumbs from her
cheek.

He looked up, weariness written in all the lines of his face.
With a faint smile he said, "In the fells beyond the frith, my
lady. None can follow here."

The horse plunged its nose into the water and sucked.
Melanthe thought of the pathless forest they had passed
through so easily. She gazed at the bare branches around the
tarn—and suddenly saw the pattern in them, the felled trunks
and interwoven framework, one twig pulled down and
anchored beneath another, a third twisted about its neighbor,
a pair spread open, braided and pruned and pinned to the
ground to start a new shoot, all growing together into a wall
of thorn and wood.

"Avoi," she breathed. "It is a *plessis* barrier."

"Yea. And ancient, my lady. Since before the northmen
came to this coast, before anyone remembers, hatz been kept
so."

She looked at him. "What does it protect?"

He came to her and held out his hand. Melanthe took it,
rising. He led her to a place that seemed impenetrable: only
when he stepped into it did she see that she could follow. They
walked through a dark hollow, skirting the downed trunks of
trees. He climbed ahead of her into another cleft in the rocks,
and offered his hand.

Melanthe gathered her skirts and let him hike her up. The
space was barely large enough for both of them, with wind
whining through the fissure of slate. He flattened himself to
the towering sheet of rock and let her sidle in front of him,
pulling her back against his chest so that she could see
through the rent in the cliffs to the open country beyond.

"There," he said, and pointed.

The mountainside fell down so steeply from where they
stood that she could not see the tops of trees except far below,
where the forest swept to the valley floor. Ragged mists
moved across, forming and fleeing, rising in wisps to flow up
the cliffsides, blurring her view. At first she thought the valley empty, only more forest, and more, with the hint of a river

running along the bottom and frozen waterfalls on the far side. She scowled against the wind-tears in her eyes, trying to follow where he pointed.

She blinked. What she had thought to be a waterfall seemed to be a tower; she blinked and it was a waterfall again, its lower cascade hidden by the spur of a ridge—but it had a strange slate formation at its source. Triangular; and another, a little lower, dark cones of stone, each with a bleeding white tail at its base . . . the mists drifted and broke apart, and suddenly, for one instant, she saw a castle, bleached white, turrets with battlements and slate-blue conical roofs, the glint of golden banner staves—and then it was only a misted cliff marked by icefalls once more.

"Do you see it?" he asked, bending close to her ear.

Melanthe realized that she had drawn a sharp breath. "I cannot say—is there a hold? The mist befools me."

"There is a hold." He put his hands on her shoulders. "Wolfscar."

"Depardeu," she said as the mist cleared again. "I see it!"

"This is mine, from six miles behind us to that second peak, to the coast on the west and the lakes east. Held of the king himself—and a license and command to fortify it with a castel." His voice held a note of defiant pride, almost as if he expected she might disagree with him.

Melanthe turned away from the icy wind. "Thou art a baron, then!"

"Yeah, we haf a baron's writ, to my father's grandsire and before. Did ye think me a freeman, my lady?" he demanded.

She slipped back from the crevice, down into a wider and quieter space between the rock walls. He came behind, the familiar chink of his mail compounded by the ring of steel as his scabbard hit the stone with each step.

She stopped and turned, smiling. "Nay. Bast son of a poor knight. 'Twas Lancaster thought thee a freeman."

He bristled, his eyes narrowing. But before he could speak, Melanthe said, "Why should we imagine more of thee, Green Sire? When thou wouldst not name thyself."

"I cannought," he said. He gazed at her grimly, his eyes dark in the shadow of the walls. He shrugged. "The letters patent be lost. My parents died in the Great Pestilence. The abbey—" His mouth curled. "They were to holden my ward in my non-age. And they forgot me! I went there when had I five and ten years, for I ne'er heard word nor direction, nor had aid of them. And the monks said I was an open liar and in fraud of them, that this land escheated to the abbey in the last reign, and ne'er watz revoked by the king. Ne did they e'en know of the donjon—" He set his fist on the stone. "My father's castel, that was seven years abuilding! To them is naught but impassable forest, and all else unremembered!"

His indignation at that seemed greater than at being disavowed himself. But Melanthe saw instantly the heart of the blow. "Thou canst not prove thy family?"

He leaned against the rock face, his heel braced on it. "They all died."

"All of them?"

He contemplated his knee, his head down. He nodded, as if he were ashamed of it.

Melanthe frowned at him. They were of an age—if his kin had perished in the first Great Death, he would have been no more than seven or eight when he was orphaned. "But—from then, till thou went to the monks at ten and five—who cared for thee?"

He looked up, with his trace of a wry smile. "My lady— come thee now and greet them, if thou wilt deign."

PLUNGING INTO THE valley of Wolfscar, carrying Gryngolet on her wrist once again and clinging to Ruck with the other arm, Melanthe felt a stir of superstitious wonder. She had traveled with him in wilderness and desert, so she had thought—but this place seemed farther from church and humanity with each step.

The way down was a slide and slip into murky trees that groaned with the wind in their tops. She stiffened as she heard the distant howl of a wolf—or was it a woman's scream? The shriek went on and on, changing pitch from low to high, growing louder as they descended, but Ruck gave it no notice. They made a sharp turn and abruptly the wail was a roar; the wind through a pile of slate teeth, transforming again to a living screech as they passed it.

"God save us," she said below her breath.

He squeezed her wrist. She was glad that he had tightened his hold on her, because in the next twisting in their progress, she looked up over his shoulder and near leapt from the pillion in her recoil.

It was a huge face; thrice taller than the destrier, staring at her with baleful black eyes out of the depth of the tree-shadow. She made a choked sound in her throat, but neither horse nor master made a sign of fear; they moved steadfastly downward, and at a different angle the face became stone and bush and branch, an illusion of reality.

She remembered the strange fusion of dream and waking of the night before, the silent woodwose they had sailed with, the boat that seemed too small to bear them and the horse safely . . . she began to doubt what sort of guardians watched over him.

The ground became gentler. A cold mist enfolded them, a sudden pale blankness, with only the next bush, the next tree trunk looming out of it and vanishing. The horse put its head down as if it smelled its path the way a hound would. Melanthe shuddered, hiding Gryngolet under her cloak as the mist sent the chill to her bones.

As she sat huddled as close within her mantle as she could, her fantasy began to imagine that she heard music. She told herself that it was the wind, another illusion like the scream she could still hear from above them. And yet it had form and melody; it was a song that she knew, or thought she knew, sweet and sad and beguiling. The horse's hooves beat in time to it. Ruck said nothing; his head seemed to nod in the same rhythm, his hand loosened on hers—she thought that he was falling asleep, the direst lapse of all with such enthralling spirits.

She grabbed his shoulder and shook him hard. "Wake!" she hissed. "In God's name, wake up!"

"Avoi!" He started upright. He lifted his head and jerked it back, neatly smashing her nose as he reached for his sword.

Melanthe yelped, squeezing her eyes shut against the pain. She put her hand over her face, blinking back tears. When she got her sight back, the forest was silent but for the high wind and the sound of Hawk's hoofbeats.

"On guard!" she whispered. "Thou moste not let thyself sleep, or they shall have thee!"

He took a deep breath, gripping the pommel of his sword. "Whosome shall haf me?" he asked in a bewildered tone.

She shook him again, until his armor rattled. "The fays," she said. "If they have thee not already. Didst thou hear the tune?"

He seemed to come a little into his wits. "You heard music?" His hand loosed the sword. "What melody?"

"I know not. Fairy music, sweet and slow."

He grunted, looking to the left and right into the mist. Then, to her dismay, he idly began to whistle the selfsame air. Hawk's ears pricked, and his pace increased.

As the mist thinned, the distant flute took up his tune again. The path dropped below the fits of the wind, into a calm that seemed warm after the driving chill of the vapor. The fluting music seemed to always recede before them, never closer, never farther. She did not know if it was some prearranged signal, or if the fay folk themselves put the whistle in his head and gave the weary horse a new energy to stride forward. It was such a mournful and familiar tune . . .

The memory of where she had heard it came to her. Aboard ship, leaving Bourdeaux—with the man who rode before her now upon the deck above.

In one fell moment her mind flew over the impossible sequence of events that had brought her here, and she thought that he was bewitched, that his purpose was always to draw her into the fairies' power, to this place where they ruled.

Part of her thought it folly, and part of her feared, and part of her felt a strange excitement, a keenness to behold such as she had only read and heard about.

He ceased his whistle suddenly, halted the horse, and thrust his fist in the air. "*Ave!*" he shouted in a voice that reverberated off every wall of the valley.

A horn answered, a trumpet's call. The note held and climbed, blending with echoes of itself, until it seemed a whole company of horns.

He touched his heels to the horse, and the stallion seemed to forget fatigue. It rocked into a canter down the last of the slope, thundering across a bridge and frozen river that appeared beneath them before Melanthe half knew they were there. There was a road before them now, well-trod, following the bank and skirting the base of a rock-strewn ridge.

They passed the descending claw of slate, and the view burst open beside them. A whole valley spread below, thrice again as wide as the one they left, broad and level with tilled fields striped by snow, a palisaded park, a lake. And at the head of it the castle, shimmering white, its walls plummeting deep into the water, its garrets iced by traceries, lacy delights cut in stone, as intricate as paper fantasies.

The trumpet called again, loud and close, this time a dizzying cascade of proclamation. It broke off suddenly, and Melanthe looked to the left. Beside the road stood a brightly dressed youth with a big mastiff, both grinning, the boy's arms uplifted as if he would leap upon the horse as it galloped by.

The expression upon this young jester's face when he saw Melanthe was near as surprised as hers. He wore the gear of a court fool, parti-colored hose, bells, and rich flutters of fabric on his sleeves and doublet, and a cap decked with feathers and trailing dags. As Ruck pulled up beside him, the young man lowered his horn with a comic look of dismay.

"Who is she?" he demanded, full as if he had the right.

"Well come to thee also, Desmond," Ruck said dryly.

Young Desmond instantly dropped to his knee. He bowed his head so low that he was in danger of toppling over. "My lord," he said in a muffled voice. "Welcome."

Hawk threw his head, as if impatient with this delay, but Ruck held him. "My lady, this is Desmond, porter to the castel. Be his task to see that no strangers enter Wolfscar withouten leave—I ne haf no doubt that is the reason he demanded your name with such diligence."

"I beg pardon, my lord," Desmond said miserably from his prostration. "Beg pardon, my lady."

"Go before us," Ruck said, "and tell them that I come with my wife, the Princess Melanthe of Monteverde and Bowland."

Desmond stood up. He held the horn beneath his arm, his head lowered, but he managed one good long slanted look at her. She saw mostly a prominent nose and a complexion red from cold or horn-blowing; his expression was still hidden.

"M'lord," he said, bobbing. "M'lady."

He turned and ran ahead with a youth's energy in the speed of his piked shoes, his dog loping alongside. The road bent right, into the valley. He stopped at the turning and lifted the horn, playing his quick-noted exhortation, sending it blaring across the land with zealous vigor.

"That," Melanthe said, "be no fairy."

Ruck glanced over his shoulder. "Nay, he is a minstrel. Didst thou prefer a fay welcome?"

"Depardeu, a few moments since, I thought me married to Tam Lin himself."

He laughed aloud, the second time she had heard that fine sound. "Yea, thou shook me till my teeth rattled!"

"And well thou didst deserve it," she said stoutly. "Now take me to thy fairy castel, for I be right weary of this horse."

FAIRY THEY MIGHT not be, but a strange company and a strange castle it was. As they drew nearer the hold, Melanthe saw why it had seemed so like a frozen waterfall from a distance. While the tracery-work in stone gave the sparkling towers and chimneys an aspect of light froth, the lime-wash on the walls had not been maintained. Long streamers of dark stone showed through the white wherever water flowed off the blue roofs and out of the gutters. The whole keep gave the ghostly effect of melting like a sugar castle at a banquet.

And the household—every man, woman, and child was dressed as if he belonged in a mummery play, from the spiked poulaines on their feet to the lavish colors and designs of their clothes. They came running to line the road, most all with an instrument, from nakryn drums to little harps to bells, and as Melanthe and Ruck rode between them, they sang a gay chorus with treble and countertenor as well executed as if they had practiced it for weeks. Those that did not sing went before the horse, tumbling and leaping and juggling—there were even women and girls among the acrobats, wearing men's hose and springing as high as the others—and a pair of little terriers that walked upright backward, performing flips and yapping.

Melanthe saw no peasants, no tools or evidence of winter toil, though there were gray sheep with white faces scattered in the pasture about the lake. "Where are thy people?" she whispered, beneath the song and music.

He opened his hand, indicating the lively troop. "These they are, who brought me up."

"These minstrels?"

He nodded, leaning down to accept a braided sheaf of wheat from a little girl who marched alongside the destrier and then pelted away, her caroling full of giggles.

Melanthe looked about her at the singing company. "Better than raised by wolves, I trow," she murmured.

They had come to the outer barbican. Before the gatehouse, at the base of the gangway, a portly fellow with a great white beard stood waiting, dignified and comic in his tight hose and barrel body clothed in rainbow hues. His companion had a smarter aspect, a man with a young face and old brown eyes, calm and intelligent, geared all in blue but for a white pointed collar and a silver belt.

As the younger man stepped forward, the music fell to silence. "Your Highness," he said, with a deep and perfect bow, "all honor is yours. May the King on High bless you, and our dear lord esteem and cherish you. I am William the Foolet, and this be William Bassinger. Do we give your lady's grace great welcome to our master's house and hold."

He held out a ring of keys to Melanthe. Looking down into his soft-lashed dark eyes, she thought him no fool, little or otherwise. She accepted the keys and nodded to him and to Bassinger. "Grant you mercy, trusty and well-beloved," she said clearly, for all to hear. "May Christ you foryield, and give all in this castel good chance."

Plump Bassinger swept a deep flourish. "The gates!" he declared in a voice that rolled across the lake like ripe thunder. "Our liege lord and lady come!"

Unseen hands bore open the portcullis and brought down the bridge. As Ruck and Melanthe rode through the echoing stone passage, handfuls of wheat kernels rained down from the murder holes in the ceiling. Their motley household followed, singing and cheering.

Crossing the moat, Melanthe glanced up from the bridge to

the towering wall. Above the inner gate was carved the device of a wolf's head, painted black on a field of azure, the colors a fresh contrast, bright against the fading white. Inside the walls the intricate lace of stonework and decay seemed stranger still. A neat garden plot occupied the center of the court, but leafless woodbine climbed and covered half the arches of a sagging wooden gallery, the last vestiges of its painted ornament almost lost to the weather. Several cattle munched on hay strewn in the dry well of a fountain, oblivious to elegant slender chimneys and the beautiful windows, delicate with traceries and glass, that soared above.

Ruck dismounted and helped her down. A pair of boys seized his sword and shield, bearing them off with the destrier. He seemed reluctant to meet her eyes, standing in his green-tinged armor amid this elvish ruin that was no ruin, a donjon that should have held ten times the folk she saw, that was too lately raised, too lovingly fashioned, to be forsaken to neglect and decline.

William Bassinger gestured, and the arched door to the great hall was opened for her, the minstrels forming a path as a harper struck up a lively cascade of notes. Ruck took her hand. Carrying Gryngolet, Melanthe stepped with him up the stairs, the icy crunch of their feet obscured by music fit for sprightly angels.

It followed them inside, past the fine screens, into the hall where the liquid sun shone down through mosaic glass from five huge windows. All defense was left to the outer wall; the inner was a splendor of airy light that glowed on plaster and tapestry, touched gilt and varnished beams, illumined long cobwebs that trailed from the ceiling. The excellent tapestries stretched and gathered dust in their folds, and the ones lit by the windows were losing their brighter hues already.

But a fire blazed in the big hearth, with benches and stools gathered round it, discarded work, piles of brilliant cloths, and unstrung musical instruments, here and there a sign of more mundane effort, such as a harness in repair. In the rest of the hall the trestles were stacked against walls.

Ruck lifted her hand, guiding her to the steps onto the dais. He looked over the gathering, the upturned faces of haps fifty people, near half of them no more than children, the whole dressed in color and caprice. The harp music lent a sweet air of fantasy, the dust made all hues softer, and Melanthe wondered if she had wed Tam Lin in truth, for everything seemed only incompletely real.

He waited until the music drew to a conclusion, as if it held precedence. And yet his waiting gave him greater attention than any seneschal bawling for quiet. In the new silence he spoke quietly, and yet with a voice that came back in soft echoes from the hall.

"Your Highness," he said to her, "my lady, my dear consort and friend, accustomed be ye to greater, deserve ye greater, but this is my hold, and my people. For what love you may bear me, I ask of you to keepen them in your heart as I do. And them I ask and require likewise to love you, and holden you in fear and respect, and I give you power over them all, to ordain and arrangen according to such as you shall see best to do. Nill I name them to you now, for our journey has been long and weary." He had spoken to a point somewhere below her chin, still avoiding her, but he lifted his eyes then and met hers. "I say you, on my life and soul, that ye are safe here, where no ill can finden you, for so long as ye wish to remain."

She held his hand, and made a small reverence toward him. "In these matters, husband, do I willingly and gladly obey thee."

His green eyes narrowed in a brief smile, abashed and mocking at once, taking full note of her reservation, that she did not promise to submit in all things, but only in these. He looked again over the hall.

"Plague comes yet once more to the world beyond the frith, so therefore do I decree for the common good that none shall venture out anon. Pierre Brokeback is dead, though nought by pestilence, may God preserve and defend him, and give his soul rest. And yet moreover my wife the Lady Isabelle, whom, God pardon, returned—after the spirit to Heaven whence she came, these thirteen years. I—" He seemed to lose the tail of his words and said abruptly, "I am shend in weariness, and my lady, also. We will speak of these things hereafterward."

He let go of Melanthe, and in his turning she saw indeed

that he was like to fall asleep on his feet. *"Avaunt!"* she exclaimed, beckoning to the nearest of the dumbfounded household. "Dispoil thy lord of his armor, and offer comfort. Ye knowen not how far he has carried me these two nights and day again."

IN THE CHAMBER of the lord of Wolfscar, cushions lay on the floor, and carpets, too, the height of sumptuous luxury. The bed was made in ermine-lined coverlets and hung with embroidered silk on red cords and golden rings. The place smelled of old smoke and damp.

Melanthe's first notion was to chastise and justle, demanding whether these acrobatic women could not find the time amid their tumbles to air the bedding, but both William the Foolet and Ruck were looking at her doubtfully, like two boys caught neglecting their studies by a severe master. Ruck, divested of his armor, went past her to the windows, leaning with his knee on the deep sills to open each latticed glass pane. Fresh air poured in from the courtyard, cold and carrying a faint scent of livestock.

"Charcoal," William snapped to the bevy of persons hanging back at the door.

"Anon!" A jester in a pointed cap came pushing through with two pails of fuel and set to work at the hearth.

"Your lady's grace," William Foolet said diffidently, "the falcon?"

Melanthe had no intention of handing Gryngolet over to this odd crew. "I will inspect the mew whilst the chamber airs," she said, maintaining a courteous tone. "A meal before the fire will do thy master well."

"Stews are preparing, and fish baked in bread, my lady. Will my lady see the kitchen?"

"I think it prudent." She looked at Ruck, who sat on a window seat, leaning against the painted stone embrasure, his expression brooding and his eyes with the distant cast of too many hours waking. Melanthe felt weary herself, but wonder and curiosity drove her. She went to him and caught his hands. "Thou wilt not come, but stay and rest," she ordered gently.

He frowned and looked as if he would object. But at last

he said only, "It is the way they left it. Ne do I wish aught changed." The note of sullen defiance did not quite conform with the way his hands closed about her fingers, detaining her, almost a pleading touch.

"No thing would I do here," she promised, "without I crave thy leave, my lord."

A fresh rue came into his face. He released her, standing. "Alter what you will, then," he said shortly, "for naught I could deny that Your Highness asked."

He moved away, kicking a stray charcoal that had rolled onto the carpet, sending the piece clattering into the hearth. With his back to her, he lifted the trestles from where they stood leaning in the corner and began to set up the small table himself.

Sixteen

SHE WANDERED THROUGH a dream of chalk-white pinnacles and vapor. Cloud wrack blew across the highest turrets, the gilt banner staves and azure peaks of the roofs vanishing and reappearing again overhead. The battlements dripped icicles on carved stonework—a face here, a winged creature there, their features made stranger and more distorted yet by the transparent masks; whole chimneys and flying arches interlaced with spires and lances of crystal and whitened stone.

Rich and cold it was, and empty, although a little flock of minstrels followed her about, staring at her as if she were as incredible to them as this place was to her. Hovering just behind her elbow like a pair of anxious dry nurses, the fat and slim Williams ordered the gaping band to disperse repeatedly, to no effect whatsoever.

She did not speak to them, but took her own path: the bailey, the gatehouse, the constable's chambers and guard rooms; weapons and armor dim with disuse. Her diligent escort offered no explanation for the deserted spaces.

It is the way they left it, Ruck had said, but she could hardly comprehend this lost place, falling by inches to time and ruin while minstrels played in the hall.

A soft ringing echoed in the courtyard. Out a window Melanthe saw a priest walking across the bailey, swinging bell and censer—he at least dressed in the white surplice and red vestments of his office and not in some extravagant motley. She followed him to the chapel, faithfully pursued by her silent troop.

Golden arches, golden cherubim and seraphim, golden chalice and paten, golden roodscreen—the sanctuary was a marvel of magnificence, all warmed and dyed by the hues from trefoiled windows, She watched from the lower end, carrying Gryngolet, while at the altar the chaplain softly sang a Mass for the Dead. When he came to the memento, he recited names aloud in a long litany, beginning with the lords of Wolfscar and intoning on and on, mounting up to more than a hundred before she stopped counting. Inscribed tablets stood upon the altar, but he did not seem to read them, droning the names with the sure familiarity of long practice. When he had done, the minstrels behind her joined him in a *De Profundis*.

She left before the chantry was done, descending the stairs, the Williams hurrying after her. Finally, in the lesser hall and the servants' spaces, she came upon something of normal life and exertion. The chimneys had fires. Beds lined dormitory chambers. Even her speechless retinue seemed to find their voices, whispering and talking behind her. As if released from an enchantment, William the Foolet cleared his throat. "Will my lady's grace judge the mews?"

Melanthe allowed herself to be escorted. The birds' quarters were not as much a shambles as she had expected, with clean sand on the floor and high barred windows for air and light. Hew Dowl was introduced to her, with some pomp, as "the son of the late lord's falconer who died in the pestilence." Hew himself was no more than an austringer, it appeared, flying only two big goshawks—kitchen birds, but hardy and practical, a meet pair to keep the larder filled. The close sight of Gryngolet was almost enough to unman him. He was struck mute and could only indicate the facilities that he kept by dumbshow and mumbles so thick with northern speech as to be unintelligible.

Still, Melanthe liked the fit look of his birds, their plumage full-summed and their weathering blocks positioned out of the wind. Gryngolet went to him without protest, and Melanthe had no nonsense out of Hew Dowl about his own opinions when she gave orders for the falcon's care. Gryngolet preened contentedly—her ancestors had flown the snows and ice rivers of the northman's country, and this chill mountain air was well to her taste.

With Gryngolet comfortably disposed, Melanthe went next to the kitchen, where she met the cook and his sister assisting him, whose parents had perished in the Great Death at Wolfscar. Likewise with the bottler, and a girl peeling onions, and the smith, all honorably descended from the castle, though they wore the gaudy livery of minstrels, and some of them she recalled with instruments from the procession outside. Forebears in the former lord's household appeared to be the only parentage worth the telling.

William the Foolet clearly acted constable, marshal, and seneschal at once, such as the offices were. William Bassinger appeared to have no tasks beyond the lending of his rich low voice to noble and gracious talking, and tasting of the stew. After she had overlooked the pantry stores and buttery, they led her to the ladies' bower.

It was a chamber like the others, frigid cold, rich in hangings and carved cupboards and carpets. For the mistress there was a bright oriel bay overlooking the court, with its own hearth and three large windows that sent shafts of light through the dust. Melanthe lifted her hand, dismissing her curious retinue. "Only the Williams," she said, and the rest had sense enough to find urgent business elsewhere.

She walked slowly across to the bay, glancing at the ceiling, where painted vines bloomed with golden flowers against a ground of stars and sky. With the hem of her mantle she brushed off a chair by the window. An embroidery rack had been left with the work still upon it. She turned and sat, fixing a straight gaze upon the two Williams, ignoring the cold.

"Now, my men," she said in French, "we will have some honest talking."

William Bassinger bowed, and Foolet knelt on one knee. "Your Highness," he said with flawless humility.

"Rise, and look at me."

She waited until they obeyed, and waited still longer, a

sustained and steady observation. Bassinger's brows slowly rose and his lashes lifted, his face growing more and more roundly innocent above the white beard, until a babe could not have appeared as blameless. William the little Fool only stood without expression, a light color in his cheeks the single flaw in his calm.

"Tell me what has happened here," she said.

Bassinger bowed. "Your Highness, as God maintains me, may I bend my poor talent to the task you set?"

"With all dispatch!"

"Your Highness, I beseech the Saviour of the world to fill me with such ardor and excellence as to give you great delight and pleasure in my tale—"

"Not a tale, but a history," she said impatiently. "Not one word but true."

He gave her a hurt look, then lifted his chin and filled his chest with air. "Then I begin forthwith, to tell Your Highness of the glorious and stirring history of my Lord Ruadrik, the grandsire of the father of the father of our present lord."

Melanthe lifted a forefinger from the arm of the chair. "Nay, let us drop a father or two. Begin with your lord."

"Ah, but Your Highness, his father the Lord Ruadrik was a great man, very great of heart and body, so I have heard tell."

Melanthe saw that it was useless to press him faster than he would go. "Very well, but say me nothing false."

Bassinger puffed up in mild indignation. "My knowledge is exact, Your Highness, from sources of faultless authority, being my lord your husband and Sir Harold."

"And who is Sir Harold?"

The Foolet spoke. "A knight of the old lord's. Our present lord's tutor in arms. Lives he in the postern tower. He waxes a little—mad, sometimes. Your Highness will have a care of him, I pray."

Melanthe raised her brows. "A most interesting household. Recommence, William Bassinger."

"Your Highness, I tell you of how our lord's father Ruadrik of Wolfscar was in his youth among the companions of our noble King Edward of England, may God protect him. It was in the king's minority, when his unwise mother the queen and that vile traitor Mortimer held sway in the land, such that any man of honor and understanding deplored the state of affairs, even to fearing for the life of our young king himself. For all know that the traitor murdered most foully the former king his father."

He paused, to see that she was attentive. Melanthe nodded at old history and urged him on with her fingers.

"But by the grace of God," Bassinger intoned, "our king had good friends and true, and Ruadrik of Wolfscar was one. Under the advice of Lord Montagu and others, the king laid a trap for—"

"Yea, at Nottingham, they went in by a secret passage and took Mortimer by surprise," she said, to cut short what was like to be a long adventure. "Wolfscar was one of the king's party?"

Bassinger appeared to have a good deal of trouble swallowing her rude interruption, but after a moment of offended silence, he agreed. "Your Highness, Ruadrik of Wolfscar led the way."

"Well, I think I would have heard of him, had he led the way, but I can believe that he was in the company. And for this service, I presume he was rewarded?"

"He was made a knight of the Bath, and his lands extended from here to the abbey in the south, and the lakes in the east, and the coast on the west, and two miles north."

"Knowest thee who held these lands before him?"

"Your Highness, I be no lawyer," Bassinger pronounced solemnly.

"They were escheated of a part of Lancaster that had no heir, my lady, and held by the abbey," the younger William said, "but the king suspended the escheat and gave them to Wolfscar for reward."

"And the license to fortify? These lands appear not rich enough for such a castle."

William Bassinger would have spun out another tale, of Scots and battle heroics, but William Foolet cut him short. "There be a mine for iron in the hills, Your Highness. The king gave my lord's father the income without encumbrance for the building of the castle, for there was no northern defense."

"Iron?" Melanthe looked about her at the silk and cushions with skepticism. "A full rich iron mine must it be," she said.

The fool's unfoolish eyes regarded her. She waited. "Gold there be in it, too, my lady, and silver," he said at last, reluctantly.

Melanthe steepled her fingers and rested her chin on the tips. For a long while she watched the slow fall of dust motes through a shaft of light.

"Why," she demanded softly of Foolet, "did the abbot not ward him as Lord Ruadrik told me should have been?"

"It were evil days, my lady. I think many monks died. None came here."

"He should have gone to them!" She looked to Bassinger, for Foolet could have been no more than a child. "After the death passed. Thou shouldst have taken him!"

"My lady, you may be assured that had I known of the arrangement, I would have moved both Heaven and Earth to see my lord Ruadrik into the hands of those who would guard and care for him, for I loved him as my own son. I was not made mindful of this warding. I think he did not apperceive the will of his father, whom God absolve, for some time."

"What time?"

"I found his father's testament, my lady," Foolet said, "among the manor rolls. My lord Ruadrik had ten and five years then, and we went to the abbey, my lady."

"And?"

Bassinger made an apologetic gesture. "The clerks had no record of the king's grant of the land to my lord's father. There was a fire, it seems. They were short with us, my lady. We left them."

"Left them! Without seeing the abbot?"

"My lady, with such a rude welcome, I advised my lord to withdraw, ere he let news abroad that might be harmful to him. It is a very covetous abbey, my lady."

"Thou half-wits, there would be record among the king's rolls, if the abbey's was lost!"

"I am no lawyer, my lady," Bassinger murmured. "We carried out his honored father's will."

"My lady," Foolet said anxiously, "we did try. But we were afraid then; we realized that he could not prove himself—"

"None knew him from the font? No retainer? No villein?"

"Only Sir Harold," William Foolet said in a hollow tone.

"One is enough, if he is a man of good standing."

"I think not, my lady. His mind is—uncertain."

"The priest, then."

"My lady, our chaplain came into the valley after the pestilence. There were a few such who came from outside, in the first years, and we made a place and welcome."

She frowned at him. "Come, they did not all perish, those who knew him. What of these you've named to me as in this valley at their birth?"

"Yea, my lady. But you saw them; they are younger than my lord. It is their parents who could have said, and they have died since." He shrugged helplessly.

"I am no lawyer, my lady," Bassinger repeated, "but I think that to make a claim stick against that abbot, a hundred peasants who could name my lord Ruadrik would not suffice. And so I counseled my lord." He drew air into his chest expansively. "He saw the wisdom of my words, and being a young man of great heart and spirit, he betook him to prove himself worthy of his lands by his own exertion. He eschewed these ink-stained clerks and lawyers and went out into the world in search of adventures and glory—as is proper to one of his knightly lineage, my lady, I'm sure you will agree. I have recorded his ordeals and victories in a poem, and will be pleased to delight my lady's grace with the singing of it. It is not finished yet, for we still await the great deed by which he will prove himself, and take his due reward, but God willing comes it soon."

Melanthe gazed at him. At first she thought that he was making a mirth. But he looked back at her with a pleased expression.

"By hap my lady would care to hear the prologue?" he asked.

"God confound you!" she breathed. "Have you made him go ragged and nameless about the world, as if he is of no account but what he wins by his strength of arms?"

"My lord does no thing but what he chooses of his own self." Foolet's voice was stout, but his gaze wavered almost imperceptibly.

She leaned forward. "The abbey should have warded him! Or better yet the king!"

The two stood silent before her vehemence.

"But if they had," she said fiercely, "they would have made short work of thy troop of minstrels sojourning here!" She swept her hand wide. "Lord Ruadrik would have held the land of his own right long since—but instead you have made him surrender his real claim, and try to win it back by foolish errantry, for fear his wards would cast you out!"

"My lady, be it nought in our power to make His Lordship do anything!"

She stood up. "Nay, you have some unholy clutch upon him! What is it? Why should he withhold his name from those who could help him, if not to hide something? He is a baron, by God's bones, and he married a burgher's daughter as if he could do no better! You have battened upon this place some-how, a troop of worthless common minstrels, and he protects you by his foolishness, and you care not that you drag him down!"

"Madam." Ruck's voice arrested them all, cold and soft. "I asked you for love of me to esteem my people." He stood in the doorway, dressed in a black doublet and hose, a golden belt about his hips, his hair uncovered and his face angry and tired. "Ne do I demand obedience as your husband," he said in English, "but I expect of a princess the honor of your word, that ye gave me nought a few hours since."

Melanthe felt a fire of mortification rush into her cheeks. She had promised—but the state of this place outraged her.

In the silence he said, "Ye does nought know what clutch they haf upon me, in troth, nor can knowen, did ye ne'er come on your home to finden it a charnel house. The death anni-hiled in this country, my lady; took it nought one in five or one in three, but nine in ten—of every living thing down to the sheep and the rats, for what sins I know nought." His breath frosted in the cold room. "Came I home from the household where I was fostered as a page, but the pestilence met us on the road." He gave an ugly laugh. "Ye speaks of warding. Oh, I was well warded. I had me full eight years of life and wisdom, lady, and dead men all about me. Ne did no passerby, ne friar nor knight, halt or linger, but stoned me for fear of my contagion if I approached them, but until I met this troop of worthless common minstrels."

"Then in faith," she answered coolly, turning to the window, "I wish thy minstrels as well as any men under God, for their great charity to thee."

The jealousy was there again, the envy of his loyalties to anyone but her. Her hands were freezing, but she refused to clasp or warm them, only holding them at her sides. She wished to explain, to tell him that it was his welfare and his rightful place that she would defend, but pride held her tongue, and the apprehension that if she made herself offensive to his men, it was she who might be sent away.

She was not accustomed to making herself agreeable to servants. To turn a smile and wiles on them to win affection . . . well, she had performed more difficult counterfeits for less, but already the need to deceive seemed a distress, an old and fatal misery. She could not, at that moment, even summon the will to begin it. She said no more. Instead she found herself turning to walk quickly to the door. She did not look up at her husband as she passed him. Lifting her skirts, she ran down the spiraling stairs, seeking the courtyard.

RUCK WATCHED HER from an arrowslit in the gate tower that commanded the whole of the meadow and the lake. His first foolish thought had been that she was leaving—but of course she would not, could not, alone. She would not have been able to find her way from the valley even if she had commanded a horse.

Knowing that, he had not followed her. He was hotly aware of Bassinger and Little Will; of how this impossible marriage must appear. Since his first warning of plague, he had thought of bringing her here for security, though more in his fantasy than in seriousness. Not once had it ever entered his head that he would bring her to Wolfscar as his wife.

But in the crisis, trapped between the hounds and the sea, he had gone by his secret way for the one place he could be certain of. He knew the decision now to be as witless as their exchange of vows—had realized it in full when he saw his castle and his people as they must look to her. Already she disdained them.

Nodding stiffly to Will and Bassinger, Ruck had left the ladies' chamber with its cobwebs and echoes, acting the lord just as if he had not cleared ditches and drunk ale and planted palisades shoulder to shoulder with the Foolet while Bassinger gave advice and complained of his back. Ruck did not wish to seem to chase her, but he could not face his old friends, either, or justify what he had done. Standing now in the empty garret, he felt utterly alone, as if he had executed his own banishment.

He leaned his forearms against the angled cut of the arrow embrasure, resting his head in the crook of his elbow so that he could keep her in his sight as she carried the gyrfalcon into the sheep pasture. She strode across the snow-crusted grass. A train of children followed, tramping behind with their arms swinging, until Hew Dowl chased them off to a proper distance. She was a hooded sweep of emerald green in the dirt-gray landscape, leaving the motley colors of the children and the austringer behind her. She stopped, and Ruck saw her beckon.

Hew ran to her, his shoulders stooped in reverent submission and his eyes fixed on the ground. As Ruck watched, she spoke to the austringer. Hew's head came up. His face was too distant to see clearly, but his whole body seemed to expand. He donned his glove and held out his arm to take the falcon. They talked for a moment, Hew raptly attentive as she handed him the jeweled lure.

As the princess stood back, Hew hid the lure and struck the hood, removing it. For a few moments the gyrfalcon sat motionless on the man's upraised arm; then it bounded free.

Ruck lost sight of the bird. From his arrowslit he could only gaze at Melanthe as she shaded her eyes and followed the flight. It felt mockingly suitable that he stand hidden, staring out at a narrow view from this crack in stone-thick walls. He grew angry at his own cowardice as he thought of it. Afraid of her contempt, afraid of his own friends—ashamed of his home.

He thrust back from the embrasure and paced across the garret, the bare planks reverberating beneath his feet. For twenty years the haunted frith-wood and fate had protected Wolfscar; there had been no need of a garrison or armed watch and none to man the towers anyway. He had not reopened the mine, he had not reclaimed the road; he had done nothing that might draw attention, waiting for the day when Lancaster his prince would call for the Green Knight and ask him what reward he would have for some marvelous deed—and then, Ruck had dreamed, he would reveal himself, and say his claim, and Wolfscar would be his without dispute, without abbots or haughty monks or any question of right.

It was all a boy's fine fantasy, built of the songs the minstrels sang, of Gawain and Lancelot, adventure and glory, of troth and loyalty between a man and his master.

He had long ago learned the way of the world. But he had been committed by then, and making a name with Lancaster, and there were tournaments and war—if not as glorious as the adventure of his imagination, at least opportunity for advancement and future, until Lancaster had dismissed him. Because of her.

Princess Melanthe could purchase Wolfscar ten times over. Ruck would have been more of a saint than he was, he reckoned, if the thought had not crossed his mind. But he could hardly stay apace with his own feelings. Outside, he had been bewildered and humbled by her vow to be his wife, but here—here, he did not want to give up his sole mastery, he did not want to explain himself and his life, he did not want to submit to her authority, he did not want everything he was to depend on her, he did not want to give her up, he did not want to deny her anything, he did not want to sleep alone again— and he did not, *did not* want her to leave him.

He returned to the arrowslit in time to see Gryngolet pounce upon the lure that Hew threw down on the frozen grass. It was a simple method, the usual way a towering falcon would be brought down. In its very simplicity, with plain Hew making in to the bird like any countryman's falconer, the sight brought the image of Melanthe lifting her jeweled gauntlet and lure, unbearably vivid, the sky and the bird and the fire of emeralds and white diamonds as the gyrfalcon came to her hand. She had been weeping and laughing, beautiful and not, a dream within the compass of his touch.

He watched her as she bewitched Hew into a hound in human shape. The man heeled to her with panting devotion,

nodding and gazing and nodding again as she spoke. While
the gyrfalcon ate, he pointed about the valley, obviously dis-
cussing the hunting.

Ruck felt his heartbeat rise. If she thought to hunt the bird,
then she did not wish to leave anon. He wouldn't have taken
her even if she desired to go, not until he could better assure
her safety, but he had not relished a quarrel with her about it.

He rolled on his shoulder and put his back to the tower
wall, leaning there and staring at the gash of light that fell
across the floorboards from the defensive slit. The stone was
so frigid that the cold seeped through his doublet to his body,
but he did not move. He knew he was not thinking clearly.
Weariness misted his wits. Had it been warfare, he would
have distrusted any humor or inclination now, holding himself
back from hasty action.

But it seemed that he had done naught but hold himself
back for all of his life. Hard-won habit ruled him: he had only
to think of her to want to couple again, and his next thought
was that he must not—and only in the eternal struggle to conquer his bodily passions did it come to him that there was no
longer a contest to win.

He stared so hard at the patch of light on the boards that
his eyes began to water.

He had made a particular study of the sin of lust, with careful questions to the priests, and a certain amount of reading in
confession manuals when he could examine one in French or
English. He felt himself rather a master of the subject. Even
on marriage, the religious did not always agree among themselves, which meant there was a little space for preferring one
set of advice over another amid the thickets of clerical admo-
nition. All admitted that there was no sin if the intention was
purely to engender children, but a few maintained that any
pleasure at all in the marriage bed could not be without sinful
fault. Others judged that the conjugal debt was a pious duty
between spouses to prevent incontinence, and the marriage
act only a deadly sin if there was excessive quest for pleasure—with many fine computations of what might constitute
excessive pleasure.

Ruck found his tired spirits lifting. He was clearly inconti-
nent, or like to be if he thought on his wife at any length at all,

and the very notion of begetting a child on her sent him into
a hot ardor of perfectly sinless passion. Not excessive ardor—
but iwysse, if he waited too long, he judged his soul would be
in certain danger.

He pushed away from the wall, finding a new vigor in the
gloom.

MELANTHE REFUSED TO allow herself to hesitate as she
opened the door. When she had returned from the mews, a girl
had been waiting with the message that Sir Ruadrik asked
Princess Melanthe to honor his unworthiness by her presence
in his chamber—courteously worded as a request, it was true,
but still her hand had lacked a little steadiness as she coaxed
Gryngolet onto her perch.

She entered the lord's chamber expecting to be confronted
by all three of them, including the two Williams, for it was
always the way with favorites that they wished to be present
when their rivals were diminished. But Ruck was alone. He
rose from a chair as she closed the door behind her.

"My lady," he said, "I would have you eat now."

He placed the chair by the chimney corner, where a white
linen cloth lay over the table, already laden with a meal. In his
black weeds he was tall and formidable, the green of his eyes
intensified by the night-hue of his clothes and hair. A fire
crackled actively, warming the chamber, and fresh-cut boughs
of pine drove out the stale atmosphere with their fresh scent.
In the late afternoon a candle gave the table extra light.

She was hungry indeed, but the flutter of dread in her
stomach made the food unsavory. She released the pin on her
cloak, and tossed it over a chest. "What did they sayen of
me?" she asked haughtily, meeting the matter on head so that
she might gain the upper hand by surprise.

He looked up at her. "Say of you?"

She washed her hands in a basin beside the door. "I warn
thee, sir—is a poor master who is ruled by his servants. But
of course, they will say thee otherwise, that to be ruled by a
wife is worse."

He gazed at her, a shadow of a frown between his brows.
She paced to the table and sat down, scowling at a dish of
wheaten frumenty, well aware that he stood close behind her.

From the edge of her eye she could see his arm, the velvet rich with light and shadow on the black curve of his sleeve.

She took two swallows of the frumenty, which was nearly cold and only barely palatable, before her throat closed and she could not eat more. She put down the spoon. "I ne cannot eat, ere I hear thy decision."

"My lady," he said, "what decision?"

"Wilt thou send me hence?"

He walked away. Melanthe slid a look after him. He stood at the window, his back to her. "Send you hence?" he demanded harshly. "A'plight, then why haf I troubled to bringen you here, in the stead of drowning you like a kitten in a bag, for to spare myseluen the toil? If that be the decision you would hear—nill I take you hence, nay, nor any here show you the way. In good time, when augurs it safe enow, then will I see you to your hold. Henceforth until then, thou moste biden here, though it displease."

She bent her head, clasping her fingers tight together. "Nay—I will not displease. I can maken myself pleasant to them. It is the easiest thing possible. I cannot thank them for their injury to thee and thy rightful estate, but I am thy wife, and n'would not have discord sown between us, for it bodes not well in the house." She took up the spoon again abruptly, plunging it into the pottage. "And such is a humble speech as I am not accustomed to making, in troth, but I love thee, even if I do not adore thy churls."

She forced herself to eat, sitting on the edge of the chair with her back straight.

From the window he spoke hesitantly. "It is nought that ye will to go?"

She did not care to admit the depth of her desire to stay. Lightly she said, "Wysse, ne do I languish for the back of a horse again soon."

The floorboards creaked beneath the carpets. He came behind her. "Haply is rest and a soft bed you desire, my lady, after your meal."

If some mannered gallant had said such to her, she would have known how to understand it. But she heard naught beyond his careful courtesy in his voice, though again he stood very near her as he took up a napkin and poured hot ale from the hob. He set the kettle back.

"Thou hast not fulfilled thy own repose," she said, watching steam rise from the gold chalice and vanish against the background of patterned silk on the wall.

"Nay," he murmured, still close behind her. "Nay, lady."

He offered no dalliance, and her court wit deserted her. All the words that came into her head seemed green and foolish. He sat on his heels beside her chair and served her a roasted apple. She ate a few bites. He did not rise, but remained there like a man at ease.

She felt herself strangely daunted by him, overpowered by his greater size, the black line of his legs, the heavy square links of the belt that hung at his hips. He wore it as if it had no weight at all, though each joint, ornate and thick, studded with the silvery sable of marcasite crystals, would have balanced a cobblestone on the measuring scale. But in his velvet he moved effortlessly. When she glanced at him, his eyes were on her, his lashes showing very dark, his face somber, almost severe. As if he had forgotten himself by kneeling there, he rose instantly, drawing away.

Melanthe was not certain of whether he had made an invitation to share the bed or not. She ate slowly, delaying the end of her clear reason for being there in his chamber. As she sipped at the honeyed ale, she felt a miserable excitement, doubtful of what he wished. He said nothing to woo or dismiss her. She did not know if he was angry with her still. In this mute courtesy he could hide anything. She did not want to sleep alone, away from him.

At last she set down the chalice. "I will leave thee respite then, to take thy rest as thou art due."

She rose. With her eyes downcast she went to him and put her hands upon his shoulders. She reached on her toes and touched her lips to each cheek, lightly, taking a mannerly leave as if he were an honored guest or close kin. "Give thee good eve, sweet knight," she murmured.

He stood still, only turning his face slightly, returning pressure in response to each kiss. She let her hands slip down his arms. His palms turned up; he caught her fingers for an instant—and then let them slide through his.

She turned swiftly, taking up her cloak as she went to the door. At that moment she would gladly have given up all of her noble estate and forgone the cold and private luxury of the ladies' chamber. At least she did not intend to sleep with the dust: she would rouse out these useless minstrels for a fire and proper comfort, be they pleased by it or not. By hap she could find a maid or two among the women, to make the bower clean without moving any item from its sacred place, and then invite him there on the morrow, when he might be—

"Melanthe."

She halted with her hand on the door hasp. He had never before called her by her name.

He stood, all black, his legs set apart as if someone might come at him with a sword. "Art thou sore weary?" He made a trifling motion of his hand. "I ne am nought one to sleepen in the light of day."

Pleasure and relief soared through her. "Nay, how is this?" She crossed the carpet to him and lifted her hand to his forehead. "Dost thou go sick? I have seen thee snore with some success in daylight ere now."

"I n'would nought have thee depart so soon, if it please thee."

"Please me?" She let her hand slip down and sighed. "What—forfeit a cold chimney and empty bower, only to suit thy liking? Verily, thou art a tyrant, husband."

He caught her waist, holding her between his hands. She had been wary of mirrors, and compliments, but in his face as he looked down at her what she saw was desire, open and vehement, unembellished.

"Wilt thou have me?" he asked softly.

Almost, he frightened her, in the lightness of his hands and the calmness of his voice. He was like Gryngolet when she hunted, a silent rage, hushed violence, riding currents beyond knowing.

"Yea," she said. "Gladly."

His hold tightened a little. "Then I would hear—how I can best please you."

She rested her hands on his arms uncertainly. "I am pleased with thee," she said.

His jaw was tense. "On hap I am nought gentle enow, or skilled enow, or—what would delight thee."

All of her experience was in denying men. For delight she knew naught beyond kisses, and lying beneath him as she had done. There was more to it, experience and skill, as he said, and a new fear sprang alive in her, that he would expect her to know such things.

She made a small lift of her shoulders, feigning sport. "Thou moste guess what delights me."

He looked down upon her. He lifted his hand and drew his thumb across her mouth. His green eyes showed a new light, a trace of amusement. "Then I shall take experiment of thee, lady. Happens I haf made me a modest study of wicked delectation."

She murmured, "I thought thee chaste, monkish man."

"Yea, I haf been." He closed his eyes and bent to her, kissing the side of her mouth. "But no monk am I in my head, God grant me pardon," he whispered. His body drew closer, velvet and taut elegance. "My confessor has chastised me oft, and bade me study on my sins at length. And so, lady"—he kissed her, the hunger in it sinking down through her like a comet falling—"I have studied."

Seventeen

———❧———

MELANTHE DREW A breath, tasting him on her lips, inhaling his scent. "And what hast thou mastered in thy study, learned husband?"

He seemed to grow abashed, turning his face away. "My lady, it is all nonsense. Better thou shouldst sayen me how to give thee pleasure. Ne am I accomplished in luf wiles, truly."

She drew her palm down the soft nape of velvet on his chest. "I would hear what thou hast learned. For my pleasure." With a light pluck she freed the topmost golden buttons on his doublet.

He made a low unhappy laugh. "I know well that ye wields more skill in this art than I."

She stepped back. Standing in the half-light, he appeared no innocent, but a man full in prime of carnal boldness, no more chaste than a stallion might be chaste, being beautiful and strong and only what it was, a creature made for life and union.

"But a child am I in the craft," she said lightly. "Thou moste be my master, or nill we proceed far."

He made no move, but stood with his hands open, a signet gleaming on his middle finger, the light sliding on his golden belt.

She lifted her eyebrows. "Or be thou courageous in war and coward in chamber, knight, for shame?"

She had not expected such a crude hit to touch him, but he flushed at her words, response so quick that she thought it a taunt he must have heard before. The severity came into his face again, the hunting coldness. He closed the space she had made between them and lifted his hands. Without speaking, he began to unfasten her gown.

Melanthe stood still. The cotehardie was not an elaborate fashion, but simple and warm for traveling, ermine-lined and buttoned. He pushed it off her shoulders. The fur hem brushed over her hands, dropping to the carpet.

Her white damask kirtle laced beneath her arms, fitting to her body. He loosened the cords. She felt the lace slip and knot in an eyelet. He worked at it, looking down, his face close to hers. A line formed beside his mouth. He gave the tie a tug, and then a jerk, breaking it, a force that made her take a step backward for balance. Without even unlacing the other side, he lifted the damask over her head and tossed it away.

Through her linen, she could feel the cool air. He opened his hands over her, his palms against her hips with only her thin shirt between.

Melanthe closed her eyes. Abruptly she put her arms about his neck, arching against him on tiptoe as she had done before, seeking that delicious sensation he had given her at Torbec.

Velvet touched her breasts. She could feel his hard belt, and silk and pressure against her belly—but somehow she could not come within reach of the pleasure. With a small sound, of frustration, she fell back onto her heels.

He pulled her closer. "Lady," he whispered against her ear. "Lie you down."

His hands slid upward, lifting the linen with them. On the eastern carpet before the chimney, he stripped her of her shirt, baring her of all but her white hose and garters, drawing her down with him as he knelt.

She lifted her chin defiantly, resting back on her elbows, refusing to be mortified by her nakedness like some fluttering novice nun given to visions and starvation. Shameless, he had called her—so let him see.

But she was terrified, her heart beating so rapidly that she was sure he must discern it. She wasn't a delicate blonde beauty, frail and dainty—she was dark-haired and white-skinned, and not a girl. Above the garters at her knees, she had two bruises on one thigh from some encounter on their wild travels, and another at her hip. He could not have spanned her waist with his two hands, and her breasts were too full to be the high round strawberries, or nuts, or even pears, sung of the ladies in romances.

He only looked at them for an instant, before he averted his face and closed his eyes, sitting beside her with his weight on his hand.

She lost her rebellious nerve and curled upright, hugging her legs to her. "Uncommon sour I am to beholden, then," she said sullenly. "Iwysse, a hag as old as thee!"

"What?" he said, in a distracted voice.

He looked strange and uneasy, frozen in place. For a moment she was in fear that he was near a swoon or a fit.

"What passes?" she demanded, catching his arm.

He moistened his lips, pushing off her hand as if she offended him.

"Avoi!" she hissed. "Do not say me thou art praying now?" She let go and plumped back upon a cushion. "Monk man!"

"I am counting," he said tightly.

She stared at him. "Counting what?"

"The chimneys."

"The chimneys!" she cried.

He opened his eyes, looking straight ahead over her. "The chimneys, the doors—for God's sake, ne do I hardly know what I count." He drew a breath. "I am—better now."

He glanced at her, and then away again. Melanthe curled her fingers in her crumpled shirt. "Depardeu, I will cover myself, to spare thee this dire distress."

His hand landed firmly over hers. "Nay—lady. If you please." He turned a look full on her, his eyes near dark as the deep evergreens, the hidden life of winter. Like a secret his faint smile touched his mouth. "In faith, is nought affliction, but too great bliss."

Melanthe regarded him a moment. His courtesy was

beyond calculating; he might say anything to maintain it. "In troth?"

He crossed himself, his face sober.

She asked suspiciously, "N'is not my body uncomely, thou think?"

With a sound low in his throat, he stretched out his legs and lay at his length alongside her. He laid his hand between her breasts and drew his knuckles downward, over her belly. His dark lashes lowered. He smoothed his hand up to her knee and down her hose to her ankle, up again, then between her legs, burying his fingers in her curls.

"My lady, thou art lickerous." He smiled, pressing the heel of his hand against her.

And there it was, the pleasure, the sensation she remembered. Her breath caught. Her body seemed to stretch, to move outside of her mindful accord, arching up to meet the touch.

"Ah," she said, and strove to check her unsteady voice. "Ah, but this is a riddle." She took refuge in a mocking tone. "Lickerous to taste or lickerous lustful?"

"The both," he murmured, "an I prove fortunate."

She gave him an arch look. "This is luftalking indeed. I will think me I'm at court to hearen such."

His thumb slipped downward, seeking. Melanthe gave a little start and pressed her legs together to prevent him.

"Lady, thou art now at my court, where I rule." He gently resisted her effort, opening her knees. He stroked her, the inside of her thighs, her quaint, up and down again, touching her openly, making her flinch each time his fingers passed over that spot.

Her breasts and her body tingled. "Stop," she said, with a sharp intake of her breath.

"Nay, thou hatz bid me teach thee wickèd delectation. This is the second sin of lust, my lady. Unchaste touch."

His thumb moved in a slow pulse. She swallowed. "That I can believe—is a sin," she said.

He shifted, moving up on his elbow. "And this is the first—" Without ceasing the stroke of his thumb, he leaned over her mouth. "Unchaste kissing." He tasted her with his tongue, then invaded deep. His fingers slid into her sheath, intruding, pressing, and stretching her. Melanthe whimpered into the double commixtion, the velvet weight and the hard graze of his jaw. Her heels slipped down the carpet; her legs strained as if she could have more.

He drew away, brushing his lips against her temple. While Melanthe searched for air, he bent to her breast. He kissed her there, at the same time thrusting his fingers full to the very depth of her.

All air seemed to vanish; she panted to regain it as he caressed her with his tongue, suckling her as if she were sweetmeat. Her body rose to him, to his mouth and his hand—unchaste beyond any recognition or heed that virtue might exist upon the earth.

"Unchaste kiss . . . unchaste touch." His breath was close to her skin, brushing and warming her as he spoke. "The third sin of lust is fornication, but we are wed, lady, so ne cannought I teach thee fornication. Ne also the fourth, o'less thou art a virgin, that I may seduce thee from they purity."

"Nay," she whispered, curling her fingers in the thick silken nap of the carpet. "Not a virgin."

"I thought me nought so." His lips moved over her shoulder, a gentle searching. She could feel him smiling against her. "Ne can we adulter, neither by single or double, ne commit sacrilege—lest thou art under a religious vow?"

She gave a breathless laugh. "Look I to thee like a holy woman, knight?"

He lifted his head. "God shield," he said, with a sudden fierceness. "Nay, ye looks like my wife, fair and mortal—and no thing that we do between us be sinning, by the word of Saint Albert."

She lay against the cushion. In her life she had made certain that men thought her iniquitous, lethal in her loves and passions. The Princess Melanthe looked like no one's fair and mortal wife. But she had never before lain naked beside a man, uncovered, without shield or mask, reckless.

"Nothing?" She made a pout, stretching her arms overhead. "Alas, thou wilt destroy all my wicked disport."

He caught her chin, rubbing his thumb across her lips. "Does thou nought drive me to inordinate desire, wench, which is deadly sin, wed or no."

She brought her arms down about his shoulders. "And is thy desire now ordinate, learned monk? Haply we will delay this loving then, and take us to the chapel for a day and night of prayer and fasting, to prove thee."

"Haply thou art the Arch-Fiend's daughter, come to harry me until I be undone body and soul."

"Nay, only thy wife, fair and mortal," she said virtuously. "Chaste, too, so far this day."

He leaned on his elbow, ungirding his golden belt. The linked bosses dropped to the carpet with a rich chink. "Thou art uneasy in the state, I trow."

Agreeable it was to trade words and luftalk. But the turn of his broad wrist, competent and brief, and the sound of the belt falling gave Melanthe pause. She drew her knees up, uncertain if he would mount her and have done—she did not object; she welcomed it, for that by God's send she would breed his child, but experience of four times, thrice with Ligurio and once with him, taught her that it marked the swift conclusion to all love-liking.

She had been most delighted with this play and was not eager to see it end so soon. As he leaned over her, she put her palm upon his chest. "What study is this, learned monk? Yet lacks my instruction. The first and second sins of lust only have I beheld."

But he did not answer, only gave her a thorough demonstration of the first again while he loosed the buttons on his doublet. She could feel the force of his intent; he had grown impatient with disport and love-amour. With a little dejection she let her hand relax, trailing it upward, sliding her fingers idly in his hair as he lifted himself over her.

She spread her legs, yielding obedience to what she owed him. Her body tensed slightly, anticipating the discomfort.

But he did not lie hard upon her; instead he held his weight up and kissed her mouth, and her throat, and her breasts. She sighed, savoring, drowning and pleasuring in the last moments.

The freed cloth of his shirt and his doublet brushed her skin. He drew hard on her teat. The sensation shot through her, half pain and half ecstasy. She clutched the loose velvet, pulled and arched, trying to bring him down to her.

"Merci." She gasped, all her muscles contracting with each tug and sweet spike of pain. *"Merci, merci."*

He made a wordless sound, moving away, downward, shaping her with his hands. She wanted him back for more; she dragged at him, lacing her fingers in his hair, but he was leaving her, pulling away in spite of it, dropping kisses down her belly.

Just as she would have exclaimed in despair of his withdrawal, he pressed his mouth to her quaint. He held her hips and touched her with his tongue.

The delicious bolt of feeling transfused her. She trembled beneath him, drinking air, moaning between her teeth, her body twitching as if seized by each lascivious stroke. She tilted her head back, lifting her breasts and her spine and her hips, pressing up to him to take the waves of lust, asking, begging—demanding with her flesh.

He rose above her. For the moment that they were separate, she whimpered in anxiety: she wanted him to go on kissing her that way, but he sat back and pulled off the doublet and shirt, baring shoulders muscled as fine and thick as the destrier's. He reached down to his hose and breeches that showed his full tarse through linen, crammed heavily against the cloth.

She felt distraught. He would use her now, and it was over, and she was near weeping for the feeling he had given her that still demanded more.

He released the lacing on his breeches. She lifted up her arms to embrace him as he came over her. She did not flinch, though he was so much larger than Ligurio; she lay herself open for him despite her thwarted yearning.

He rested on his hands, looking down into her face. "Lady," he said, with a quick grin, "in thy studies, that last that I taught thee—falls it within the thirteenth sin, indecent manner of embrace."

She made a faint wild laugh, a mindless answer, for he was lowering himself on her, this time using his body as he had used his hands and his tongue to urge that impossible pleasure. In surprise she felt it coming again as his hard member pressed at her, parting her a little with each push, until the head was inside her.

His arms trembled. He stared down at her, a blank distance in his look, a blindness. He drew air in his chest, his grin going to a baring of his teeth as he drove himself into her.

Though his size was a sore burn, she took him deep. No coupling she had ever known to be like this. His unchaste kiss, his unchaste touch, his breath a harsh sob at her ear; his weight on her and his penetration to the very depth of her. Over and over she rolled and shoved herself wantonly against him—and culmination came upon her like an ambush.

"God save!" she cried. Her back arched. Her body shuddered, beyond command. She died as he did, in full ecstasy, lost and cleaving to him in the flood.

SHE SLEPT AGAINST Ruck's chest, on the floor, turned to nestle with one leg drawn up and her hips curving, her hand resting possessively on his waist. Propped on his elbow, he watched the firelight play orange and rose over her skin.

For as long as he remembered, ever when he discharged his seed, even from the first of his marriage to Isabelle, he had come into his wits again with his spirit borne down by melancholy. A nameless sorrow possessed him, a presage and knowledge of loss.

He knew to expect it, but the expectation brought no remedy, only an acceptance of something that God saw fit to impose on him. In his years alone, when he had given in to his lusts in secret, the grief had sometimes hardly left him from one trespass to the next, only abated by his vision of his perfect lady and confession. Its durance was sometimes days and sometimes only as long it took him to fall asleep, but ever the deep trist was there in the afterward, as it was with him now.

Softly he moved his hand over her, a gentle stroke. With each breath he could feel the tips of her breasts touch him. He could lower his lashes and look at them, marvel among many marvels. Without her gowns and jewels, she had a womanly shape, all roundness and long lines, not so coldly slender as her close-cut fashionable robes made her appear, but sweetly pillowed and cushioned, full ripe in life.

In his despair her comeliness made him think of how he would lose her. It must be impossible; he could not imagine any future in which he would have this moment again.

His finger trailed down into the shadow between them. He followed an odd flaw in the satin of her skin, an irregular line from her merkin curls up to her belly. He drew his fingertip downward, tracing another beside it, and another. They were strangely feminine, faint and light, soft at the edges like no scars he had ever seen in a wide experience of battle wounds. He wondered at how she might have come by such ghostly marks, but the very idea of questioning the Princess Melanthe on such a topic as her flaws made him smile inside himself.

She would freeze him in his place. She would not understand him, that he only wished to know more of her, nor believe that because she was not perfect beneath her furs and silks and jewels, he loved her the more. Arrogance and unexpected blemish, and such courage to ride with him alone. Shameless and coy by turns, her marvelous blue-lilac eyes sulky with fear that he was repelled by her appearance.

As he traced the marks, she caught his hand, folding up her leg up with a quick move, as if to hide herself. Her eyes sprang open. "What art thou about?" she asked sharply.

He locked his fingers into hers and leaned over, caressing her brow with light kisses. "Inspecting thy great age and ugliness, wench."

She brought his hand up, making him rest it on his own thigh, trapping it firmly there over the black hose he still wore. "I've lost count of these times thou hast called me wench. Thou moste be flayed alive to atone for them all. It is a great tragedy."

"Bassinger will make a woeful lay of lamentation, to remember me."

She stared at the base of his throat, unsmiling. He regretted speaking of Bassinger, bringing the world into their seclusion. To distract her, he loosed his hand from her hold. He cupped her breast, caressing his thumb over the dark rosy crown.

She drew in a swift breath. The shade of a frown hovered between her brows. She slanted a look up at him.

"Thou hast lied to me, monk man. Thou art no abstinent from women."

He shook his head. "I have told you troth, my lady, fore God."

"Nay." She rolled onto her back, gripping his wrist. "What of this manner of—kissing and touching? Depardeu, where hast thou discovered such things?"

He lifted his eyebrows. "This?" He made a slow circle with his thumb. "Lady, I have been married. A husband will touch his wife so."

She gave him a look as offended as any scandalized abbess. "Mine did not!"

Ruck tilted his head, resting his cheek on his fist. "Did he nought? Ne cannought I say why, my lady, but that pleases me for to hearen."

"And—did I not mean only—this—but thy . . . unnatural kisses. I think me only lewd gallants and carpet knights know of such perversions!"

He ceased his caress and lowered his eyes. She seemed truly agitated by the transgression. To be sermoned by the Princess Melanthe, of all people, made him think he must verily have been immoral to the worst degree of vice.

"Forgive me, my lady." He set his mouth. "I thought— such a one as you, wise in luf-amour—I thought me you would knowen these things, and like them. Ne will I nought offend you so again, I swear it."

She curled both her hands about his. "Nay, nay, thou mistakes me. I did—I took pleasure, wee loo, how could I say thee I did not? But—" She turned her face to him. "Where indeed hast thou learned them, if not from dissolute women and harlots?"

"Ne haf I recourse to harlots." He withdrew his hand, staring down at the silken carpet between them. "I wit it from confession."

"Confession!"

"Yea, lady."

She sat up. "Priests I know who are full of impurity, but I did not think they taught it in the church."

"They ask—" He plucked at the nap of the carpet and looked up at her sideways. "Do they nought ask questions of you, my lady?"

"Iwysse. Have I been idle, or proud, and suchlike?"

"No more than that?"

She hugged her knees. "Envious? Angry? Grasping?

Gluttonous?" she recited, and lifted her shoulders in a shrug. "Had I one would clatter and carp that I adorned myself too fine, until I wearied of it, and had him disappointed and another in his place."

"Oh," he muttered. He picked at the motley silk.

"They inquire of thee else?"

He scowled. "Yea. Of my lust." He spread his fingers, rubbing them back and forth over the nap. "They ask, haf I nought engaged in lecherous touches and embraces—and when I say I haf nought, asks the confessor in another way, haf I nought touched a woman on her breasts, or her body. And neither does he trust me no more than you, my lady, when I say him nay, and asks again, as if I had said yea, then did I nought touch her womb-gate and her merkin? And did I nought kiss her there and on her teats, for to make her lewd? And did I nought mount her unnaturally, as the beasts couple, or let her mount onto me? And did I nought do it on a holy day?" He made a snort of misery. "And then do I think of little else, I say you my lady, when I go out, but what I might do if I had me a wife and might usen her."

"Avoi," she said softly, but he could hear mirth in her voice.

His jaw hardened. "So, if ye believe me—ne did I nought learn vice from harlots."

"Haps thou couldst teach them!" she suggested.

He lay back with a deep sigh, stuffing a cushion under his neck and clasping his hands behind his head. She regarded him, and then reached up and touched his bent knee.

"It is because they take measure of thy form and vigor, and cannot conceive that a man like thee would be continent. So did that priest reckon me for excess in adornment."

He had not been perfectly continent, but he was not going to tell her more of the grinding inquisitions he received on the matter, not when the worst crime she was required to acknowledge appeared to be excess adornment.

"Is true, then," she asked, "that those things be not sin in marriage?"

"Some say yea, and some nay." He remained staring between his knees.

"Thou hast studied much on this matter?"

He nodded.

She rocked back on her hips and laughed. "Forsooth, we shall send thee to confession full oft, monk man, for thy further instruction!"

He let his gaze wander up to the window, to the chimney—to her, as she sat curled with the warm firelight on the curve of her back. He smiled slowly. "As God and my liege lady command me."

Eighteen

—∞∞∞—

THE FIRST THING Melanthe knew was the roar of a voice and the chime of rings sliding as the bedcurtains swept open and gray light poured over her.

"Baseborn whore!"

A monstrous black outline flashed, and something came hurtling at her. Through the blankets a blow smashed into her neck and shoulder.

The black flashed again. She heard a shout, the thing came at her, and suddenly another weight bore down atop her, between her and the assault. A sound like an ax on wood cracked through her head. The weight on her jerked, and jerked again under another hit. Through a daze she realized that it was Ruck above her, his body pressing her down as someone beat him, raining blows on his naked back.

"She is dead!" the voice bellowed. "Get off the strumpet, ye idle whoreson! I haf slayed her!"

With each blow Ruck's body jarred, and his breath made a low sharp grind. But he held, shielding her, his arm locked over her face while the shocks hit him and the bed, wild strikes sometimes high on his shoulders and sometimes low, sending quakes of violence through to her legs.

"High morn is it!" their attacker howled. "Rise, boy, or

look ye to losen your hide! Thy commoner is killed; base whore thou took to wive, and I'll slay her bastards to clean the nest! She was unworthy of you! Adaw, the swords await." His weapon cracked down again. "Up! Will ye jape a bloody corpse? Get up!"

The hits had lost a little of their energy. Ruck lifted himself. He raised his arm; she saw a grizzled man beside the bed—the descending wooden sword whacked into the palm of Ruck's hand. He held the weapon off and jerked it from their assailant's double grip.

Ruck rolled away from her. He cast back the bedcurtains and rose, hurling the wooden sword. It struck the open door and woke a thunder of echoes in the spiraled stair beyond.

"Cease off!" Stride-legged and naked, his back reddened by beating, Ruck glared at the savage old man. "Keep ye, that ye trespass no further!"

The man didn't even glance at Ruck. "Stinking bitch-clout, does thou breathe still?" He came for Melanthe, gray and powerful, his beard an untamed mat. "Hey and ware, I'll soon strangle thee!"

Ruck sprang to prevent him, ramming him back, holding him with an arm across his chest. "Nay, sir, 'tis folly! Heed to me!"

"Heed ye!" The man fought, big and strong enough in spite of his years to force Ruck to arm's length, but none of his struggle could break him free. "Heed ye, ye pillock, whilst ye degrade your mother, God assoil her! Whilst corrupt your father's line with common blood!" He spat toward Melanthe.

"Enow! Cease off this blundering!" Ruck caught him by the shoulders. With a grunt of effort he forced the old man to his knees. "Abase you!"

The man made wild efforts to rise, but Ruck held him down. "I have no children," Ruck said fiercely. "Ye knows this. I haf said you many times. Now listen to me. Isabelle is dead years agone. My lady's grace is the Princess Melanthe, of Monteverde and Bowland. And my wife. I would you wist it clearly, and repeat my words, that I trow I may release you."

The old man ceased his combat. Melanthe clutched the

sheet and her hand over her bruised shoulder. He turned pale, lifting his face to her. "Bowland?" he said, his voice suddenly atremble. "Lo, the daughter of Sir Richard?"

Ruck let him go. The old man's body shook. As he bowed down his head to his knees and began to weep, Ruck looked quickly toward Melanthe. "My lady—are ye hurt?"

Her arm throbbed, but the quilts had muffled the impact of the sword. She was more stunned than in pain. Wordlessly she shook her head. He turned, kneeling to embrace their groaning attacker, holding him tight, as if he were a child.

"Who is this?" Melanthe exclaimed.

"Sir Harold." He did not say more, but gently urged the other man up. "Come, ye mote depart anon, sir."

Sir Harold pulled himself away. "Sir Richard? You have wed Sir Richard, boy?"

Ruck touched his shoulder and indicated Melanthe. "His daughter," he murmured. "The countess."

The grizzled knight twisted and pulled at his hair, possessed with frantic mumbling. He seemed to lose his strength, falling with his forehead to the floor, begging mercy, muttering in confusion of her father and Bowland and killing. Melanthe watched Ruck try to coax him away with no success.

"Come forward, Sir Harold," she said curtly. "Now speak plain words as a good trusty knight, or take thyself off."

The sharp command seemed to reach his scattered wits. He stopped his moving and mumbling, and crept to the bedside, his scarred hands knotted together. He raised his face to her. "My noble lady's grace," he said, "I haf a demon!"

"Yea, that is clear to me, Sir Harold."

"My lady," he said hopelessly, "me thinks I mote slay myseluen, to kill it."

"Nay, thou wilt not. Nill I nor Lord Ruadrik give thee leave. 'Tis against God, Sir Harold. And would deprive my lord of his rights to aid and counsel of thee." She softened her voice. "When the demon tries to seize thee, thou moste remember to ask God for counsel and solace, for He comes to the aid of those who wish to do good and act faithfully."

The old man gazed at her, dawning adoration in his face.

"Blessed be you, my lady. Oh, my lady, ye be the wisest and worthiest of the world's kind."

"This is not my wisdom, but my honored father's, God give his soul peace. I only mind thee of thy duty."

Sir Harold still wept, but he gave a little sigh. "Gentle lady, truly the Lord God blessed this house on the day your lady's grace wed my lord. It was the unworthy bitch-mare I designed to slay, to keepen clean my lord's noble blood."

"God has saved thee from that mortal sin," Melanthe said. "Take thy near escape to heart."

He bowed his head. "My lady."

"Lord Ruadrik will adjudge thy punishment for striking me, but if it be heavier than a day in the tumbrel, then I will try to intercede for thee."

"Gr'mercy, my lady," he said humbly. "I beg my lady's favor."

"Thou hast my favor. Leave me now." She held out her hand from beneath the sheet to be kissed. He reached for her so quickly that for a moment she regretted the move, but he took her fingers gently, only the rough pads of his palms touching her as he made a courteous gesture of bending over her hand.

"God preserve your lady's grace." He rose, falling back from the bedside with his shoulders squared and his head lifted. Ruck had stood all the time beside him, as if ready to drag him out at any moment. Sir Harold gave him a deep bow, pronounced himself at his lord's mercy whenever he should be pleased to devise a just punishment, and strode from the room.

Immediately Ruck closed the door and barred it. Without speaking, he took up his shirt, pulling it over his head, covering the fiery marks on his skin. For the first time Melanthe became aware of rain that pelted against the window glazing and the cold dimness of the room.

"Depardeu!" She sank back into the pillows. "What next in this place?"

"Ye ne are nought hurt, my lady?"

His cool tone warned her away from japing. Her shoulder throbbed painfully, but she held the silken quilt up close, watching him. "I live."

"He is formaddened, my lady," Ruck said. "Ne can he help himseluen when the fits are on him."

"Who is he?"

"My master in arms. In his prime he tooken a blow to his head that lay bare the brain, and since then has he no command of his rage. But he is a great knight, my lady, and taught me the best that I know of fighting."

"The secret of thy prowess. Thou dost fight like a madman because a madman instructed thee."

He shrugged. "Peraventure, it may be." He bent over a chest and took breeches from it, dressing himself without service. "Sir Harold esteems him gentle blood and bobbaunce above all things. Isabelle he despised, though ne'er did I bring her here. Only to hear her name arages him. He would haf had me taken a princess to wife."

With a little twist of his mouth and a glance at Melanthe, he acknowledged what he'd said, as if he'd just heeded his own words.

"Then I shall crush him with my magnificence, so as to gladden him," she said.

He took clothes from the chest and shut the lid. "Ye delighted him greatly, my lady, with your noble talking."

"It is a talent of mine, noble talking."

"Witterly," he agreed. "Enow to make a man's head spin."

"That is the purpose of noble talking. It has saved many a prince from certain death."

He rested one foot on the ornamented and embellished settle, lacing his hose. The gear was of gray silk, a fitted tunic embroidered in black and set with jet stones, trimmed in sable fur. She was pleased to see that amid his many-hued retainers, he alone went uncolored. It set him apart as no fantastical finery could, and did his comeliness no hurt at all, but underscored it.

"Will ye rise, lady?" he asked when he was done. "Or sleep away all your lifetime?"

She slipped down and pulled the sheet over her head. From beyond the white warmth she heard him move. The door bar made a grating slide.

She sat up. "Wait."

He stood at the door, his hand upon it. Melanthe held the blankets up to her.

"Ne do I wish thee to go," she said abruptly.

He made a slight bow and waited at the door, as if for an order.

"Ne do I wish thee to *go*," she repeated.

"My lady, they expect me in hall. Long haf I been absent, and many matters will await." He scowled down at the hasp. "Though it seem a strange place to you, I am master of it."

She understood a lord's duty as well as she understood how to breathe. But some imp inside her—it did not even seem to be herself—made her plump her body on the mattress like a spoiled child. She turned over with her back to him.

"When you rise, my lady," he said, "I will be below."

She heard the creak of the door and rolled over, flinging a pillow at him. It hit his shoulder. As he turned, she hurled another that struck him full in the chest.

She dropped down into the bed and yanked the coverings over her, curling facedown, her hands gripped together under her chin. She heard the door close. The sound of the boards beneath the carpets traced his coming to the bed. Then she was miserable and angry, not even knowing what to say, beyond a bare demand for his company and his indecent embraces. Too low to sink, to ask for what she had always denied; and too terrible if she should be refused, chosen over, and he went to his minstrels that he loved.

It was not witful to feel so. She herself would have gone to her duties first. She said into the mattress, "Thou art discourteous. Thou hast not even bade me good morn ere thou depart."

"Good morn, then."

"Good morn. And I hope thou dost break into boils and die."

She felt his hand on her back, then both hands sweeping aside the sheet and kneading her bare shoulders. He buried his face in the nape of her neck, his weight bearing down the mattress. With a whimper of relief, she turned up to him, ignoring the pain where he pressed her bruised shoulder, eager for his kisses.

"Ne do I hope for it," she said against his skin, against his cheek rough with new beard. "Ne do I. I would perish without thee."

"Melanthe." His fingers gripped her. "My sovereign lady," he whispered, and gave her freely what she wanted, without the asking, company and unchaste embraces and his body deep in hers, until she perished another way, blind with delight.

RUCK FELT HER sleep—always sleeping, this wife of his—this drowsy miracle, slumbering in his arms as if she were in some enchantment. He pressed his cheek to her loosened hair. The melancholy fathomed him, grief and fate encompassing him while he held on to her.

He waited for it to pass. He listened to the rain and thought of her, how she masked and dazed him. In her easy arrogance she did not confound him; nay, not her commands or noble talking. She was meant to be so, born to be so—it was only what was right.

But she threw pillows at him. And sand. A woman full grown, as old as he, a princess in one look and a looby the next. He had known court ladies to play the child, to pose and flutter and speak in small voices for to draw the men, but she was so unreken and left-handed at it, and so abrupt. He would have thought her more smooth and artful in dalliance. In good faith, he was more comely with love-sporting himself when he tried.

Sometimes it was as if there were another soul inside her. Or by chance it was all false leading, to mock him. He had allowed her in, carried her through the woven wood: she knew Wolfscar now. She would go out, speak of it to the world, jape at him and rob him of what was his. There was only Sir Harold left alive to say that he knew Ruck without nay or doubt. One mad old man to bring in favor of Ruck's claim, against the richest abbey in the northwest. And all hope of Lancaster's esteem and support with the king lost.

Yet she was so soft and slight in his embrace, her arms about him, as if he were her sole defense against any peril. He had shown her through the frithwood, but she had not slipped so quietly through the thickets that he had raised about his heart. She burned them down to find him, and then left him smoking ashes.

It was too late. She was here. He was at her mercy, as he had been from the moment he had beheld her.

"YOU HAVE NO choice, if you hold any hope for this sister of yours," Allegreto said, low and harsh. He leaned across the table. "You're a bungler, Cara. You're hopeless. You haven't got the nerve to work alone."

In the miserable little alehouse, the light through a barred window fell on his face, making a mask of him, an ancient pagan statue in the shadow of some ruin. Smoke from the open fire in the floor permeated every crevice and flavored her ale. She drank a sip, forcing herself to swallow the sour brew without looking down. It was cloudy and cold, like everything in this godforsaken northern land. Outside it snowed, when it was not raining. She put down the vessel and stuffed her hand back in the muff he had bought for her.

A sennight she had been with him. Once, she had tried to steal her silver as he slept—a futile chance, and almost fatal. She had cut the length of his stiletto on the side of her neck, where he had nearly impaled her throat as he overturned upon her.

"How can I go in there?" she whispered desperately. "She said she would have me killed!"

"If she had wanted you killed, you would be dead." He leaned back, draining his ale. "She would have told me to see to it."

"So she said, that she would loose you upon me—only she would not say when, but she would not make me suffer to wait long!"

He laughed. "Naturally. And what did you do, goose? Bolted, just as she designed."

Cara glared at him. "As did you, Navona."

He nodded, his grin becoming a sneer. "Yea. I did. And I will pay for it in full, do I not remedy the matter."

His eyes slid away. He stared into the dark corner. Twice, when they had slept in barns and cow-byres on the journey, she had heard a faint sound in the night. He wept, she thought, but she was not certain. Perhaps he only dreamed.

"Well," he said, "she has outwitted herself. She never meant for her escort to leave her to a man, of that we can be sure. I wager even the green fellow deserted her in the end— or died for her when the bandits fell on them, more like, as these love-drunk champions are wont to do. So we've only to see to her ransom, and she's delivered back to us tied up in silk ribbons."

"Haps they killed her," Cara said, feeling guilty and hopeful.

"They're a foolish lot of brigands if they did. She's worth their wildest dreams, and I'll wager they know it. We'll have her back for the right price."

"Mary, if you're so anxious to save her, you should have gone to the prince of that Chester city and begged his aid."

"The cities don't have princes here, or patricians. I don't know what they have, but you can be sure that whoever rules so close to that nest of outlaws is like a hand in their glove. And even if she made a fool of me with her cursed plague trick, still pestilence might lurk in the cities, though we've seen the countryside clear. Nay, we will work from out of the princess's own hold, where we can have some command of matters."

"I can't go in that castle!" Cara kept her voice low, watching the alewife who watched her. No one here spoke a civilized language, only a few words of broken French, but they did not seem oversurprised at foreign travelers. She feared that meant the Princess Melanthe's retinue from London had already arrived. Her stronghold of Bowland was but an hour's ride from here, if the alewife's nods and babble could be depended upon. "What if the others have come?"

"Hah! Who did she leave to charge of them? Sodorini, that fluttering old buffoon! They'll go in such circles they won't be here for weeks. And why should you fear them anyway?"

"I—" She stopped herself suddenly.

Allegreto smiled in the barred light. "Who is it, Monteverde goose?"

She took another gulp of her unpleasant ale.

"Cara," he said patiently, "do you suppose I don't know there is a Riata among them? You have no choice. I tell you.

Come to us—we serve and keep our own, not like the Riata dogs—and Monteverde is gone forever." He leaned forward across the table. "I'll speak to my father. We'll even get your sister back, if she's still alive."

"You cannot promise that," she said.

He shrugged. "Nay, for she may be dead already."

"You cannot promise for Navona." Her lip curled. "He broke my family. My father—"

"Was a foolish man," Allegreto said soberly. "If he had cared for his family, he would have done what was asked of him. And your mother did not fare so badly when she married again."

She turned her face away from him, so full of hate that she could not even speak to uphold her father. She did not know what Navona had asked of him; she only knew that he had been tortured to death on a false accusation, and Navona had caused it.

She pushed away from the table and stood up, flinging her muff onto the smoky fire. "My mother was terrified to be wed to Ligurio's brother. She lived the last days of her life in dread that she would bear a son and see him killed by Gian. I cannot deal with Navona."

He rose as quickly, at the same time that the alewife darted forward and snatched up the muff. The woman held it uncertainly, and then retreated to the far corner like some stray dog with a scrap.

"Cara." He stood between her and the door.

"I cannot," she said.

"Cara!"

"I will not."

"Oh, no, have mercy on me."

"On you!" she shrieked. "Who ever had mercy on my father or my mother or my sister or me? Nay, why should I have any mercy on *you*, ten-times damned creature that you are!"

"Cara." He was pleading. "For God's pity! I'll have to kill you!"

She stilled, knowing it and yet shocked by it. He had already trapped her; she could not reach the door beyond him. She stared at the knife at his side.

"Don't try," he said. "Don't try. Please."

A cat rose from a pile of rags and stretched. In the moment that she glanced at it, the stiletto was in his hand. The alewife whimpered, backed in her corner.

"Only say it." He held the knife relaxed at his side. "Only say you're with us. I'll trust you."

The fire smoked sullenly.

"I cannot. Not for my life."

He made the same grieving sound that he made in his sleep. His fingers moved on the weapon, rotating it in his hand. "Do you hate me so much?"

"Oh, yes," she said. "More."

"I'll save your sister. On my soul, I'll see her safe."

"You have no soul to swear upon." She was shaking. "Liar and murderer." She began to walk past him. "Hell will embrace you."

He moved. Cara flinched, her pride withering into a humiliating recoil. His hand gripped her; the tip of the knife touched her rib through the coarse wool.

She could see the pulse in his throat. She was trembling so hard that the stiletto goaded her, stinging like a pinprick, forcing tears to her eyes.

"So do it, Navona!" She showed her teeth like a cornered animal, to defy him.

His beautiful black eyes stared into hers. The knife tip touched her again, and she jerked.

"Don't!" she cried. "Don't taunt me!"

"You're with us," he said.

"Nay, I'll kill you if I can!" The fear possessed her. She heard herself, long past reason to mindless, witless, hopeless defiance. "I'll work for the Riata; I spit on the name of Navona; I'll wipe it from the face of the earth!"

He pressed the knife to her, and the tears spilled over. It stung violently; she imagined the blade sliding in, a thousand times greater pain. She waited for it. She had a panicked thought that she would be unshriven; but she could not even confess in her heart; she kept saying farewell to Elena, over and over, until it took up all of her perception.

When he let go of her, it happened so suddenly that she

fell backward against the trestle table. It rocked beneath her weight as she clutched the edge.

A shadow passed the window. She heard a horse, its feet squelching mud. A voice hailed from outside.

The alewife ran forward. Allegreto stopped her, pressing his fist hard to her mouth and jerking his knife in her face. He freed her slowly. She shrank back and slunk into her corner again.

"Ave!" The door swung open, rain splattering on the sill. A young man walked through, pushing his hood back, showing blond hair. "Ave, godday!" He carried his own drinking vessel. He plunged it into the cask himself, dropping the cover back with a bang, and asked something of the alewife. It was English, but the word *Bowland* at the end of his question was roundly clear.

The wife ducked a nod, her glance flicking to Cara and Allegreto. The newcomer turned.

"God bless," he said in a friendly way, and waved toward the door, whooshing another English comment through his teeth, obviously a complaint on the weather.

"May God protect you," Cara said boldly in French, seeing a savior in him. She held her fingers pressed over her side, staunching her stinging cut.

He bowed. "Grant merci, and God smile on you, lovely lady," he replied, his French accent ungraceful but his words distinct enough. He nodded at Allegreto. "Good sir."

Allegreto bowed, indicating the table. "Honor us."

"Gladly." The young man smiled, doffing his cloak and shaking the drops from it before he hung it on a peg. He wore flesh-colored hose with dirty wool bandages wrapped up to the knees for protection. They were an absurd color, but after a week with Allegreto, an open face and easy smile were enough to please Cara. "I'm Guy of Torbec," he said. "But I think—you aren't English, sir?"

"We serve the Princess of Monteverde," Allegreto said.

"Ha! Mont-verde? Then Bowland it was, by God! I guessed it." Guy straddled the bench. "I am on the right road at last. Has he got your lady safe back, praise God?"

Allegreto grew very still. "Back?"

Guy seemed suddenly to realize that he might have been

indiscreet and set the pot down, glancing over his shoulder. "The lady of Mont-verde and Bowland," he whispered. "She was not—away?"

Cara put her hand over Allegreto's arm. "She was attacked," she murmured. "We were in the party. Do you say she is safe?"

"Or bring a ransom demand?" Allegreto asked sharply.

"Nay, nay—by God's love, *I* had no part of any such notion!" Guy leaned forward. "I only bring news. I wish to help."

"What news?" Allegreto murmured.

Guy chewed his lip, eyeing them warily. "I was bound for the castle. I thought the green knight might give me a place in his company."

Allegreto's arm relaxed beneath her hand. "If it's reward you want, then tell me. I'll see you get a place if you deserve it."

In spite of his peasant clothes, Allegreto had that easy arrogance about him that bespoke authority. She could see the Englishman puzzling over it.

Guy tapped his fist rapidly against his knee. Then he sighed through his teeth. "Can you? But I don't have much news, I fear. Only that I saw her, with a knight who named himself by his color green, at Torbec Manor, in Lancashire." He nodded in a direction that meant nothing to Cara. "But they fled west, with my—with the man who holds Torbec Manor at their heels. He lost them at the coast. We—he thought they must have gone south along the shore, but I thought the green knight clever enough to come back through the pursuit. And I remembered Bowland, on the falcon's varvel, and that the old earl's daughter was wed to a foreign prince. So I came here, because I couldn't stay at Torbec." He wet his lips. "I hoped they would have come by now. I—did him a little good, the green knight, I think, so I reckoned he might look well on me."

"When was this?" Allegreto demanded.

"Four days past."

"And she was with the green man alone?"

Guy nodded.

Allegreto smiled at him. "Well done," he said. "Well

done, Guy of Torbec. Come with us. We're for the castle. I
think you'll find a place."

IT WAS THE finest bed to sleep in that Melanthe could
imagine. She did not leave it for three days, but lay
enveloped in warmth, enfolded in slumber and safety while
the rain slid down the windows. Ruck leaned over her,
already garbed, and kissed her beneath her ear.

"Thou moste be in some witch's thrall," he murmured.
"The alder-most slothful witch in the world."

She flipped the sheet over her nose, languid in the aftermath of their morning love. "Send drink and bread. And
return to me full soon."

"I wen well where to finden thee, at the least."

She smiled with her eyes closed. "Melikes thy mattress,
my lord. By hap will I never leave it."

He did not answer, but pushed away from the bed. She
heard him cross the chamber. The door opened and closed.
Before, each morning as he left, she had settled into the bed,
satisfied and sated with their coupling, sustained on the
wheaten bread and ale someone left on a trestle beside her,
drowsing until he came again. She had not thought of where
he went; she had not thought of anything at all with more
than a torpid interest that passed into pleasing dreams.

But a small doubt crept into her mind, because he had not
answered her when she had said she might never leave. The
two Williams would be out there—unlikely they were
singing her praises to his ears, or urging him to prolong her
stay. She opened her eyes.

She sat up and swept back the bedcoverings. Chill air
touched her skin.

Fool. Fool! No woman held a man with bed-play alone,
not with his favorites whispering poison in his ears.

She had felt safe. She *was* safe. But if there was one lesson greater than any other Ligurio had pressed upon her, it
was that to give a man what he wanted was to lose all mastery of him. Ruck was so sweet and stirring when he came,
she had not sensed the danger until this moment.

She thrust her feet from the bed. There was no maid, of
course. She had to serve herself as he did, but in rooting

through the chamber chests she found a linen smock, stiff and unworn. It smelled very faintly of herbs. There were robes too, but she refused to appear in the raiment of the former lady of the castle like some resurrected ghost. She put on her own faithful gown and azure houpelande over the clean linen.

Her hair she could only cover with a kerchief, with no one to dress it for her. She found one clustered with jasper and chalcedony. All of the clothing in the chests was richly adorned with embroidery and gems. No poor knight's hold, this Wolfscar.

She thought of the minstrels who sojourned here at their ease, and narrowed her eyes. But she would move carefully. A man's favorites could be delicate matters, not subject to common reasoning with his wit, as the history of any number of kings could attest.

THE STAIRWELL FROM the lord's presence chamber opened onto the high end of the great hall. Melanthe heard voices and music and laughter before she reached the floor, but in this castle there were no convenient spying peeks to oversee the hall, or none that she could find.

She stepped into the doorway, then hastily pulled back. Ruck was there, seated at the table on the dais, facing away from her. He had a child on his shoulders, a half-grown babe with feet balanced on either side of his head and hands planted in his black hair as he bent over rolls and counters spread across the table. In her brief moment of view, Melanthe had seen William Foolet counseling with him, and minstrels all around the hall, some of them congregated about the dais, some at work, and one pair juggling a great wheel of apples up toward the roof.

Melanthe sat down on the stair out of sight. The fantastic aspect of it struck her anew. She felt unsure of herself, a somber crow at the feast. It would not be wise, she thought, to go to him amidst their smiles and laughter. Later, when he came to her alone, she could try to reckon how the Williams might have damaged her.

But she did not want to go back to the empty bedchamber now. She sat in the stairwell, listening to the easy talk, the murmurs of mirth. They spoke of lambing and the fish in the lake, things she knew but little of. She could predict what would happen if she stepped through the door. They would all turn and stare, and she must be her lady's grace the princess then, for she knew nothing else to be.

Quick small footsteps sounded on the wooden dais, and a little girl in gaudy-green appeared through the door. She put her plump hands on Melanthe's knees and leaned forward, dark-eyed and rapt, her black locks flying free of any braid. "Why hide ye?" she demanded.

Melanthe drew back a little. "Ne do I hide."

"Ye does. I saw you. But I found you!" She turned and wedged herself into the space between Melanthe and the wall, taking a seat on the narrow stair. She put her arms about Melanthe's neck and kissed her cheek. "I love you."

"Thou dost not love me," Melanthe said. "Thou dost not even know me."

"Ye are the princess." She said it with an enraptured sigh. "I am Agnes." She laid her head on Melanthe's shoulder and took her hand, toying with the rings. "I play the tympan and the cymbals. I haf a white falcon and lots of jewels."

Melanthe watched the small fingers trifle with hers. "Thou art a great lady, then."

"Yea," Agnes said. "I shall sleepen all the day when I be grown. Ne likes me nought to nap now, though," she added scrupulously. "I shall marry Desmond."

"Desmond. The porter?"

"He will be the king then."

"Ah," Melanthe said. "A man of ambition."

"A man of what?" Agnes looked up at her. "Oh. Are you sad?"

Melanthe shook her head.

"You weep, my lady."

"Nay. I do not."

"I love you." Agnes climbed into her lap and put her face into Melanthe's throat. "Ne do nought weep."

"I do not."

"Why do you weep?" The girl's voice was muffled.

Melanthe held the small body close to her. "I'm afraid," she whispered. She drew a breath against fine black hair, as if she could drink it like some fragrant long-forgotten wine. "I'm afraid."

"Oh, my lady, be nought." Agnes hugged her. "All be well, so long as we bide us here as my lord commands, and go nought out beyond the wood."

Nineteen

⸺⟨≋⟩⸺

THEY HAD PLEASED Ruck, those days that she spent tumbled in his bed like a dozing kitten. He would have thought she was ill, but that he knew her for a master in the art of idle slumbering, and she awoke well enough when he came.

While she had stayed in his chamber, Wolfscar was his yet. He spent the days in ordinary work, in spring plans and lists of repairs, the most of which would never get done, but he did not have to make explanations or excuses to her. She had asked nothing, but only besought him in bed with her blunt and unhende wooing.

He did not dislike it. A'plight, he lived all through the day in thought and prospect of it. His clearest memories of Isabelle were of bedding her, and those were dim, overlaid with years of throttled desire and fantasy. But he did not think that any woman on Earth or in imagination could compare with Melanthe, her black hair and white body, her sleepy eyes like purple dusk, the feel of her as she used him, mounting atop him in her favored sin. To have seen her so was worth a thousand years of burning to him. If he went to Hell for it, he only prayed God would not take away the memory.

Still, nothing about her came as he expected it. When finally she had left the bed and appeared in the hall, he was girded for her queries and objections. He saw her look about. He had grown taut in readiness for her censure—saw dust and decay that he had never noticed before.

But he was forwondered once again by his liege lady. She did not speak of Wolfscar's unkept state at all. She smiled at him like a shamefast maid, looking up from beneath a kerchief. She became modest; at night she withdrew from him and eluded his kisses. In the day she went about with a crowd of small girls. It was as if she had arisen from her spelled sleep transformed, turned from a haughty princess into a nun's acolyte.

Will Foolet was terrified of her. Bassinger was not daunted to speak to any person alive—he would have sung his lays to the Fiend himself given the chance—but even he gave her a wide breach. All three of them, Ruck and Will and Bassinger, had heard her speak her mind about Wolfscar and its history.

The others gathered around her, enslaved as easily as she had vanquished Hew Dowl and Sir Harold. Will was complained of and called a hard taskmaster, only for directing that the ground-breaking begin in the fields. Performing before her lady's grace, their first new spectator in a decade of years, was much to be preferred.

Ruck and Will rode out alone to the shepherds and lambs, making rain-soaked notes of the fences and fodder, and lists of needed work. They ordered the labor by its importance, for never did they have enough bodies or skills to carry out all that cried to be done. Before there had been willingness and ready hands, at least. Now the fields and the bailey were empty, and Ruck walked into the hall to find it full of tumbling and singing before Melanthe.

He lost his temper. Flinging his wet mantle from his shoulders, he strode into the middle of the clear space, halting a pair of somersaults before they were begun. The music died.

"Is a feast day?" Ruck glared around him. He threw his cloak onto the floor, sending droplets from it to spatter on the tile. "How be it that my gear is drenched and my rouncy in mud to his belly, while ye maken mirths and plays? Am I your lord or your servant?"

Everyone fell to his knees. A tympan tinkled in the stunned

silence as a small girl crawled from Melanthe's lap and knelt, holding the belled drum before her.

"Thorlac," he snapped to one of the poised tumblers. "Stable my mount. Simon, take Will's. Stands he outside in the rain with the order of laboring. Nill no one be seen in this hall nor heard to singen or playen until Lent is passed. Eat in the low hall, and give ye thanks for it."

At once the great room emptied, light footsteps and shuffles and the odd note of a justled instrument. Only Melanthe was left, sitting on a settle drawn near the huge chimney. The gems on her kerchief gleamed as she bent her head, rubbing one hand over the back of the other.

"My lady mote forgive me for ending your sport," he said tautly, "but the work demands."

"I ask thy pardon," she said, without lifting her face. "Ne did I know it. I thought they were at leisure."

"Nought in this season, my lady. Spring comes."

"Yea," she said.

No more than that. He was damp, his hands still cold, though the fire beside her rumbled with more than enough wood and charcoal. "Haf I displeased you, lady," he said harshly, "that ye refuse my company?"

He had not meant to speak it out so abruptly. Her hands folded together in her lap, nunlike.

"I ne do not refuse thy company, my lord. I am with thee now."

"My embraces," he said.

She slanted a look up at him beneath the kerchief and her lashes, and then gazed down again, the picture of chastity.

He paced away. "Peraventure ye tire of this place and wish to go anon to Bowland."

"Nay, and risk the pestilence?" she asked quickly.

He turned. "Was little sign of it enow, my lady. Only at Lyerpool."

"Who speaks to thee of this—that I would go?"

"I think of your place, and your holdings. Ne cannought ye look to sojourn here long, to your lands' neglect."

She stood up. "Who spake thee so?"

"Is common wit, my lady. I should have seen you to

Bowland, as we intended. Nis nought fitting I should have brought you here to detain you."

"Thy minstrels said thee so!" she exclaimed.

"My minstrels?" he repeated blankly. He stopped in the face of her vehemence. "Nay, they said no such."

"William Foolet has whispered in thy ears, and the Bassinger, to sayen thee of my lands' neglect, and plague is no danger to me!"

"Ne did they."

"Dost thou care less for me than for thy people? They are commanded to stay within your *plessis* wood for fear of pestilence!"

"Watz nought my meaning, forsooth!" He found himself near to shouting in response to her wild accusations. "Faithly—ne did I wist you feared the plague so much."

"I do."

Her violet eyes regarded him, shaded in black lashes. She had never seemed overconcerned to Ruck. She did not seem so now. With her head lifted, her kerchief sparkling with gems, she seemed more angry than alarmed.

"Ye does nought choose to make all haste to your lands, then," he said.

"I fear pestilence."

He shook his head with a slight laugh. "My lady—ne do I trow that you e'er speak me troth."

"I do! I fear to go out, for the pestilence."

Her lips made a strange pressing curve—an aspect there and gone, a shadow between her brows before she smoothed her face again to cool composure. Always she was a secret, impossible to read. It could have been a hidden smile or a hint of tears. But he thought it was not a smile.

She faced him wholly. "Thou said that I may stop here, where no ill could come, so long as I wished!" She made it a challenge, as if she expected him to deny it.

"Then do we nought go, my lady," he said, "until I know it to be safe for you."

"Oh," she said, and closed her eyes.

"I thought me that you would wish to depart anon."

She made a tiny shake of her head.

"Melanthe," he said, "will I ne'er understand thee?"

Her eyes opened. "When I wish it."

He bent and retrieved his wet mantle, throwing it across his shoulder as he stepped up onto the dais. "My lady," he said, giving her a brief, stiff bow before he went through the door and mounted the stairs.

He had stripped himself down for dry weeds when she came. She closed the door and looked at him with a look that made the blood run strong in his veins. He could not hide himself, though he turned away from her—but she came to him and touched him and put his hands at her waist.

He kissed her. He held her hard and laid her on the bed, knowing he had been befooled somehow, that she meant to wile him by her days of denying and now giving, heartless ramp that she was. But she had only wiled him into what he wanted anyway, to keep her here and love and overlie her until she gasped in frenzy beneath him, her hair escaped from the kerchief to spread all about the pillows.

He buried his face in the black silken strands, groaning his release through clenched teeth. He lay atop her and felt her breasts rise and fall against him, her sheath tight and delicious, faint throbs in her that ran through him like sweet kisses.

She turned her lips beside his ear. "Now," she said, "thou dost understand me."

He gave a laugh, his teeth still clenched. "No, Melanthe. Only you make me cease to care if I do or nay."

IN A CAREFUL fold over her arm, Cara carried an altar-cloth and the vestments she was to mend. She crossed Bowland's dim and busy hall, jumping back from a wood-man's bundle of fagots as he stopped suddenly in front of her and dropped the load. The wood thudded almost on her toes.

"Ware thee!" she exclaimed, one of the English expressions she was learning well among these savages.

The servant turned with a great show of surprise, but he was smirking beneath it. He did not even bow, but only leaned down to grab the roped bundle.

"Thou didst that on purpose!" she cried in outrage. "Disrespectful oaf, thou wouldst have broke my foot!"

He didn't understand her French, or pretended not to. She

pressed her lips together. In less than a fortnight here, the small slights were mounting to open disdain. She hated this place, and these people. A hot sting threatened behind her eyes.

Someone stopped beside her. Still in his travel mud, the English squire Guy seized the woodman's collar and dragged him up close. He growled something in English. The servant's insolence vanished as he tried to choke out words and bow at the same time, his face turning red with effort.

Guy spoke again, short and fierce, and shoved the woodman back. He fell over his own pile of fagots, landing on the rush mat with a loud thud and yelp. Guy made a gesture toward Cara. When the servant was slow in heaving himself up, Guy stepped over the bundle and aimed a kick with his armored toe.

The man yelped again, scrambling into a kneel before Cara. He begged her pardon humbly, in perfectly adequate French.

Everyone in the hall had paused to watch. Guy swept a look over them. "Surely a noble house serves its ladies with good cheer," he said, his quiet voice carrying to the corners.

The hall was silent. Slowly, as Guy maintained his arrogant stare, one or two of them bowed, then more, until finally every servant in the hall had acknowledged him.

He gave Cara a curt nod and strode back toward the passage beyond the screens, his blue cloak flaring from his shoulders. She looked down at the still-kneeling woodman and the respectfully bowed heads around her, and hugged the vestments close, turning to go after him.

She caught up with him in the passage. "Sir!"

He stopped, looking over his shoulder. When he saw her, his face broke into a boyish grin.

"I must thank you, sir," she said, halting a few feet away from him and lowering her face.

"Did you see that?" he exclaimed. "It worked. I can't believe I did it."

The excitement in his voice made her look up. He was still grinning, with a streak of mud she hadn't noticed on his jaw. When she had first seen him, his blond hair had been damp and plastered to his head—she hadn't realized what a bright color it was, shining like a golden crown in the dismal passage. He didn't wear the flesh-colored hose now, but a soldier's armor. He did not appear silly at all.

"It's the manner," he said. "Soft and steady. Confidence."

"God grant you mercy, sir, for your aid," she repeated, taking a shy step backward.

He bowed. "It was an honor to serve you, my lady."

She almost retreated, and then paused. "You've been traveling."

He lowered his voice. "Seeking after news of your mistress. Navona and Lord Thomas have divided a few of us to search and report."

"You've found something?" Cara asked anxiously.

He shook his head. "I'm sorry, my lady. Nothing. But you must not fear that we will fail." He gestured toward the door. "I must give my account to them now, and so haste, if I don't offend you."

"Oh no—of course you must go." She moistened her lips. "Where do you lodge?"

"Over the postern gate, with the squires."

"I will see that a bath is made for you, and see that your robes are ready when you wish them." She wrapped the vestments close about her arm and went quickly toward the hall. She hesitated at the screen, glancing back.

He stood looking after her, his golden hair a faint gleam against the stone. She smiled, making a little courtesy, and hurried into the hall.

THERE WERE ALMOST no other women in the castle—none at all of Cara's rank, and, she had the upper rooms of the household range to herself except for the infrequent servants passing through. She had found herself a place by a window and sat in the embrasure, bending over the vestments in the rain-soaked light and picking the seam loose with her needle.

Allegreto came upon her before she knew he was there. She reached for scissors and looked up, starting to see him leaned against the stone chimney mantel with his arms crossed.

"Blessed Mary!" she exclaimed, her hand on her breast. "You're as sly as a stoat."

He inclined his head, as if it were a compliment. Dressed in the Bowland livery, all scarlet but for a simple gold slash diagonal, he might have been a crimson angel or a devil from the fires below. Cara slipped her needle into the fabric, pretending to go back to work. He came sometimes to watch her, and then left again without saying a word—spying, she supposed, though to what purpose but to unnerve her she had no notion.

The disastrous news they had brought to Bowland of Princess Melanthe's disappearance had worked heavily on the peace of the castle's constable, as well Cara could imagine. Sir Thomas seemed an able and efficient man enough, to see the sound state of the hold and garrison, but in this crisis his management failed him. She was aware that Allegreto had played no small part in the man's consternation, encouraging him in terrifying notions of who would be blamed if the news spread and the king heard. Allegreto ever had the natural presence of his father if he pleased to use it, and he did now. A bare sixteen years he might have, but Sir Thomas hung upon his advice as if he were a hundred.

"Put down your work," Allegreto said softly to her. "I have news."

A bolt of fear made her fingers jump. She barely missed pricking her finger. "Tell me!"

"A runner has arrived. The rest of our people will be here before night." He made a humorless chuckle. "And only a month since they left London! Sodorini outdoes himself."

She was glad she did not hold the needle, for in her shaking hand it would surely have pierced her. Allegreto watched, a flame and a darkness.

"I have waited, Cara. Now you must decide."

The castle suddenly seemed a huge weight around her, pressing down upon her.

"Riata or Navona," he said.

She wadded the vestments in her fists. "My sister. My sister."

"We will ruse them. But I must know who it is."

"I can't tell you!"

"Little fool, do you think I can't find out for myself? I'll know by who kills you." He pushed off the chimney. "We came here together. I brought you. Cara, *I* brought you!"

She fixed her eyes on his crimson figure. With a blinding vision, she understood him, saw how it would appear in Riata eyes. The princess was still alive, free of any nunnery, outside of all reach—and only Cara and Allegreto, together, had returned with the word. Even a child must believe that they had conspired to effect it.

"Only tell me," he said. "I can safeguard you."

She closed her eyes.

"I beseech you. I beg you."

"Ficino," she whispered.

With a soft rustle across the rushes, he came close to her. "You're with us now. With me. I'll keep your sister if God wills."

He stood before her, the devil's perfection, invoking God. Abruptly he went to one knee and gathered the vestments and her hands within his, pressing his face into the cloth. As suddenly he let her go. He thrust himself back, as if he had touched a flame, and went to the passage.

He stopped there. Without looking at her, he said, "You must send him word to meet you in the cistern cellar, the one where the oils are stored."

She stared at him, bereft of words at what he had just done.

"Cara!" he snapped over his shoulder. "Repeat me, that I know you won't blunder it!"

She started. "The cistern cellar, for the oils," she said. Before she was finished speaking, he had gone.

THE ALARM BELLS came deep in the night, dread tolling and shouts of fire. All the ladies rushed about in the dark, trying to find their way among the half-packed baggage and chests. Cara was the first down the stairs, knowing her way, holding her candle aloft for the others to see.

The hall seethed with torch shadows and confusion. She tried to stop a servant, but none would mind her, and the ladies were screaming and pressing around, pushing for the door. She was carried with them out into the bailey, where the low clouds reflected light onto a chain of men passing buckets.

No flames showed, only a black boil of smoke pouring from the base of the farthest tower. Even as she watched from the hall steps, it began to dissipate, and then vanished, carried away into the night. A hail began at that end of the bailey, a cheer that rolled toward the hall. The bucket chain began to break and scatter into knots of men, most of them pushing toward the tower.

Cara drew a deep breath. It appeared to be quenched. She almost turned to go in, but a figure caught her eye, a gleam of bright hair among the men. He carried two buckets in one hand, striding out from the crowd. She watched him turn and shout at a page, and trade the empty buckets for a torch.

The brand lit Guy's face, showing him smoke-blackened and his shirt stuffed hastily into his breeches. A sudden cough racked him; he bent over, holding the torch awkwardly as he choked.

Cara forgot her undress and cold feet. She ran down the steps and grabbed up a bucket that still had water in it, hauling it with her in spite of the sloshing that wet her gown. She came to him as he straightened up, still spluttering.

"Drink, sir." She set the bucket on the ground and reached for his torch.

He looked down at her blankly. For an instant she feared that he had already forgotten her, but then his gaze cleared and his open grin dawned. "Grant merci," he croaked, and squatted beside the bucket, scooping water into his hands. He drank deeply, then splashed it on his face and stood, wiping his arm across his eyes.

Cara smiled at the wild smear of blacking that he made. "Your bath is wasted, sir, I fear."

He rose, making a small bow. "Ah, but I did delight in it," he said hoarsely, "and that is not wasted, good lady." He looked beyond her, lifting his hand in salute to another smoke-blackened man passing.

His companion stopped, with a nod toward Cara. "They say there was a poor devil in there, by Christ," he said.

"'Fore God." Guy blew air through his teeth and made the cross. "He has passed to his reward, may the good Lord save his soul. I know not what was in that cellar, but did burn like the flames of Hell."

" 'Tis where they keep the oils," the other man said. "Good fortune that the stock was low—here, ma'am!"

Cara had dropped the torch. She could not get her breath.

"My lady." Guy's face swam in front of her. "For love—John!"

She did not swoon. A horrible shaking fit possessed her. She felt she must scream, but she could not scream. Her knees were sinking beneath her. Before she reached the ground she felt herself lifted up.

"We shouldn't have spoken of it in front of her." She heard Guy's voice, but she couldn't command words. He carried her into the hall, and next she knew the ladies were crowded around him and hart's horn and vinegar thrust into her face as he set her down.

"No—" She pushed them feebly away. "I'm well. I only—lost my breath."

Guy knelt beside her, looking up into her face with a frown of innocent concern, black streaked all across his nose and temple. Cara clutched his hand. She swallowed, trying to command herself. But when she lifted her head, she lost all mastery.

Beyond him, past the ladies in nightgowns and the men in shirts, above the curious faces and tumult, Allegreto stood on the dais, dressed in gold and fire.

He was utterly still, watching her, the only silent figure in the commotion.

She moaned, shaking her head. Guy pressed her hand and patted it. He asked her something, but she did not hear. She pulled away and stumbled from the bench. Guy called after her, but she couldn't stop; she had to run, turning and twisting blindly, like a doe trying to find some break in the deerpark wall.

Twenty

———

THERE WERE TRAPS set all over Wolfscar. They were feminine traps, light and easy to escape, but no man tried too hard. On the day after Easter, with Lent past and Ruck's grievous interdict lifted, the sport of Hock Monday became an occasion for high glee.

Ruck found himself hocked at the door to the great hall, barred by a rope from passing until he paid a groat to the mirthful women who stopped his way. His was an easy escape—the other men were bound hand and foot, voicing loud protest, struggling at their fetters, refusing to pay and altogether making the most of their imprisonment while it lasted.

Having bought his freedom, he reached the gatehouse and crossed the bridge safely. Crocus bloomed alongside the road, saffron yellow. Alone but for the grazing animals, with the shouts and song left behind him, he walked beside the furrowed and readied fields, his breath frosting in clear air.

He stooped and probed in the mud with a stick, pleased with the results of the new draining ditches. The mill needed repair, but the mill always needed repair. They had pressed the oxen to plow near four virgates of land, even reclaiming some that had gone to brambles.

He sat on his heels, looking out over the valley and the high slopes. Protection and boundary, the purple-green walls. So easy to forget the world beyond them. He stared at the long morning shadow of the castle across the fields, the dark ripples of turrets and chimneys on red soil.

For weeks they had lived as man and wife, lived as if nothing existed beyond Wolfscar. Not once had she said that the time neared for leaving.

He flipped a clod of mud from the end of the stick. It fell with a plop. He flipped another, watching it hit the ground, thinking of why she would not want to go, why she would sojourn here so long without even desiring to send word of herself to her home. There were dangers, yea; always peril— but he had never thought she would stay so long.

He should speak, he knew, though it was easy to bide silent. Easy to stay his tongue, hard to find the moment. He had never been so loath to think beyond the frith-wood.

A chimney shadow took on life as someone came up the road behind him. He did not rise, but flipped mud from his stick, waiting for Will to discuss the seed corn.

Instead a rope dropped over his shoulders. A tug pulled him off his feet. With a startled flail and exclamation, he over-turned onto his back in the cold grass.

"I have thee!" Melanthe said.

She fell on her knees, pinning the rope down with her hands next to his shoulders. He lay looking at her upside down.

"How much?" he asked.

"All thy land and chattels, knight, shouldst thou hope to rise again."

"I paid the others but a groat."

"Ha," she said, "I make no such paltry bargains."

He pulled her down and kissed her, holding her head between his hands. "All is thine, brazen wench," he said against her lips. "'Ware thee what I levy on the morrow, when will be the men's turn."

"Thou moste catch me first."

He rolled over and sat up, casting the rope about her. "Haply I haf thee already."

She squealed and wriggled like a village girl. "Thou

treacher! Never!" Their frosted breaths mingled in the sun as he held the cord against her struggles. She tried to push him away, laughing. "No trumping wretch shall cheat me of my lands!"

He stilled, standing on his knees, looking into her eyes. "Melanthe," he said soberly, "ne do nought accuse me of it, e'en in jape."

Her hands lightened on his shoulders. Then she gave him a push. "Whence this gravity, monk-man? Thou wilt be sorry, to fatigue me with earnest speech."

"Nay, my lady, I have bided silent too long." Ruck let the rope fall. He stood up and walked a step away. "I let bliss conquer my wit. Ne can you nought linger here lost for e'ermore."

He looked back at her. She sat on her knees, holding the rope across her lap, staring down at it. On her hair she wore the golden net. From her shoulders a mink-lined cloak of amber flowed carelessly onto the muddy grass. He did not recognize it; she must have found it among the fabrics and chests that filled abandoned wardrobes all over the castle, more richness than Ruck had ever been able to use. And yet a hundred times more wealth belonged to her beyond the mountains.

"My lady—if it be our marriage that checks you from returning—I ask no open espousal of you. For as long as you will, it shall be secret and private betwixt us."

"Is this repentance," she asked lightly, "that thou wouldst conceal our vows?"

"Nought repentance, ne'er mine, forsooth. But I think me the world will looken harsh upon your folly, and therefore you tarry here for fear of consequences. Ne did I wed thee to obtain thy fortune or place. I am willing to biden, without I am acknowned to the world as thy husband, till some meet time as you choose. Be it long, e'en."

"Such heavy thoughts!" She reached over and plucked a tiny snowblossom from the grass. "Thou dost weary me."

"We moten set our faces to this, and take you to your rightful place."

"The plague," she said. "We dare not venture out."

He shook his head. "I will go alone. After Hocktide, to

ascertain what is in the world. A day or twain, peradventure, to discover if plague still imperils."

She curled the rope about her hand, crushing the flower in it. "Thy talk annoys me," she said. She cast the blossom away and rose. "Come, I would have luf-laughing, and not leaving."

With her hands about his arms, she pulled him to a fierce kiss, drowning why and wherefore and reason. She could make him forget time and sense. She could make him forget his own name.

ON THE WEDNESDAY after Hocktide, Ruck came upon Desmond far up the mountainside, plucking doleful tunes on a gittern and staring at the blank wall of mist that shrouded the hills. Although in his gloom the boy appeared not to notice Ruck, he was situated where he could be sighted easily from the trail, a brooding figure in yellow and green like a forlorn elf-prince of the wood. Since it was well known that Ruck intended to make scout-watch outside the valley today, he viewed this melancholy vision with a dry smile, understanding it to be a request for audience. Ruck had a fair guess as to what matter troubled Desmond. Maidens.

He tied the bay mare and hiked up the rocks, coming to where the youth sat cross-legged on a ledge. Desmond made a creditable start of surprise, striking an off-note.

Ruck leaned against the ledge. "Lost lamb?"

Desmond jumped down from his perch. "Nay, my lord!" He opened his mouth, as if to go on, and then remembered himself. He went to his knee. "My lord, I have been at work on the green wood."

Maintaining the frith as an impenetrable tangle required constant labor, uncounted twigs staked down or coupled to their neighbors, logs felled and sharp-needled leaves and thorns encouraged. It gave an excuse to be outside the valley and past the tarn, as Desmond was. Ruck made no comment on the boy's lack of industry at this worthy labor, but loosened his wallet.

"Rise," he said. "Stay with me whilst I break fast. I be gone for scouting outermere today."

"Is it so, my lord?" Desmond said, just as if this were fresh news. He climbed back onto the ledge and sat with his legs dangling while Ruck shared out oatcakes and small ale. They ate and drank in silence. The mist drifted past, dewing the rocks with black tear streaks.

"My lord," Desmond said suddenly, "yesterday, and the day afore—Hock Monday, you know—"

He broke off. Ruck took a swig of ale, not looking at the boy as he struggled with his words.

"My lord, watz no woman to binden me up on Monday. And yesterday, when were the men's turn—and I be six and ten this year, so I am to join in—I ne could nought—you nill haf counted, but I can tellen for you, my lord, that all the women are taken, and Jack Haliday so jealous of his wife that he shouted at me ere I put a rope about her, my lord, which I ne would nought ha' ventured but she's my sister's friend, and twenty and one, with three bairns!" His voice rose, throbbing with his sense of the injustice of this event. "My lord, I—"

He seemed to get tangled in the tail of his sentence again. Ruck finished his oatcake, brushing the crumbs from his palms. He leaned his elbows back on the ledge, waiting.

"There are no maids, my lord!"

The despairing exclamation rang back off the rocks. Desmond flung a stone. He hurled another pebble after the first.

Ruck watched them take the leaf tips off a holly branch. Desmond had impressive aim.

"They're all too young, or too old," the boy muttered.

"Didst thou bring a mount?" Ruck asked.

Desmond glanced at him warily.

"I am in hopes that thou didst. I be loath for the mare to carry us double down and back."

The boy stared at him, then leapt off the ledge with a whoop. "Ye will taken me?" He threw himself down at Ruck's feet. "Grant merci, my lord! Grant merci! I brought Little Abbot to ride, and plenty of food, for chance!"

DESMOND WAS BY no means the first youth to venture out of Wolfscar with maidens on his mind. He followed Ruck's mare on the little white-footed ass, kicking to keep up, and carried on a flow of fine talk and song about love all the way down through the frithwood. Ruck listened, half inclined to his old jealousy of the minstrel wit to hear it. Full grown, he had never been so confident and easy as this unfledged orator was at sixteen. The first time Ruck had come down from the mountains himself, he had been too shamefast to make a bow to a female, far less sing of love.

But Desmond lost a little of his boldness after they had dropped below the mists and come into where the dark woods thinned. The air held a heavy scent of smoke, the mark of the charcoal-burners who worked the abbey's iron ore, and a sign, Ruck hoped, that no pestilence interrupted ordinary labor.

They skirted high above the abbey works, descending by steeper slopes to the land beyond what the abbey claimed, passing by stages out of the forest. At first the clearings were small and overgrown, no more than a little pasture for the horses loosed to breed, then better kept, with a meager space for winter oats hacked out of the trees by some poor cotter, gradually increasing in size and density, until suddenly the woods were coppice instead of trees, and the lowland fields lay ahead of them. Desmond had long since ceased his humming and appeared willing enough to wait at the last white water ford.

Ruck was already certain that plague had spared the country before he spent a shilling to find out the news from a shepherd. What might have come to pass in the larger world, the man knew not, but a band of pilgrims had descended upon the abbey for Easter, and they seemed healthy enough to complain of bedbugs and the sour ale as they went through. There had been one raid by Scots reivers, but the worst trouble was between the abbey and some knight who sent his men in livery to seize supplies on purpose to gall and vex the abbot. The shepherd was like to think these hot-spurred nobles were a worse plague than Scots or pestilence, either.

Ruck looked past the shepherd's flock, where the hills opened to farm and pasture. There was no plague, and no reason to delay longer. If not for Desmond's hopes, he would have turned back here, for he knew what he had come to discover.

But the youth was waiting, having lost interest in love and conceived a lust for travel. He kicked Little Abbot along eagerly. The wider horizon had worked strongly on his mind, and he was full of questions about far places and cities Ruck had seen.

"I shall go to London," Desmond announced.

"Mary, 'tis a sore journey only for a maid," Ruck said.

"How far?"

"Weeks, an thou walks—which thou wilt, as Little Abbot does nought accompany thee."

"Ne would my lord haf me go," Desmond surmised gloomily. "Ne'er will I go nowhere."

Ruck smiled. "Ne'er. I forbid it."

The youth sighed. He squinted longingly at the distance and sighed again.

"Ne'er, that is, but for the journey I command thee," Ruck said idly, "with the man I send to my lady's castle, to fetch back her guard."

A grin broke over Desmond's face. "My lord! I may go?"

"Yea."

"When, my lord?" he demanded. "How far be it? And who wends with me?"

A pair of cows lifted their heads as the mare passed. Their bells clanked roundly. Ruck watched them, weighing the matter in his mind.

"Soon enow when we return," he said finally. "I charge Bassinger to go."

"Uncle Bass?" Desmond cried. "But he'll ne'er stir himseluen!"

"Will he or nill he," Ruck said. "None other but myseluen knows the road as he."

"Were a hundred years ago, my lord!" Desmond kicked the ass up even with him. "His knee will pain him. His back will ache upon the horse. Nill nought he riden from the gatehouse as far as the sheepfold now, my lord! Send Tom with me, my lord."

"Thomas plants. And Jack, and all able bodies. Someone be caused to taken up thy slack, and that be full enow."

Desmond scowled. "Will Foolet."

"Will is afraid and afeared to go out of the valley, as thou knows well. Take thy satisfaction that I allow thee leave, 'ere I regret it."

"Yea, my lord." The youth swiftly ceased his complaint. "So will I, my lord."

LITTLE ABBOT ANNOUNCED their arrival by planting his hooves and braying lustily in spite of all a red-faced Desmond could do to whip him along. But the animal's voice was hardly noticeable amid the disorder and stir on the green. Horses tied too close nipped at one another or nosed hopefully in laden carts. Servants hustled packs and boxes. A pair of nuns stood together guarding their bags with the ferocity of wimpled mastiffs, while a stream of people passed in and out under the long pole and brush that marked the tavern.

"Pilgrims," Ruck said, but it was an unusually large party, and even conducted by an armed guard. The carts were full of larder and wool. "They go out with the abbey's trade."

Desmond was gazing at the soldiers, his eyes alight. "Will they have to fighten?"

Ruck took stock of the large guard. They were mounted all, and well turned out, holding patient watch while their charges refreshed themselves—the kind of escort he wanted for Melanthe. But they wore the abbey's livery, and he had no notion to ask for aid there. "They will accounten themseluen well, if they do." He turned away. "Dame Fortune likes thee, Desmond—e'ery maid in the country will be here for such sight."

Even as he spoke, three girls hurried out of the inn and began rooting for something in a baggage cart. One of them cast a glance at Ruck and Desmond and instantly pulled her veil over her face, huddling into hisses and giggles with her companions. All three turned and stared.

Desmond turned bright red. He was common enough in his green and yellow dags in Wolfscar, but here his vestment shouted amid the common grays and browns. Ruck could see him shrinking. Little Abbot chose that moment to lift his head and send forth another raucous bray.

Desmond turned from red to white. He looked as if his stomach warmed.

"Were I thee," Ruck said under his breath, "I would show them that I had a right to my minstrel's gear."

But the youth seemed daunted into impotence. Ruck dismounted. He took hold of Abbot's halter.

"Is this the king of lovers whom I met this morn? Hie, tumble thee hence to the tavern door," he said, "three springs off thy hands, if thou canst."

Desmond threw his leg over Abbot's back and hit the ground. He bounded off his feet onto his hands, flipping backward, a green-and-yellow wheel across the grass, five handsprings and a midair tumble at the finish before he came up flushed, sent a glare at Ruck, and stalked into the tavern without even glancing at the girls.

They were openmouthed with astonishment. A few of the guards shouted and clapped. Ruck raised his hand to them and gave the maids a light courtesy. He tied his beasts, then carried Desmond's gittern into the tavern.

DESMOND HAD FALLEN in love. It was his misfortune that his choice was the comely redheaded maid who served the shoemaker's wife and traveled with the rest of the pilgrims in the abbey's party. Ruck, sipping ale in a corner well removed from the white-robed clerks traveling with their abbot's goods, foresaw lengthy pining over doomed love as the harvest of this day.

It was hopeless to try to direct the youth's attention to the nut-brown daughters of the village. They were shy; Desmond was shy; it had taken the city maid's coaxing smile to cajole him into performing, and then she had chosen a love song and added her clear untrained voice to his—and Ruck saw himself fifteen years past, beguiled past all wit.

"Come, ye will wenden with us?" the shoemaker was saying to him as Desmond sat down on the bench beside his love, having just proven he could stand upon his hands to the count of fifty. "Your boy's good—ne do I doubt me you can play the better, my man, and it's a weary mile to York."

"York?" Desmond said between pants, before Ruck could deny that they wished to travel. "How far is it, sir?"

Ruck gave him a quelling look. Desmond hid his face in an ale tankard while the redhead smiled benignly at him.

"Ah, ten days, or twelve, peraventure. Little enow on the way, in troth, naught but Lonsdale and Bowland, and Ripon—

but such lone places welcomen minstrel folk, for 'tis little oft they're seen."

Ruck turned to him in new interest. "Ye came that way?"

"Yea, and will return by it, for with this guard we have no fear of reivers, God be thanked."

"How fare the roads?" he asked, but missed the shoe-maker's answer, for Desmond had suddenly choked on his ale and begun twitching his head in a strange manner.

He was looking fixedly at Ruck. After a moment he stood up, bowing frantically. "My lor—sir! Sir, mote I speaken you, sir!"

Ruck thought he must be ill, he seemed so agitated. He pushed back the bench and followed the boy hastily outside.

"My lord!" Desmond turned just beyond the door and dragged Ruck behind the horses. "My lord! Bowland!" He had no appearance of sickness. He was bouncing on his heels, his face radiant. "Bowland! Is my lady's hold, is nought?" he demanded.

"Yea, I know it."

"My lord, I can go! I can go with them anon!"

Ruck released a heavy breath. He shook his head. "Nay, Desmond, I want Bassinger—"

"My lord! Only consider! The Scots raid, and Uncle Bass ne ha'nought seen the road for years! Haps is all changed, if e'er he knew it! These folk haf just come o'er from York— they'll nought be lost nor stray out of the way."

Ruck started to refuse again, but Desmond went down on his knee.

"My lord, I beg you! When will another armed company be that way? Will ye senden Uncle Bass and me alone?"

The pleading made no impression on Ruck, but the thought of Bassinger and Desmond traveling alone across the barren reiver country was enough to arrest him. When he looked about the green, he saw that the guard had been divided and an evening watch posted. The men off duty did not idle in the tavern, but went about business with their horses and armor, efficient and experienced in their moves.

Desmond was gazing up at him in the late evening light, full of desperate hope and excitement. Ruck leaned against the wall and frowned, calculating. There was the chance that

Desmond in his lovesotted state would not stop at Bowland, but trail behind the object of his heart all the way to York. Ruck suspected, though, that this redheaded maid would grow bored with a rustic swain long before York, and probably before they reached Bowland. She had the look of experience on her—a lesson that might not be a bad one for a boy who had seen nothing of the world.

But it was just that greenness that made him loath to send Desmond. If it had been any older man of his hold, he would not have hesitated. The advantages were obvious, and just as Desmond stated. It would not be soon that a stout armed party would wend from here direct toward Bowland.

"My lord," Desmond said, "if you think I'm too young— 'tis said you ne had no more than five and ten when you first went out! And I am older."

Ruck nodded, barely hearing him. In his heart he was glad that Melanthe was not here now, for he could hardly have demanded that she stay in Wolfscar with such a favorable company to conduct her.

It was that thought that decided him. He was delaying; if he did not send to Bowland now, he would go back and find another reason to delay; Bassinger would protest his rheum, the planting would need management, the weather would be untoward—he could find a thousand reasons, and they were all shirking and tarrying to avoid what must be done.

He took Desmond by the shoulder and hauled him behind the granary. "If I say thee yea, Desmond," he hissed through his teeth, "and thou fails by some idle chance, or for this maid or another—I shall profane thy name with my last breath, does thou comprehend me?"

Desmond's face lost a little of its zeal. He stood soberly and nodded.

"Ne art nought to letten two things pass thy lips, to no creature man nor woman. Thou art nought to sayen whence thou came, ne the name of Wolfscar. Nor aught of my marriage to my lady. Swear to it."

"Nay, my lord. I swear by my father's soul, my lord, ne will I speak of Wolfscar nor whence I come, nor aught of my lord and my lady's marriage."

Ruck pulled the top buttons of his cote open and searched

beneath his shirt. "Now listen, and learn thy message. Her lady's grace is safe and free from harm or restraint. Ere Whitsunday, a guard and company with all things suitable to her estate is to comen to the city of Lancaster and await her there. This is her free wish and command, as attested by her chattel here sent." He held out the leather bag that he wore. "Lay this about thy neck, and guard it. Will prove thee from the princess. Say me the message."

Desmond repeated it instantly by heart, well-trained in minstrel's learning. Ruck gave him the whole contents of his wallet, silver enough to tide him there and back, and saw the leather bag stowed safely about the boy's neck.

He felt a terrible misgiving as Desmond tucked his green scarf back into place. "Stray nought out from the party," he said. "Keep thee with the shoemaker if there be fighting. Ne do nought think thou canst aid in any combat."

"Nay, my lord."

"When thou returns, signal from the tarn. Ne do nought come farther. I will meeten thee."

"Yea, my lord."

"Desmond, this red-haired maid—"

Desmond lifted his eyes, so innocent of all love's dangers that Ruck only sighed and shook his shoulder.

"Ne do nought fail me," he said. "Do nought fail."

"Nill I, my lord!" Desmond said fiercely. "Ne for no maid nor any other thing!"

Ruck stood back. "Then fare thee well, as God please."

Desmond went down on his knee, crossing himself. "God ha' mercy, my lord!" He leapt up and ran, leaving Ruck in the deepening shadow behind the barn.

Ruck took the mare and left Little Abbot tied. As he rode out, the ass called after with a mournful braying. The echo of it rang in his ears long after he could no longer hear the sound. Ruck made a cross and prayed to God that he had not done a dearly foolish thing.

Twenty-one

"I KNOW NOT why you ask me," Cara said. "I've no help to give you."

Allegreto stood with his back to the trefoiled window. He never paced. She wished that he would, or do anything but be so still and yet seem as if he would spring.

"You did not like what I did before," he said. "So I ask you."

Cara sat straight in the chair he had given her, staring at a tapestry of the conversion of Saint Eustace. It was a finely detailed piece, full of greens and blues, the white stag with the miraculous cross between its antlers gazing fixedly at the hunter.

"I don't know what you mean," she said.

"Ficino," he whispered. "Ficino is what I mean."

The stag, she thought, was a brave creature, to stand trapped on a ledge that way, even for a miracle.

"He was dead before the fire," Allegreto said, "if that is what upset you."

She closed her eyes. "Don't speak of it."

Weeks had passed, all of Lent and Easter, and more, and still she could smell the smoke and see him standing in red upon the dais. He wore white and blue today; he had not worn red since, which was the only reason she could look on him.

He turned suddenly, facing away out the window. "This messenger from her—I know it's a ruse! I have to do something. Christ, I can't bide till Whitsuntide—and then find that it's some wile to bait me!" He put his hands over his face. "God's mercy, where *is* she?"

Cara looked down. Lint flecked her gown from the wool she'd been spinning when he summoned her. She picked at a bit, rolling it around and around between her fingers. "The messenger will not say."

"Nay," he snapped, turning sharply toward her. "Not for love, in any case."

"It may be he doesn't know."

"He knows. She's with the green man—she sent the falcon's varvels, the ones she gave to him. She's using the knight somehow, but for God's rood I can't make out her intention." His voice held a cold strain. "And my father—I've not sent him word all this time. I don't dare, not even to pray him to protect your sister. Cara, this messenger—" He stopped, as if he had spoken what he did not wish to say.

"What of the messenger?" she cried, rising suddenly from the chair. "You want to torture him, don't you? And you ask me if I have a better means, when you know I've no notion what to do!"

"I thought—haps if you spoke to him. I frightened him. He's but a boy, and innocent as a virgin."

Cara laughed. "You're more fool than I think you, if you believe I can succeed where you've failed."

"Or your friend Guy might do it," Allegreto said, ignoring her denial. "He's back from searching again, empty-handed."

She lifted her eyes, feeling her heart contract. But Allegreto showed no sign of malice. There was nothing in his gaze when he looked at her but the faint longing that she had come to recognize. He had never touched her since that day before he'd killed Ficino. He did not press her. She would have thought it had been imagination, that one touch, if she did not see it in his face every time now that he was near her.

"If you would only aid me, Cara," he said in a strangely helpless tone. "I'm trying."

For no reason she could say, her eyes began to blur with tears. "I don't understand you."

He walked the wall from the window to the tapestry. "Nay," he said distantly. "I know it."

He stood before the woven stag. The woven hunter stared at him in wonder.

"You can't do anything," he said bleakly.

He was so beautiful. She had never seen a living man or a work of art so beautiful and terrible. She swallowed tears. "Allegreto, I will try, if you wish it."

"Nay, it is hopeless," he said. "You'd only blunder, and Guy the same." He smiled at her, wooden as a carved angel in a church. "A hopeless pair, the two of you."

SHE DID TRY. She took food to the messenger in the room where he was kept, careful that she did not do anything to let him escape. He was very frightened, as Allegreto had said. He would not even eat, but sat hunched on the stool, a youth with a long nose and long musician's fingers. Allegreto had even left him his instrument, but Cara doubted that he played. The turret room was frigid.

A boy, Allegreto had called him, and yet she thought them of an age. But he could never be as old as Allegreto, not if he lived a hundred years.

"Do you speak French?" she asked.

He did not answer, but looked away from her. She thought he must understand her, though. She took a deeper breath.

"I have come to explain to you," she said. "You must tell Allegreto what he asks."

His look flicked toward her, and then back. A stubbornness came into his jaw.

"He only wishes to find my mistress and see that she is safe."

"She is safe," the youth said.

"How can we be certain? Why can't we go to her, or she come to us?"

"I have said all I can say!" He stood up, prowling the cold turret and chafing his hands. "Persecute me as you will!"

Cara rose from beside the tray that he scorned. "You don't

know what danger you're in," she said sharply. "You don't know what persecution means."

"What, hot pincers? The wheel? Go ahead. I have sworn my word. I will not speak."

She shook her head in amazement. "Are you so blithe?"

"I'll die before I speak!" he said wildly.

"This is not courage, I think, but mere ignorance!" Cara's angry breath made a keen flash of frost in the air. "Do you know why you're sound now? Because of me. Because he does not want to displease me, you foolish boy! How long do you think that can last?"

He drew himself straight and gave her a sneering look. "Tell your lover to try me as he will."

"Oh!" She whirled, banging her knuckles upon the door to be released. "I shall tell him to serve you as a fool should be served!"

The guard let her out, locking the door behind. She ran down the spiraling stairs, her hand on the cold plaster curve of the wall to support her. At the first landing Allegreto stepped out to meet her.

She had not told him she would go to the boy, but of course he knew. His dark eyes questioned her.

"I learned nothing," she said, "but that he is a witless mouse among cats."

Only by his silence, and the slight casting down of his shoulders, did she realize that he had truly hoped she might succeed. But in the next moment he was the sculpted angel, living stone. "Then you must visit him again tomorrow. And tell him that your lover's patience wanes."

FOR MORE THAN a week they played the farce. Cara feared every day that she would come to the turret room and the young messenger would be gone, forfeited to Allegreto's ruthless practice. She did not have to feign the growing urgency of her pleas to the youth; Allegreto would not, could not keep this forbearance long.

She saw the struggle in him. Even the seneschal had begun to mutter of stronger measures. Sir Thomas did not approve of involving a lady in such matters as imprisoned messengers, and shrugged and glared and said, "So there," each day when

Cara reported her failure. "Her lady's grace is held to ransom, mark me," he said. "We'll have a payment demand yet if we don't deliver her."

Allegreto sat at the heavy council table, staring as if he looked far beyond the seneschal's white head. He seemed to grow farther away as each day passed, reclusive and distracted. Only in the moments when Cara came from the tower room, before he heard that she had learned no more, were his eyes alive and quick, asking for fulfillment.

She knew that her efforts were no use, as he must know it. But instead of bringing the game to its foregone end, he withdrew into a strange languor. He had no counsel for Sir Thomas, no insults for Cara, nothing but those instants of living hope once a day.

She was coming to hate Desmond. As she grew more vehement, he grew more cocksure, as if he took pot-courage from her visits. Well he might, she thought, hearing dire warnings from a female, threats that must seem more impotent by the day.

"You must do something more," she said, after another fruitless session in the turret.

Allegreto gave her a level look. "Must I?" he asked softly.

She thought of Desmond, so proud of his boy's stupid courage, trying to protect someone who in all chance deserved no protection, worst of all if it was her fiendish mistress and her wicked schemes. She thought of Ficino, who at least had known the way of things. And Allegreto, standing in crimson on the dais, the color of blood and fire.

Somehow, after that night, he had given over his soul to her, as if she could protect it for him. He waited for her decision.

"You must talk to him again," she said.

He smiled. He laid his head back in the chair and laughed. "Cara," he said. "Ah, Cara."

He said it as if he were in despair. He cast a look about the room, a prisoner's search for some weakness or crack in the walls. Then he pushed back the chair and sprang like a cornered cat from a pit, leaving Cara and Sir Thomas alone.

• • •

SHE WAS LYING awake when he came in the dark. She had heard the single clarion that heralded some late arrival, and sat up hastily. Allegreto's outline against the low candle confirmed her in fear and wild relief. "She has come?" she whispered.

He put his hand over her mouth, moving with utter silence, pulling her urgently up from her bed. Some of the other ladies stirred, but he pushed her from the chamber before their sleepy mumbles gained sense. Cold air welled up the stair; he held her and went before her at once, half dragging her with him down the black descent. She could hear the voices of men in the bailey—louder at the arrowslits where the night air poured in.

He brought her to the landing, hauling her with a fierce grip toward the unshuttered window. His breath was harsh, coming fast and uneven next to her ear, as if he could not get enough. He pushed her into the embrasure, his hands on her shoulders.

Cara leaned over, looking down at the torch-lit scene with the night wind blowing in her face. She blinked, trying to see, trying to recognize the voices in French and Italian. One soft command to a porter drifted up to the tower window—someone turned a lanthorn and lit a man standing quietly beside his horse.

She covered her mouth.

The castle, the world, seemed to turn over. Allegreto clung to her, his face buried in her shoulder.

"*Gian*," she said, and made the cross in terror. "Blessed Mary, have pity on us!"

"What he will do to me," he whispered. "Oh, God—Cara—what he will do to me."

SHE DID NOT know how Allegreto possessed himself. Gian Navona said nothing, watching each of them in turn: his bastard son and Sir Thomas and Cara—and Desmond, shackled to a bench in the council chamber, where only a single candle burned on the table, lighting them all and leaving Gian in shadow.

Allegreto had explanations. What they were, Cara didn't hear. She could hear nothing but her own pulse. At some moment her name came through it, and she felt herself observed.

"Lift up your face, Donna Cara," said that quiet voice from the shadow. "You preserved your mistress from these poisoned shellfish?"

She could not command her tongue. Allegreto gave her a look, one of his old looks, full of amused disdain. "Not by her wit, as you may see. She thought they smelt badly."

Gian chuckled. "But it's a good girl," he murmured. "A miss be as well as a mile, so they say."

Allegreto made a snort. His father's gaze turned toward him momentarily, and then to Desmond.

"Sir Thomas," Gian said, without taking his eyes from the youth, "your patience is praiseworthy. You will not wonder at my concern in these matters when I tell you that the princess and I are to be wed. Perhaps my son has not mentioned it?"

The seneschal cleared his throat. "He acquainted me, my lord, with your interest and solicitude for my lady, and has stood here as your chief man and hers, to give aid in this fearful matter."

"I hope he has been of some benefit to you, but his tender years need not bear such a grave weight longer, now that I am here."

"The castle be at your service, my lord," Sir Thomas said. "My only aim is my lady's welfare. I have not called in the king's aid, because—"

"Quite right," Gian interrupted him. "To broadcast news of this misfortune too hastily would have been the worst possible mistake. You have done well, Sir Thomas, as Donna Cara has done well, each to his own talents." As he spoke, he had never ceased watching Desmond. "I am a little dissatisfied to find that Donna Cara has turned her domestic arts, invaluable though they might be, to matters my son might have been thought to manage better."

Allegreto sat calmly, lazily, gazing back toward the dark end of the chamber at his father. He still had the faint lift of disdain to his lips, his lashes lowered in sleepy watchfulness.

"I am proud of thee, Allegreto, thou art so brave as to be here," his father said. "Thou art a devoted son."

"My lord," Allegreto said, acknowledging the compliment with a nod.

"But then, I neglected to send word ahead. I must give thee my regret for the oversight. No doubt that is the reason for this unfortunate reception."

Allegreto said nothing. He did not move.

"Take this"—Gian indicated Desmond—"somewhere that I may deal with it, as you have not."

Desmond's face was white. He wet his lips as Allegreto rose and loosed the fetters from the bench. The boy had the fear in him; he understood her warnings now, when it was too late.

"Donna Cara," Gian said, "you must take care that the chambers are well prepared for your mistress. I think she will be among us ere long now."

CARA KEPT A vigil in the chapel, for she could no more sleep than she could flee. She prayed for the souls of her parents and for her sister. She prayed for Desmond. The priest looked at her curiously when he rang the little bell for hours. She left then, unwilling to draw attention, pulling her headscarf close to her as she pushed open the door. The bailey lay silent and still under the cold stars before dawn.

A black figure stopped away from the wall beside the arched entrance. It was Allegreto, shaking in the frigid air. "Wait," he said, his voice a faint tremor in the quiet.

She felt sick. "Is it over?"

"Nay," he murmured. "Nay, he holds yet. It is early." A shudder ran through him. In the starlight she saw him grip his fists tightly. "I'm sorry."

She bit her lip. Then she shook her head. "It is your father."

"I did not know—I never thought—" Another shiver broke his words. "You must stay away from him. I never once thought he would come here!"

A soft frightened sound seemed to seep from him against his will. His shaking increased. She reached out to him, for she thought he would fall, and he caught her hand and held it hard against his face. She felt wetness there—ice, his tears and his cheeks were, as if a marble statue wept.

"Don't!" It frightened her beyond wit to feel him shake. She pulled him close to her, against her breast to make him stop, pressing her back to the wall and holding tight to force him to be still. With a groan he brought his hands up around her shoulders and kissed her.

She said, "No," but his cold lips and cheek touched hers, drawing life, taking away what warmth she had with desperate greed.

"No!" She turned her face away. She twisted her fingers in his hair to check him and yet still hold him—hold him like a child with his face buried in her throat, her arms tight around him.

She kept him there, stroking his hair. She held him until her arm ached with the strain. The tremors passed through him to her, easing, but before they had left him, he shoved suddenly away from her and turned his back.

"Monteverde bitch," he said, but he had no venom in his voice, only anguish.

His figure cast a faint, smeared shadow on the wall beside her. She opened her palm against it, but it was only cold and darkness, an illusion. She did not have life enough in her, she thought, to give him as much as he needed, even if she gave it all.

"Come with me," he said coolly, as if he had never trembled in her arms. "I have a scheme; I need your help." He flashed a look at her, his face stone white in the starlight. "But if you slip, Monteverde, you kill all three of us."

SHE COULD NOT look at Desmond. She was afraid to look; he made a sound as the heavy door opened that was pain and terror, choked off into wordless pants. There was no guard—Allegreto had told her to watch, and speak when she was told to speak. She no more asked what he had done to the guard than she looked at what they had done to Desmond.

A candle had been left burning in the larding cellar, lighting ordinary things. Allegreto's shadow passed across smoked meats and a bushel of apples. "Now, my stubborn little ass, you've made acquaintance of my father," he said quietly. "You may take your choice between us."

Cara wet her lips, her eyes fixed on the open door and the

stair beyond. No sound came from Desmond but the faint gasping of his breath.

"You have one hope to live," Allegreto said. "You can tell me where she is, and I'll take you out of here before my father comes again."

"Nay," Desmond whispered.

"Then tell me where I can get a message to her. She must be told that my father is here. She will not expect it. None of us—expected it."

"Nay, you—will—tell him," Desmond said, his voice a weak grate.

"Cara."

She had to turn. She looked only at his face, his white face, his head lying against the wall. His face was whole.

"You would not listen to me," she hissed. "Listen to me now! Allegreto means to get you free. You can't fight Gian; he'll kill you by inches, or let you live, which will be worse. And we'll die, too, if he finds we came here to aid you! We tried—we tried to spare you this, and you would have none of it! Well might you help yourself now, stupid boy, that Allegreto risks life and limb for thee!"

His eyes closed. He rolled his head to the side, mumbling in English.

"Speak French," Allegreto said harshly. "We can't understand you."

"I don't know," the youth muttered. He swallowed and groaned. "I don't know. It hurts."

"Here's my dagger," Allegreto said. "Do you see it? I'll cut you free, and you won't hurt. As soon as you tell me where to send, I'll cut you loose." He turned Desmond's head, to make him see the knife before his eyes. "I give you until she counts to twenty, and then we leave you here to God and my father's mercy."

He nodded to Cara. She began to count, as slowly as she dared, staring at Desmond's racked face. He turned his head from side to side, panting. From somewhere up the stairwell, a dove cooed, waking.

"Eighteen," she said, and closed her eyes. Nineteen."

"I can't tell you," Desmond gasped. "But I can—take . . ."

Allegreto slashed the knife across one set of cords. Desmond cried out as his arm fell.

"Take?" Allegreto demanded, the dagger hovering.

"Take . . . near. You—give me . . . the message. Wait for—answer. I swear. Help me!"

Allegreto cut him down.

A BAND OF deep gray-blue threatened rain along the tops of the hills. As the wind blew a warning of late frost from the north, the black branches tossed, showing their tiny green buds in shafts of sunlight.

She had not flown Gryngolet long. Her moult would begin soon, and in this weather any stray gust might sweep the falcon beyond a ridge and out of sight. The horses plodded along beside the river, taking snatches at new growth. Melanthe rode dreaming, her mantle close about her ears, thinking of ways she might coax her husband into bodily fellowship.

The music at first seemed like part of the wind. She lifted her head, listening. In a lull she heard it again, or thought she did. Sometimes it seemed a melody, and sometimes only single uncertain notes. She turned in the saddle to look at Hew.

"Yea, I hear, my lady." He scowled up at the ridge. "Desmond, my lady. I think me."

Melanthe's hand closed on her reins. "He's come." An old foreboding fell over her, hearing that elvish measure on the high wind—but wavering and broken, a travesty of the song.

Hew was still looking up over the sweep of trees to the heights. He reached for the horn slung over his shoulder.

"Take me to him," Melanthe said.

He paused, the horn lifted. "My lady, Lord Ruadrik said—"

"Take me!" She turned her horse. "Or I will finden my way alone." She urged it down the riverbank. The animal plunged in, fording the stream in knee-deep splashes. They heaved up onto the overgrown track on the other side.

Hew came behind. Without another word he splashed out of the water and pricked his rouncy past her.

RUCK PULLED UP Hawk from his last gallop. While the destrier recovered its wind, shedding a furry winter coat along with winter fat, Ruck guided him out of the lists. He let his feet dangle out of the stirrups.

He smiled at the May pole that stood ready in the middle of the sheep meadow, ribbons bound tight, the spring blast whistling through them as he rode Hawk in a circle around it. The weather would not smile on their celebrations, he feared; it seldom did, but hope sprang anew each year. If the sun failed them, they would move the pole and festival into the castle bailey.

He left his ax and mace leaning outside the wooden rail of the lists, ready for him when he returned after eating, and let Hawk amble up the slope toward the road. There were already twenty lambs, leaping and running, or staring fixedly at him as if he were some pressing secret to be unraveled. Joany Tumbster stopped him at the gatehouse and demonstrated how she could vault up behind him over Hawk's tail. The destrier bore it patiently, as lenient with girls in fluttering dags as he was intolerant of full-grown men in armor.

They rode into the yard with Joany standing on Hawk's rump, her hands on Ruck's shoulders. Her brother, scraping cow dung into a barrow, yelled at her to let go and stand straight. Just as she dared to chance it, a horn sounded from far outside the walls, taken up by another at the gate.

"Desmond's come!" Joany slipped and snatched at Ruck's neck, bounding free just before she strangled him.

"Nay. Hold!" His command caught her halfway across the yard to the gate.

She and the others halted, turning their young faces to him, wind-burned and innocent.

"No one goes to him until I know that he does nought bring pestilence." He reined Hawk around. "Joany, you come with me, far enow to fetch the princess back—she and Hew have gone downriver with the falcon. Tell her that I wait on her in the bower when I return."

UNTIL HE HAD heard the horn, Ruck had not known how much he dreaded it. After he dropped Joany at the crossing, he let the destrier walk across the bridge, as if by going slowly he could gain back the time that had slipped away as the ice had melted from the river.

Hawk hoisted himself up a turn in the familiar path, his hooves sucking in mud. He went without Ruck's guidance, knowing the way out as he knew the way in. They had climbed high on the slope, where the hawthorn buds were still tight and purple-black instead of bursting, when the sharp scent of fresh droppings jolted him from his brood.

He halted Hawk. The tracks were fresh, ascending instead of descending. They had not been on the lower path—they had come in on a side trail.

It could only be Melanthe and Hew. Ruck scowled, unhappy that they had rushed up here to meet the boy. Desmond had not been outside before; he was young and impetuous; he might be fetching anything back—plague and more.

Ruck whistled, but the wind in the upper crags was whining too high for hearing. He slapped the horse, urging him to a swifter pace.

Hawk heaved and blew frost, his ears flicking as they drew up to the howling rock and passed it by. The slate cliffs loomed above. Ruck kept expecting to hear Desmond's flute, to meet them all coming down; his nerves grew more taut as Hawk climbed on alone.

The destrier gathered himself for a lunge up onto the stony ledges. Pebbles skittered down from under his feet as he made the shelf and broke into a brief trot on easier ground. Ruck's hair whipped his cheek in the wind. Another ledge up, and another—and he guided Hawk into the stone fissure.

The sudden hush of the tarn was like a sound of its own. Beyond the moaning crevice, the pool was tranquil as it always was, black, still ice-skimmed in the cold shadow of the cliffs. As they entered, Hawk shied violently. Ruck grabbed for his sword as a figure rose from the bushes.

It was Hew, without the horses or Melanthe. Ruck controlled the destrier, spurring him forward. "Where is she?" His alarm echoed off the slate, mingling with the ring of Hawk's hooves.

Hew sank to one knee, his head bowed. He had no blood or look of a fight on him. Ruck threw himself from the saddle and grabbed the austringer's shoulders. *"What happened?"*

"My lord—a message, my lord. For you, my lord."

For an instant, sight and heart and lungs failed him. She was abducted. Blindly he grabbed for Hawk, to remount. "How long? How many of them?"

"My lord!" There was a hot strain in Hew's voice. "A message from my lady!"

Ruck paused, leashing his urge to throw Hawk into a pell-mell charge down the path. As soon as he turned, Hew stood up and closed his eyes. He looked miserable and scared, squeezing the wool mitts on his hands.

"My lord, my lady commanded me. I am to sayen you as if she herseluen spake, my lord, and her message to you be thusly—" He wet his chapped lips. " 'I leave thee of my own desire. Desmond says that Al—Allegreto lives, and his father comes in this country to wed me. I love this man as my life, better than e'er I loved thee.' " He took a breath while Ruck stared at him. " 'What was between thee and me is naught and nis,' " he recited with a nervous flick of his tongue. " 'I sore repent it. Ne do nothing to abashen me, for henceforth nill I desire to beholden thee, ne'er again, for base shame and disgust of such a connection.' " He opened his eyes and flung himself down on his knees. "And so did she charge me to sayen exactly, my lord!" he cried. "I swear to you, for ne'er should I speaken such words else!"

"It is false!" Ruck shouted. "The horses are gone! They took her; they forced her!"

He gripped his hands together and bent his head down. "Nay, only Desmond watz here, my lord, and she went apart and spake to him within the sight of my eyes, lord! And she mounted him upon my horse, and said that he would haf it to carry him, and bade me on pain to stayen you from following her."

"Nay." Ruck took a step forward. "She did nought!"

"My lord, she instructed me to sayen you, if ye would nought abide her word"—Hew lifted wretched eyes—"to remember, my lord, that she warned you once, that always she deceived."

Twenty-two

HE HAD NO memory of coming down from the mountain. Hawk was galloping, pounding down the road before the castle. The May pole stood in the meadow. He sent Hawk flying off the track, drawing his sword, careering down the slope with his arm outstretched.

The sword hit, slashing through the ribbons, a violent impact in his hand. The stave vibrated wildly as he swept past. He reined Hawk on his haunches and spurred the destrier at the pole. He was yelling as he rode it down, swinging his sword overhead. The bright silks flew in the wind. The blow rang through him, opening a white gash in the wood.

Ruck carried away strips of blue and yellow; they fluttered and curled around his gauntlet and the guard. He flung the weapon from him as he passed the lists, leaning down to catch the haft of the battle ax. His arm took the heavier weight. He swung upright in the saddle and charged the May pole howling fury in his throat.

The blade flashed and bit deep in the wood. With a crack the pole bent drunkenly. Hawk carried him by it as the upper half listed. He drove the horse around with his legs, hefting the length of the ax in both hands. He cut at the stave, spurring Hawk in ever smaller circles around the fractured pillar, swinging again and again as wood chips flew past his face, chopping until the log fell with a squealing groan.

He raised the ax over his head and brought it down, cleaving the standing wood down the center with a crack like a lightning bolt. He yanked the weapon free and dismounted amid trampled ribbons, assaulting the downed spar.

The wood splintered beneath the blade. He lifted the ax and swung it, lifted and swung, grunting, mangling the pieces, driving them into the muddy ground. He had no thoughts, no idea of time. He hewed until his hands went numb with the work, until he could not pull the blade from its seat but stumbled forward over it when he tried.

He fell on his knees amid mutilated silk and sundered wood. His breath burned his throat. With his dagger he stabbed at a scarred length of pole beside him, the only thing in reach, grinding the knife tip around, deepening and widening the wound, stabbing at it again.

He could hear nothing but his own heaving breath and the sound of the point impaling wood. Sweat trickled down into his eye, sharp salt. He wiped it with the back of his leather sleeve.

The cold wind bit his cheeks when he looked up. All of his people stood at the edge of the lists, a cluster of color and silence except for one little girl who was weeping. Their May stave and garlands lay maimed and dismembered about him.

He shook his head. He shifted the dagger and speared the mud beside his knee. He pulled it free and gored again, his fist rising and falling weakly. He shook his head once more.

"My lord." It was Will Foolet's voice, heavy with fear and question.

"I cannought speak of it." Ruck's throat was hoarse. He shoved himself to his feet. "I cannought speak of it. Ask Hew."

He took up the ax and walked toward the lists, wiping his muddy knife on his thigh. The tear-stained girl came up to meet him as he passed, reaching for the hem of his surcoat. "Won't we have a May then, m'lor, if you please?" Her large eyes fixed him. "My lady's grace said me that I might carry her flowers to the stave—" Her mother hurried up, trying to lift her away, but she clung stubbornly to him. "And ne can I now!" she cried.

"Beg grace, my lord!" her mother exclaimed, yanking the small fist free.

Ruck saw a lone figure walking toward them from far away down the track. Hew. Soon enough they would all know, and stare at him, and pity him for a wretched love-sot, more fool than they could invent in their best playing at fools.

"I'll fell another." He turned from them, hefting the ax onto his shoulder. "Ne do I desire company at it."

DESMOND HAD TOLD Melanthe nothing more, but that Allegreto's father had come to Bowland. She had not asked. He did not use his bandaged hand, and he moved like an old man, his young face unsmiling, his eyes bleak.

He brought her to her senses. She had looked on him, the boy who had left with a merry melody that knew nothing of pain, and she had known that she must go.

She could not let this come to Wolfscar. And it would come, if she stayed, if Gian was here. The world would come no matter the depth of the woven wood barrier. Gian would hunt her until he found her.

As dreams and vapor vanished, as a laughing youth came home a cripple, so would such things perish if she tried to hold on to what she could not possess. She had not forgotten who she was, but she had let herself forget what it demanded.

She had looked back once, halting the horse at a crossroad where a monk and a farmer worked to repair a harrow. Gryngolet sat on the saddlebow, asleep, her head tucked beneath one white wing. The wind blew warmer here, pushing fat low clouds and showers off the sea. The lowland was alive with the work of spring, with cleared fields and flowers, church bells and children chasing birds off the new seeds.

Behind her the mountains rose, catching the rain against their flanks—a dark watch, a malevolence that made the eye long to turn to the new foliage and fresh red soil. She stared at the boundary. High and impenetrable it seemed, and yet precious frail, vanishing at a glance for anyone with the key.

Her message to Ruck had been a more powerful kind of barrier, designed to kill all trust and love. He would have followed her—she made a pit of broken faith between them to prevent him.

Desmond did not halt or look back at her. His fat sluggish rouncy, taken from Hew, carried him step by step. She had seen him wrap his good hand in the mane, his mouth drawn hard against every jolt. Sometimes, when his face grew too white, she had told him they would rest, and gave him time to recover himself.

She wondered how many fingers he had left beneath the bandage. But someone had been kind to him—it was only his left hand, and he could still move his joints, if stiffly. He had not been racked for long.

So far from Gian, she had let herself drown in foolish visions. She had done a thing unforgivable and irreparable, disdaining the danger. She had loved, and let it command her.

If she had not, Desmond would be whole. He would still be in Wolfscar, playing his mirthful flute. But she had never thought Gian would come. She had thought Allegreto dead. She had thought she was free.

Free! Better she had obeyed Ligurio and gone into the nunnery. Better she had flung herself from the highest tower of Monteverde. Better that she had never, never known what she knew now—a man's faint smile and the depth of his heart and his faithfulness. She did not deserve it, she had never deserved such, she had mistaken herself for someone else. Ligurio had trained her, Gian would have her; it was beyond defying.

Even God Himself had stayed his hand. She had not conceived; she had seen the signs denying it each month with regret—but she understood now what mercy had been given her, that she was barren.

Fantasies and a lover she left behind. Only one thing did she do for herself, brutally cruel as she could do it, so that she might have a hope of sleeping. She made him hate her, so that he would not follow.

THE MOMENT THAT they rode within sight of the massive gatehouse and red sandstone walls that guarded the abbey, Allegreto came striding out. He did not keep to a walk—he began to run, avoiding puddles and a flock of peahens, coming to a halt before her horse.

"My father," he said.

His face held no expression, his voice no panic, and yet he radiated a fear so deep that he seemed to breathe it in and out of him.

"Is he here?" She nodded toward the abbey.

"Depardeu, no!" He seemed to get a little hold of himself and shook his head. He bowed to her. "No, lady. At Bowland. We came away in secret."

"Let us go in, then. Desmond must have rest and food."

Allegreto looked toward her drooping companion. He walked to the horse and took its reins, reaching back to grip Desmond's good hand. "Well worth you," he said, "for bringing her lady's grace. You see I did not follow."

Desmond gave a hollow croak of a laugh. "Not for lack of trying."

Allegreto turned and clucked the rouncy into a slow walk. He looked back at Desmond. "How were you injured, when they ask?"

"A mishap," Desmond said weakly. "A mill wheel."

Allegreto nodded. "Clever enough," he said to the horse.

Melanthe saw Desmond smile feebly. He looked at Allegreto with bleared and worshiping eyes.

"I have said a lady doing penance is expected," Allegreto informed them. "A great lady traveling poorly, to atone for her pride and vainglory. A falcon brought the message to her in a dream."

Melanthe sighed. "Ah, Allegreto—and I thought thee dead." She pulled her hood about her face and lifted the bird who had delivered the unfortunate news of her pride and vainglory, pressing her horse toward the abbey gate.

SHE KNELT BESIDE Allegreto in the sanctuary, telling prayer beads with her fingers. While the monks sang compline in the candlelit church, he spoke softly to her, his voice a tight undertone to the motet and descant.

"I know not what you want, my lady. I don't know what you intended by fleeing. I have thought on it these three months, and still I cannot fathom your desire."

"It is not important," she said.

"Yea, my lady, it is important to me. I am yours. You won't believe me. I cannot prove it. But if I must choose between you and my father, I have chosen."

She looked aside at him, keeping her head bowed. He was staring intensely at her, the smooth curve of his cheek lit by gold, his eyes outlined in shadow as if by a finely skillful hand. "Thou hast chosen me?" she asked, with a soft incredulity.

"You do not want my father. That is all I can make of your move. Is that true?"

Such a blunt question. She forced her fingers to tell the beads, her mind to think. Was this Gian, trying to wrest words from her that he would use somehow? Allegreto was his father's creature; he had ever been, born and bred to his devotion. As frightened of Gian as all the rest of them, loving his father as a wolf cub loved its parent, in cringing adoration.

"You need not tell me," he said quickly. "I well know you cannot trust me. What can I do that you will trust me?"

"I cannot imagine," she said.

He was silent. The monks sang an alleluia and response, voices soaring up the dark roof. The straw beneath her knees made but a rough cushion; she was glad to stand when the rite allowed it.

"Lady," he said when they knelt again, "two years ago, my father wished me to journey with him to Milan. Do you remember?"

She made a slight nod, without taking her eyes from her fingers.

"We did not go to Milan. We spent the time in his palace, lady. He told me I must keep you from all harm. He taught me such further lessons as he thought I needed, and watched me spar and fight, and—tested me."

A tenor answered the treble song. Melanthe started the beads over again, her head bent.

"My lady, there was a man who had done my father a wrong. I know not what. He was loosed in the palace, and my father said I was to kill him, or he would kill me." Allegreto was unmoving next to her. "He was a master, this man. He was better than I. I was at the point of his dagger when my father delivered me." Amid the chants, Allegreto's voice seemed to become distant. "I failed. My father told me that because I was his son, he saved me, but I had to remember not to fail again. And so I was bound in a room with the man I should have killed, and they took his member and parts."

Melanthe shook her head. She put her hand on his arm to stop him, to silence him.

But he kept speaking, trembling beneath her hand. "And while they did it, my father came to me and said to remember I was his bastard, and he could sire more sons, but was better for Navona that I could not. He laid the blade on me, so I should feel it and bleed, but then—because he loved me, he stayed it. He made me know that if I failed him again, that should be my reward. I should not be reprieved." He looked up at her, breathing sharply. "And I have not failed, until this time."

Melanthe's hand loosened. She stared into his face.

"It has been deception, my lady, that I was gelded. He let me go and bid me play it well, or it would be done to me in truth. It was so that you would bear me to sleep near you, that I might keep you from your enemies. He knew—" Allegreto's mouth hardened. "He knew that he could trust me in all ways."

She closed her eyes and drew a shaky breath. "Christ's blood. And I am to trust thee?"

"My lady—" He put his hand over hers, gripping hard, desperate. "Lady, this time he will do it. He promised it."

She shook her head, as if she could deny all thoughts.

"I can't go back without you, my lady!"

"Ah," she said, pulling her hand from under his, "is that all thou wouldst have of me, for thy vast loyalty?"

"Not all," he said in a painful voice.

She looked sideways from under her hood. His hands were clenched together on his thighs as he knelt.

"My lady." He bent his head down over his fists. "Donna Cara is there. If you tell my father of what she tried to do to you—"

His words broke off, requiring no completion. Melanthe gazed at his hands and thought, *Cara*? Cara the bitch of

Monteverde, whom he had scorned so savagely and strained
so hard to have sent away?

*Away, away, out of Monteverde, Riata, Navona. Away,
where she would have been safe.*

In profile he looked older than she remembered, his mouth
and jaw set, his beauty more solid. Growing. And a man, with
passions in him that he had kept dark and silent.

"Oh, God pity thee," she whispered. "Allegreto."

"She is not for me. I know that. There is an Englishman."
He took a long breath and spoke coldly. "I believe he will wed
her. But if your lady's grace accuses her to my father—" He
shrugged, and his elegant murdering hands twisted together.

She might have thought he was lying. He was player
enough, verily, for any part.

He squeezed his eyes closed, lifting his face to the high
arches. "I am yours. I'll act only for you. I will do whatever
you ask to prove myself. Only—I cannot leave her there, and
I cannot go back without you, my lady."

Three monks in procession came from the chancel down
the nave toward them, singing, their faces underlit by the candles they carried. Melanthe watched them turn and leave the
church by a side door.

"Listen to me, my lady. Your white falcon was there—
when my father punished his enemy and forewarned me."

She looked toward him. "What?"

"My father fed it," he said. "He said that he had trained it
to know me."

"That is impossible."

"The falcon hates me, my lady."

"Your father has never touched Gryngolet."

"He told me that if I betrayed him with you, that the falcon—" He looked at her imploringly. "My lady, he *fed* it."

He did not say more; he let her understand the monstrous
thing he meant. Through her horror Melanthe bared her teeth.
"If he had a gyrfalcon, it was not Gryngolet!"

"I will carry her." Allegreto gazed at Melanthe with a
straight and terrified intensity. "To prove my fidelity—that I
do not lie to you."

She suddenly realized that the church was silent, the
prayers completed, the sanctuary dimmer. What candlelight

was left hardened the sweet curves and comeliness of his face, erased the last hint of childhood, revealed the untenable compass of his fear.

He should have tried to appeal to Melanthe's welfare if he wished to entrap her. Her desires, her ambitions. But he had admitted that he did not know them.

He asked her what he could do, as clumsy and open as Cara in her folly.

It did not seem a great thing, this offer to carry a falcon, for a manslayer, a lovely boy with the soul of a demon. If he was lying, and she trusted him—then she walked open-eyed and helpless into Gian's clasp.

Three things Allegreto dreaded. Plague and his father, and Gryngolet. He knelt in the church and offered to defy two of them. For lying.

Or for love.

"Thou needst not carry her," Melanthe said. "I trust thee."

His lips parted; that was the only sign he gave of elation or relief.

"If thou art mine," she said, "then attend close to me now. Thy father did not have Gryngolet, nor ever has. I flew her at Saronno, all that week that I supposed thee in Milan. She was not in Monteverde for him to use in such vice. It was another bird obtained to daunt thee, we must assume—and contemptible abuse of a noble beast."

His jaw twitched. She deliberately disdained his father's horror as a mere offense against a falcon's dignity, to shrink it to a thing that he could manage.

"Gryngolet has hated thee because I have not been over fond of thee, I think." She shrugged. "Or haps she dislikes thy perfume. Change it."

He closed his dark eyes. He drew a deep breath into his chest, the sound of it uneven.

Melanthe stood up, the beads sliding through her fingers. She turned and left the church, pausing after she had made her obeisance. "Allegreto," she said quietly as he rose beside her from his knee, "if we fear him to a frenzy, we are done."

He nodded. "Yea, my lady. I know it well, my lady."

• • •

SHE HAD NOT seen Bowland for eighteen years. Against spring thunderclouds, the towers did not seem as monstrous huge as she remembered, and yet they were formidable, the length of the wall running a half-mile along the cliff edge to the old donjon at the summit. Its massive height stared with slitted eyes to the north, defying Scots and rebels as it had for a hundred years and more.

Strength and shield—her haven—and Gian held it of her. She had not sent word. She arrived at the head of a guard provided by the abbot when she had revealed herself to him. Their approach had been sighted five miles back, of that she could be sure, for Bowland overlooked all the country around, with signal towers to extend the view. He would know by now a party came.

And he had surmised who it was. A half-mile from the gatehouse, a pair of riders sped out to them, bringing breathless welcome, and a few moments later an escort of twenty lances showing signs of hasty organization trotted to meet them, wheeling to form proud flanks.

A few drops of rain spattered her shoulders, but she did not raise her hood. She rode over the bridge and into the immense shadow of the barbican with her face lifted and her head bare but for a golden net.

Woodsmoke and cheering shouts greeted her as her rouncy jogged into the open yard. The lower bailey swarmed with people and animals, as if every member of the hold had dropped his task to come. They wished to see her, she knew, their mistress returned.

Among the English she recognized no one, but that was beyond reason to expect. All her old servants, her parents' men, they would all be changed beyond knowing. But a babble of Italian and French equaled or outpaced the native tongue, and there were ones she saw of Gian's knaves whom she knew better than she cared to, and her own familiar retinue awaiting—her palfreyour to take her horse, and her chaplain, and yes . . . Cara, smiling, with a trapped rabbit's fright in her eyes.

Melanthe ignored her. As she dismounted, Gian came striding from the donjon.

He was grinning, his arms open. His houpelande of crimson flared behind him, guards of gold embroidery skimming the ground, and his spiked harlots impaling the air elegantly with each step.

He went low to his knee, lifting the hem of her gown. "God be thanked for His might. God be thanked." He made the cross and touched his lips to the cloth.

"Your Grace," she said. "Give you greeting."

He sought her hands as he rose, kissing her eagerly on cheeks and mouth. "Princess, you know not what I have endured."

He tasted of perfumed oil, his beard dressed neat, blackened by dyes of cypre and indigo. She offered her hand.

"I was the one lost in desert," she said lightly. "Ask what I've endured. Depardeu, I have not heard a word but in English these three months."

"Torture indeed!" He took her arm and led her up the stairs into the donjon. "You shall tell me all, when your ladies have done with you. Come—oh, come, my sweet." His fingers tightened on her suddenly. He halted, gathering her hands in his and kissing them.

"Gian," she said softly.

He straightened. "Christ, I am undone, to treat you so." He released her. "Go to your women. Call me when you will."

With a swift turn he walked away from her. At the screen he passed Allegreto, who bowed down with his forehead to the very floor tile. Gian did not glance at him. He crossed the hall and disappeared into a stair.

IT WAS NOT until she was in her bath, with the silk sheets hung about and Cara setting a tray of malvoisie wine on the trestle, that the full scope of Melanthe's defeat came upon her. She had held herself insensible to what she did; refused to think backward instead of forward, to move in weakness rather than strength.

But she had lost, and lost beyond all her worst imagining.

Gian held her. And Bowland that was to have been her security, her refuge where every servant was safe and known and no alien countenance could be concealed. She had thrown away the quitclaim to draw him off, she had rid herself of Allegreto and Cara only to have them back, she had played bishop and queen and king—and lost. Bowland. Her safety, her freedom. And more—but she could not think of him; she would break if she thought of him, and Gian would see.

Cara washed her hair. Melanthe could feel the maid's unsteady fingers—she wanted to scream at the girl to summon her nerve, for one weak link was enough to kill them all. Instead she took the washcloth and wiped soap across her mouth, preferring the flavor of it to Gian's taste.

"I hear thou art repentant," she said coldly. "What proof canst thou give me of it?"

"Oh, my lady!" Cara whispered. She bent her head, her wet hands clenched together. "I'll do anything!"

Melanthe gazed at her. "Hardly reassuring. What of thy sister?"

The girl shook her head. "My lady, what am I to do? I would give my life for her if it would make her safe, but it would not. Allegreto has said—that he has tricked the Riata for a little time—I know not how, but I was to account to them by Ficino, and within the day of when he came here, before he tried to seek me out, he . . . he must have caught a candle in his clothes, my lady, and . . . there was a fire. It was a terrible accident, my lady. All said so."

Melanthe hid the jolt of discovery about Ficino in a brief laugh. "Thou hast found thyself a useful friend in Allegreto, it would seem."

The maid kept her eyes lowered. She did not answer.

"Thou wilt go between us. He must stay near his father and away from me," Melanthe said. "He has told me I may trust thee, which is why I do, and the only reason, since thou givest me none other. But remember that Gian is here, and at thy least indiscretion I will give thee to him, and even Allegreto could not save thee then."

"Yea, my lady. I could not forget it, my lady."

SHE RECEIVED GIAN in the chamber that had belonged to her father, with its paintings of jousts and mêlées all along the plastered walls, a newer wainscoting below them that she did not remember and a line of diverse shields hung above. Again it seemed not so vast as it ought, the colors duller, the curtained bed smaller and the red and blue ceiling beams not so high as she recalled. But her father's chair still stood near the chimney, with a cushion in it that was shabby and almost worn through, an imperfect embroidery of the Bowland arms that Melanthe recognized at once.

Every year since her marriage she had made him a new cushion, and sent it. This one had been the first. Some others lay about the chamber, early efforts, when she had been so sick for home that she had spent hours at the task. In latter years she had chosen elaborate designs and caused the best craftsmen in the city to execute them in expensive materials, but she did not see any of those richer pillows in the room.

She was glad they were not here. The thin cushion worn through in her father's chair was better comfort and courage. She did not rise from it as Gian entered, but only indicated a lesser chair drawn up near.

He bowed to her. Melanthe went through the ritual of ordering spices and drink. While a servant waited at the door for any further charge, they exchanged greetings of exquisite courtesy. Gian sat down.

"My lady's father left his holding in good order, may God assoil him," he said in French. "I've seen naught but signs of the most excellent management here since he passed to his reward."

Gian was a master. Word of that compliment would soon spread throughout the bailey.

Melanthe smiled. "I think you are a little amazed, sir. Haps you thought we lived as savages here in the north."

"My dear, none such as you could have sprung from savages, or from any but the most noble blood."

"I told you that my English estate was well worth my journey. This hold is but a fraction; I have numerous manors to the west and south, and five good castles, garrisoned all. I've made homage for them to the king, but there's much work yet to be done—I must meet my vassals and tour my holdings. I'll be truthful with you, my lord, and hope that you did not come sallying north in the expectation that I would return immediately."

He was silent, looking at her in an unfathomable way. She tilted her head and put a question in her glance. She had worn a high-necked gown and dressed her hair in a wimple of purple silk, so that the pulse in her throat would not show.

"I would have thought you well occupied at home," she added, defying caution to make a swift attack.

He grinned, lifting his eyebrows. "And well you should, my lady. After such a kindness as you did me with your quitclaim."

He appeared quite at ease, even amused. But of course that could hide anything. She shrugged. "A mischief, verily—but not too great, I hope. I regret I had not time to warn you, but I was pressed upon too closely, and then of course—this fearful adventure I have experienced—"

She left it there, without supplying details that might entangle her.

"We must thank God that you're safe," he said. "These other matters are trifling. The Duke of Lancaster has graced us with a company of men and lawyers in Monteverde, to press the claim you gave his father. My son tells me you have met the duke?"

There was the heart. His real concern, in a casual question tagged to the end of his words. Armies might move and lawyers argue over the paper claim she had given away, but the real threat she still carried in herself and her marriage. Lancaster was ambitious and powerful, with the throne of England behind him; if already he sent a force to assert her quitclaim, how much more aggressive might he be with the princess of Monteverde as his wife?

"Indeed yes," she said, "I stopped at Bordeaux until the new year. A gracious and hospitable man, truly. His brother the prince is sore ill, I fear, and so the duke takes all the burden of Aquitaine upon his own shoulders. I'm surprised he had the resource to pursue any business in Monteverde."

The refreshment arrived, saving her from saying more. Gian watched as the English steward tasted the wine and spiced cakes, and then his own man did the same. When the drink was poured, Gian dismissed both servants with a flick of his hand. It was the first usurpation of authority he had taken—not having been so tactless as to lodge himself in the lord's chambers or issue orders to her attendants. Melanthe made no remark on it, but she did look deliberately at his hand and up at his face.

He smiled. "Forgive me. I'm an impudent fellow—but how shall I not be anxious to have you to myself?" The door hasp clanked shut like the bolt on a prison. For a long moment he sat with his wine cup in his hands, gazing at her. "My life has been a joyless desert without you."

"Come, Gian—we're alone. You needn't exert yourself to love-talk now."

He rubbed his thumb over the rim, looking down at it. "It's no exertion," he said softly.

She realized that he wished to play at love-amour. She thought of his perfumed kiss, and a terrible loathing of the course she must take came over her. He was no Ligurio, to leave her in peace in her bedchamber, but the man who had made sure by murder that she took no lovers. He had waited for her—without a legitimate heir, for his own enigmatic reasons, for a logic she had never plumbed, nor ever would.

"It would be exertion for me," she said. "I am too weary now to trade compliments."

His eyes lifted. He smiled and drank. "Then I'll waste none upon you, without my fair share in return. Tell me of your dread adventure, if you cannot praise my manly beauty."

"Nay, I should not like to disappoint you, if it is compliments you desire," she said. "Shall I say that your own son could not flatter that elegant garment better?"

He did not move, but the pleasure seemed to flow through him, from a slight twitch of his spiked slipper to a deeper expansion of his chest when he inhaled. "Do not say it, my dear lady, if it would tire you too much."

"I am weary in truth, Gian." She nibbled idly at a cake. "I really don't wish to hold a long conversation."

He rose abruptly, walking to the oratory, her father's little chapel where light from a narrow window of stained glass dyed the altar and rood. He was handsome enough, in his own way—older than Melanthe by near a score of years and yet lithe as a youth—an Allegreto with the sureness of age and power on him. Gluttonous indulgence was not his vice; he lived austere as a monk but for the fashions in clothing that he liked to set. For their interview he had abandoned the staid floor-length robes in favor of the single color of Navona: white hose and a short white houpelande. Often he embellished the milky ground with gold alone, but now he was embroidered in spring flowers, his voluminous sleeves longer than his hem. It showed the lean legs of an ascetic—and his masculinity—very well.

"Concede me just a little description of your ordeal, my love." He smiled. "Your escort comes from an abbey, they tell me. Have you been safe all along in a religious house, then, while our Allegreto tore his hair?"

"Why, yes—has he not recounted to you?"

"He seems to have become shy." Gian leaned against the carved arcade of the oratory. "Gone to earth somewhere, like your English foxes."

She did not know whether to bless Allegreto for his forethought, or fear that Gian had indeed questioned him and now wished to compare their stories. "He has a great fear of your displeasure," she said, a description so patently inferior to the actuality that she found herself returning Gian's smile with a wry curl of her own mouth.

"Still, a son should not hide from his father's just wrath. Or the world would become a wicked place indeed, don't you think?"

She gave him a surprised look. "Wrath? But what has he done?"

"Failed me, my dearest lady. Failed me entirely, when he allowed this calamity to befall you. And acted beyond himself in another small matter, not worth mentioning. If you should come across his burrow, you would not be amiss to tell my little fox that delaying the chase only puts the hunter out of temper."

"If you mean that he failed in my protection—surely you did not expect him to take on a pack of murdering bandits?"

"Ah, we come now to the bandits." He examined a painted and gilded angel's face carved at the base of the arch. "Was it a large body of outlaws?"

She shrugged. "I think it must have been. I was woken out of a sound sleep to flee."

"You're very easy about it, my lady! Were you not dismayed?"

She made a sound of impatience. "Indeed no, I was so delighted that I stayed to offer thêm wine and cakes! Truly, I am not eager to live the experience again only for your entertainment."

He bowed. "I must ask your pardon. But these outlaws should be brought to justice."

"That has been taken care of, you may believe."

He raised his brows. Melanthe looked back at him coolly, daring him to put her to an inquisition, or hint that she did not rule here in her own lands.

"Alas, I arrive too late to rescue you, and now I cannot even take your revenge. A paltry fellow!" He drained his wine. "Hardly the equal of this mysterious green captain of yours, I fear."

She leaned back in her chair and gave him a dry smile. "Verily, not half as holy."

"Holy? I was told he is a knight of some strength and repute."

"Certainly he is. I retain only the best for my protection."

"But where is he now, this paragon?"

Melanthe turned her palms up. "I know not. I believe a great hand comes down from heaven and lifts him up to sit among the clouds. Haps he prays and parleys with angels, which is as well, for his conversation is too pure to be borne on earth, I assure you."

"Even when he shares a bed with you, as I'm told?"

"A bed!" She stared, and then laughed. "Ah, yes—a bed. At that delightful manor house, you mean. But how come you to hear of that farce? Most notably holy when he shared a bed with me." She grimaced. "My ears rang with his prayers."

He observed her a moment and then chuckled. "My poor sweet, you have had a hard time of it, haven't you?"

"Worse than you know! I fell from the rump of his repellent horse and broke my cannal-bone. Three months have I sojourned in the most contemptible little priory, among nuns! The prioress could barely speak French and did naught but pray for me. She and my knight got along excellently."

He laughed aloud. "But I must meet him, this knight. And the prioress, too. Such intercessions might save me a little time in Purgatory."

"Gian, do not flatter yourself. Prayers are wasted on you, as they are on me. I told her so, but she was relentless. God is weary of hearing my name, I quite assure you."

He strolled back to her chair, standing near. "Surely, though, some gift or reward should be—"

She turned an angry eye on him. "Do not forget that I am mistress here. I do not require your advice or your assistance in it."

"Of course not, sweet. But I think—hearing of your trials and adventures—that I do not like you riding about the country on the rump of some nameless knight's horse. Or falling off of it. Or sharing a chamber with him, however holy he might be. You have had your way, and paid respects to Ligurio and your king, and seen to your estates." His hand skimmed her cheek. "I think, my dear love, that it is time and past for our betrothal."

She stared at the colored window in the oratory. "Yes, Gian." She kept her breathing slow and even. "It is time."

His finger pulled back the silken scarf, tracing her jaw and the telling pulse at her throat.

"If he touched you in desire, fair child," he murmured, "he is dead."

Melanthe rose, moving away from him. She locked her hands and stretched her arms out before her. "If the man ever felt desire, I warrant it would kill him. Now indulge me, Gian, I want to rest. My shoulder pains me." She smiled at him. "And do leave poor Allegreto alone if you love me, my lord. I want to dance with him at our wedding."

Twenty-three

THEY HUNTED WITH ladies' hawks, summer birds, a blithe company passing through the meadows with laughter and elegant disport. Melanthe wore a garland that Gian had presented her. The sparrowhawk she carried felt no heavier than one of the blossoms from the spray, tiny and fierce, pouncing upon thrushes and woodcock and returning with them to the glove, a delicate court lady with savage yellow eyes.

Melanthe rode beside Gian, tame as the sparrowhawk returned to hand. Their time at Windsor drew near to a close. He had completed the contracts and assignments; the king's license was sealed at the price of only two of her five castles, the quitclaim to Monteverde purchased back from Edward for a proper princely ransom. They hawked today; in three days the betrothal feast began, a week more of such pleasures; of gifts and minstrelsy—then Italy, and their wedding. Gian was not eager to wait.

He chafed at their separate residences, but Melanthe had held adamant on that point and his proper behavior beforehand. He laughed and cajoled her, but knew her better than to believe she would give anything away for nothing. That was what he thought and said of her, not knowing that she would give everything away for nothing. For the nunnery, as the only place she could avoid fornicating with him.

When she lay awake at night, as she did every night now, she laughed silently until she wept at the mockery of it all. The place she had walked through wilderness and fire to avoid, the abominable nunnery. She did not dare attempt to evade him in England again. Once they were back in Italy, she could fly to the abbey that she and Ligurio had endowed. She had Allegreto's promise that he would help her. And vows upon vows, lies upon lies, until she forgot who she was, if she had ever known.

Amongst the betrothal gifts there were already three mirrors, carved ivory and sandalwood and ebony, all buried as deep in her chests as she could bury them, so that she would not chance to look into the glass and see no one there.

"It's a great shame that your gyr is still in mew, my lady," the young Earl of Pembroke said, while the others complimented a fine flight for Gian's hawk on a blackbird. "What a day she might have given us!"

"'Tis a lighter weight to carry, this!" Melanthe held up her little bird. "And only think how fat Gryngolet will be, come autumn."

Laughter rippled over the company. The spaniels put up a bevy of quails, and two ladies cast off. Courteous clapping and a discussion of the full bags and prospects for a sparviter's pie of partridge and larks and wheatears followed their success. Turning away from the late afternoon sun, they allowed the horses to ramble toward Windsor and the castle, its highest banners just barely visible over the far trees.

The shade of a narrow lane spread the party out, with Melanthe and Gian paired at the head as if by design. "You look a mere maiden in your blossoms," he said to her, smiling. "Flowers become you."

"Do they?" she asked lightly. "Nay, I think you suppose to flatter me, sir, so that when I ask for diamonds you can satisfy me with daisies."

She expected some smooth wit in response to hers, but instead he tilted his head. "Never do you consent to a tribute to your beauty, my lady. Is it the compliments or the complimenter?"

"Neither, but myself. A maiden, Gian? Daisies? I fear I am too shrewd to believe such pleasant fancies."

"I think you should believe them, my lady, for they are true."

She slanted a look at him. The leaf dapple passed over his white velvet shoulders and turban hat. "Why, Gian. Can this be love?"

He returned her look steadily, speaking barely above his breath. "Is it possible that you don't know it?"

She felt a flush rise in her throat. He did not take the easy tone of gallantry.

"Why, then of course the betrothal must be off," she said. "Love will not do, if we are to be wed. People will think us a pair of burghers!"

"Ah. But this is a puzzle. If love is not acceptable in marriage, does it follow you have no love for me now, since we are betrothed?"

"You must go to the Greeks for logic," she said.

"And to a lady for love. Do you not love me, my dear one?"

She pricked her horse to a trot. "Inquire of Cupid, my lord, for the answer to that!" she called gaily over her shoulder.

She straightened about in the saddle. The shaded lane curved, descending to a ford. Sunlight glistened on water through the trees—glinted on something more. She dragged her horse to a jerking halt.

On the far side of the stream a pale destrier waited, caparisoned all in green, the rider armored, his sword drawn, emerald and silver like a dream in the glowing yellow light of afternoon.

The black eyeslits watched her silently. Gian came up behind her. She heard the others, the thud of hooves and the sudden stifle of easy talk.

The knight shoved his faceplate up. Melanthe felt Gian beside her, felt a helpless frenzy.

"My lady wife." Ruck's hard voice rang across the stream that divided them. "I would have let thee live separate and alone. I would not have abashed thee, if thou hadst only wished to deny me for cause of pride and place. But thou art my wife, Melanthe—and 'fore God, I will not let thee forlie with another man, nor live together with him in dishonor of us both."

She thought of laughing. She thought of screaming. She thought of disclaiming any knowledge of him; all those things came to her at once, but she said, "Don't approach him. He has gone mad."

In her dismay the words held utter conviction. She felt Gian's eyes shift.

Ruck did not move. "It may please thee to claim so, my lady," he said coldly. "But you know as I that it is not true. I bid thee now to honor thy word and obey me. Leave this place, and this company, and come with me."

"He is mad," Melanthe repeated stupidly.

"Make way, fool," Gian said.

He started to press his horse forward, but she seized his sleeve. "Gian! He's dangerous."

She thought it sounded convincing: Gian paused, and Ruck's mouth lifted in contempt.

"Only in defense of thy virtue, madam." Sunlight slipped down his bare blade. "I will not endure thee to whore with him."

One of the ladies behind her gasped. Gian pulled his sleeve from Melanthe's hand. "Thou harlot, I'll kill thee for that, mad or no."

"Gladly I'll fight," Ruck said.

Gian spit on the ground. "Baseborn churl," he said with deadly softness, "I would not soil my hands. Thou wert born upon a dung heap. Out of the way, madman, and run far."

The destrier turned on its haunches, making room in the road between the thick hedgerows. "You may pass, if you will. And the rest, but for my wife."

Gian reached out and caught the bridle of her horse. He spurred into the stream, pulling her along. At the sloped bank, the white courser moved before them, blocking passage. Ruck's sword came down between their horses, the blade suspended over Gian's arm.

"Unhand her," he said quietly.

Gian made a move to go around. Hawk kicked out with a vicious force that sent Gian's mount shying back. He lost his hold on her bridle as his horse slipped and stumbled at the edge of the stream. His sparrowhawk fluttered free. At the same moment the Earl of Pembroke came splashing through the water.

"My lady!" he shouted, slapping her horse's rump. "Go now!"

Her rouncy jumped forward, colliding with Pembroke's as he passed, but the destrier held the narrow road. Ruck fended off the young earl's dagger with an armored elbow, keeping his own sword clear. The war-horse backed hard against Pembroke's bewildered mount, shoving him beyond knife reach.

"Pass." Ruck swept his blade point upward, allowing a slim opening to the earl. "I have no quarrel with you, but you may not take my wife."

"Thou staring madman, she's no such thing!" Pembroke exclaimed. "How dare thee say it?"

"Ask her," Ruck said.

Melanthe felt their all attention fix. It was high disport, this; a play to them—except for Gian, who had silent savagery in his eyes. He had suspected; she knew he had suspected, but she had lulled him and beguiled him, and now he knew. Not the marriage, no, for that was too fantastic for credence—but jealousy burned behind his calculating stare. He would not bear lt.

"Am I thy true husband?" Ruck held the destrier in taut check, staring at Melanthe. "Tell them, my lady."

She looked up into his eyes, his green cold eyes, and saw the last slender flame of trust still there. He asked her for the truth, because he did not conceive of dishonor. He did not know the depths of treachery—standing armed and armored, and defenseless against it.

She shook her head, with a small disbelieving laugh. "Thou art a silly simple," she said. "Thou art not even a man, I think, save by hap in thy dreams!"

In the slight flicker of his lashes it died, the last tattered rag of faith. He smiled, a baring of his teeth. "Thou dost not answer my question, lady."

"Then let me make my words clear to thy fevered brain!" she exclaimed. "I am not thy wife!"

"I say that you are, but that you dare not speak according

to conscience or the pleasure of God, for fear evil might be done you." He spoke with an even force. "I say that we were in the manor of Torbec at the end of Hilarytide, in the solar chamber above the hall, and thou said thou took me there and then as thy wedded husband if I willed it, to have and to hold, at bed and at board, for better and for worse, in sickness and health, till death us depart—and of this thou gave me thy faith. And I said that I willed it, and plighted thee my troth the same, and more, for I dowed thee with all that is mine, which thou didst not do for me in return, nor did I ask or wish for it. I had no ring nor garland for you, but swore all this by my right hand. And we had company and use of each other in the same bed where we spoke, to seal our vows, and afterward I wept."

"A vivid dream indeed!" Melanthe said.

"No dream," Ruck answered her, "but what passed between us in truth. We lived as man and wife, and the last time lay together ere you left me for Bowland on the day before the May."

It was working upon their witnesses as he meant it to, a detailed and rational list of circumstances, no madman's vision. She saw Pembroke's expression change from disbelief to wonder—saw him look at Gian to measure his response.

"You lie!" Gian's shout rocked off the water and the trees. "Whoreson, who paid you to say this?"

Ruck's gaze went instantly to him, like a wolf that had sighted its prey at last. His sword made a singing sweep into guard. "I do not lie, nor speak for gain. I am no son of a whore, but I'll be pleased to kill thee for thy slander.

"No." The earl held out his arm. "Nay, sir—Dan Gian is not armed."

Without hesitation Ruck reversed his sword, offering it to Pembroke. As the earl grasped the hilt, Hawk lifted his great hooves, treading sideways, shouldering into Gian's horse. Gian didn't flinch—he made a murderous stab toward Ruck's eye with his poison-dagger. For an instant they grappled together, and then Ruck had Gian's wrist in his grip, the horses splashing and circling.

Hawk sidestepped against Gian's mount, shoving, his bulk compelling the other horse to scramble for footing as Ruck forced Gian's arm overhead. Like a slow ram, the destrier impelled the lighter horse to move, to lurch and falter in the stream. Gian wrenched free and threw himself toward Ruck, driving the dagger at his face as the rouncy went down with a floundering splash.

Heavy drops sprayed over Melanthe as her mount shied back. The ladies screamed, clinging to their reins and their bating hawks. Amid a flail of hooves and water Gian was half-trapped, his leg beneath the horse, but the animal rolled and heaved forward, struggling upright in a glistening sheet.

Frantically she scanned Ruck's face, dreading to see a poisoned scratch within the shadow of his helmet. But there was no blood, only the forbidding set of his mouth as he met her eyes.

It was this he had wanted from the start, she saw. Not his command to her to go with him—but Gian, dripping and humiliated beyond human bearing, shamed into challenge and combat.

"She is my wife," he said, looking on Gian as the downed man groped to his feet in the middle of the stream. "Thou wilt not touch her or see her again."

"Thou art an open liar and false knave." Gian's leg gave beneath him, and he went to one knee, but even his soaked velvet did not diminish the proud savagery of his response. "I'll have thy contemptible life."

"Name the occasion. And come armed."

Gian drove himself to his feet. "Thou wilt receive my messenger."

"I await him. The Ospridge at Colnbrook." Ruck tossed Gian's dagger into the water. He turned Hawk, reining the destrier up onto the bank, and halted beside Melanthe. "For courtesy, I do not compel my lady's grace to attend me at a common inn."

"Mary, I would not attend thee at Westminster Palace, thou poor deluded churl." Her rouncy pirouetted. "Begone thee. Gian, your little sperverhawk has taken a stand in that oak—" She spurred her horse, gesturing urgently at the sparviters who had held the spaniels and gaped all through the scene. "Come quickly, we must retrieve her ere she escapes us!"

•   •   •

ALL THE TOWNS and villages about Windsor Castle were full while the king was in residence. For a fortnight Ruck had sat in taverns and listened to the talk of clerks and squires, of knights in waiting. He'd heard it all—how this Italian lord would wed her, what terms he bought and how he bought them in his dealings with the king's ravenous mistress and her favorites, where he resorted, and how often he attended the Lady Melanthe at her bury hall of Merlesden.

Navona kept his own lodging three miles off, in the town hard by the castle. If he had not, Ruck thought, he would already be dead.

Warm air, smelling of dust off the street, flowed into the upstairs window of the inn. Ruck sat with his feet propped on the sill. He could see Merlesden from his chamber, an admirable court hall of pale stone on a wooded hillside across the water meadows, the sun sparkling from its many windows.

He hated it. He hated her, with a fine relentless hate, a cold will down to his heart and sinew.

He would not endure her to make mock of him. To discount him, as if he did not exist. How long she must have planned it, he could not fathom—she had rused and wiled, and he had been so sotted and glad that he had not pressed her. Or haps she had never planned it, but only heard that her great love had come for her, this Dan Gian, this Italian lord—father of her lap-dog lover; vice beyond conjecture—and she forgot all else but to warn Ruck not to presume on her for shame of him.

He swung his legs down and stood, pacing the width of the private bedchamber as he had walked the towers of Wolfscar. She had called him mad, and he had gone near mad in truth, lost he knew not how long in silent ferocity, a violence locked up in himself, so that he could not speak even when he heard common voices talking to him.

He was out of his right mind yet, he knew. She would have her way, he did not doubt: he would not have her back—nor wanted her. She had not even looked as he remembered. Ever the witch, she had changed herself again: thinner, delicate and narrow like a phantom spirit clothed in richness, her eyes deep and dead when she gazed upon him. Her flowers were a japing mock, virgin's blossoms to adorn a ramp.

He leaned his hands on the painted boards and put his forehead to the wall. He listened to the sound of his own breathing.

Ruck wanted to slay her as she slayed him, but he could only take the oiled and painted carpet knight. By the church or by the challenge, he would deprive her of that connection. In his madness to prevent her, he was blessed with detached reason, as if he were two men, one who burned and one who was ice.

He had hired counsel in canon law. He made his case to the bishop, giving solemn oath of his truth—on the morrow she would have notice of that, and peraventure her foreign lord's great preparations for a feast would be gone to waste. Ruck had even found his green tournament plate, stolen in the Wyrale and ransomed back from an armorer in Chester, missing the emerald yes, but fit for use. He had chosen his place and time with perfect care—to speak before witnesses who would put the word about court and countryside swift as gossip's wing could carry it.

If they dared to carry on with their betrothal, Ruck intended to sour the wine in their mouths.

The canon clerk had advised him to assert that she could not speak freely for fear of someone near her, a trick to counter her foregone denial. That Melanthe had ever feared anything, even unto Hell itself, Ruck greatly doubted, but he could see the usefulness of the pretense. He had also given a hoard to the clerk's safekeeping, in case they should try to have him arrested on charges of deceit and falsehood, and set down names of men who would let mainprize for his surety. He trusted her as he would trust a viper in his bed.

He lifted his head at the sound of a horse coming fast in the road. Two days had he waited for Navona's agent. He turned eagerly, to hear if the rider came to a halt, but the hoofbeats did not slow. The horse rushed beneath the window.

A pale object flew through the open glass, startling him. It thumped on the floor, a small white sack, while the horse passed on without a pause.

He swept it up, yanked open the string, and poured pebbles from inside. A folded paper fell after them into his hand.

For an instant his whole heart changed—he pressed open the folds with a hope that lasted only long enough to see that it was French. She would not write him in French, not if she meant well. Neither her name nor her sign marked the paper.

"On guard," it said only. "The wine."

He held the paper, rubbing it between his fingers. There was no hint—but it must be her, to warn him of this wine. Who else . . .

Comprehension came to him. He had seen Desmond here, at a distance, loitering with Allegreto and a crowd of honey-fly gallants and laughing ladies, dressed in a short hamselin coat with delicate embroidery and fur tips. Desmond, too, she had perverted, but this much faith the boy must have left, to forewarn Ruck—in French no less—that his wife or her lover tried to poison him.

He made a small laugh, tearing the parchment and flicking the pieces away. And when Navona's agent came at last, bearing a flask of wine and news that Dan Gian, his ankle broken in the fall beneath his horse, would have a champion in his place rather than delay their reckoning, Ruck did not drink to seal the arrangement.

A champion. But let him cower behind tainted wine and champions, the fisting cur. He would not have her.

Ruck gave the wine flask to the landlady and told her to poison rats with it—for which she thanked him in the morning and said that it had done very well.

THE CHAMPION WAS to be imported from Flanders. Ruck learned of it when he went to the jousting ground in search of exercise, and found no dearth of offers.

He fought in the lists all morning. He did not usually encounter so many who wished to trade spars with him, but he was glad enough for the fierce activity. The betrothal feast had not been set aside; it went forward at Merlesden after a promise on the church porch—the canon lawyer assured him that the priest's words would include "if the Holy Church consents," a caution Ruck could depend upon to protect his interest, but he knocked a squire clear from his saddle with a wooden waster when he thought of Navona's face.

It came now to forbidding the banns. He would not have to stand up in church and object; his clerk already worked to present his case, and at least until it had been investigated, the betrothal could be carried no further. Ruck chafed at these bishops and clerks, but it was a rite that had to be observed. He expected no success; she would deny him to the bishop as she had denied Ruck to his face, and so it was his word against hers. He had but one way to prove himself, with a sword.

He dismounted, starting to take a ladle of water from a page who ran up to offer it—and then hesitated. He let the water pour onto the ground and called another waterboy from outside the lists.

"Wary bastard!" A knight halted beside him, some foreigner with an accent of the south. He said in a loud voice, "These stinking coquins must watch their backs."

Ruck ignored him, squatting down to cup his hands and drink from the bucket.

"Miserable wretch, how much money dost thou think to get for renouncing your foul tale? Tell me, and I'll take the message to Dan Gian, to save thee the toil."

Ruck stood up. "If thou hast come from Navona," he said, calm and clear, "then advise him to save his silver, for to hire the man who dies in his place." Ruck wiped his face with a towel. "Since he's too much a woman to fight himself."

"He's injured, caitiff."

Ruck smiled up at the knight. "I'd be pleased to wait, but I think his ankle won't be so brave as to knit soon."

The foreigner looked about at the crowd that gathered and deliberately spit on him. "Fight me. Now."

Ruck wiped his *cuir bouilli* with the towel and threw it down. "With the greatest delight, thou son of a mongrel bitch." He turned to Hawk and tightened his girth. Immediately the spectators split, pages and squires pressing up to serve him with helm and a steel sword instead of the wooden wasters for practice. The blunt-fingered squire who held out the helmet dropped it an inch from Ruck's hand.

As they both bent to retrieve it, the squire hissed, "Your friend says beware the sword."

Ruck looked up at him. He was a stranger, backing away with a quick bow. A quick scan of the spectators lined along lists revealed no Desmond, nor any other friend.

They were sympathetic to him, though, halloing him vigorously as he mounted. He turned the sword he'd been given, running his glove along the edge. Light flashed up and down it. He could see no flaw, but he was not fool enough to chance it. He called for another—and as he handed down the first blade, he saw it: a ghost across the metal, the faintest flaw of color.

"Who gave me this?" he shouted in English. He held it overhead, reining his horse in a circle, spurring toward the quintain. "Who gives me a sword nought worth ambs-ace?" With a violent sweep he brought it flat against the stout practice post.

The blade broke, the sundered half flying through the air to land with a skidding puff of dust.

"Witness this, that I was goaded into combat by no will of my own, and given that to fighten with." He glared around at the staring faces. "I am in health and whole today—if I die afore I prove my truth against Navona's slander, then I pray you, for your honor, to search into the cause." He threw away the broken hilt and turned his mount toward the gate. "I ne do nought fight with a foul nithing."

They jeered; he supposed it was at him, until he reached the rail and they started to duck under it and run into the lists. His challenger did not make it to the gate, surrounded by an angry swarm. They pulled him from his horse, tearing his helmet and weapon away the better to beat him.

Ruck watched for a moment, with a habitual urge to stop the disorder. He was not certain that the man had been behind the flawed sword. But there were boys taking hold of Hawk's bridle, excited squires and pages escorting him out the gate. He remembered that foreign voice and deliberate spit, and turned his back.

He realized that the bull-shouldered squire who had given him the warning was walking beside him, hand on his stirrup.

When he dismounted, the man took his shield and helmet with a seasoned efficiency.

"Who does thou serve?" Ruck asked in English.

He made a smart bow. "My good lord Sir Henry of Grazely died at Pentecost, may Lord Jesus grant him grace. I be withouten place since."

Ruck frowned. "Who spake thee as my friend?"

"Ne do I not know, sir, but will I try out the creature and find him, an you liketh." He looked at Ruck with a sober expression that did not quite disguise the glint of hope. "John Marking is my name. My lady Grazely will write a letter to attest me, should it fall out that you be in need of a humble squire, God save you, sire."

"Then let her write anon," Ruck said, and handed John his gloves.

AT THE ARCHBISHOP'S pleasure, Ruck knelt with his canon in the inner closet where the prelate was lodged at Windsor. He listened to the canon review his case, as he had listened to it laid before priest and archdeacon and bishop. When the clerk had finished, the archbishop sat in silence for a few moments, and then said he wished to speak to Ruck alone.

"Sit there." The prelate waved him to a bench, holding the papers, all in Latin, and spreading them out on the table before him. "This is not a cause in which I would intervene," the prelate said, "but that since I came here I have heard of nothing but the marvelous case of this unknown knight, who would have it that he's married to the Countess of Bowland— who would have it that he's not."

Ruck said nothing. He sat straight, looking at the archbishop's peaked and embellished mitre that he'd taken off and set upon the table. The churchman sorted through papers.

"You press your cause ardently, with nothing to make proof," he murmured, reading. "But of course, I'm told that the widow is an heiress of great fortune."

"Your grace," Ruck said, "I do not want her fortune, nor will have it."

The prelate ran his finger across a line. "I see that you have so testified, that you quit all right in her estate. And yet such a marriage cannot be a disadvantage to you, for you have no property or place that you name. Sir who? Of where? What county?"

"Honorable father—I am under solemn vow, that I will not undertake my right name before the world until I prove worthy. But I have written it, and lies it sealed there." He nodded toward the parchments on the table. "The Duke of Lancaster is my liege lord. Six gentlemen and knights of good character vouch upon me, that I am no felon nor outlaw, but a true Christian man ready to keep the peace."

The archbishop made an irritated flick of his hand. "The Lord would be better pleased if young knights were not so hasty to swear such extravagant and profitless vows. But you must keep to your sworn word. Still—this want of conformity and open truth seems sufficient to arouse suspicion that you make your claim with worldly and wicked motive."

"My lord, I make claim for cause the Princess Melanthe is my wife, before God, and no other man may marry her while I live."

The archbishop tapped on the papers. Strong light shafted across the table from a lancet window, making a long shadow from his finger. "You testify that the Princess Melanthe took you to husband by your right name and knows your place."

"Yea, my lord. She lay at my hold, from February to May."

The churchman frowned at him thoughtfully. "Say me, in your own words, what passed."

Ruck had told the story often now; he related everything from his dismissal by Lancaster to the bed at Torbec. The archbishop did not break in to question him as the others had. He simply listened, shifting the papers on occasion. At the end he said, "My son, I fear that you have been wiled by a wicked and lewd woman. If those at Torbec could have testified to witness of the vows, the case might be different. I do not say that you have lied, but you have no proof."

"If I do not lie, then she is my wife," Ruck said. "She cannot marry another."

"I have seen her. I spoke to her right plainly, and put her in remembrance that her soul is at stake in this matter. She denies the words, and that you had company of each other, with great vehemence."

Ruck lifted his eyes in shock. He had not known she had already spoken her story.

But he did not trouble to repeat to the archbishop the foolish claim that she spoke under duress. Thrice in as many weeks Ruck had received warnings from his "friend"—and thrice had he lived to value them. He wrestled between believing that his wife was attempting to murder him and hoping that she was behind the warnings that spared him.

He shook his head. "My lord, she is my wife, and she cannot marry another. I do not lie in this, on my soul and any other oath required of me, though for saying it Dan Gian Navona accuses me of deceit and falsehood. I defend my words by arms against him, with leave of the king's justices in the court of chivalry, honorable father, if by God's will you accord."

The archbishop scratched his forehead and read the paper before him again. "He does not fight himself, but sends a champion."

"His ankle is broken, my lord."

The prelate gave a slight laugh. "I see. God in his wisdom prevents a direct meeting, that you may not be charged with a killing to clear your way to his betrothed."

"She is not his betrothed, but my wife, my lord."

"You are zealous," the archbishop said. "So too was the princess in her denial. But—if you speak true, then she married without the king's license and now has a great lord for a suitor. Many a man and woman, rightly wed, has made mock of their vows for less than this." He leaned back on the settle and rubbed his nose. "And when I asked of her where she lay for the months of February to May, in her impudence she told me she had spent the time so deep in prayer that she did not recall the place." He lifted his brows. "I be little convinced that such a female can benefit your spiritual welfare, my son in Christ."

Ruck knew that she could not. His spiritual welfare was in bloody shreds. But he bowed his head and said, "Good father, I wish to honor the bonds of holy matrimony."

He did not dare raise his eyes, for fear the man of God would see the depth and heat of gall in him. He listened to the scratch of the quill as the archbishop made a note in the margin of the document.

"I will forbid the banns and delay sitting of the canonical court on this matter until the outcome of the combat," the churchman said. "If God sends that you are successful in your defense against the charge of falsehood, then follows it that between you and Dan Gian, the weight of truth is yours. The court will take fitting account of the point. If you fail—and live, by God's mercy—then I forbid you as a proved deceiver to make further cause before the church. In absence of any earthly witness, let the Holy Spirit direct."

THEY LEFT THE archbishop's lodgings, Ruck's canon triumphant with success and John Marking striding ahead, clearing a path through the orderly confusion of the courtyard with oxlike resolution. Even John had to pause for a moment as the horns rang out and an opulent procession came through the gate.

Ruck felt his elation grow cold. Behind a scarlet vauntguard, Melanthe rode beside Navona, who did not appear much discommoded by his ankle. She was robed in red and gold; he all in white. A tall knight trailed them, armed and horsed and squired—the Flemish champion, without doubt, looking about himself with a keen interest.

The rest of their company came behind, faces shocking in their strange familiarity in this surrounding—Allegreto, the gentlewomen—and Desmond in the scarlet livery, wearing gloves in high summer and sitting a delicate palfrey with bored arrogance.

"There he is!" John suddenly leaned close to Ruck. "Your friend, my lord, who gave warning of the sword."

Ruck looked at Desmond, so unfamiliar and familiar in his finery.

"Rides he the fourth," John said under the rising sound of halloes and grumbles, "the first in the white surcoats. Young and comely."

"Nay—" As the company halted, Ruck's gaze shifted from scarlet Desmond to the first rider in the milk-white livery of the Italian. It was Allegreto. "Nought in white?"

But at that moment Allegreto's lazy glance passed along

the crowd. He looked directly at Ruck. His dark eyes took note, expressionless. With a deliberate move he pulled his light sword from its sheath and examined the blade.

Ruck found the area around himself opening. Someone pressed him forward from behind. The Flemish knight had dismounted; the space between them was suddenly empty—a confrontation, and the voices around rose in shouts of "Saint George! Saint George!"

The champion was a tall man, younger than Ruck by years. He skimmed the cheering English with a smile of delight and made a bow that held just the right touch of mockery, as if they were hailing him. It brought the shouts to a peak.

Ruck stood alone but for John. The Fleming examined him and then made a courteous nod. Ruck acknowledged it. He looked past the knight to where Melanthe sat her black palfrey. Though every eye in the courtyard was fixed on him and the man he would fight, she dismounted as if neither of them existed.

Her path lay away from Ruck. Her Italian lover took her arm, showing only a slight hesitation in his walk as he led her toward the great double tower entrance of the royal lodgings. The Flemish knight saluted Ruck and turned to follow.

Ruck had been prepared for their first encounter by the ford, armored in hate and determination. He had wanted witnesses. This time he wanted witness as he would have wanted staring eyes on him while a lion tore his heart from his chest.

She denied him. To his face, to the church, before the court. And Desmond—who did not look at Ruck, who did not pause or speak—Desmond saw it, and that was worst of all.

"THE MADMAN HAUNTS me," Melanthe murmured, before Gian could mention it.

He smiled, patting her arm. "Put him from your mind."

She paused in the echoing gate passage, lowering her voice below the sound of talk and movement, speaking Italian. "Avoi, Gian, I pray you not to have him killed before this cursed duel! Or after, if you please, for they'll never let you leave this misbegot country then!"

"You upset yourself for no cause, sweet." His eyes went briefly to Allegreto. "Put your faith in me, and say no more."

"Gian! You do not understand the English! If he dies by any way but in this combat, you'll not go unscathed. Let the lawyers pay him off. Or the—"

"I have told you not to speak of him." His fingers closed cruelly on her arm. He made her walk slowly on.

"I only—"

"My dear princess, if you add another word, I shall be forced to think you plead for his life because you love the poor devil."

She bore his painful grip without wincing. "My dear Gian," she said, "if you do not heed me, I shall be forced to think you are a great fool."

"Shall you?" He slanted a look down at her. "But in truth, Melanthe—I do not think I am."

Twenty-four

———⚬⚬⚬———

INSIDE THE TENT the sound of the spectators was a steady mutter embroidered by music, the king's favorite airs. John knelt at Ruck's feet, fastening on spurs. His green plate was polished and restored, the dents beaten smooth and the silver bosses renewed.

Ruck wore her colors, but he went to the fight not knowing her. She was the argent and green of Monteverde, or the red and gold of Bowland. She was his murderess, or she was trying to save him. She kept Wolfscar a secret to preserve it, or to discount him as a nameless adventurer. She had sent Allegreto with the warnings, or her lapdog betrayed her.

He did not know if she wished for Ruck to win and free her, or if she hoped that he would die and free her. He did not know.

But he shook his head to clear away fantasy. He knew. If she wanted him, all she had to do was speak what was true.

The flap of the tent flashed open, and Allegreto stepped inside, dragging the silk full closed. "I've only a moment," he said quietly. "My father must not smell me here. The Fleming has been told that you cannot withstand blows to the head. 'Ware your bascinet."

John instantly snatched up the helm. It glowed with the

new burnish as he turned it over in his hands. Nothing showed
on the surface. He lifted the aventail to examine the staples
and then smoothed his hand over the outside curve.

With a sudden exclamation he seized his dagger, slashed
through the padded lining, and scored the inner surface.
"God's death." He held out the blade. "Look at this, my lord."

Dark bluish shavings lay curled on the shining surface.
Ruck knocked them into his palm. "Lead."

John clouted the helm with the hilt of his sword. It cut a
dent in steel too soft to withstand even a one-hand blow. He
tore the leather out and explored the interior with his fingertips. "There." He pointed inside. "You can feel the place, my
lord."

The patch had been made with masterly skill, sheathed on
the outside by a thin skin of finer metal. The flaw was invisible, but rubbing his fingers over the inner and outer surfaces
at once, Ruck could detect the faint difference in the finish at
the edges of the place, and the slight hollow in the thickness.

It was too late to fit another bascinet. "I'll have to use the
great helm and a mail coif," he said.

"My lord!" John stood up. "This is too much. Lay it before
the marshal!"

"Nay," Ruck said softly. He looked to Allegreto. The youth
tilted his head, a smile on his mouth that never reached his
black eyes. "Why dost thou aid me?"

Allegreto put his fingers around the tent pole. He examined the ruby ring he wore. "You were kind to me once." He
shrugged, with a short laugh. "I remember it."

"Who tries to kill me?"

"If you will make mischief—many people."

"Thy mistress?" Ruck's voice was strained.

Allegreto lifted his brows. "Show a little wit, green man."

Ruck felt a tightness leave his muscles that he had not
known was there. "Then it's she who sent thee."

"Must someone send me?" Allegreto made a smirk. "I
come for love of you, Green Sire. How else?" He swung
about the pole and paused. "Be wary," he murmured, and vanished outside.

•   •   •

THE SOUND SHIVERED Ruck's head: pain first, a bright arc through his brain, and then his ears aching in the peal of metal. Each time he took a stroke, the clang stopped in his ear, building pressure, until the roar of the crowd and even the blows grew distant. He could only hear himself panting, sucking hot air through the pierced breaths in the helm; he could only see black and his opponent through the eyeslits and feel the violent swacks when he could not parry them.

In spite of the padding his great helm shifted whenever a blow caught it, obscuring his vision for an instant. The Fleming didn't take advantage; he flailed over and over at Ruck's head and only shifted a few times to any other assault. The strong onslaught left the man's body undefended on the side opposite his shield, but he rained blows so swiftly that Ruck was too occupied with deflecting them to attack.

If the helm had not blinded him, Ruck would already have cut under this crude beating and had the man on the ground. But he dared not leave his head unprotected long enough to strike, for fear the helm would be knocked askew too far to seat again and screen his sight entirely.

He defended with shield and sword, watching the Fleming's arm strokes. He squinted through the slit, blinking back the sting of sweat. Stepping backward, he let the champion have control of the rhythm, retreating slowly from the blows. Through the dint and clang, the dim shouts of the spectators rose to passion as he gave way.

The Fleming heard them, too: he renewed the vigor of his onset, faster and harder. Ruck parried in his attacker's cadence, falling back. Inside his brain, with the ringing clash, he sang a song of war that Bassinger had taught him, the swords tolling each note. The Fleming pealed the steady motet; Ruck answered in even time.

Then he took up the hocket—a hitch in the rhythm, counterpoint as he dropped the parry and swung his blade in attack.

Brilliant pain flashed in his ear, a tumble of light as the inevitable strike came. His sword bit, silence to him amid the belting in his head, but he felt the jolt and pause in his arm, swung through and past it, blind entirely. The Fleming missed his motet note, but Ruck sent the hocket back in treble, up and up, a half breath off the beat, a full double-handed swing overhead and down.

He killed the man. He could not see it, but he knew it: an instant of impact as his sword cleaved steel—and the collapse, a perception, and a dull chime of metal falling to the ground.

He stood in sweltering darkness, gasping with exertion, the skewed slash of eyeslit a white radiance above his line of sight, the cheek padding pressed painfully against his nose. It gave him a horrible moment of helplessness, his ears ringing and his eyes blind, without defense.

Then John was there, divesting him of the helm. It did not come off easily, beaten and wedged as it was, but when Ruck bent over and let the squire give the steel a bang from behind, the helm loosened. Ruck could barely hear the hit; he couldn't tell if the roar in his ears was the crowd or his head. As the helm fell, the warm summer air felt like a blessed rush of coolness on his face.

At his feet the Fleming champion lay in the trampled grass. His attendants and a physician clustered around him, but he was lifeless, his helm sundered through. Ruck stood straight. He lifted his bloodied sword and turned about to the stands. The constable and earl marshal sat beneath a canopy. A cross and Bible lay on the tapestry-covered table where Ruck and the Fleming had sworn their oaths. Beside them, on a slightly higher dais, sat King Edward himself, leaning forward, his face red with excitement, his long beard flowing down over his robes like a living and gleeful statue of Moses. The well-fed Lady Alice stood behind him, unashamed to have her hand on his shoulder.

Ruck barely found enough breath to speak. "I wish to know—if I have done my duty—to my honor," he asked of the justices. His own voice sounded strange to him, muffled and remote. When the marshal answered that he had, it seemed that the man spoke from very far away.

Ruck handed his sword to John and walked forward to the king. As he knelt, the block in his ear burst, and he could hear again.

All was silence, but for his own heart and heavy breath,

and the rustle of the pages of the open Bible. The crowd in the stand waited.

"Rise, bold knight," the king declared in English. "Thou hast defended thy honor before our court of chivalry with hende sword as proper." He chuckled. "A great dunt it was! A delight to see."

Ruck stood up. He lifted his eyes. The king was grinning, a little childgeared as they all said of him, but still a royal presence. He stroked his beard, his smile fading as he looked down into Ruck's face.

"But why dost thou wear those colors?" the king asked on an aggrieved note. "We ne do not like thee to changen, Ruck. Did we give thee leave to changen thy arms?"

He spoke the name without hesitation or title, as if he knew Ruck like an old friend. A faint murmur passed over the crowd. In his amazement Ruck could not find his tongue to answer.

"Why doth he wear green?" The king turned to Alice. "It should be azure ground, and the device a well huge werewolf depainted in black. Where is our herald of arms?"

While Ruck stood with his limbs and his speech beyond command, the herald came forward to wait on the king. The ladies in the stands craned over the railings, staring. People whispered and leaned near one another.

"Lord Ruadrik of Wolfscar," the king said, waving at Ruck. "Tell his arms."

The herald bowed. "Sire, the lord of Wolfscar of the County Palatine of Lancaster may bear him a blazon of bright azure, the device a werewolf of sheer sable within."

"There, we are exact in our memory!" The king looked triumphantly at Ruck. "We command our subject Lord Ruadrik of Wolfscar to divest himself of these and bearen his right device and colors."

"Sire," the herald said softly, "Lord Ruadrik died in the year of the great pestilence, and all his household with him."

"Nay." Ruck heard his own voice, still short of breath from his fight, but strong and clear. He fell on his knees before the dais. "Sire, I have sworn to conceal my name and place until I was proved worthy of it, but if God has sent to you to descry me, by what grace or method I know nought, then I avow that

I am Ruadrik, son of Ruadrik of Wolfscar and my lady mother his wife Eleanor."

The audience broke into a clamor. The king looked bewildered.

"What proof hast thou of this, sir?" Lady Alice's sharp voice cut through the noise.

Ruck ignored her. She was the king's mistress. He had heard that she would have profited greatly from Dan Gian's betrothal bargains.

"Sire," he said to the king, "my sovereign and beloved lord, gladly will I obey you and resume my own arms of Wolfscar from this day forward."

The king nodded, his perplexity brightening to simple satisfaction. "We are pleased. Full oft have we been glad to see thy blazon spread in battle with our enemies. Thou mayest rise, our trusty and well-loved Ruck."

Lady Alice put her hand on his arm and whispered into his ear. He frowned and shook his head as he listened to her. "Nay, my dear lady, we are not mistaken." He patted her hand. "The herald supports us. It is the azure-and-black wolf. Lord Ruadrik himself doth admit our verity."

"*Voire.*" Ruck stood with his smile breaking, impossible to restrain. The king had recognized him. Or mistaken him for his father, but that was no less a triumph, and an elation in itself, for he had not known it possible. "Truly, sire, it is as you say." He felt sweat trickling down his temple and had to prevent himself from wiping it away.

"Thy prize," the king said, looking about him. A man came from among the attendants, offering the king a wallet of coins. "How much?" the king whispered audibly as the attendant bowed at his knee.

The man murmured. King Edward frowned and nodded, beckoning Ruck to approach.

"One hundred mark," he declared.

Ruck stepped onto the dias and bent knee, his armor clunking loudly as it hit the wooden platform. He accepted the modest purse and rose at the king's command. Edward stood up with him.

"A dear fight! God and Saint George!" The king clouted Ruck's face between his palms and kissed him on the mouth.

Then he fumbled at the golden clasp on his robes and pressed the jeweled pin into Ruck's glove. "And here—a small love-drury, for thy service at Nottingham."

Ruck lowered his eyes, shaking his head at the mention of Nottingham and the king's love. "Sire, ne can I nought accepten this. My father it watz who climbed from the cellars with you and the others, sire, at Nottingham Castle. Ne yet watz I e'en born upon earth that day."

The king held the clasp, blinking down at it. He rubbed his thumb across the gold. "Not born, by God," he muttered. "Not born." He gave a deep sigh. "Yea, it is long ago now." He looked up, his eyes vague. "Thou wert not born?"

"Nay, sire. Watz my father who was with you, sire."

The king seemed to grow shamefast. "Ah. Thy father. Who is he?"

"Ruadrik of Wolfscar, sire. You called him Ruck, as I am called, too."

"His son!" A pleased smile grew on the king's face. "But how thou art much like him, in thy face, and thy uncouth northern tongue! Remember when we—" Then he shook his head. "But he is dead. All of them dead, Montagu and Bury—the best of men." He suddenly took Ruck's face between his hard old hands again, the clasp pressing into Ruck's cheek. "The most remembrance that I have shall be upon thee, and on thy needs. Keep this, I command thee."

He pushed the clasp into Ruck's hands and strode from the dais before Ruck could even say his thanks. Alice and the royal attendants hurried after—he might be wavering in his mind, but the king's body was in no wise impaired.

Ruck made a belated bow. He stepped down from the dais. In a maze of joy he walked toward John and the gate as noble spectators flooded down from the stands, crowding about him offering compliments and cheer. John gave him a towel to dry himself. Someone thrust a cool goblet into his hand. He glanced and saw it was Allegreto, with a triumphant grin and wink—Ruck's dark and strange savior, her envoy.

Beyond the crowd around him, beyond the knot of men still on the grass beside the Fleming champion, a chariot was drawn up beside the lists. Ruck stopped, lifting the goblet to his mouth. She was still there, beside her treacherous lover—

watching him with a faint smile. He drank, washing exertion and passion down his dry throat in one great swallow, taking boldness in with the wine. He started toward her, to demand that she come to him, his wife, the wine a bitter sourness on his tongue.

Her smile widened. She touched Navona's arm and nodded toward Ruck.

The moment that she did it, the cold enveloped him. His fingers numbed, his feet and his legs. As he took a step, his knee collapsed, cold rising to his waist, poisonous cold.

The wine killed him. He felt it stop his heart. Like a murderous hand, it strangled his throat. His lungs froze; his limbs seized.

His mind failed him. He felt himself die, the ground hurling upward to meet him.

PRINCESS MELANTHE SAT on the window seat that curved within the oriel recess. She leaned her elbow on a pillow, looking out an open glass, staring down into the garden. Cara stood in attendance, gazing at the painted window glass where two angels held the message "Love God and dread shame."

"My dear one," Gian said, bending before the princess, "I beg your pardon for my delay." When she only lifted her hand for a kiss without turning from the window, he left her in the sunset glare and went to pour himself wine. "But entertaining it was, you may be certain."

"What have they decided?" Princess Melanthe asked idly.

He set down the brass ewer. "For two hours did they debate over whether this green fellow had upheld his word after all. It turned on a fine point, my dear. A fine point. Did he leave the lists before he died or after? Had it been after, the case might have been different!" He put on a mock solemn face, imitating a justice. "For then no one could assert that he had been killed by the Fleming, without a mark on him. But he was still in the lists when he expired, so it could be argued that the Fleming killed him with one of those blows to the head, but the effect was belated. You'll delight in the verdict, my love."

"Will I?" the princess asked. She turned her face to him.

Cara thought her cold—so cold that there was not a shred of living feeling in her.

"Since the green fellow did not lose, his cause was just and true. So he did not lie." Gian shrugged and smiled at her over his cup. "I suppose it must follow that you did, then, but we will pass over that lightly in the circumstances, as our clever justices of chivalry chose to do. They have determined that God could not allow the green churl to lose, precisely—but clearly He did not think it a satisfactory match, and so put period to your late husband with a flourish, rather in the style of striking him with lighting. Be it a lesson to all abductors and rapists of innocent females."

The princess narrowed her eyes. "I will not remain here another day. We leave tomorrow, Gian. No more of this!"

He did not answer her, but roamed the solar, his white velvet turned to rose by the late burn of the sun through the tall open windows. "So, my betrothed—you are a married woman and a widow in the space of a few moments. With all thanks to my precious boy—" He stopped beside Allegreto, who lounged against the bedstead. Gian stroked his son's cheek lovingly. "Ah, Allegreto, thou art forgiven everything. Thou didst so well. I saw his face as he died—and he knew it. He went to Hell knowing, and he'll burn there knowing. I could not have asked for more, my sweet son. I do love thee beyond words."

He took Allegreto in his arms, a long and hard embrace. Allegreto's hands curled into the rich flowing cloth of his father's houpelande. He gripped the velvet as if he would not let go, near as tall now as Gian but holding to him like a child. He pressed his cheek against Gian's shoulder, his face squeezed into a grimace of passion, a terrible thing to see.

"How can I reward thee?" Gian murmured, stroking his son's black hair. "Wilt thou have Donna Cara? I see thine eyes when she enters the hall. She is not worthy of thee, Allegreto—I would have better for thee, but if it would please?"

"I am betrothed, my lord," Cara said sharply.

Allegreto's face was hidden in his father's shoulder. Gian made him lift his head. "Wilt thou have her?"

Cara began to tremble. She knew that she should not; it

was the worst thing she could do, show her thoughts and feelings. No one else showed his heart.

"I will have what you want for me, my lord," Allegreto said. "I am ever yours in obedience."

Gian smiled. "And in love," he said, touching Allegreto's cheek.

He looked into his father's eyes. "And in love, my lord."

Gian's thumb moved over his cheek. "Thou hast thy mother's comeliness," he murmured. "And my wit. We'll look far higher for thee, sweet son. Let her have her English clod, or take her as thy mistress. But nay—" He grinned, tilting his head back. "Nay, I forget, thou art a virgin still, poor Allegreto, on account of playing the role I gave thee. And didst well at that, too, as Lady Melanthe informed me with some wrath. Let me find a woman to teach thee pleasure first, lovely boy. Then canst thou decide if this sour little milkmaid will satisfy thee." He stepped back, disengaging himself gently from Allegreto's still clinging hold, and gave him another kiss.

"So touching!" the princess said viciously. She stood up. In the last shafts of light from the window, she was only a black device against it, her hair haloed, sunset sparkling on the golden net and the besants lined down her sleeves. "Where have they taken the body?"

Allegreto shrugged. "The charnel house, I suppose."

"Fool! Thou shouldst have found out!"

"My lady, I made sure he was dead and left him with the doctor and one weeping squire. I was not required to follow him to the grave!"

"Thou art certain of this poison," she said.

Allegreto lifted his brows. "I put a misericorde in his heart, my lady," he said. "He did not bleed."

She made a faint sound in her throat. Cara was afraid for her mistress suddenly; afraid she would swoon, afraid Gian would see and kill them all in his jealousy.

But Princess Melanthe only stared for a long moment at Allegreto. Then she said, "I will not have him thrown in a paupers' grave. He will be buried properly, by a priest, in a church. There will be a stone made, marked by that name the king called him. I wish a chantry endowed for his soul." She moved toward the door. "Find him, Allegreto, and see to it. Tonight."

Gian caught her arm. "My lady," he said coldly, "you pay him such respect?"

"He prayed too much," she said. "I do not wish some tedious ghost haunting me with aves and hosannas." She pulled her arm from his hand. "And I do not care for restraint, from you or any man, Gian. Do not touch me so again."

He smiled down at her. "You're an unruly little dragon. I would not have you slip your couple."

"Hold me with love, Gian," she said smoothly. "That works best."

"Nay, my dear," he murmured. "The fear that comes of love works best."

"Then am I on a long leash," she said, sweeping from the chamber. "Come, Cara—why stand there like a gaping trout? See that Allegreto does my bidding." She paused at the door. "And pay no mind to this talk of looking higher for him. Marry thy English squire—and if thou art clever, thou wilt still have Allegreto panting after thee as Gian does me. And then we may rule the world, I promise thee."

Twenty-five

⎯⎯⎯❧⎯⎯⎯

THERE WERE VOICES. It was a great well of stone, its compass lost in darkness, echoing, with shadows that moved and hulked across the curving wall.

He had no body. He could see and hear, but the voices made no sense. It had been only an instant's shift, a blink between crowds and color and the poison cup in his hand, then strangling death and this place. A deep horror possessed him. He was in Purgatory; demon-haunted; he had died without shrive or absolution of killing a man.

One of the demons counted. It was invisible, but he could hear the clink of its claws with each tally. "Two and fifty hundreds," it said with a lurid satisfaction.

Was that his sentence? So many years? Fear drowned him. He tried to speak, to plead that Isabelle had prayed for his soul, but he could not speak. He had no tongue. He remembered that there had been no prayers. Isabelle was dead, as dead as he, burned for heresy.

The well echoed with fearful murmurs, with scrapes and footsteps, and then a great crash that thundered and rolled about him. He heard something come toward him plashing and dripping, and wanted to scream with fear of what monster it would be to gnaw and tear at his flesh for two hundred fifty years.

"He does look dead," the monster said in bad French. "A merry poison, this. I could make good use of it in my art."

"What, to physic thy patients to death and bring them out again! Dream, thou mountebank—thou couldst not buy it in a thousand years."

Allegreto's reverberating voice shocked him. Like a demon-angel, the youth floated in the air, appearing and vanishing. He had not expected Allegreto to be here.

"I would have him wake." Now it was his squire John Marking. "Never did I contract to be party to murder."

Had they all died? Their voices and faces kept slipping away from him. His nose hurt. He was dimly surprised to have a nose. He tried to open his eyes to see if the monster was gnawing on it, but he only had eyes sometimes, and other times not.

They were demons, he thought. Demons with voices and faces that he knew. He refused to answer them when they demanded that he wake. It was the Devil calling him. If it called in Melanthe's voice, then he would be sure it was the Devil.

The monster touched him, cold and wet. He tried to jerk back, his head hitting stone—he had a head suddenly, because it hurt. He had never thought of this. He knew that his dead soul would be like a body so that it might be tortured for his sins, but he had not imagined it would be by single parts, with the rest still gone.

The wet thing licked over his face, a loathsome cold tongue, water in his eyes and on his chest. He had a chest. And a heart. The Devil spoke in the voice of a maid.

"Wake now, my lord." It was the gentlewoman who had served Melanthe. He could see her through slitted and dripping eyes, and felt sorry that she had died, too. Wolves, he thought. Wolves had eaten her. "Try to wake," she said. "Drink this."

He turned his head away. "De'il," he mumbled, the word barely passing his throat. "Deviel."

"He's alive," Allegreto said. "Art thou satisfied?"

He could not make sense of it. Alive. Dead. Purgatory, and

these were his demons. He did not think the worst could have begun yet, for Melanthe was not among them, but he had no doubt that she would come and take delight to torture him. She had smiled as he drank her poison, knowing that she killed him.

ALLEGRETO RETURNED FROM the river, beckoning to Cara from the door at the top of the stairs. She was glad to leave this awful place, abandoned as it seemed to be by the monks who had built it, indeed, by God Himself. The great round cellar still held a few ale-kegs, but the water well dominated the brewery, a black pit as wide across as a castle turret.

She hurried up the arch of stone steps, leaving the water bucket full and one candle burning for their prisoner. Allegreto closed the heavy door, barred and locked it.

"I'll walk with you to the lodge," he said. "There is a horse, and a guide to take you back."

She followed him up the wide, sloped passage. At the outer door he opened the wicket and doused the candle. They both ducked through the small door.

A half-moon was rising, shedding light on the empty monastery. Buildings rose about them in black and gray bulks, shapes without colors. She pulled her hood over her head and lifted her skirt as he led her across a grassy plot. Her footsteps echoed softly as they passed onto the paved cloister.

A half-year past she would have been terrified out of her mind to walk here in the silence and emptiness. But Allegreto was with her, and not even the ghosts of dead men could frighten her. An old monastery on a summer night, only abandoned because the monks had preferred some better place, held nothing so fearsome as he was.

He walked ahead of her, noiseless, turning through another passage where the moonlight shone in a pale arch at the other end. They followed the overgrown road to the gatehouse, and Allegreto gave her his hand to help her over the slanted timbers of the half-fallen door.

He let go of her instantly. But he stopped, facing Cara in the starlight. "Is it true—or did you say it for my father?"

She could not look into his face. Since they had left

Bowland, she in Princess Melanthe's household and he in Gian's, there had been naught but the briefest dealings between them, messages passed for her mistress and no more. She was safe with him, she knew; she did not even fear ghosts with him beside her, but Guy had been given a place with the princess as a yeoman of horse. He was well within Allegreto's reach.

"No," she lied. "No, I just said it, so that—"

She stopped.

"So that my father would not force you." Mortification hovered in his voice. "I wouldn't have—I didn't, did I? I could have said yes to him."

"Let us not speak of this." She started past, suddenly fearing him as she had not before, fearing that they were alone here in the empty dark.

"Are you betrothed to him?"

"No." She said it too quickly, too breathlessly. That was to protect Guy, but she had no lie to protect herself if Allegreto chose to constrain her by strength.

"Do you think I'll kill him?" he said. "I won't kill him."

She stopped and looked back across a distance of a yard. He propped his foot on the warped and canted door, the moonlight on his shoulders. "I only wondered if you would go home with us."

"Of course. My sister."

In a silken tone he asked, "Will Guy save and keep your sister?"

"You sound like your father."

"How not? I am his son. And Navona alone can steal your sister safe from the Riata."

"What does that mean? Will you make me choose between Guy and my sister?"

He lifted his head. "Then you are betrothed."

"You swore Navona would keep my sister safe."

"You *are* betrothed. You are. You are. Monteverde bitch." It was not an execration; it was like an endearment with him. He swung away and walked on, passing her, a moonlit shadow.

Cara went behind him, keeping distance. The faint path led across a water meadow and up onto higher ground, where she could look back and see the sheen of the river beyond the dark priory. Night dew made her shiver.

"So—will your Englishman remain with the princess, that you may go home with us?" Allegreto asked.

She did not answer, but walked on behind him. He hiked himself over a stile and waited on the other side until she climbed it.

"You should see that he asks her for a place soon." Allegreto wove around a black patch of bushes. "You heard her say tomorrow she leaves—it won't be that swift, but as soon as she can have my father upon a ship without his suspicion, she will. We can't hold the green man long."

"Who is to set him free?" Cara had a sudden ghastly thought. "Mary, what if some mistake is made, and he's left down there after we're gone?"

Allegreto turned to face her, so suddenly that she almost fell over her skirt. "I would not let that happen!" he said fiercely. "And if you care so much, then stay here with your precious Guy and see to it yourself!" He snorted. "But I wouldn't put it beyond the two of you to drop the key down some gong-pit, so I guess I'd better do the thing."

He pivoted and strode on along the path, ducking a branch.

"You'll stay here?" she asked, trailing him.

"I'm to miss the departure and catch up in Calais. I think I'll let my father give me a good whore," he said bitterly, "and have her teach me about pleasure until I can't crawl out of the bed to travel." He took Cara's arm and propelled her in front of him. "There's the lodge. Her father had all this enclosed for a hunting chase, and there's none but a parker who likes good Bordeaux. The princess gifted him with a tun of it, so you need not expect he will ask questions." He pushed Cara ahead. "The guide will see you back to her. Farewell."

He was walking away before she realized the finality of his tone. She turned and gazed after him.

"Farewell, Allegreto," she called softly.

He did not pause. He vanished in the dark.

"I KNOW YOU can hear me."

It was Allegreto's voice again. Ruck had all of his body now. His stomach walmed, and he shook in every limb. It was

a Purgatory he had never conceived, but no less appalling for
that. He thirsted. He could not get his breath, and these insis-
tent demons plagued him. He swallowed, trying to lift his
hands, but one was weighted down with iron and the other
would not do as he expected, moving aimlessly at the end of
his arm.

"Open your eyes, green man, if you can hear me," the
Allegreto-demon said.

He remembered that he had a name. "Ruadrik," he muttered. He stared bleakly at Allegreto, trying to see the shade
of a monstrosity behind his comely face.

The demon smiled a wicked smile. "Ruadrik, then, if
you'll have it so. Listen to me, Ruadrik. Try to remember this.
You have food and drink here. There's a pail, if you need it.
I'll return in the morning. Remember. Don't lose your head.
Do you hear me?"

Ruck tried to lift his hand, to catch and strangle him, but
he could not.

"Wink your eyes if you hear me," the fiend ordered.

Ruck closed his eyes. When he had eyes to open again, the
demon was gone.

"HE WAS WAKING, my lady," Cara said very softly.

Melanthe laid her forehead down on the pillow. She had
been waiting at the window, waiting and waiting. She had not
thought Cara would ever come.

It might have killed him, the poison they had used, a grain
too much, a drop of wine too little—but Gian's would have
done it with mortal certainty.

"He spoke, but made no sense, my lady," Cara said.
"Allegreto sent word to you that he is weak, but will be well
by morning."

Melanthe lifted her head. The night air flowed in the open
window. She put her hands on her cheeks to cool them.

"My lady—" Cara said. "I wish to tell you—when I
spoke—when I said I was betrothed. I had no right to make a
contract without your leave. Forgive me!"

Her words seemed distant to Melanthe. She flicked her
hand in dismissal. "Later. I cannot think of that now."

"My lady. Please! I have no wish to marry Allegreto."

Melanthe made an effort to turn her mind to Cara's distress. "After all he has done for thee? Poor Allegreto. Thou dost have thy claws in his heart."

"I never meant to do so, my lady! He frightens me. And—I fear for Guy."

"Such a tragic face. Guy? That Englishman from Torbec, I suppose. He is beneath thee. He hasn't a florin to his name. Silly girl, his lord lives in a pigsty. Thou mayest believe me, for I saw it."

"My lady—I love him."

Melanthe gave one short laugh. "Verily, this is what comes of letting foolish female creatures sit at windows and look out upon the street, is it not? We dream stupid dreams, and fall in love with any unsuitable man who walks past."

Cara bowed her head. "Yea, my lady."

"I spoke to thee once of love."

"Yea, my lady."

Melanthe pulled the window closed. She could see the reflection of candles in the glass, and a wavering darkness that was herself. "What did I say of it?" she whispered. "I have forgotten what I said."

"My lady, you said to me that great love is ruinous, my lady."

"And so it is." She put her hands over her hot cheeks again, watching the obscure movement in the glass. "So it is."

"My lady—if it would please you—if Guy might find a place in your retinue when we return—"

"God's death, dost thou care no more for thy betrothed than to lead him into the viper's nest?" Melanthe turned angrily on the girl's brown-eyed innocence. "And what of Allegreto? Is he to sing a gleeful carol at thy wedding?"

"My lady, it was Allegreto who proposed it"—Cara made a courtesy—"that Guy find a place with you, so that I might go home."

Melanthe gazed at her. She could not see in the soft face anything but a tame doe's stupid trust. "Do not press Allegreto too far." She rose, flinging the pillow aside. "Nay, if thou must have this Englishman, then you will both remain here. And count thy blessings."

Cara bowed. She went to Melanthe's bed and began to turn down the sheets. The manor bells tolled matins.

"I'll go to the chapel," Melanthe said. "In faith, I cannot sleep!"

SHE WOULD HAVE preferred to go to the garden, or the mews, but Gian had spies on her in the household, and she did not dare arouse any curiosity. As well accustom herself to altar and roodscreen—it would be the whole scope of her life soon enough.

She thought perhaps she would surprise everyone and be a fiercely austere nun. The ladies who retired as religious and still kept high estate had always seemed pathetic to her—acting out a play without stage or spectators. No, she would give everything to the church, and fast, and have visions. And they would all be of a man who had loved her once.

He hated her now. She had done all she could to drive him to it. She had a conversation in her head with him about it, to explain to him. She had poisoned him, yes, but it was to spare him. She imprisoned him, but it was to keep him safe until she and Gian were gone. If she denied him as her husband, broke her vow and murdered his heart, it was so that she did not have to live knowing that he did not.

She could not kill Gian instead, she told him. She had thought on it long and deep. She knew of wives who had slain their husbands—one had been flayed alive, but the others had only paid fines. But it was no easy task, not with Gian, who had eluded the best of killers, and if she failed once, there would be no magistrate to sentence her, for she would not live so long. Allegreto would not aid her in it, nay, but oppose her.

And if she succeeded—she would be theirs. She would belong to the Devil wholly.

She told these things to Ruck. But it was not a conversation. He never answered. In her mind he stared at her with unyielding silence. He would not understand. Could not. Her deliberate dishonor was beyond his comprehension, as the black depth of Allegreto's love was beyond Cara's.

They knew themselves—she and Allegreto. They knew how close the Devil had them. She could almost pity Allegreto, who still held to his own mysterious honor by a thin thread. If he had wished to rid himself of Guy as a rival, he would have done it, and yet this subtle suggestion of his that Cara and her lover return to Italy boded of darker intentions, or else foolish hopes. He was not so old, Allegreto, that he might not have hopes, but Melanthe would not allow Cara to drive him beyond endurance. She and Guy must stay in England, far away from him.

In return for such a kind favor from Melanthe, Allegreto would make certain that Ruck hated her. He would say all the things that Melanthe did not have the strength to say herself, kill pride and hope and future. And Ruck would go home to live in his enchanted valley, where Melanthe had never been meant to go.

They were old allies, she and Allegreto, strange friends and familiar enemies.

"THIS IS YOUR last lesson, green man. Have you learned it?"

"Ruadrik."

"Ruadrik, then." Allegreto made a courteous bow. "Lord Ruadrik of Wolfscar."

His voice echoed in the old brewery, calling from all sides, whispering back from the high slits of light made in the shape of holy crosses, the only windows in the curving wall. Ruck had shouted until his voice was nearly gone, but if anyone passed outside those windows, they did not come into his prison.

She had done this. Allegreto made no secret of it. Ruck was to be kept here until she was gone from England, and if he followed her, he would die by some means just as unclean and secret as her sleeping poison, but lethal this time.

His last lesson. If he did not appear to have learned it, then he did not leave this place.

Allegreto sat on the far edge of the huge round well, his legs dangling in it. He pilled one of Ruck's oranges and tossed the rind. Ruck heard it strike the water with a faint plop. A queer imprisonment, this, with food befitting a banquet table—or a princess—fruit and almonds, fresh cheese and white bread. The brewery was ancient, but his bonds were new and strong, the anchor sunk deep into the wall, the fetters no mere bands about his wrists and ankles, but a whole steel boot on his right foot and a fingerless metal glove that extended up his left arm to his elbow, padded inside, both fitted to him so perfectly that they must have been patterned on pieces of his own armor.

John Marking, without nay. Ruck cursed his own witlessness. To suppose that she ever meant him well, to trust Allegreto for one instant—old Sir Harold had never been so mad and simple as Ruck when he had thought he had won.

He remembered her face in that brief moment of his victory. Smiling at him. In the death-dreams, it was that expectant smile that had tortured him worse than demons.

Allegreto sucked the juice from a segment of orange and spit the seed away. "She told me why she let you live," he said. "She said you prayed too much, and would haunt her to tedium if she killed you."

"Tell her I'll haunt her into Hell itself if she marries Navona."

"Then prepare your howls and shrieks, for that's what she's going to do, green man."

"Ruadrik."

"Ruadrik. Late of Wolfscar."

With a light move Allegreto stood up, pitching the last of his fruit into the well. He came around to Ruck's side to draw water at the great crane. It might have lifted a ton of water. The bucket hooked to it now seemed absurdly small. Allegreto did not even work the elaborate machine itself, but only dropped the bucket in. The plash echoed, a memory of dreams, scaping and sloshing as Allegreto hauled the bucket up by hand and set it within Ruck's reach.

The youth sprang up the stairs three at a time. At the door he paused. "I leave you to ponder—will I return, or will I not? Her mind is much occupied with her wedding. She might forget you entirely, green man."

"Ruadrik," Ruck said.

"Did I tell you this was a walled park, my lord Ruadrik? Nothing but deer for two miles in all directions. And the river. I think you should shout, and hope they hear you on the river. Enlarge your skill at haunting." He gave Ruck a charming smile. "Verily, a place like this needs a ghost."

The door boomed shut behind him. Thin crosses of light angled down, illuminating the stone floor, vanishing into the enormous well.

CARA KEPT HERSELF in the background as she was bid while Gian visited them with his daily presence at supper. She was hopeless at concealing things, Princess Melanthe had said, and well Cara knew it. She could never have contended so coolly as her mistress did with him, insisting that they set forth at once for Italy against his new determination that they marry here in England.

"These fools make a martyr of the fellow," Gian said. "There are a thousand candles for him after just a seven-night—next we'll have a miracle, and his fingerbones sold in the market square."

"All the more reason to depart." Princess Melanthe watched Gian's own sewer, always with him, make a tasting from a platter. "Look, there is a fresh salmon, the best of the year, they say. I could almost be pleased that it's a fish day."

"Nay, we will not flee from deluded rabble. We've only to wait a little time for the banns, and then a feast to make them forget their saintly Ruadrik ever crawled out of whatever wolf's cave he inhabited. I prefer it, my lady."

"Gian, this business had disturbed your wit. So you are not popular here. You are foreign. What matters it? Let us go home and leave this unpleasantness."

"You've been in no such hurry. Why so anxious to leave, my love?"

"By hap I do not care for the ugly looks I receive when I go out," she said sharply.

"Peasants," he said. "If anyone dares insult you, tell me."

"I would rather not wait until it happens. I am telling you now, I wish to leave as soon as we may. If you love me, you will agree."

He set down his wine. "That, my dear one, is a device you will do well not to invoke too often."

"This fish needs spicing." Princess Melanthe examined the platter with a frown. "Cara, send to the kitchen—a fried parsley, I think. My deepest pardon, Gian, I cannot say why the herbs were forgotten."

Gladly Cara left the chamber. She sent a page with the parsley, and did not return herself, for it was certain that Gian in this difficult mood might take any unholy notion into his head. With one of the laundry maids for chaperon, Cara slipped out into the yard instead, passing under the gate to the stables.

In the late evening light Guy curried Gian's horse himself. Cara stood in the shadow, too shy to approach him. She admired his hair, golden as it was in the last sun rays, and twisted her skirt and the present she'd brought together in her hands. She was glad he had stayed with the princess, even when the green knight had come. She hoped that he'd made his choice to be near her, though it might equally well have been only because the princess could reward him far more generously.

He reached, sweeping his comb down the rouncy's smooth gray haunch. All of her heart seemed to run out after him, just watching his sure and simple motions, the shape of his hand, and the breadth of his back.

One of his grooms said a soft word, and all the men looked at Cara and the laundress. Guy straightened, turning. When he saw her, his face grew pleased, but he immediately looked down at the currycomb in his hand as if it held some vital mystery.

It was the first time she had approached him in public since their private speaking. His men grinned, and one of them pitched a pebble at Guy. It bounced off his shoulder. He lifted his hand and brushed at his sleeve absently.

Cara handed her present to the laundress. It was a silk lace. The maid went up to Guy and held it out to him. "From Donna Cara," she said simply. Cara thought she might have had the wit to embellish a little, but she was English.

He looked about at the men instead of at Cara. She held her breath, worried at the solemn set of his mouth. But then he reached out and took the lace, holding it between his hands. Amid whistles and mockery, he grinned at her.

Suddenly one of the grooms came under the gate and snatched her about the waist. He pulled her back. Cara gave a shriek, resisting him, but it was not a very serious abduction, for Guy chased him off with a few hard cuffs and caught her back against his chest. He smoothed her hair and went down on his knee before her, pulling his good white gloves from his sleeve.

"Donna Cara," he said, "I give you these on condition that you will marry me. Will you agree?"

She felt everyone in the yard looking at her. One of Gian's men called to her in Italian not to be a fool, offering himself as a better choice. She gave him a glare and took the gloves. "Yea, sir. I agree."

Amid the clapping, Gian's men made ugly mutters. A sudden scuffle erupted, the English grooms converging, but as Cara gripped Guy's arm, a boy came running from the house.

"Make ready! My lord departs!"

Instantly the fight dissolved. Guy shouted for the saddles, hastening to the gray rouncy. The meal could not possibly be over. Cara feared that Gian and her mistress must have come to open battle. She caught the laundress's hand to run with her toward the kitchens, but already Gian appeared at the door, walking with such long and angry strides that his white cloak flared out in spite of its heavy embroidery and gold bosses.

He came under the gate, passing Cara without a glance. Then to her horror, he halted, looking back at her.

With a slight move of his hand, he made his men go past. The yard was full of confusion. Cara looked desperately for Guy, but he was swinging one of the elaborate saddles onto a horse's back. And as she looked, she knew Gian saw her look, and cursed her own weakness.

He smiled at her in a kind way and stood beside her as if he had suddenly become patient with waiting. "Donna Cara. It is a pleasant evening to be abroad in the air, is it not?"

She made a slight courtesy, all she could manage on her weak knees. "Yea, my lord."

"A pleasant evening for lovers. But where is Allegreto?"

A flash of utter terror swept over her. She dropped her eyes. "I know not! I know not, my lord."

She should not have repeated herself. She should have said it with more surprise. She did not know. Why should she know?

"Why should I know, my lord?" She spoke it aloud, an attempt at the cool tone Princess Melanthe would use.

"Indeed," Gian mused, "why shouldst thou?"

His thoughtful tone dismayed her. She made another courtesy, afraid to look up at him.

"He has been a little absent of late," he said softly. "He told me that he had a lover. I had thought—but thou wilt forgive me, Donna Cara, if I offend thy modesty—I was so dull as to suppose it must be thee."

She did not know what to do. She never knew what to do. All she could think was that she should never have let him trap her.

"Ah—but this is thy young man, is it not?" Gian asked in French as Guy led up his rouncy. When Cara answered nothing, her tongue frozen, Gian said to him, "My compliments to thee. A fair and chaste maiden for a bride."

"Grant merci, my lord." Guy bowed deeply. "Donna Cara does me great honor."

To Cara's vast relief, Gian mounted. As he settled in the saddle, he looked beyond her. The rouncy threw its head and danced a step, though Gian made no visible move.

Cara turned to see Princess Melanthe crossing the yard. Several of the other ladies hurried behind her, lifting her trailing skirts. She stopped beneath the gate. In the dusk her skin seemed white and cool, her breasts rising and falling evenly beneath the low neckline of her gown.

"I came to see you well, Gian," she said. "I would not have us part in anger."

"My lady," he said, "I would not have it, either, but you have tried me sore this night."

She tilted her head, smiling slightly. "I did not think you chose me for my docile nature."

"No more did I, but I would have you know who rules between us."

"Then choose your battles more carefully, my love. For I make my respects to the king tomorrow and leave for London before sunset—and to Calais from there. It will be a lonely wedding without a bride."

In the whole yard there was not a sound but for the chink and soft breath of the horses. Such brazen defiance was beyond Cara's grasp—all the alarm and confusion that

Princess Melanthe should be feeling seemed to be concentrated in Cara's trembling limbs.

"Then you have won, my lady," Gian said at last. "I'll be at your side. But take care that your victories are not often bought so dear, or you may find that you've purchased defeat."

She sank into a deep courtesy, spreading her skirts. The rings on her fingers caught light. "As you say, Gian. I look forward to your company on the road."

CARA FOLDED AND packed. It had all come much faster than she had expected. They were to leave, everyone to go home, and she was to be left behind.

With Guy, she told herself. But still she was afraid. The house was in confusion and disorder with Princess Melanthe's command to be gone by sunset, chests and trunks piling up on the wooden dock below the manor. When Cara had finished emptying the princess's bedchamber and seen the baggage safely aboard the waiting barges, her duties here would be completed.

She had no desire to linger until her mistress returned from the king's audience, having leave to go at once to Guy. He was to take the horses to some castle Cara knew not where, but not too far away; he had a letter commanding that he be given charge of the stables and stud there, a great advancement, he had told her, an unbelievable stroke of fortune. He had said her mistress must think a great deal of her, to give him such an elevated place after so little time in her service. They could marry immediately, thanks to her benevolence, without waiting for him to become established as he had feared.

Cara was not foolish enough to suppose that Princess Melanthe loved her so very well. Such favor did not come free. Cara had a charge on her—but only one, and not difficult. She was to make certain that, after Princess Melanthe and Gian had left the country, Allegreto certainly freed the poor chained madman in the abandoned brewery. When she saw that it was so with her own eyes, Cara was to write a letter herself to her mistress, and somewhere in it that letter was to contain three times the words *by the grace of God*, and then the princess could be sure.

Cara thought that when she could pen the last "God" of the three, it would truly be by His grace. She made a cross and said a prayer of thanks, begging Him to let her somehow free her sister, too. And she felt a strange certainty that it would be so. Allegreto had promised, and against all reason, Cara believed him.

But there was the way Gian had looked at her. She knew she had aroused his suspicions. If only he had not mentioned Allegreto to her. But surely, he would only think that she disliked him speaking of love with another, when Guy was so near.

She finished filling the chest, spread strawberry leaves and rose petals over the top layer of linen, and hastened downstairs to call a page to bind and carry it. The princess would expect the barges to be loaded by the time she returned, but there was nothing to stay Cara now that her part was done. She was to meet Guy at the smith, where all of the horses were getting their shoes set before the journey to their new quarters.

For a moment, on the stairs, Cara had a moment's vision of what life might be without the princess and Gian and Allegreto. Without thinking each thought in fear of their response, or listening each moment for some fatal word. At this time tomorrow, they would be gone. She would be almost alone in an alien land, but they would be gone.

A tremulous joy filled her. She took a deep breath, thinking of Guy with secret pleasure, and hastened down the curve of the stairs.

At the bottom Gian waited. He stood in the open door, looking out at the barges and the river. His cape swept about him as he turned to her, the golden bosses clinking heavily against one another. "Donna Cara," he said, smiling. "Well met! It is thou I came to see."

Twenty-six

SHE HAD THOUGHT of throwing herself in the river. She had thought of calling out to the one boat they had passed. She had thought of refusing to speak, pretending she did not recognize the place. She thought of everything, but in the end she only wept.

She could not lie. She had never been able to lie perfectly, and with Gian she was beyond even being able to think. *Her sister*, he murmured, and she babbled out what he asked to know. *Guy*, he said, and she went with him when he commanded it, without a word to anyone, without a scream or a plea, a rabbit carried helpless away by the wolf.

He would kill the poor mad knight who loved her mistress. She did not want to see it, and put up her greatest resistance at the old stone wharf, half-hidden in reeds. But he laid his fingers close about her neck and crushed her throat until she gave in to pain and fear. Gasping air into her bruised throat, she crawled out of the boat and led him up the path through the reeds.

The wicket door to the brewery passage was unlocked, standing slightly open. Cara had a moment of wild hope. She drew a breath—a scream, a warning—but Gian's hand came across her mouth. He stroked his fingers over her neck, pressing lightly.

"Silence," he said into her ear. "Please me. That is thy only hope now. This open door—has he escaped?"

She shook her head.

"Then someone else is here. The princess?"

She wet her lips and made a small shake.

"Thy Englishman?"

Cara shook her head violently. Her nose seemed full of the scented oil that he used. Allegreto's voice drifted from the wicket door, far away and echoing, a faint derisive laugh.

His father did not move. Gian held her. He turned his head. Allegreto's lazy tones were beyond doubting, and yet Gian squeezed her throat and hissed, "Who is it?"

Then he suddenly shoved her down through the door. She fell onto her knees in the sloped passage with a yelp, her palms scraping. Gian had already passed her, dragging her up with him.

"*Allegreto!*" he shouted, a sound of savage anguish that reverberated down the passage and rolled back from behind them. The brewery door hung a little open; he hurled it wide and stood upon the landing, staring down at the huge chamber: Allegreto beside the well, the mad knight with his fettered arm resting against the wall. The last of Gian's voice still muttered frenzy back from the hollow spaces.

"Allegreto," he whispered.

In her desperate hope Cara had been glad to see the doors ajar. Allegreto, who could frighten demons—but he did not move. He sat on the edge of the well, his eyes on the water. An orange rind dropped from his motionless fingers. It fell far down below his feet and hit the water with a faint plink, a bright patch floating on the surface of a huge black moon.

Gian said softly, "Look at me."

Still Allegreto did not move. He closed his eyes.

"Not even this?" Gian said. "Not even this that I ask thee? My son." His teeth bared. "My son. Look at me."

Allegreto turned his face upward. He saw Cara. A faint sound, like a dreamer's whimper, came from his throat.

"Now stand up."

"My lord—"

"Do not speak to me. I do not wish to hear thy voice. Stand up."

Allegreto raised himself. He wore a sword and dagger, but he touched neither. He stood up, and then, as if his limbs failed him, he fell onto his knees.

Gian turned to Cara. With a courtly gesture he directed her down the stairs. She went in helpless tears, the only sound in the great chamber. He brought her before his kneeling son.

"Donna Cara—look upon a great love," he said. "For thou, he has betrayed his father. For thou, he has slain himself."

"Oh, no," she mumbled. "No."

"No? Is it not for thee? But it must be. He looks at thee—thou art somewhat fair, no great beauty, but such sweetness, such innocent light—and his heart turns to treachery. But what has he bought with it? Thy safety, thy life . . . ah . . . those poisoned mussels, that he told me you were so clever as to save your mistress from. By hap you did not save her? I have been a little stupid. I have loved my son, and been stupid."

Allegreto was silent, his eyes glazed dark and empty.

"But haps I will forgive him. Perhaps someone else has been more false even than he. My betrothed was in such concern to haste me toward home." Gian turned his back on his son and walked to where Princess Melanthe's knight stood watching. "I may thank what wit I retain, I suppose, that I am not chained up like this poor hound, to await her pleasure. Does she love him?"

He observed the knight, who looked back with a grim and even stare.

"Does she love thee?" he asked in French.

"She is my wife."

"Nay, but does she love thee?"

"Ask her."

Gian tilted his head. "She denies thee. And yet—thou art here, instead of under a pile of dirt where I would have thee. She forgives Donna Cara for poisoned mussels, because she can buy my son's service by it. She has lain in bed beside thee, and feared for thee, and lied for thee!" He put his fists to his head. *"Melanthe!"*

The knight moved. His steel fetter caught light, a flash and slam, the chain hitting the end of its length a bare instant before it would have struck Gian's temple. The sound went around the chamber in discharges like hands clapping.

Gian recovered from his recoil, standing beyond the other man's reach, his hand on his sword.

"He is mad," Cara said desperately. "My mistress says that he's mad. She is to marry thee. Don't kill him."

Gian's attention came to her, and she regretted speaking. She thought of the stairs so close behind her, of Guy at the smith, waiting for her, and new tears blurred her eyes.

"Why, Allegreto, what a kind heart thy maiden has. Did I say she was not worthy of thee? She is too good for thee."

His son said nothing. He stayed on his knees, his gaze on the stone pavement. Gian walked around the well and stood before him.

"There, I will not run the poor hound through, dost thou see, Donna Cara? I cannot resist a lady's pleading. Verily—verily, thou art far too good for my black-hearted son."

Allegreto was trembling, breathing as if he would weep and could not.

"Look at him. So frightened. Shall I forgive him, Donna Cara? His life is in thy hands."

"Oh, yes! Forgive him!"

"Come, rise, my sweet son." Gian touched his shoulder. Allegreto jerked as if he'd been pricked. He rose to his feet, but there was no reprieve or relief in his face. He seemed to have gone beyond any thought at all, closing his eyes when Gian took him by the shoulders and pressed a kiss to each cheek.

Gian stepped back, shoving his son hard away. Cara screamed, watching in disbelief as Allegreto reached and failed and fell, his arms outstretched toward his father. He disappeared at the edge. A moment later the water broke in immense echoes.

She ran forward without thinking, looking over the edge. His head came up, his shoulders, the water surface shattered into silver and jet. She grabbed for the bucket and rope that hung from the huge crane, but Gian jerked her back. He crushed both her wrists together in his hand.

Allegreto held his head out of the black water, pushing his

hair from his eyes. He looked up at them. The blankness was gone from his eyes. Water plashed softly as he kept himself afloat.

Gian walked to the edge, still holding Cara. She struggled, terrified that he would throw her in, too, but he did not. He only stood, looking straight down the wall into the water. Allegreto swam toward them. His upturned face looked deathly white against the dark liquid. He put his hand on the wall, searching it.

Gian shook his head. He pulled Cara with him, walking around a quarter of the well, still staring down the edge. Allegreto followed, as if a magnet drew him. His hands slid on the well-dressed stone, finding no hold.

She realized that Gian was making certain he could not. Slowly he circled the whole well. When he came to the water bucket and rope, he picked up the bucket and set it beyond reach of the knight, who watched them from his bolted chains.

No one spoke. Cara thought it must be a nightmare, but for the pain as she pulled and twisted to free her hands. When Gian forced her to the stairs and up, she tried to look over her shoulder. Allegreto seemed a ghost in the huge well, his wet face already confused with the shining black water in her eyes. His father closed the door, and the one beyond it, driving down the bars.

THE BRIGHT MORNING outside burst upon her. It seemed for a moment that it could not be summer, and day, but should still be that dim cold twilight they had left behind. The numb burn in her hands was like the speechless horror in her brain. It was day; there were birds and grass and the river sparkling.

Down among the reeds Gian stopped, loosing her hands. "Now, Donna Cara," he said reasonably, "for the sake of thy sister, and thy Englishman, thou wilt forget this morning, and this place forever."

In the summer warmth it already seemed a dream, and his calm voice seemed part of it. She was stricken with dumbness, like a sleeper unable to speak.

"Thou hast been a brave child, and done well for thy sister. We will have her safe from the Riata for thee. And thou hast helped thy husband, too." He led her up onto the wharf.

"For coming with us, I'll make him a greater man than he dreamed of being."

The boat waited, tied. Cara stood on the stone quay, her toes over the edge. Gian let go of her and pulled the boat closer.

She heard her name. *Caraaah*—faint and hoarse and distant, a howl of fear and pleading.

Gian heard it, too. He straightened, looking at her with a faint concern, as if he worried for her. "Come. We all must make our choices, Donna Cara."

She jerked away from him. He grabbed, catching the liripipe on her sleeve as she flung herself toward the path. She felt the fabric part, tearing loose, freeing her with an unexpectedness that made her stumble. He shouted; there was a great plash behind her, and suddenly she had a chance. She scrambled, not looking back, not thinking, only running.

Oh hurry oh hurry oh hurry; the sound of her own breath obscured anything else. She did not know how long it took him to get onto the wharf, how close he came behind. She hiked her skirt and slipped and ran *hurry hurry* her mind on nothing but the bucket, the door—could she bar it behind her? Allegreto must have the key to the knight's fetters—if he would not fight his father, the mad knight surely would.

RUCK STRAINED AGAINST his steel bonds with impatience as he watched the weeping maid fumble the bucket and the crane.

"Give it to me!" he snapped. "Give me the rope! God's blood, you can't raise him on that thing!"

She ceased trying to work the heavy machine and ran to him, panting, with the bucket. He did not need the bucket— what wit she had appeared to have completely deserted her— but for escaping Navona and barring the door against him, Ruck blessed her with every blessing that he knew. He tossed the bucket into the well and braced the rope across his steel boot, taking a loop around his arm fetter.

"Now!" he exclaimed.

The girl was down on her knees, crying and urging Allegreto in Italian. The rope strained, slipping a little as it took the youth's weight. Ruck heard water surge and plash.

He held firm with the boot and his arm against the hard jerks of Allegreto's climb.

The boy's black head appeared. He grasped the rope above the edge and heaved himself up. With a grimace he thrust onto the stone on his hands and knees, water spilling off his dragging clothes.

"Where is he?" Frenzy edged Allegreto's words as he looked toward the door. *"Where is he?"*

"He fell in the river! I ran, but he'll be here any moment!"

Allegreto stood with his eyes on the door. "Mary, oh, Mary—save me."

"The key!" Ruck slammed his arm against the chains. "Dost thou have it?"

The youth was so gone in terror that he stared at Ruck without comprehension for an instant before he looked down and fumbled the key from his soaked wallet. His hands, dripping and white, were shaking hard enough that he could not get the iron in the lock.

"Keep thy head, whelp," Ruck said, gripping the boy's arm.

Allegreto nodded wordlessly. He stabbed at the lock twice, and at last got it free. Ruck pulled the key from his fingers and opened the boot himself.

"Give me thy sword." Ruck reached to Allegreto's belt and swept the light weapon from its sheath. He made for the door, threw off the bar, and flung it open without caring what was behind it. Released from seven nights and a hellish death chained in this pit, he was willing to slay anyone to get out of it, and more than pleased to make Gian Navona the first.

ALL THREE OF them saw it at once, in the reeds at the edge of the current. Donna Cara made a garbled sound.

"I heard him behind me." Her voice was shaking. "I didn't stop."

Allegreto said nothing. He stood for an instant, and then threw down his dagger, plunging into reeds and water up to his waist. He caught the white cape and pulled frantically.

It was too late. Ruck crossed himself and helped haul the body up onto the shore. The pale velvet dragged in the grass, heavy with golden coins and besants. Allegreto dropped to his knees. He clutched his father's hand and squeezed it convulsively between both of his.

Navona's half-closed eyes stared at nothing. Ruck was still full of battle blood, his teeth clenched as if he would swing a sword at the enemy at any instant.

"Take Cara away," Allegreto said. "You must go, both of you."

Ruck hesitated, scowling down at the body. He knelt and pushed the man over on his side, with a thought to pressing the water from his lungs. But there was no motion, no struggle or life beneath his hands.

"Go to the princess, before she leaves." Allegreto's head was bent, his voice muffled. "Go to your Englishman."

Donna Cara plucked at Ruck's shoulder. "Let us go, sir," she whispered. "Please. I'll show you where your horse and gear are hid."

Too sudden it was, too brief and effortless a thing to embrace. The river lapped softly at Navona's feet, glittering in sun and shadow between the reeds. Ruck thought of the black well behind him, and looked at Allegreto's wet hair, and marked the cross on himself again.

"Go!" Allegreto looked up fiercely, his eyes drowning. "Leave me with him."

MELANTHE STOOD IN the screen passage of the near-empty house. "My books?"

Old Sodorini pulled at his sleeves gravely. "On your own bark, your grace, but not where you may reach them. I am sure, your grace, if we only had another week—"

"Thou dost not have another week. Nor another day."

Sodorini clung to the notion that he was directing the move instead of his nephew, but Melanthe had been no such fool as to suppose that he could have the household packed and leaving on close notice. The hall was already cleared and the chests aboard only because his nephew, who had been displaced from his position as steward for the journey to Bowland, was back in authority. But Old Sodorini was loath to give up his moment of glory.

"I fear for the hurried way things have been packed," he

said ominously. "My lady's grace will find nothing at her convenience."

She ignored this gloomy warning. "Has Dan Gian arrived yet?"

"The boats and baggage are here, and the lower servants. His grace has not come with his men."

Late sun through the open front door made Melanthe's shadow a long distorted shape. "Hold all of my people at readiness on the dock. As soon as I am changed, we depart. Dan Gian's servants may do as they please, but I will not wait for him past the time that I set. I wish to be at London by midnight. I will want a supper on the boat. See to it." She almost ordered that Cara attend her, but remembered that the girl would already be off with her beloved Englishman. "Send Lisa to me."

She left him, climbing the stairs to her solar. The bareness of the house did not sadden her—she was glad enough to leave Merlesden. She had no childhood memories of the place; it had merely been convenient while the court was at Windsor, and full in its way of Gian's presence.

But her steps were slow on the stairs. Leaving here, she broke the final thread. There would be London and Dover and then the sea, but it was here that the end came.

She passed under the arched door. The last chest lay open for her to change into traveling gear. The great bed was dismantled and gone, the stone walls bare of tapestries and the floor of carpets. Colored light poured in the oriel windows, green and gold and red and blue, intense with sunset.

A shadow stepped into it. She started. "Gian!"

But he was too tall, too broad in the shoulders. He was all black against the light but for the hard curve of his cheek and the red and blue hues on his shoulders.

Melanthe turned and slammed the door, barring it. She pressed her back against the wood. Lisa's knock came, and her perplexed call, muted through the door.

"I do not need thee!" Melanthe strove to keep her voice steady. "Go to the others. Wait at the wharf!"

"Yea, my lady." The maid's voice was barely audible through the wood.

Too late, Melanthe realized that she should have given

some order that would keep Gian and everyone else from the house. But her mind seemed simple, her heart sending too much blood to her brain with wild beating.

"Ye wends you anon," Ruck said.

"A'plight, art thou to annoyen me yet, mad churl?" She thrust herself off the door, but stayed near it. "Go, ere I have thee arrested for trespass!"

"My lady, ye stonds betwix me and the way."

She could not let him leave—at any moment Gian would come. So close, she had been so close to drawing the danger safely off. Even now, if she could get Gian aboard the barks and on the river, if she could hold Ruck bound just long enough—

"Ne would I leaven here by any way," he said. "I have come for you, wife."

"Thou hast a wooden head."

"So haf I said myseluen, as I lay in chains of your making, my lady."

"Behoove thee to mark them well!" In her agitation she glared at him with real savagery. "I know not how thou art here, but by Christ's rood, I tire of thy impestering of me!"

"And I tire of thy faithless deceits!" He walked nearer to her, out of the glare. His dress was nothing from a prison—he wore his black velvet, with the gold belt and marcasite, stones that were silver and pitch at once, like the face of water at night. "Where lies thy heart?"

"I have no heart. Did I never say thee so?"

"I had a message of thee, that thy great love, this Navona, had come to wed thee. Allegreto hatz poured news of it in my ears, how ye cherish his father and forget me for love of him. N'is nought thy heart?"

She turned his words. "Hast thou slain Allegreto to get free?"

"Nay, he is safe enow, but nought here to twisten and turnen for thee, my lady. Nor Navona to harbor thee."

"Gian comes anon."

His eyes flickered, as if he heard a sound behind her. Melanthe stiffened, gripping the door hasp, but there was nothing, no noise of feet on the stairs, no voices below.

"Faithly, does he? Then my lady has only to wait. He will slay me, nill he nought?"

"Slowly," she agreed. "With the greatest agony he can serve thee."

He smiled slightly. "So would I serve him, if I could."

She saw with despair that fear would not move him. He had no dismay of Gian, but she was possessed with dread of what would happen if Gian and his men found him here. It would be no quick poison this time. It would be torture, and she would have to watch.

Melanthe tilted her head back against the door. She looked at him beneath her lashes. "Come, wilt thou be such a poor love-sotted wretch, to die for me?"

"Yea," he said simply. "I would."

"Fool!" She pressed against the door. She must have him out of here, away, and yet she could not think of how. "When I despise thee! Wilt thou torment me to my grave?"

"To thy grave. Jouk and duck and tumble, and guile as thou wilt, I am still thy husband, Melanthe, and I will have thee."

"Never did I wed thee, fool. How should I? It was a jape, an idle disport, monk-man, to make thee forfeit thy vaunted chastity!"

His green eyes held steady. "Thou hatz as many deceits as a fox has turnings, my lady, but thou art well skewered on this jape of thine."

She laughed. "I love another man. Thou art nothing to me."

He took a step at that. She sought desperately for a way to turn it to advantage.

"Melanthe—"

"I loathe and scorn thee!"

He lowered his hand. With a sharp turn he paced to the far end of the chamber, lost again in shadow. The rays of the sun were longer and lower. Gian must come, any moment he must come.

"Ye ne'er told of Wolfscar to them," he said, his voice coming with a soft echo from the dark corner. "Why did ye nought, lady?"

"Why?" She shrugged. "But why should I? Ne did I wish to make my lover jealous."

She could not see him, but she sensed that she had found a chink. An inspiration came to her, if she only had time to employ it. She reached to her throat and released the catch on her silken mantle. It fell to the floor, and she kicked it from her.

She stood in the light and stretched her arms luxuriously overhead. "But Gian is not here yet. Haps I will bedevil thy chastity one more time before I go."

She turned, looking toward him, unable to see past the shafts of colored sunlight. He said nothing.

With a wicked smile, she moved into the shadow. "One kiss," she murmured. "For farewell, monk-man."

He caught her hand before her eyes adjusted, pulling her up against him. "Is this loathing and despite?" he asked low.

She lifted her eyes, the sun-haze still in them, his face dim and veiled; his mouth on hers all feeling. He kissed her hard. She breathed him, familiar heat and plain scent, a man's unadorned skin and the taste of him on her tongue—memory and delight and pain. The last time. The last time his arm pressed her into his chest, the last time his fingers slid upward behind her throat, straining her closer still.

She almost lost herself in it, but the declining sun burned on her eyelids. Her hand crept up his shoulder. She pressed the point of her dagger beneath his ear.

He jerked at the prick of it, his breath hissing inward.

"Now," she said, "thou wilt do as I bid. Thy hands crossed behind thee."

His dark lashes hid his eyes as he looked down upon her. Slowly, slightly, he shook his head. "No, Melanthe."

She breathed deeply, holding the tip against his skin. "Dost thou think I have not the skill, or the strength?"

"Nought the will."

"Fool! Ne do not try me!"

His mouth was a taut line in the half light. "I try you. Do it, if you will."

She gripped his sleeve, turning the blade, pressing harder and praying.

"Ye thinks to tie and imprison me until you go," he said

bitterly. "But thou moste slay me, Melanthe, if thou will to be free, for nill I concede it while I breathe life."

She cut him. He flinched, but he held her, his arms tightening as a bright trickle of blood ran down his neck. She was trapped in his embrace.

"Fool! Fool! If Gian comes now, he will flay the skin from thee alive."

"What matters it to thee, who hates and loathes me?"

She heard horses. Hoofbeats sounded in the courtyard, and the voices of men. "He is come!"

Ruck seized her tight. "Decide, my lady. It is beyond lies now."

"He is come!" she cried. She tore herself from him. "Go!"

"Is he you want, then?"

Her mastery shattered. "Go!" she screamed. "Thou simple, dost thou think it is between you? He will slay thee—I cannot bear it, God curse thee, he has killed all that I ever loved only because I loved it. Go! The kitchen, the postern door—"

But he did not go. Melanthe stood in the midst of the streaming light clutching the dagger, staring at the blind shadow of him, hearing the sounds below.

"He knows, he knows," she moaned. "He will find thee here—how didst thou come? Thou wast safe, I made thee safe, go, go now, if thou ever loved me . . . please—I cannot bear it." She could see nothing, only light and the window, the last sun pouring past her in rainbow hues. "I cannot bear it."

He caught her wrist, wrenching the blade from her. His body made an outline against the light, the rays shifting and dancing around him. She heard the knife clatter on the stone floor.

"Melanthe—" He held her hands up, and she saw blood on them, felt the sting where she had cut herself. "He is dead."

"Go," she whispered, but it was hopeless, too late. She could hear them in the hall and on the stairs.

"Navona is dead, Melanthe."

She shook her head. "He is not dead. He comes."

"Nay, my lady." He held her hands. She couldn't see his face. She wanted to see his face, but tears and light and dark were all she had.

"He comes."

"No," he said.

There was a scratch upon the door. She shuddered. She could not move.

"My lady, thou said me once, ne'er was I to tell thee false. Gian Navona is dead. I saw him—my lady, my sovereign lady. Believe me. Thou need nought fear."

"My brother, and Ligurio," she whispered. "And my daughter. And any friend I ever thought to have but Gryngolet. I did not mean to love thee. I did not mean to. It was so far away. I never thought he could find out."

The sun rays shafted around him as he lifted his hands to her face. He smoothed her hair, his fingers catching in the net and passing over the jewels.

"She only had two years. My baby. And she was so fair. I always remembered how fair—and I thought—with thee—if God willed—" She licked tears from her mouth. "But then I was afraid."

"I would thou had told me. Melanthe. If thou had told me!"

"I was afraid." Her face crumpled, and she could not see again. "I was afraid for thee. And then Desmond came, and I knew that I had brought it all there, and I had to go away." She shook her head. "Ne did I want to, but I could not say thee so, for thou wouldst come."

"I did come. How could I nought?" His hands squeezed tight on her shoulders. "How could I lose thee? Ah, Christus, a child . . . Melanthe, my lady, my life—e'en that? And thou kept all from me, and made me think—" He shook her and then pulled her to his chest. "Helas, I have nought known thee; thou hatz blinded me."

The scratch came at the door again. She put her hands on him, closing her fingers.

"Gian is dead," Ruck said. "It is not Navona."

With an effort she released him. He let go of her and went away. She stood facing the shining window, the tall traceries of colored glass. Her hands stung and throbbed.

Behind her, someone spoke softly in French. Ruck answered them, the words too low to understand. Melanthe turned around, and for the first time she saw him clearly, not a shadow against glare, but real and distinct. He closed the door and came back to her.

His face in the light was sober, his black brows and lashes stark. He touched her hands gently, and then her cheek. "Is Allegreto below, and Navona's men." He took her wrists.

She lifted her eyes, a new terror rising in her. "Who killed Gian?"

"No one, lest it were the Arch-Fiend himseluen."

"Thou art certain he is dead?"

"Without nay, I am certain." He held her face between his hands. "Luflych, make thy soul easy." He gathered her close to him. "He is gone beyond where he can reach thee e'ermore."

A quiver ran through her. He held her harder, pressing his lips to her hair. The gentle kisses seemed to draw fear from her in a surge, breaching walls and barriers, transforming it into endless tears that spilled from her eyes and washed her cheeks and his black velvet.

"It cannot be." Her voice was hollow, muffled against his shoulder. "It cannot. Art thou sure? Didst thou kill him?"

"Husht, Melanthe," he murmured. "Be still." He rocked her softly. "I haf said thee true."

She wanted to push back and look at him, to make herself believe that he was with her, but she did not want to leave his embrace. She closed her eyes and felt him instead, his broad back beneath her palms, the height of his shoulder and the breadth of his body. She pulled him into her as if she could make the steady rise and fall of his breath supplant the jolting sobs that shook her.

"Husht now." He drew her down onto the window seat. His arms enfolded her tight against him. He kissed the nape of her neck as she pushed her cheek to his chest. "My liege lady—my heart. Husht. Thou art safe with me."

Twenty-seven

THE MURMUR OF many lowered voices drifted to them in the stairwell. Ruck felt Melanthe's hand on his, colder than the stone walls. He stopped on the stair, enclosing her fingers between his palms to warm them. In the dim light he could barely see her face.

She rested against him for a brief moment, and then stepped down. At the foot of the stairs she paused, looking into the manor hall.

Silence fell over the gathering. In candlelight Gian Navona lay on a straw-covered hurdle, only the stone floor beneath him. He was white, his skin and his clothes, already an effigy with painted black features and gilt embellishment. A priest knelt beside him; the others left a space about the corpse, standing back clustered in the corners and along the walls, except for Allegreto.

The youth stood beside his father's body like a white alaunt guarding its master. Ruck had not sensed the depth of resemblance between them before. In his frozen pallor Allegreto was a mirror of his father: comelier, younger, perfected. He still wore the milky livery, showing damp yet, as if no one had thought to let him change.

Beneath the rafters painted red and gold, against the dark

slate floor, Allegreto and Navona and the priest were like a scene from a miracle play—only the look of Allegreto's face was no playing. His pitch-black eyes turned to Melanthe, watching her as she left Ruck at the screens and crossed the floor.

She stood looking down on the dead man for a long time. The priest murmured his prayer softly. Ruck could not see her face.

Navona's men waited, a score of them ranged beyond Allegreto. Most of Melanthe's retinue gathered nearer to Ruck, at the lower end of the hall. Set apart, an Englishman stood with another, unmistakably a clerk by his writing roll and pen. Local people pressed forward through the open door into the passage, goggling and hushing one another, staring at Ruck harder than they stared at the corpse.

He jerked his head at them to leave. The ones in the front tried to comply, but the others behind jostled them forward. Melanthe turned, glancing toward the whispering spectators.

"Place a shroud on him," she said. She looked at her maids and spoke in Italian. One of them ducked a courtesy and went quickly out past Ruck.

"My lady," the Englishman said, stepping forward and speaking mannerly French. He sank to one knee and rose again. "With all reverence—John de Langley, our lord the king's justice of the peace."

"What happened?" she asked, lifting her chin. "How did he die?"

"Madam, I am—"

"He fell from our boat into the river." Allegreto's voice cut across the justice's, sharp and cold. Then despair seemed to burst from him. "My lady, I tried to save him. I tried!"

"Madam, I am—"

"Will you believe such a thing?" One of Navona's men stepped toward the justice. "Nay, the bastard speaks false— my lord never fell from that boat. They have murdered him, these three together!"

A murmur ran through the onlookers. *"Madam,"* the justice said tightly, "I pursue an inquisition to determine this matter, whether it be an accident or a crime to be brought before the jury."

Melanthe said nothing. Langley inclined his head to her.

"I have found no witness but this youth, the name of, ah—"

"Allegreto," she said. "He is Dan Gian's bastard son."

"Yea, my lady. And this is—?" He looked meaningfully toward Ruck.

"My wedded husband. Lord Ruadrik of Wolfscar."

The spectators didn't even attempt to remain quiet. A clamor broke out among them. Ruck walked to Melanthe's side.

"Yea, and so I have said," he declared, glaring about him to silence them. "I have defended my word before the king. The archbishop himself has heard my plea that my wife went in fear of her life from this man Navona, and could not say the truth." He faced the justice. "If this is not proof enough—that she speaks my name now, when he is dead—then will I gladly prove it by my sword again, against any who deny it."

"Hear him!" The single cry came from the passage, and instantly all the English took it up. The hail even rose from outside, the sound of a substantial crowd. "Hear him, hear him!"

"*Oyeh!*" the clerk bawled. "Silence for my lord justice!"

They settled into muttered grudging. Langley made a courteous nod toward Ruck. "I hear your words, Lord Ruadrik. I was in attendance on your honorable combat. You will understand that I am justice of the peace. A complaint and accusation is lodged here, which I must see into. If I adjudge there is not evidence of a crime, then no arraignment be required."

"They have murdered my lord Gian, may God avenge it!" the Italian shouted. He pointed toward Ruck. "Look you, that this Ruadrik threatened my lord, and assaulted him, and desired to steal his promised wife! All know it! Where has he been, this fine Lord Ruadrik, I ask you, that he was mourned for dead and now we find him here with her, almost in the very hour of the murder? They've conspired together, these vipers; Allegreto to have his own father's place, and those two to congress together as they will!"

"Where is the proof of this, I ask you once again," the justice said evenly.

"Will you not look to find another witness? Will you take the word of this lying baseborn?"

"He has spoken under oath," Langley said. "All this day I have conducted a search for other witnesses, and found none to deny his story."

"My lord would not fall from a boat!" the man said fiercely. "He was no such fool."

"Verily, any man might lose his balance, I think. And he wears weight enough in gold to drag him under."

"Pah!" The Italian made a motion as if to spit at Allegreto, though he did not do it. "You know nothing! Ask him what he gains, this bastard! A fortune for himself, instead of a lawful born brother to take his place!"

"I did not kill my father," Allegreto said in a fragile voice. "Morello, you know I love him."

"Such love!" Morello snapped. "When he lies dead at thy feet!"

"*I love him!*" Allegreto cried, his anguish echoing back from the roof.

Melanthe's hand tightened for an instant on Ruck's arm. The whole hall was silent as the sound of the youth's grief died away. Ruck watched, afraid that Allegreto would break in his misery, losing his wits and his tale. But he only closed his eyes, and then opened them, with a long and unblinking gaze at Morello.

The man looked away. He muttered something viciously in Italian.

"And still I hear no credible proofs, to say the boy speaks false," Langley said. The justice turned to his clerk, requiring Bible and Cross. "Lord Ruadrik, will you take oath to your innocence in the matter?"

"Verily," Ruck said. He placed his hand on the holy book and swore by his soul that he had not killed Gian Navona. He kissed the rood and crossed himself. As he stepped back, the spectators murmured approvingly.

"My lady?"

Melanthe made a courtesy as they brought the Bible to her. In a clear, quiet voice she swore the same.

The justice leaned over and spoke in his clerk's ear. The man nodded, and nodded again. Ruck put his hand on Melanthe's elbow, holding lightly. The onlookers were so still that they seemed to hold in their breath.

"I find no cause to convene a jury," the justice said.

A hail burst from the English, and a shout of anger from the Italians, quickly subdued when Langley gave them a furious scowl and his clerk demanded silence.

"In the case of murder, we are advised never to judge by likelihoods and presumptions, or no life would be secure. Therefore, without a witness who is willing to step forward and swear otherwise, the accusation of murder appears unfounded. I have no material reason to doubt the drowning of Gian Navona was accidental, may God pardon his soul."

He had to pause once again until order was restored, with two of the Italians bodily restraining Morello. The justice looked on him with raised brows.

"My lord Ruadrik has said that he will uphold his sworn word by his sword, as he has done before. Do we understand then that you wish to fight him?"

Morello jerked himself free of his companions, glowering. He cast a glance at Ruck and said nothing.

"If not," Langley said, "then I declare that the king's peace be best served by the swift dispersal of those who have no business here—and by the absence of some two-score foreigners of Italy from my county on the morrow."

ALL THE VILLAGERS had wanted to touch Ruck. In spite of the justice's command, they managed to crowd near him, until Langley shouted that they profaned the corpse with their disrespect and used his staff smartly against a few rumps.

Navona lay enshrouded in scarlet cloth and silence now, awaiting a lead coffin to take him back for burial to his own country. The priest and Allegreto kept vigil, Navona's men banished to uneasy, torchlit waiting by the river with Melanthe's retinue. She did not even keep a maid from among the Italians, but commanded them all to depart. Only the gyrfalcon and some chests had been brought back from the barks, and the bed, set up again in her chamber without its hangings. The boats were to leave as soon as the coffin could be placed aboard.

Ruck watched her face as she moved about giving direction and order to her distracted retinue. She was so much more slender than he remembered, brittle pale beneath her jeweled net, her rings and the golden buttons lined down her sleeves the only flash of life about her.

When the gray friars came with a coffin of lead, she turned away and went upstairs. Ruck would have followed her, but he looked back and saw Allegreto standing alone, gazing at the friars as they began their work of washing the body and sewing it up in its shroud.

Ruck did not go to him, but stood by the screen until Allegreto saw him there. Ruck made a curl of his fingers to beckon. The youth seemed lost; he hesitated and then came quickly, like an uncertain dog that overcame its doubt, following Ruck into the shadowed passage. He put his hand on Allegreto's shoulder. "Thou art still wet. Hast thou dry clothes?"

"On the boats." The boy looked up at him, his cloak of mastery vanished—strangely young, as if they had all forgotten that he was hardly yet more man than child. "Should I change now?"

"Yea. I'll have something brought up from the wharf for thee."

Allegreto caught Ruck's arm as he turned. "Cara?" he asked, the name a whisper.

Ruck paused. The youth looked off toward the pool of light falling into the passage from the hall, where the friars did their work with quiet words and soft plashings. In the set mouth and proud chin, Ruck saw that it was no fear for the girl's telling tales that concerned him. "I took Donna Cara to her betrothed, as she asked me. They have left now with the horses."

The youth glanced at him coolly. "Where?"

"My lady's castle by the forest of Savernake, so they said me."

Allegreto's eyes narrowed. He nodded. Then a shiver passed through him, and he leaned his shoulders back against the wall, crossing his arms. "Depardeu, I wish they would be done with him, so that we might leave."

"Thou wilt return with the others?"

"Navona is mine, green man. So I will take it. And Monteverde and the Riata with it."

The names were no more than names to Ruck, castles or

kin or cities, he knew not. But it might have been Gian Navona himself standing in the half-light. Ruck only said, "'Ware your friend Morello, then."

"Morello!" Allegreto shrugged, with a faint sneer.

"The rest of them will follow thee if thou art swift to move," Ruck said. "Choose a captain tonight and divide their stations where they cannot whisper among themselves."

The dark eyes flicked to him. Allegreto wet his lips and nodded.

"Make them carry pikes," Ruck murmured. "It will slow them from freeing their sword hands."

Allegreto raised his brows. His mouth curled in a slight smile. "I did not know you were so sly, green man."

"I think me thou art too sly. It will take more than guile and poison to rule, my fine pup. Before they can love thee, they must know thee beyond a shadow and a comely face."

The priest's bell began to toll. Something happened to the mocking curve of Allegreto's lips. He stared at the dim-lit door to the hall, his mouth trembling.

Ruck turned, watching as the gray friars carried the coffin from the hall, eight of them, bent down by the weight of it. Allegreto took a step back into the stairwell, looking down on his father's bier.

The priest walked behind, swinging his censer. Allegreto came down as if to follow, then held back with his hand on the corner of the stair. He stood looking out the door at the end of the passage. Cool air flowed in, ruffling his dark hair.

He slanted a glance over his shoulder to Ruck, as if he had some question that had not been answered. But he did not speak.

"'Ware Morello," Ruck said, "and put on dry clothes."

"Morello will be dead before we reach Calais." Allegreto let go of the wall and strode toward the door.

"Dry clothes," Ruck said after him.

The youth paused, turning. "Are you my mother, green man?"

"Life hangs on the small things, whelp. Why die of a fever ague and make it easy for Morello?"

Allegreto stood in the doorway, the breeze blowing in past

him. He gave a brief nod, then turned into the darkness, following his father.

NO TEARS GREETED Ruck when he went to Melanthe's chamber. She stood waiting in her linen smock, her hair loose, a phantom in the light of a single candle, dry-eyed as the white falcon that stood motionless on its block.

"Ne do not tarry away from me," she said angrily. "Where hast thou been?"

"Below, my lady. They have carried the coffin out."

"Witterly, that could not come too soon." She held herself straight and distant, without advancing to him. Ruck closed the door and stood with his back to it. She was ever difficult in such a mood; he recognized it, but did not know the remedy.

"Say me what happened in troth," she demanded. "Who killed him?"

"No man. Donna Cara was with him on the wharf at thy brewery place. She bolted away, she said me, and he caught her sleeve. The cloth parted. She heard the plash." Ruck gave a slight shrug. "And we returned to finden him."

Melanthe stared at him. Then she laughed and closed her eyes. "It is too witless."

"Too witless it was that thou chained me to a wall, my lady," he said tautly, "but God or the Fiend has him now, and is too late for my vengeance."

She lifted her lashes. "Wouldst thou have tortured him, green sire?" she asked in a scoffing tone. "Torn him limb-meal in pieces? Only for me?"

"Melanthe," he said, "ne do nought be so this way tonight."

"What way?" she demanded, turning from him. She went to the bed and flung back the sheets, sitting down on the edge of it, her bare feet on the board.

"His."

She pressed her toes downward, her feet curving until they showed white. Her eyes seemed too large and dark to be human. She was like an elven, elegant and sheer, as if light would pass through her.

"How wouldst thou have me, then?" she asked.

"Disporting? Meek? A worthy goodwife, or a whore? I can be any—or all, if thou likes."

"Readily I would haf thee in a sweeter temper, my lady."

She threw herself backward onto the bed, lying among the sheets. "'Tis all? How simple." She made a web of her hands and flung them wide. "There. I am sweet. I am honey. Come and taste me."

Ruck unbuttoned his surcoat and dropped it with his belt and sword over a chest. At the harsh clatter of the gold links, she sat up again.

"A'plight, a man of swift reply," she said mockingly.

Ruck continued to divest himself. When he was naked he went to the bed and took her down with him on it. He could not speak to her, or he would shout. He opened his mouth over hers, kissing deep. She arched her body up beneath him, her hands greedily about his loins to pull him into her.

Delicious lust possessed him, compounding with his anger. He used her without indulgence, taking no time but for himself. Still she inhaled and dug her nails into him and spread her legs to twine them about his. She pulled frantically at him, her hands gripped in his hair so hard that it hurt.

The pain brought him back from blind hunger, caught him sharply from his own passion. Her eyes were squeezed shut, her face a mask of ferocity, as if she fought with him instead of straining to him.

He slowed, gentling his moves, but she would not have it. She made a bitter cry, forcing their union as hard as her strength could force it. Even though he stilled, she clung to him and strove to reach her pleasure.

Ruck let her use him, his own wrath sliding away. He brushed his lips over her hair as she shuddered and seized in his arms, her skin dewed with moisture.

She fell back, panting, her fingers digging into his shoulders. The blunt pain eased as she slowly released him. Her palms explored, sweeping up and down his arms, touching his hair and his face.

She never opened her eyes as her labored breathing slackened. She skimmed her hands down his body, then spread her arms out wide on the bedsheets. All her limbs softened.

He bent his forehead to the base of her throat, resting there, drunk on the scent and mystery of her. He felt her twitch, drowsing. As he lay atop her, in her, still full and hard, the last of waking tension drifted from her limbs. Her breath became a steady feather at his ear.

He began to move again, finding his own pleasure deep in her body. But though he came to the height of his lust and discharge with a heavy tremor and a sound of ecstasy, she did not wake. His lost and bespelled princess, beyond his reach even as he possessed her.

IN THE EARLY morning, in a manor house empty of all but a few servants, he left her sleeping hard and deep. He bathed and shaved in the kitchen and walked outside, where a little huddle of villagers surprised him in the yard, eager hands reaching out to touch him. He was, he discovered, a miracle arisen from the dead—a notion he found repellent. He dismissed them with the trenchant suggestion to seek out his excellent doctor instead of miracles, which produced an efficient clearing of the courtyard.

Fog lay on the river surface, shading to mist and clear air. He stood looking down through it toward the shore, where trampled grass and the black clods of burned-out torches were all that remained of the departed barks.

He had not expected this morning, this moment. He had never since the day she left Wolfscar believed in his heart that he would have her to wive again. Even before, it had never seemed perfectly real, but a thing of fantasy with no tie to the earth. They had not spoken of the future, because they had both known that in truth there was to be none.

But abruptly, he was in it—future and present, anchored by his own battle to prove their vows and her public words of acceptance in the hall.

Amid birdsong and wet flowers, he walked aimlessly toward the empty stables. He heard someone behind him and turned, half expecting Melanthe, but it was not.

It was Desmond. He wore his court clothes, her fine scarlet livery, limp with the mist.

"My lord," he said, and went to his knee. "My lord!" His face crumpled into tears. "Will ye letten me go home?"

Ruck reached for him, and the boy came into his embrace, holding on as if to life.

"My lord," Desmond sobbed against his cote, "ne'er did I break my word! Ne did I say aught of Wolfscar, nor that ye kept wedlock with my lady, e'en did they rack me! But Allegreto said me nought to comen to you, that I mote nought, for my life and yours. And I saw you die, my lord—I—"

He lost his voice in weeping. Ruck crossed his arms over Desmond's neck, rocking him fiercely.

"My lord, can I go home? Oh, my lord, I made blunder and wrongs and failed you, but I beg you."

"Desmond." Ruck put his face down in the boy's shoulder. "I will taken thee home if I bear thee on my back in penance. God forgive me, that e'er I sent thee out alone."

CARRYING WINE IN a blue-and-white jug and waster bread from the pantry, Ruck mounted the stairs to her chamber. A thin mist of daylight fell from the open door above, painting a faint golden stripe in a curve down the stone wall.

He had expected to find her still asleep, but instead she was up, kneeling in her linen beside an open chest. Her head was bent over something in her hand.

He saw that it was a mirror, fine and rare, made of glass instead of polished steel. She held her loose hair on her shoulder, looking at the carving on the ivory back. As he came into the room, she held up the glass, reflecting his image onto him.

"What dost thou see, monk-man?"

"Myseluen, my lady. Wilt thou break fast?"

She rose as Ruck laid the napkin over a chest and set the food and tankards on it. He shut the door.

"Here." She held out the mirror to him, turning casually toward the window seat, as if he were one of her maids meant to place the thing away.

He stood holding the glass. She did it by design, he knew, to bedevil him, and it succeeded. He felt the difference in their stations sharply; he thought that if he let it pass now, her small disdain, he would have to live like a servant evermore.

"My lady wife," he said, pouring wine and handing it to her along with the mirror, "ne do I require this glass for looking."

"Hast thou no vanity?" She laid it facedown in her lap. "But I forget—thy choice of sin is lust."

He poured for himself. "If I mote choose," he said, "yea."

"But verily, thou art a comely man. Thou might be vain with some justice. Look." She held up the glass again.

"Is aught amiss with my face, lady, that thou wilt bid me stare in this mirror so oft?"

She gazed at him, still holding it. Then she smiled slightly, bringing the glass up so that her face was half-hidden behind it, like a shamefast girl. "Nay. Aught amiss, bestloved."

The mirrored surface gleamed and flashed at him, her eyes above it unreadable. But she pierced him through when she smiled.

"I saw Desmond below," he said.

The mirth vanished from her. She lowered the mirror and stretched out her bare feet on the window seat.

"I take him to Wolfscar as soon as I can," Ruck said.

"Nay, thou dost not leave me. I send a courier to deliver him, if he mote go."

"I take him, my lady." Ruck drained his wine.

"No."

"Dost thou poison me and chain me to prevent it?"

She sat up. "Does that wrathe thee? By God's rood, thou wouldst be dead, had I not!"

"God a'mercy that I am alive, for is none of thy doing, Melanthe! What demon was in thy head, that thou didst nought say me true of that hell-hound Navona, that I could serve thee?"

She turned her head, looking out the window with a lift of her shoulder. "I could not."

"I well know that troth is like bitter wine on thy lips, but thy falsehood is beyond absolve for this."

"I could not!"

"Melanthe! Thou took me for thy husband, and yet could not say me?"

"He would slay thee."

Ruck made a furious turn. "And so that he mote nought, thou left me, and went to him to be his wife?"

"He would slay thee."

"His *wife!*"

She gathered her knees up against her. "Foolish simple! Ye know naught of it. He would slay thee."

"Yea, and so would I choose to be slain than to see thee in his bed, but I think me that I would nought die so tame!"

"I did not bed him, ne would have. I was for a nunnery instead, so thou moste be easy on that point."

Ruck shook his head in disbelief. "Thy brain is full of butterflies! A nunnery, by God, when thou hadst only to say me of thy need. Is my place to protect and defend thee, Melanthe; is my honor."

She sprang to her bare feet. "Yea, thy honor! And where is honor when the bane finds thy lips? I have said thee why I did it. I would do it once again, and lie and cheat and steal the same, so be it, to save thee."

Carefully he set his clay tankard on a chest. "Then I haf no place with thee, by thy own word." He lifted his sword belt, girding it. "I take Desmond to Wolfscar, and thence to my duty to Lancaster."

"Lancaster! Thou art not his, but mine. He will not abide thee."

"For the ill way things go in Aquitaine, he mote needen seasoned men. A lord will forgive much to a captain of experience."

"Nay!" she said sharply. "Thou shalt not go away from me!"

"In this, my lady, thou does not command me."

"Thou art my husband. I will have thee at my side."

He buckled the belt. "Lady, is a lapdog thou wouldst have at thy side. I will buy one for thee at the marketplace."

"Ruck!" Her frantic voice made him pause at the door. She stood with the mirror clutched to her breast.

He waited. For an instant she seemed to cast for words, her lips parted, her eyes darting over the room, but then on an indrawn breath she pressed her lips together and stared at him royally.

"Nay, thou dost not go away to France, sir. I so command!"

"My lady, I have been your liege man. Now ye hatz made me your husband, and named me so to the world. It is I, lady, could command thee if I willed, and no man would say me nay."

Her brows lifted. "Shall it be war between us then, monk-man, for who commands? 'Ware thee my force in that battle."

He put his hand on the door, to yank it open, and then dropped the hasp. He turned on her. "I doubt nought that I should beware the force of thy guile! Well do I know the depth of it—much time had I to ponder in thy prison!" He shook his head with a harsh laugh. "I am no match for thee, faithly. Thou couldst skulk and slink to Lancaster, and poison me in his ear, so that I mote nought go to France. Thou couldst take Wolfscar from me if it pleased thee, so that I haf no thing of my own. I doubt nought thou couldst command me, and hem me, and keep me by thy side. Thou does value thy falcon better, for you set her free and trust her to return to thee, though it be e'ery time a peril. Thou might mew her in the dark for e'ermore, to keep her. But I see thy face when she flies, and thy joy and wonder when she comes." He shook his head again. "Nay, lady, there is no war between us. What use a war with a dead man? For ne could I live mewed up at thy pleasure, nor e'er love thee again as I do now, in free heart and devotion."

She pressed her palms over the mirror, holding it to her mouth. Then she turned to the window. "Gryngolet comes to the meat upon the lure—not for love."

Her shoulders and arms were pulled tightly inward as she held the mirror against her. Her smoke-black hair cascaded down her back. The colored window light turned bright white at her smock, drawing a fine outline of her body within.

"Happen I am a man, and not a falcon," he said gruffly.

"Ah. Then I cannot tempt thee with a chicken's wing."

"Nay, my lady."

She sighed. She sat down on the window seat, frowning down at the carved mirror back.

"Wilt thou nought look into thine own glass," he said softly, "and see what I would return to?"

Her body stiffened. She squeezed her eyes shut, averting her face a little. "What if I am not there?"

"How couldst thou nought be there?"

"Haps I am a witch, with no reflection."

"Times there be that I think thee a witch in troth, my lady."

"Why?" She gave him a quick glance. Her eyes had an uneasy vividness, that imperfect blue smudged to violet.

"By cause I love thee when I would rather strangle thee."

"But—haps I am a witch. Haps I am no one. Haps the Devil came and took me while I slept. I dreamed it once, that he took me, and left naught but a thing fashioned of lies, to seem like me." She gripped the mirror. In a small voice she said, "Ruck. Wilt thou look into it, and see if I am there?"

He went to her and knelt beside her, taking the glass from her nerveless fingers. It was a perfect mirror, the size of his spread hand, flashing light from the transparent surface. On the back an ivory lady gave her heart to a vain-looking knight. Ruck saw his own face as he turned the glass, a brief glimpse of jaw and nose and the golden buttons down his surcoat.

"Wait!" She stopped him as he rotated the mirror. "Wait— I am not ready." She pressed her eyes shut. Her face was taut, her hair in wild curls about her pallid cheeks. She held his hands still for a long moment. "All right," she said weakly, loosing him. "Now. Look. What dost thou see?"

He did not even glance at the mirror.

"Sharp wit," he said. "Valor past any man I know. Foolish japery and tricks worse than a child. Lickerous lust, hair like midwinter night. A proud and haught chin, a mouth for noble-talking—that does kiss sufficiently, in faith, and slays me with a smile. Guile and dreaming. A princess. A wench. An uncouth runisch girl. My wife. I see you, Melanthe. Ne do I need a glass."

"Look in the mirror!"

"Luflych." He wrapped his hand about her tight fist. "I see the same there."

She gave a rasping breath of relief, without opening her eyes. "Thou art certain? My face is there? Thou dost not say me false?"

"I fear for my life do I e'er say thee false, my lady."

"Oh, I am lost! I need thee to sayen me true. I need thee to say me what I should be. All is changed, and I know not what I am."

"Then will we keepen watch and see. And if ye be some-one new each morn, Melanthe—God knows thou art still my sovereign lady. Nought will I be at thy side in e'ery moment, but in spirit always, and return to thee with my whole heart, to see what bemazement thou wilt work upon me next."

Her hand turned upright beneath his, clinging. "I pray thee. Ne do I command thee, but I pray thee—do not go to France and leave me. Not—so soon. I would not maken thee my lap-dog, but—" She moistened her lips. "Verily, I know naught of sheep. And I have thousands, so says my seneschal. Haps I will require thy good advice."

"I am a master of sheep, my lady. E'en to shearing them, if I mote. I know some of oats and other corns, and how to instruct the bailiffs. The garrisons and men-at-arms I can command to good effect, and o'erlook castles and crenella-tions for what repairs and enlargements may be required."

Her hand eased, but still she kept her eyes closed. "All this? Thou art supreme in merits."

"I haf thought me a little o'er what my service could be."

"And what is left to me, but breeding?"

"Iwysse, I think of it each time we keep company, that we may not sin."

"Monk-man!"

"There be chambers at Wolfscar in need of dusting. I wen well how my lady wench likes to sweepen a hearth."

"Wench?" she uttered dangerously.

He rubbed his thumb across the back of her hand. "If Your Highness finds time heavy between thy lazy sleeps—I be nought much hand at Latin, my lady, nor lawyers and court dealings such as a great estate mote always have."

She opened her eyes, looking out the window. "All these plans and devises! Methinks thou art a great trumpery, who never meant for a moment to go back to *chevauchee* in France!"

"If thou hatz truer need of my service," he said with dig-nity, "then shall I nought, lest our king commands me."

She put her hand on his, preventing the mirror from mov-ing. Her face diverted, she looked warily from the corner of her eyes. With a cautious move she shifted the mirror in his hand, turning it slightly toward her.

"Look into it, my lady," he said. "I ne haf nought lied to thee."

She turned it all the way, staring down into the glass. Her

brows rose in outrage. "Why—I am not comely! I am *not*!" She slapped the mirror facedown. "I knew it was all dishonest dwele, these songs and praises to my beauty. Wysse, when is a rich woman plain?"

Ruck smiled at her. "Art nought comelych? Is my fortune to be blind, then."

"Pah!" She reached out, catching him off balance with a hard shove at his shoulder. He fell back off his heels, sitting down with a grunt on the bare stone. "Any woman would look comely to thee, monk-man, after ten and three years of chastity!"

Epilogue

CARA SAT IN the solar, her toes by the fire and the cloth of gold spread over her lap as well as she could with the child so great in her. The ciclatoun was to make a coverlet for an infant's cradle—none of hers, of course, but Lord Ruadrik's gift for his lady's churching, along with a robe of scarlet trimmed in ermine. He had left the fabrics at Savernake as he passed through just before Christmas, and bade her have them sent back to Wolfscar by Easter to be well in time.

She lifted her head, taking a deep breath after bending over the labor. She was flattered to have been chosen to embroider the gifts; Lord Ruadrik had taken special note of her work among Lady Melanthe's apparel, and brought the fabric to her. She shoved herself to her feet, carrying the cloth to the cold window, where she could inspect the fine detail in what was left of the cloudy light.

She glanced out over the snowbound yard. The cloth fell from her fingers. *"Elena!"* she shrieked.

The door, the stairs, the way that was so slow in her cumbersome state vanished beneath her feet. She burst from the door onto the porch without even stopping for a cloak.

"Elena, Elena—"

Her sister was just dismounting, her small feet disappearing in the snow. Cara swept her up and buried her face in the thick woolens, panting with exertion.

"Here now!" Guy's chiding voice barely reached her. She clutched at Elena as he lifted her away. "Inside." He hiked her sister in his arms, carrying her as Cara ran alongside, almost dancing in spite of her bulk. Elena was chattering in Italian; it sounded strange and wonderful to hear; Cara took in not a word of the childish talk, only heard the gay high voice and knew all was well, that Elena was whole and unhurt. She was weeping too hard to see more than Guy's outline in the passage. Someone came in with them—a woman, a nurse; there were others in the yard; it was all confusion as Guy went back out to see to them, but Cara could only hold her sister tight.

"You're so big!" Elena said, her dark blue eyes finally coming clear. "We have had a great adventure, coming through the snow! Dan Allegreto's horse fell in a drift! Will we live here? It is so cold! Dan Allegreto says that I shall like it when I grow accustomed. I threw snow at him, but he said it didn't hurt. When will the baby be born? Will I be its auntie?"

Cara's hands loosened. "Allegreto?"

Guy came in the door, knocking snow from his boots. No one followed him but another duenna, an older lady who crossed the threshold with offended dignity as he held open the door.

"Donna Elena, thy decorum!" she snapped.

Elena stood straight in Cara's arms, making a little courtesy. "Dan Allegreto says that if I wish to marry him," she confided to Cara, "I must learn to be a lady, for I am now a hoyden."

Cara stood straight, her heart thundering. "He is come?" she said to Guy in French.

"Nay," He shook his head. "This is all the party, but the guard that I sent to the stables."

"Oh, Dan Allegreto is here. He brought me to you," Elena said, slipping easily into French.

"The yard is empty," Guy said.

Elena pulled away. She ran to the door, pushing it open. Cara hurried after her as the little girl ran out into the snow without her cloak, calling.

Cara could not run so fast—her sister had raced across the yard and past the gate before Cara could prevent her. The duennas made shrill helpless cries after their charge, but it was only Guy and the porter who caught up with Elena after she crossed the bridge.

The little girl had already stopped. She stood gazing down the empty road. She put her hands about her mouth and cried, "Dan Allegreto!"

The name echoed back across the snowy fields. Two horses in the nearest pasture lifted shaggy heads.

"Oh," Elena said in a tiny voice. "He didn't say goodbye to me."

"Elena, thou wilt catch thy death, standing in the snow." Cara spoke sharply. "Guy, she must go inside."

"Come then, little donna." Guy lifted her high in the air and set her on his shoulders. "Mama speaks, and we listen."

Elena made no protest, but she craned her head to see behind her until Guy had carried her through the gate. Cara watched them out of sight. She turned, looking down the road—waiting.

No one came. The tracks made a long thin shadow in the snow, vanishing out of sight where the horse pastures met the forest.

"God grant you mercy," Cara said. Cold tears spilled down her cheeks. "I'm sorry. Grant mercy. Thank you."

The snow chilled her feet. She stood with her arms hugged close to herself, stood until the cold went through her to her heart. When she realized she was shaking with it, she turned back, and left the empty road to night and frost.

Acknowledgments

FIRSTLY, SUZANNE PARNELL, for "Fun with Middle English." Readers should know that there exists in the world a manuscript of this book in which *all* of the Middle English dialogue has been rendered accurate in both spelling and grammar, a labor of love for the language by Suzanne, which allowed me to water it down for modern consumption—and Suzanne, I wept for every "arn" and "ert" and "hopande" that wenten, forsooth, by cause our moder tonge mei maken swich luflych layes, and gets inside your head and sings. All errors introduced by editing are mine alone.

SECONDLY, "Tercel" on GEnie Pet-Net, and Don Roeber of Texas, for introducing me to falconry. Through the strange magic of computer networking, Tercel (*not* to be mistaken for a car) passed his love of hunting birds and this ancient sport—and more of his patience and sweetness of character than he knows—to me when I didn't know a falcon from a hawk. Don generously answered my questions and loaned me books and gave me the opportunity to watch a real falcon on the hunt—and if it wasn't the most perfect weather in the world, we got the mud part right, anyway. Next season—less fog, more ducks! All exaggerations and technical mistakes I may have made in creating my "superfalcon" once again are mine alone.

THIRDLY, Mary Wilburn of the Zula Bryant Wylie Library, for ever-patient ordering of inter-library loans, and taking time out of her London trip to provide me help beyond the call of duty.

FOURTHLY, Commander Bill Ashmole and his wife, Joan, of Devon, who generously spent part of their holiday visiting English abbeys and priories under my orders—for showing Mother and Daddy the best of good times as usual. They always come home smiling.

LASTLY, but never leastly, Mother and Daddy themselves. Braving the roundabouts and shipyards, and nearly sucked into the Liverpool tunnel, my father managed to locate Birkenhead Priory tucked among the drydock cranes, when even the fellows at the petrol station down the street didn't know where it was. Another of the world's small ironies: the little priory that lay deep in the wilderness of the Wirral some five hundred years ago—still used for worship, recently renovated as a pleasant, tree-shaded civic center for the city of Birkenhead—still difficult for the average pilgrim to reach. It takes a man of true determination like my father, and very glad to see him the priest was, for it seems they don't get as many visitors as they deserve down there in the midst of the Birkenhead shipyards where no one can find them.

In addition, the Hundred Years War gamers on GEnie, who not only provide some pretty slick role-playing in the fourteenth century, but helped me obtain my own copy of Froissart; the Oxford University Press, for publishing the *Oxford English Dictionary* on CD-ROM; and Travis, the only guy in the universe, as far as I know, who can successfully install an internal NEC-84 CD-ROM drive.

And finally, most of all, an unknown poet or poetess, for *Sir Gawain and the Green Knight.*

To each of you, my heartfelt thanks.

Glossary and Notes
on Middle English Grammar

— ⚬⚬⚬ —

I'VE PROVIDED THIS glossary in the new edition of *For My Lady's Heart* as a small glimpse into the fascinating history of our language. Some of the words listed have other definitions, but here they are limited to the meanings I used in this book. I've given alternate spellings, for those who wish to investigate further in dictionaries, and a couple of grammar hints for those of you who like to go around talking to your friends like this. You know who you are!

Abbreviations: ME (Middle English); OE (Old English); OF (Old French); L (Latin)

aghlich (also awly; OE, ME)—Terrifying, dreadful
alaunt (OF)—A wolf-hound
ambs-ace (L, OF "both aces, double ace," the lowest possible throw at dice)—Worthlessness, nought, next to nothing.
a'plight (OE, "pledge")—In faith, truly, certainly, surely, in truth
austringer (OF)—A keeper of goshawks
aventail (OF, "air-hole")—The movable mouthpiece of a helmet

avoi (also avoy; OF, unknown origin)—General exclamation of surprise or fear

besant (also bezant; OF "Byzantium," where it was first minted)—A type of gold or silver coin; a gold button

caitiff (also caytif; OF)—A base, mean, despicable wretch

camelot (also camlot, cameline; OF)—A light, plush fabric supposedly made from camel's hair; a garment made of this fabric

cheap (OE)—A purchase, a bargain

ciclatoun (OF, possibly from Arabic)—A precious material; cloth of gold or other rich material

comelych (ME)—Comely, lovely

comlokkest (ME)—Comeliest, most handsome

coquin (also cokin; OF)—Rogue, rascal

cotehardi (also cote-hardie, OF)—A close-fitting outer garment with sleeves, worn by both sexes

cuirass (OF)—Breast-plate and back-plate armor

cuir bouilli (OF, literally "boiled leather")—Leather armor

cuisses (OF, "thigh")—Armor pieces for the upper leg

depardeu (also depardieu; OF)—In God's name; by God

descry/descrive (OF)—To discover; to describe or reveal

destrier (L *dextra* "right hand" because the horse was led by the squire with his right hand)—A warhorse or charger

disturn (OF)—Turn away

drury (OF)—A love-token, a keepsake

enow (ME)—Enough

escheat (OF)—To confiscate from; or more specifically the reversion of a fief to the lord, commonly when the tenant died without leaving a successor

fermysoun (also fermisoun; OF)—The close season, when it was illegal or uncustomary to hunt the hart (a male red deer)

fette (OE, "fetch")—Lay hold of

forn (ME)—In front, forward of

foryield (OE)—Reward, repay

fourchee (OF)—A skewer for the special tidbits reserved for the lord from "unmaking" or butchering of the hart at the end of a hunt

frith (OE)—wooded or waste land, underbrush

frumenty (ME)—A dish made of hulled wheat boiled in milk, with spices and sweeteners added

fustian (OF, possibly from *Fostat,* a cloth-making section of Cairo)—Coarse cloth made of cotton and flax

gambeson (OF)—undecorated body garment of quilted material or leather, worn under armor to prevent chafing

greaves (OF, "shin")—Armor for the leg below the knee

haf/hatz (OE, ME)—have

harlot (OF)—A rogue, rascal, villain, low fellow, knave; also applied to the pointed boots worn in the fourteenth century

hastilude (L "spear-play")—A tilt or tournament

havercake (ME northern dialect)—Oatcake

houpelande (also houpland; OF, unknown origin)—A tunic with a long skirt, sometimes with train attached, worn by both sexes

iwysse (OE, *gewis* "certain")—Certainly, assuredly, indeed

lay (OF)—A short lyric or narrative poem

leman (also lemman, lemmon; ME)—A lover or mistress

lickerous (OF)—Delicious; lustful, wanton

liripipe (L)—A long tippet hanging from the peak of a hood or from the elbows

lovelokkest (OE, ME)—Loveliest

luflych (OE, ME)—Lovely; gracious; a fervent expression of admiring or delighted feeling

lymer (OF, "leash")—A leash-hound; a dog bred for tracking the quarry by scent without disturbing it, similar to a modern bloodhound

menskeful (ME, *menske* "courtesy, honors")—Elegant, ornamented

misericorde (OF, "compassion, pity, mercy")—A dagger

mote (OF)—A note-call on a hunting horn

mote/moten/moste (OE)—Expressing permission, possibility, or obligation; might, may, or must

ne (OE, ME)—A simple negative; no, not. Sometimes formed in contraction with a verb, as in "n'ill I" for "ne will I" (I will not). Our modern term "willy-nilly" comes from " Will ye or nill ye!"

passager (OF)—A wild falcon trapped during migration and trained; sometimes used only for a season and then released

pillion (from Celtic *pill* "cushion")—A kind of saddle, esp. a woman's light saddle. Also, a pad or cushion attached to the back of an ordinary saddle, on which a second person (usually a woman) may ride

plessis (OF)—Felled trees, young trees, brambles, and thorn bushes woven and grown together as an impenetrable barrier and defense; plessis were common all over Europe in the Middle

Ages, some so ancient they dated back at least to the Germanic tribes of Roman times.

poleyn (OF)—Plate armor for the knee

poulaine (OF, "souliers à la Poulaine," shoes in Polish fashion)— The long pointed toe of a shoe, as worn in the fourteenth and fifteenth centuries

rache (OE)—A hunting dog that pursues the quarry in a pack by scent, like modern foxhounds

ramp (OF)—A bold, vulgar, ill-behaved woman or girl

rechase (OF)—The horn call to denote the hounds are running, or to release them to run

rouncy (OF)—A riding horse

runisch (also runish, renish; ME, unknown origin)—Fierce, violent, rough

sabaton (from L "shoe")—Armor for the foot

shend (OE)—Overcome with fatigue; bewildered, stupefied

sparviter (OF)—A keeper of sparrowhawks

Tam Lin—A traditional name for the King of the Fairies

trow (OE)—Trust

unhende (also unhend; OE)—Ungentle, rude, rough

varvel (OF, "bolt, hinge")—A falconry term for the metal ring attached to a bird's jess, on which the leash is tied; usually engraved with the owner's name

vauntguard (also avantguard; OF)—the foremost part of a troop or army, the vanguard

vewterer (also fewterer; OF from the Gaulish word "run")—A keeper of greyhounds

voire (OF)—In truth, indeed

waster bread (also wastel; OF "cake")—Bread made of the finest flour; a cake or loaf of this bread

wit/wis/wist/wen/wot (OE, ME)—Know, understand

witterly (OE, ME)—Clearly, plainly, evidently; for certain; without doubt

woodwose (OE)—a wild man of the woods

wrathe/wrothe (also wrath; ME)—annoy, vex, anger

Negatives—The modern idea that multiple negatives in a sentence are bad grammar and that "two negatives equal a positive," has no historical basis. In Middle English, the more you wanted to negate something, the more negatives you stuffed into the sentence. "No I ain't done nothing," would be perfectly proper Middle English.

Word order—Negative statements, commands, and questions often invert the typical subject-verb-object word order. "Ne care I nought," for "I don't care." "Swear thee now." "Why sayest thou so?"

Conjugation of verbs—As a very general rule, the first and third person singular are similar to our modern forms. *I hear. He hears.* Middle English differentiated between "thou" and "you," for the second person pronoun. Between equals, or to inferiors, "thou" was used. This informal second person singular adds an *-est* ending for many verbs. *Thou hearest.* When addressing a superior, "ye" or its plural "you" was used. This polite address, plus the infinitive and all other plurals typically use a *-en* ending. *You hearen. To hearen. They hearen.*

There are only two tenses, past and present. The past tense follows the same general rules: *I heard. Thou heardest. He heard. They hearden.*

There are of course many irregularities and complications, and grammar was never my strong point, so I'll recommend *A Book of Middle English* by J. A. Burrow and Thorlac Turville-Petre for those who'd like to take a further peek into the grammatical rules and a more extensive dictionary of Middle English.

When the characters in *For My Lady's Heart* are not speaking Middle English, I used simpler conventions. When they are speaking French, the universal court language of the time, I generally used the informal and polite forms of address, *thou* and *ye*. When the characters are speaking Italian between themselves, I used modern grammar.

And now a special preview of
Laura Kinsale's eagerly awaited . . .

Shadowheart

Available from Berkley Books!

"GOD'S TOES, WHY should I toil any farther up this cliff to honor some foreign rubbish!" Lady Beatrice exclaimed. She leaned upon her cane, breathing heavily, and glared about the empty tower room. They had come to be presented to the lord of Il Corvo, climbing a steep narrow stair, escorted by Captain Amposta in the lead and an armed guard behind. "Let him wait upon me. Come, girl!"

The captain reached out and caught her arm as she turned. "I think not, madam."

"You wretched devil!" Lady Beatrice hissed, jerking away. "Unhand me! Are you possessed by the Fiend himself?"

His lively demeanor had changed. "You speak more truth than you know. You may find that you fancy the Fiend better than my master."

The countess ignored him, limping with quick conviction toward the tower door. When the guard moved his pike, barring the stairs, Lady Beatrice shoved her cane into his belly-plate. "Stand aside!" she declared, her voice ringing off the rough walls.

Elayne stood silently, watching. The understanding slowly bore in upon her that they were made prisoners.

"Remove the weapon, varlet," Lady Beatrice ordered, flipping her famous reed cane under the man's helmeted chin, pushing his head up and back. Elayne well knew that murderous tone of voice: it had reduced dukes and archbishops to quailing pageboys.

But the guard stood his ground. He merely looked over his nose at the captain, who laughed and shook his head.

Lady Beatrice's translucent skin flushed with rage. She whirled about quickly, belying her fragile figure. She was three hands-breadth smaller than Amposta, and had not a single means to enforce her command as a countess here in this savage place, but her lip curled and her back arched as she spat, "You insolent harlot!" Her cane sliced the air, a supple snap of her wrist. The captain had not the reflexes of Lady Beatrice's servants, or perchance he had not thought she would dare—his hand came up too late and the blow caught him smartly on the ear, a resounding smack that sent him recoiling, his shoulder colliding with the stone wall as he bent over himself.

"I do not suffer fools," Lady Beatrice said calmly.

The captain straightened, sucking air between his teeth. For an instant, Elayne thought that he would leap at Lady Beatrice like a wild animal. The countess had lowered the cane, but she held it lightly, drawing a circle with the tip on the floor.

"My dear lady—has this fellow been disrespectful?"

The quiet voice came unexpectedly, a shock in the small tower room. Elayne saw the captain's face change—beneath the vivid red mark across his cheek, his skin drained stark white.

She turned about. There had been only the four of them present. Now, though the guard beside the door had never moved, there was a fifth.

He stood tall and still, watching them—arriving from nowhere, as if he had created himself out of the ether. Jet-dyed folds of silk fell from his shoulders to the floor: an iridescent cape of black. Beneath it he wore silver, a tunic fitted perfectly to his body. His hair too was black; the color of fathomless night, long and tied back at the nape of his neck. He was like a statue of pure metal, something—some *thing*, inhuman—elegant and fantastic. Elayne was not even certain for a moment if he were real or a marble figure come to sudden life, but dark as sin, as gorgeous and corrupt as Lucifer himself.

For he was corrupt—and the master of this place—no one need bow to make that evident, although both the captain and the guard fell to their knees with haste. Elayne dipped into a reverence, keeping her head lowered, though she watched him from under her lashes. She could not tear her eyes away. Even Lady Beatrice leaned upon her cane and made a brief curtsy.

He smiled. "My lady, you must not bow to me. I do not require it." Though his words were deferential, though he smiled, it seemed less a courtesy than a mandate. "You have been served ill, I fear, to be asked to climb so far. My regrets, Countess. You may beat the man senseless if you like."

"And who might you be?" Lady Beatrice demanded—with considerable audacity, Elayne thought.

"Alas, I have no noble titles, my lady. They call me only Raven, after the name of this island—Il Corvo."

He might have no title, but he carried himself as if he were a prince. His cloak sighed and stirred like something living, light woven into black.

"Humph," Lady Beatrice said. "A graceless cur, I think, if it be your order that I wait upon you. I am the Countess of Ludford, on Christian pilgrimage, fellow!"

He studied her, and then his glance drifted to Elayne. She wanted very badly to lower her face, but it was as if a viper had her for its mark, his black eyes glittering with that subtle smile. She did not dare to look away.

"By hap you will muster the patience to enjoy my home and table while you are here, my lady Countess," he said, still watching Elayne. "My port-master tells me that your ship is in need of some repair—I hardly think it safe for you to venture forth in a leaking vessel."

"Trumpery!" Lady Beatrice exclaimed. "Do not suppose I am any such fool as sails into your harbor every day! That ship is sound enough. We shall not impose upon your idea of hospitality a day longer."

"I fear that you will," he said softly. He wore no ring or jewelry, but on the shimmering black robe there was a strange emblem embroidered in silver, not a coat of arms, but some entwined letters or symbols, like an astrological sign, or Mistress Libushe's characters, but neither of those nor anything Elayne had ever seen before. "But your ladyship will like us better after I have Amposta here tossed onto the rocks below."

The captain made a dreadful sound, as if a protest had been choked to a gurgle in his throat. The man called the Raven looked toward him. Elayne could see Amposta freeze under that faint smile just as she had.

"A poor jest, though," the Raven said. "I see that you do not comprehend my humor."

The captain grinned, baring his teeth, the red mark on his cheek burning.

"Come and dine with me privately, my dear friend," the Raven said amiably. "We'll talk of Moors and pirates. *Mes dames*, the sergeant will guide you to your accommodations. We do not keep great ceremony here, but it is my hope that you will find them comfortable."

"So we are hostage," Lady Beatrice snarled, pounding her cane on the tiled floor. "Sold like sheep! Those treachers of St. John sold us!"

Elayne said nothing. The spell of the Raven's presence still seemed to hover about her, strange and familiar at once. Besides, the countess would not like to be reminded that it was she herself who had chosen to go aboard the captain's galley.

"Judas knights!" Lady Beatrice gritted her yellowed teeth. "You may be sure that their Grand Seigneur will hear of this, if I must go to Rhodes myself to complain!"

They did not seem to be going any place at present. The chamber allotted to the countess was richly furnished, covered with Eastern rugs and silken hangings, lit by enameled oil lamps that burned without smoke. But the arrow-slit windows looked out on a moonlit sea lying so far below that Elayne could not even see the shoreline. The tower wall and cliff beneath were invisible to her, as if the room floated high above the water by sorcery.

A servant had come, a Moorish girl who seemed to speak

no language that Elayne knew, but only brought a tray of superb fruits in syrup—figs and grapes and oranges. She placed a vase of flowers too, poppies, such a dark purple they were black, and then vanished silently. Elayne served Lady Beatrice, who never ceased railing against the Knights Hospitallers as she ate. But the countess grew weary at length, and willing to lie down on the feather mattress. Elayne drew the bed hangings, and heard the countess snoring before she had even shielded the lamps.

Elayne sat down on a bench at the foot of the bed, toying with the stewed fruits. This Raven was a pirate, of course. They were his prisoners, had walked open-eyed and guileless into an elegant snare. She could not seem to quite comprehend it. She licked at the syrup on a fig, and took a very small bite. Eating was still a burden to her. On Lady Melanthe's strict injunction, she took enough to keep herself from wasting, but had no enjoyment in it. She lifted a section of orange, and then ate it. Her fingers grew sticky. She dipped them in the little bowl of water on the tray. When she looked up from drying them, she was not alone the room.

Elayne started so that she upset the water as she came to her feet. "Sir!" she murmured, staring at the dark lord of the place as he stood in shadow not two yard's length from her.

"My lady," he said, bowing.

"I did not hear—" She glanced toward the planked door, which she herself had barred from within. The heavy rail was still in place. She blinked nervously. "How came you here?"

"Talent," he said. "And study." He moved near, standing over her. Elayne stiffened as he touched her. He took her chin between his fingers, tilting her face up to him. She suffered his leisurely inspection, having no choice. He lost none of his inhuman perfection at closer range. His face was still that graven image of proud Lucifer, fallen from Heaven to stand over her and examine her with eyes as deep black and wickedly beautiful as the poppies.

"I know you," he said pensively. "Who are you?"

She lowered her eyes. "Elena," she said simply, using the name of her Italian christening, which had long ago transformed on English tongues to Elayne.

She hoped it would sound common and unremarkable in this part of the world, the name of a girl who had no ransom value to anyone. But his hand fell away as if she had just uttered some dreadful iniquity. Like a priest probing a heretic under inquisition, he leaned closer, searching every inch of her face.

"Who sent you?" he demanded.

Elayne swallowed. She shook her head slightly. She was afraid—and yet she felt remote, as if she were not really in this chamber, but safe somewhere, watching from afar.

He took her chin hard between his fingers. "Who?" He smiled with an affection that seemed warm and terrible at once. She stared at him. Though she had no intention of speaking, she felt the answer hover on her tongue, as if his smile alone could compel her.

"Tell me now," he said gently. "You must tell me."

"Lady Beatrice," she whispered, clamping her lips closed against saying more.

His black eyebrows lifted. "Nay, tell me who sent you. Who put you in her service?"

"The countess," Elayne mumbled. "I serve the countess."

"The countess of Bowland?" he asked kindly, his voice very quiet. "Melanthe?"

Elayne's eyes widened. But he seemed now not so threatening, more human. He looked at her with a fondness that made regret well up inside her; it was the way she had longed for Raymond to look at her, with love and tenderness. It seemed that if she did not tell him what he wished to know, she would be wrong; unfeeling. "The countess," she murmured. To gaze up at him made her dizzy. "She said . . ." She tried to remember, but all the voices of the past months seemed to clamor together in her head, a tumble of instruction and warning. "She said . . . she told me . . . trust no one."

She felt his hand tighten on her chin. He drew in air with a soft hiss. "Did she?"

"I don't know," Elayne said in confusion. She put her hand on the bedpost. "I'm not sure."

He smiled, like the Devil speaking from the shadows. "Then trust me," he murmured, or Elayne thought he did. She could not seem to see him clearly. He faded, or the light faded, or the shadows crept into her eyes. The lamps went dark, leaving her standing in the blackness, with nothing certain but the wooden carving beneath her fingers and the sound of Lady Beatrice's snores.